★★★ SONS OF ★★★
VALOR IV
FALSE FLAG

Books by Brian Andrews and Jeffrey Wilson

Tier One

Tier One

War Shadows

Crusader One

American Operator

Red Specter

Collateral

Dempsey

Ember

Tier One Origins

Scars: John Dempsey

Sons of Valor

Sons of Valor

Sons of Valor II: Violence of Action

Sons of Valor III: War Machine

Sons of Valor IV: False Flag

The Shepherds

Dark Intercept

Dark Angel

Dark Fall

Dark Rising

Stand Alone Novels

Four Minutes

The Sandbox

Tom Clancy's Jack Ryan

Act of Defiance

Defense Protocol

W. E. B. Griffin's Presidential Agent

Rogue Asset

Books Written as Alex Ryan

Nick Foley

Beijing Red

Hong Kong Black

Books by Brian Andrews

The Calypso Directive

The Infiltration Game

Reset

Books by Jeffrey Wilson

The Traiteur's Ring

The Donors

Fade to Black

War Torn

Julian's Numbers

ANDREWS & WILSON

★★★ SONS OF ★★★
VALOR IV

FALSE FLAG

BLACK
STONE
PUBLISHING

Published in 2025 by Blackstone Publishing
Series design by K. Jones

Printed in the United States of America

First paperback edition: 2025
ISBN 979-8-8748-8195-5
Fiction / Action & Adventure

Version 2

Blackstone Publishing
31 Mistletoe Rd.
Ashland, OR 97520

www.BlackstonePublishing.com

For Rick Bleiweiss, who has championed our work and been our friend from the start. Thank you, Rick, for everything.

PROLOGUE

SUPERYACHT *TRANQUILITY*
ANCHORED IN FIRON BAY OFF OIA
THE ISLAND OF SANTORINI
MEDITERRANEAN SEA
MAY 2015

Wealth, power, and influence: This was the holy triad that defined what it meant to be a member of the royal Saudi family. As brother to the Crown Prince, Faisal bin Ahmed al-Saud was one step removed from power, but he was right where he wanted to be when it came to wealth and influence.

Two out of three—he could live with that.

Besides, with power came responsibility, and Faisal didn't need either of these things to live a life of pleasure and privilege for the rest of his days. Grinning, he looked over at his college classmate and friend Arash Reza, who was reclined on the cushioned chaise lounge next to him, soaking in the Mediterranean sun. Arash's eyes were closed, his handsome face looked content, and the drink in his hand—a virgin daiquiri, as his

Persian roommate had not succumbed to the temptations of alcohol—seemed about ready to slip from his grip onto the mahogany deck.

"I should feel guilty saying this, but I could definitely get used to this lifestyle," Arash said, his voice tinged with wistful regret.

"And why would you feel guilty, my friend?" Faisal asked. "We have worked hard this semester, and we deserve a holiday. Do we not?"

"Of course," Arash said, opening one eye and holding up his left hand to block the brilliant sun. Morning was nearly over, and soon it would be afternoon. "But do you imagine that any of our fellow classmates are enjoying such decadence?"

"Some," Faisal said with a shrug, though the *Tranquility* was one of the ten most luxurious yachts in the world. Arash himself was from a wealthy and well-connected family in Tehran, but wealth was a relative thing. The royal family al-Saud had redefined the meaning of the word, especially since Faisal's older brother, Khalid, had become Crown Prince.

"Any other Muslims, do you think?"

Faisal smiled and waved a hand. "Unlikely," he relented. Justice—or more to the point, *in*justice—was Arash's favorite soapbox, and one he stood on often in the international relations classes they shared at Oxford's St Antony's College. "But if we refuse the blessings Allah has chosen to shower upon us, would that change the circumstances of a single one of our classmates? Who are we to question where Allah chooses to send rain or sunshine? Should we not simply accept His gifts with respect and gratitude?"

"Perhaps you are right," Arash Reza said. Perhaps he was too relaxed in the luxury of the moment—the smell of sea salt in the air and the kiss of sunshine on his skin—to pursue his usual predictable arguments. "But," he said, taking a sip of his drink and then closing his eyes again, "you must admit the cost of this boat is enough money to feed an entire impoverished Muslim country."

"That is likely," Faisal conceded. "More than one, maybe. But I, for one, am too devout in my love for both Allah and my country to question the gifts He sends me."

"Ah, too *devout*, are you?" Reza said, and they both laughed.

"It's a ship, by the way, not a boat. And anyway, how would we meet the women we are intended to conquer without my brother's yacht?"

"Indeed," Reza replied. Women were a vice his Iranian friend had most definitely succumbed to during their time together as roommates at Oxford. "Faisal, may I ask you a serious question?"

Faisal sighed. He might not know the question, but he could predict the general topic. He was not in the mood for discussions about how they might one day lift their fellow Muslims out of poverty in the Middle East. He did not share Reza's global concerns, despite his studies. He wished only to prepare himself for service to Saudi Arabia—and, more to the point, for service to his family. Frankly, he was content with the blessings Allah had bestowed. If his future was simply to enjoy those blessings while his older brother, Khalid, executed the duties of Crown Prince—and one day as King—then he was more than satisfied with that.

"Of course, my friend," Faisal said with a patient smile, expecting a lecture on the suffering of the Muslim world. The question Reza actually asked, however, was not what he expected.

"Have you wondered, Faisal," his friend began, "what our region of the world might be like if only the power of Iran and the Kingdom of Saudi Arabia could come together? Can you imagine the good we could do for Muslims? For the whole world?"

Faisal laughed softly. He couldn't help himself.

"I imagine you may well be right, Arash," he said, trying to be patient. Wealth and real royal power were very different things, after all. Reza could not possibly understand the absurdity of what he proposed. Saudi Arabia's future was now irrevocably linked to the economies of the West. As for Iran, the hard-liners in Tehran had chosen an irreversible path as well, antagonizing the West even if doing so led to Iran's economic demise. "But that seems rather unlikely, my friend. Our countries do not enjoy the friendship we have, Arash. They are on very different paths."

"They don't have to be. Bold leadership with a fresh perspective is all that's required. It is easy to imagine an alliance that could benefit both nations. And I will say it again—such an alliance would also benefit the world. The wealth of our region does not have to be controlled by America and the Zionists. It should be controlled by our people. Only under the flag of a holy caliphate will the entire world one day have peace."

Faisal thought about this for a moment.

"A lovely thought," he said finally, and took a sip of the drink in his hand. Unlike the drink his friend sipped, Faisal's was laced with generous amounts of rum. "But my brother has forged a path forward built on cooperation with the West that I doubt he will ever waver from. He is a moderate—"

"He is more than that, Faisal," Reza said.

The edge in Reza's voice made Faisal turn to his roommate. Reza looked down, embarrassed or perhaps just deferent.

"I'm sorry, Faisal, but it's true. I know he is your brother, but it seems he cares more about appeasing the Americans and the Jews than about the future of the region. The Kingdom of al-Saud could raise the entire region, with the Kingdom at the head of the table. If only you were Crown Prince . . ."

At this, Faisal laughed out loud.

"I'm afraid that will never happen, Arash," he said. "My brother is but a few years older than me. He will be Crown Prince until he is King, and I will be advisor to his son when he becomes Crown Prince. Allah, it would seem, does not share your enthusiasm for my ruling the Kingdom."

"Ah, well," Reza said, watching Faisal closely and taking a sip of his own drink. "A man can dream, can't he? And anyway," he added, laying back on his chaise and closing his eyes now, "one never knows the will or plans of Allah. He works in mysterious ways."

"He does indeed," Faisal offered, laying back himself.

Faisal stared out at the Mediterranean Sea and the sunbeams glistening off the gentle waves. What would it be like if Arash's dream were possible?

If I were Crown Prince, could an alliance between the Kingdom of Saudi Arabia and Iran truly be formed, uniting Sunni and Shia in an economic and military caliphate the Middle East has never known?

It was an interesting thought, after all . . .

PART I

"Believe none of what you hear and half of what you see."

—Benjamin Franklin

CHAPTER 1

AN NARJIS APARTMENTS
AL-QIRAWAN, RIYADH, SAUDI ARABIA
0643 LOCAL TIME

Jonathan Bin David curled his lip in displeasure as he poured a cup of coffee into one of the four mugs that he and his roommate, Ziv Gabbai, had available in the sparsely stocked apartment. Ziv had served with Shayetet 13 before being recruited to Mossad's Tzomet division, and the Naval commando lived the stereotype of Navy men: He liked thick black coffee.

But this swill was indigestible.

"Hamza," he hollered out from the kitchen, using his partner's nonofficial cover name. Assuming you were always being listened to was a pillar of survival in their line of work. He stared at the steaming black goo and wondered if enough sugar and cream existed in all Saudi Arabia to make the brew palatable. "What do you think about stopping at Starbucks on our way to the office?"

"But I made coffee," Ziv said, toweling off his hair as he emerged from the second bedroom of their flat in dress slacks and shoes, but still in an undershirt. But his grin told him everything Jonathan needed to know.

Jonathan smiled but shook his head, pouring the coffee down the sink. "We're stopping," Jonathan announced.

"It is out of the way, Peter," his partner said, using Jonathan's own NOC: a junior banker from Germany, doing a one-year training program at the capital investment company Fenaa Alawwal. "We'll be late."

"We won't be late," Jonathan said.

A knock on the door brought their eyes together. Ziv raised an eyebrow in unspoken question.

In answer, Jonathan slipped his hand into the kitchen drawer where he kept a SIG Sauer pistol. He watched his partner walk to the door and peer through the peephole. A breath later, Ziv's shoulders dropped, relaxing.

"It's Oren," Ziv said, referring to the third member of their covert ops cell, who operated under the name Jamal Osman.

Ziv cast him a smile over his shoulder as he spun the lock.

But when the door opened, Oren didn't walk in—he was shoved through, sprawling onto the tile floor in a heap as heavily armed men in suits followed. Before anyone could react, the butt of a rifle smashed into Ziv's face, and he collapsed beside Oren.

Jonathan pulled the handgun from the drawer, spinning left as he did. He raised the Sig, but the soft burp of a well-suppressed round from a short-barrel assault rifle signaled the arrival of the bullet that tore through his right shoulder, shattering his clavicle where it met the shoulder. His hand instantly became both numb and useless as nerves were severed, and the impact drove him backward. He stumbled and fell, the back of his head hitting the stove painfully on his way down, bringing stars to his eyes and disorienting him. His cloudy brain registered muffled voices as hands dragged him from the kitchen and rolled him onto his stomach. His shoulder screamed in pain as he worked furiously to recover and plan his moment of resistance. He was Mossad—he would not go quietly—but it seemed clear that the Saudi secret police had somehow pierced their cover and discovered him and his roommates for what they were. This would most certainly end badly for all of them.

I have no intention of being tortured slowly to death by the brutes of the Mabahith . . .

It took his reeling mind a moment to understand what was being said as he shifted his thoughts from Hebrew to Arabic. The unofficial language of the private sector—especially in banking and business—was English, so his mind took an extra moment to process.

"Stanch the bleeding. Gently—do not hurt him," one said in Arabic, the helpful instruction incongruous with the man's harsh tone as Jonathan felt hands apply a dressing to his shoulder.

The knee between his shoulders certainly did not feel gentle. If they wanted them intact, that seemed like bad news indeed—unless Jonathan and his fellow agents were to be traded for something? In the old days, Mossad agents carried cyanide capsules as the last resort in situations like this, but he had no such luxury today.

Jonathan opened his eyes and saw Oren's frightened and angry face beside his own, blood dribbling sideways down his countryman's forehead.

Then he felt a sharp jab in his left calf muscle.

"Not too much—they need sleep only for the drive."

The room tilted, and he couldn't keep his eyes open . . .

He blinked and he was somewhere else. Time must have passed, but he'd felt none of it.

He blinked again, realizing the world was tilted now only because he was lying on his left side, staring across an expanse of marble floor tile. He heard Oren moan somewhere behind him. He tried to raise his head, but before he could, rough hands jerked him up to his knees. His shoulder screamed in painful protest.

"*Jaealahum yaqifun ealaa 'aqdamihim,*" a booming voice demanded.

It took a second for his drugged mind to translate the words: *Get them up on their feet.*

As Jonathan Bin David stood on wobbly legs, he began to recognize the room he was in from his briefings back home in Jerusalem. He glanced beside him and saw Ziv, his fellow operative and former Navy commando, also getting to his feet and taking in their surroundings. This was the official reception room of the Crown Prince of Saudi Arabia, Khalid bin Ahmed al-Saud.

The images from his briefing had been of an empty room, but today the ornate two-tiered desk flanked by the flag of Saudi Arabia was not empty. Instead, the throne-like chair behind it held Khalid bin Ahmed himself, his head back and his lifeless eyes staring at the ceiling. Jonathan could stare into the gaping slash where the man's throat had been cut all the way to bone, the trachea splayed open and the blood vessels flanking it on either side weakly spurting a mix of bright red and dark purple blood. The spray pattern reached several meters beyond the desk, onto the marble floor before and wall behind the corpse. Dozens of deep stab wounds bled through the white tunic over the man's chest, soaking the expensive fabric dark red.

An Arab man in a suit stepped up beside Jonathan and

pressed something into his right hand. Still woozy, he looked down to see a large, curved blade dripping blood in his grip. He scanned the room, trying to make his sluggish brain process what he was seeing. A groggy Oren also held a blade; Ziv had dropped his to the floor. As Jonathan took in the carnage, he slowly became aware of other men holding machine pistols, flanking the gory corpse at the desk.

Now another man, dressed in the formal robe and keffiyeh of the royal family, appeared like an actor cued to stage for a scene in some macabre play. Jonathan recognized the man instantly. He was smiling, a pistol in his hand.

"*Alqatala*!" Saudi Prince Faisal bin Ahmed al-Saud screamed as he leveled his pistol at Jonathan. The panic in the Saudi prince's voice did not match the smile he wore. "*Laqad qutiuu 'akhi*!" he screamed in fake anguish: *Assassins! They have murdered my brother . . .*

And that's when everything suddenly became crystal clear.

The pistol in the hand of the Saudi heir flashed. Gunfire erupted all around Jonathan, and he felt dozens of bullets tear through his flesh. His face split open with their impact as he fell backward, dropping the bloody knife.

He never heard it hit the marble floor.

CHAPTER 2

ALLY PIT BOX
HOMESTEAD-MIAMI INTERNATIONAL SPEEDWAY
1 RALPH SANCHEZ SPEEDWAY BOULEVARD
HOMESTEAD, FLORIDA
1420 LOCAL TIME

Chunk sat in the oversized lounge chair in the cool of the air-conditioning as the noise outside the floor-to-ceiling windows rose to a fever pitch. The race was about to start, the excitement more than NASCAR races he'd attended in the past, in part from the intimacy added by the VIP tour of the pit and meeting many of the drivers before the race—a once-in-a-lifetime kind of thing for a fan like him. But as Chunk sipped his craft beer and smiled, he realized there was more to it too. He felt something that was different—not better, necessarily, but definitely different—from the moments of shared joy with teammates he'd experienced since graduating from college and joining the Teams.

Family.

Gold Squadron was Chunk's "family," but the brotherhood of the Teams wasn't the same as the belonging he saw and felt this weekend with the Sawyers. This was a more innocent happiness that took him back to being a kid himself. It took him back to camping trips with his family, to baseball games and long summer nights, to vacations and even his own first NASCAR race at the Texas Motor Speedway with his dad. He'd been much older than five-year-old Connor, Saw's son, and still remembered the weekend like it was yesterday. The thought made his smile broaden. It had just been him and his dad. After the race, they'd eaten pizza in their room at the Holiday Inn and watched a movie his mom would *not* have approved of—a war movie.

That time bonding with his dad was still precious for him.

He glanced over to where Whitney Watts, Gold Squadron's intel lead and his closest non-SEAL friend in the world, chatted warmly with Ellie Sawyer, wife to Gold Squadron Alpha platoon sniper Nick "Saw" Sawyer. Ellie had three-year-old Maggie in her lap, but the little girl was more interested in dipping a finger in the now–room temperature cheese sauce beside a half-eaten pretzel and drawing on the paper place mat with her cheesy digit. Chunk watched as Maggie crawled into Whitney's lap, leaving a cheese fingerprint on her T-shirt. Some women would have been annoyed, but Whitney just laughed, wiped the three-year-old's chubby fingers, and kept talking with Ellie.

Watts, he realized, would be an amazing mom.

The thought threw up a yellow flag inside him. He'd been compartmentalizing the feelings he had for "Heels" for a long time now, because the nature of the work they did meant they could never ever cross that line. *Not while we're both at the command, at least*, he rationalized, and the thought moved the flag from yellow to red. Whitney looked at him, and he felt his face flush crimson, which made her smile and give him a quizzical look.

Mercifully, Saw picked that time to return from the buffet, little Connor's hand gripping the SEAL sniper's left hand, several plates balancing precariously on his right.

"Omigosh, Nick, let me help you," Ellie said, rising and saving two of the plates that wobbled dangerously near his elbow. "You can make two trips, baby. That's what *all-you-can-eat* means at a buffet."

Saw laughed good-naturedly and kissed his wife full on the mouth, pulling her in tight against him once the plates were safely on the table.

"I'm all about efficiency, babe," he said. "Why make two trips when I can accomplish the mission in one?"

Ellie rolled her eyes but smiled widely as she gave her man another big kiss.

"Here, Mommy," Connor said, sliding a plate full of cheese and crackers onto the table beside her. "I know you like cheese with your wine, and maybe wine will help you get lucky, Dad."

The adults burst out in laughter. Ellie punched Saw in the arm, but she was genuinely amused.

"Don't teach our five-year-old to say stuff like that, Nicholas Sawyer," Ellie chided. "What if he says something like that at preschool?"

"Then the teacher will laugh like we did," Saw said, taking a seat beside her.

"And she'll know Connor's dad is a Team guy," Whitney added.

"That's for sure," Ellie said.

The rising noise meant the race had started. Chunk realized they had missed the flag, and he was surprised to find he didn't really care. Being present with his friends was worth so much more than catching the start of the race.

"Sorry again about missing yesterday's race, bro," Saw said as he dug into a plate of hot wings.

"Nah, all good, brother. We had a great time at the park," Chunk said, grabbing his own thick wing from the plate.

The race weekend package for today's NASCAR Cup Series had also included the doubleheader with passes for yesterday's race, but Saw had opted to take Ellie and the kids to Universal Studios for the day on Saturday instead. The package had been donated by an anonymous sponsor, and it had been a no-brainer for Chunk to offer it to the Sawyer family. But there were six tickets, and Saw had insisted that Chunk and Whitney—who had become close with Ellie over the last six months—come along. They could have gone to Homestead Saturday just themselves, but instead Chunk and Whitney had tagged along with the family at Universal. Chunk was glad they had—and not just because doing the doubleheader and the Saturday night just the two of them might feel awkward. He'd loved *embedding* with the Sawyer family. Saw and Ellie seemed so genuinely happy that Chunk found himself already worrying less about his sniper and Master Chief, who had made the very difficult decision to stay in the unit after the attack by the al Qadr terrorists on his home in Tampa. A lot of wives might have given their operator a mandate, or at least been angry for a time, but Ellie and Saw seemed practically like newlyweds.

"Wanna go out on the terrace and see the cars up close?" Chunk asked, eager to see NASCAR magic from the terrace seats right behind the pit area.

Saw looked down at Maggie, who'd scampered up on his lap and was digging into a plate of chicken nuggets. "Maybe later, bro. Way too loud for Maggie, and right now I'm hanging with my girl."

"I can take her so you don't miss it, babe," Ellie said sweetly. "And Connor, too, if it's too loud for him."

"It's not too loud for me," Connor said, trying to look as grown up as a five-year-old can. "I like fast cars and fast women."

Everyone laughed again as the kid grinned, his face saying he had no idea what the expression meant, but that he liked how the one-liner Saw had fed him made everyone laugh.

Ellie punched Saw again, still laughing. "Nick, I'm serious. You can't teach him to say that sort of stuff. He's going to get in trouble with Ms. Vath at school."

"I don't know where he picks up this stuff, babe. I swear," Saw said innocently.

Chunk watched the Sawyer family giggle together. They looked like any normal American family in that moment. An outsider would never guess that the father had served on the most elite and secretive SEAL team in the country and was one of the most blooded and lethal snipers in the world.

"Come on," Whitney said, rising and grabbing her own beer. "I'll watch with you, Chunk."

Chunk rose and followed Whitney through the glass doors, pressing earplugs into his ears as he did and watching her do the same. He'd warned her she would want them—and had even kicked around the idea of bringing a couple of pairs of noise-canceling Peltors so they could chat normally—but had decided that might be too conspicuous.

"They seem like they're doing great," Chunk said, leaning in close to Whitney's ear after they took two seats in the back row. The smell of her perfume cut through the engine exhaust and burning rubber that mixed with the odor of hot asphalt. He blinked away the feeling the smell of her brought with it.

"Yeah, they're awesome," Whitney said, turning to him and leaning close to be heard. "I think Ellie is one of the coolest women I've ever met."

Chunk agreed, but he'd been fishing a bit, hoping he might get a little more inside scoop on how things were going for his teammate at home. But if Watts knew something more, she was staying mum and respecting Ellie's trust. Either that, or maybe—probably—things were as good in the Sawyer house as they seemed.

"Universal was more fun than I expected," Whitney said, leaning in again, her shoulder touching his. Chunk found himself worrying if his breath smelled like hot wings.

"Agreed. Hell, I'd go back just to ride the velociraptor again," he said as the field of cars whizzed past them.

"*Velocicoaster*," she said, correcting him. "We rode a roller coaster, Chunk, not the actual dinosaur. You do realize that, right?"

"Har, har, har," he said, grinning back. "Glad you tagged along."

"I'm glad *you* tagged along," she teased. "My invitation was guaranteed. It's your participation I had to lobby for with Ellie."

"Good point," he said, holding her gaze.

She looked at him quizzically, seemingly confused he wasn't dishing it back. Suddenly, sitting so close to her made him feel uncomfortable, and he shifted in his seat to open up a little space between them.

"Saw is a great dad," Whitney said. "And I love Ellie to death. They're an awesome couple . . . an awesome family."

"You ever think about that, Heels?" he said, subconsciously

hoping that calling her by her team nickname would reconstruct the wall they kept building between each other. "You know—being a mom?"

Her expression turned wistful. "Yeah. But that's something I might have to postpone to another lifetime, you know? Not sure how *that* fits with the work we do."

"Yeah," he said. "Same."

Ellie and Saw made marriage and parenthood look doable—even easy. But only one of them worked at the Tier One. It would be impossible if both members of the couple served at Gold . . .

"Hold on," Whitney said, leaning in again—closer, Chunk thought, than needed despite the roar of the race cars. "Are you saying that the professional bachelor-warrior Keith Redman has thought about being a dad?"

Chunk turned. Whitney's face was so close to his that he could feel her breath on his cheek. His heart skipped a beat, and a compulsion to kiss her overwhelmed him. His resolve was about to falter when—thank goodness—his secure mobile phone vibrated in his pocket.

"Shit," he said, leaning back in his seat and jamming his hand into his pants pocket to fish out the tactical phone he was always obligated to answer. He read the message:

Possible Tasking

RTB as soon as practical

Call directly when opportunity available but within the hour

CSO Sends

He turned the screen to show Watts, but she was already reading over his arm.

"That sucks," she said, stealing a glance behind them.

Through the glass window, they could both see Ellie sitting with Maggie in her lap, and Saw standing at the glass with Connor, pointing at something on the track while he talked to his boy. Chunk looked at the screen and slipped the phone back into his pocket. Bowman's order read *Soon as practical*, which sounded like a relative directive about which he, as the commander of Gold Squadron, was afforded a certain degree of interpretative leeway.

"What do you say we hold off telling them and let them enjoy the rest of the afternoon?" Chunk said, turning to Whitney and meeting her gaze. "We can leave after the race and still be back at the compound within five hours. What do you think?"

Whitney flashed him an approving smile. "I think that's a great idea."

"I'll find somewhere away from the noise to check in with Captain Bowman," he said, rising from his seat, simultaneously sad and relieved for the excuse to cut the intimate moment with Watts short. "That'll give me a better sense of the urgency."

"I'll save your seat," Whitney said.

He tried to think of something clever to say in response.

Failing, he nodded, rose, and hustled up the steps to find a quiet corner to learn what new world emergency was bringing the best weekend he'd had in forever to a premature end.

CHAPTER 3

THE SITUATION ROOM
THE WHITE HOUSE
WASHINGTON, DC
0740 LOCAL TIME

Kelso Jarvis was annoyed. He'd barely had time to catch his breath since being sworn in as President of the United States, and already the universe felt compelled to deal him a geopolitical crisis that could turn the Middle East upside down. Was it too much to ask to have a couple of crisis-free weeks so he could finalize staffing changes, sit down for one-on-one meetings with his Cabinet members, and help get his wife, Petra, settle into her new public role as First Lady and private role as White House liaison to Task Force Ember?

He looked up at heaven.

I guess it is.

"A world leader is assassinated in his own home, and I'm only just now learning about it?" Jarvis said, fixing his gaze on the Chairman of the Joint Chiefs, Peter McMillian.

"It's the Saudis, Mr. President," McMillian grumbled. "They kept the entire thing a secret until just now."

"Our people suspected something strange was happening, Mr. President," Director of National Intelligence Reggie Buckingham said softly, reading the President's mood. "The Crown Prince had all but disappeared, canceling several appointments and staying out of view entirely."

"Well, now we see why," said Jeff Trussler, the newly confirmed Secretary of Defense, while gesturing toward the horrific image in the center of the middle monitor on the far wall. The former submarine officer and retired two-star Admiral had been appointed by Jarvis to replace Robert Franks, the Cabinet member who'd been murdered—alongside President Warner and Indian Prime Minister Chopra—in the terror attack in New Delhi.

Jarvis looked again at the image on the screen of the Crown Prince of Saudi Arabia, Khalid bin Ahmed al-Saud, throat slit so deeply that his head hung backward at an impossible angle. Jarvis let out a long sigh and tried to rein in his frustration. Feeling a slight tremor beginning in his left hand, he clutched his hands together in front of him on the large conference table.

This is a disaster . . .

"What evidence are the Saudis putting forward about the assassins?" he asked. "What on earth makes them believe it could possibly be the Israelis? Not only would this be out of character, but what do they have to gain? If you're a country surrounded by nations and terrorist organizations dedicated to eradicating you from the planet, then why risk an operation to assassinate Khalid in the middle of a very public campaign to normalize relations between the Kingdom and Israel?"

"And we agree, Mr. President," Buckingham said. "Obviously, behind closed doors, there is no love of Israel in the Saudi Kingdom—nor of the United States, for that matter. But Prince Khalid has been pragmatic and forward-thinking in terms of international affairs and seemed to understand the need for coexistence. We believe his overtures toward recognizing Israel officially were sincere. Nonetheless—"

Buckingham tapped his laptop and ran through a series of photos. These showed the bullet-ridden corpses of three men on the marble floor around the ornate desk holding the body of the dead Crown Prince. These men appeared well-dressed, except for one, who wore only dress slacks and an undershirt. All had large, curved knives beside their bodies, covered in blood.

"—they claim they caught the killers in the act. In fact, the younger brother, Faisal bin Ahmed, was the one who came into the room and discovered the killers and sounded the alarm. He shot one of the intruders himself with a pistol he apparently always has with him, before the security team arrived and mowed the rest of them down."

Jarvis stared at the photos of the assassins who had supposedly murdered the Crown Prince. Khalid bin Ahmed—or KBA, as he was popularly known—had ushered in a new era of stability, foreign investment, and reform in the Kingdom. Jarvis had interacted with the man twice while serving as Vice President, and in both meetings, Khalid had been a smooth operator. Despite himself, Jarvis had felt a grudging respect for the royal. Yes, the Saudis acted solely in their own best interest, but Khalid was reasonable, moderate, and seemed genuinely interested in reform and prosperity for his people. He seemed to understand that, in the modern world, governing meant fostering relationships not only with the

West but also with Israel, the one true democracy in the region, if for no other reason than their close friendship with the United States. Nothing about this assassination made any sense. Israeli Prime Minister Shamone and Crown Prince Khalid had been working through a rough patch in negotiations after a conflagration in the West Bank, but Khalid had publicly expressed interest in an agreement normalizing relations with Israel. The historic move would have meant much for Israel's security.

Why would Shamone authorize the assassination of the first Saudi ruler in generations interested in brokering a new era of cooperation with the Israeli government? Why wreck the fragile peace Israel was enjoying now in the Middle East in exchange for war with Saudi Arabia, the one nation actively negotiating a diplomatic relationship? To jeopardize such an enormous step forward without any clear gains just made no sense, especially when it could lead to a world war in the Middle East, something Shamone would be well aware of.

"Has Israel confirmed that these men are theirs?" Jarvis asked.

"No, Mr. President," Buckingham said.

The title made Jarvis cringe, despite how familiar it was becoming. *A few more months, and then I'm out of here . . .*

"But we also don't need their confirmation," Buckingham continued, tapping his laptop again. The horrible, bloody image of three dead men was replaced with three passport-style photos, displayed side by side. "As you know—maybe better than any of us—we keep our own records of Israeli operatives as we discover them. Facial recognition on the images has confirmed the three dead men in the palace attack as Israeli operatives working in the Tzomet division of Mossad."

The DNI went through the images one by one, identifying Jonathan Bin David and Oren Allon as young but experienced Mossad operatives working together on their second deep-cover operation together. The third man was identified as Ziv Gabbai.

"Commander Gabbai is the oldest of the group and perhaps the cell leader. He is former Shayetet 13, a Navy commando with considerable combat and covert ops experience. We did not have him at Mossad, but the transfer from Shayetet 13 would not be unusual for a man with his skills. He is well-known to us, as he did an exchange tour with our JSOC SEAL team for a year, deploying to Afghanistan with the JSOTF in 2016."

"Well," General McMillian said and pulled at his face, the weight of the situation evident to him, "these men don't seem like the type to go rogue and whack a head of state—especially when doing so would seem likely to plunge their country into a conflict that would be disastrous for Israel. The hard-liners and jihadists will use this as a launch pad for an intifada like we've never seen."

Jarvis stared at the picture of the Shayetet 13 operator. Had they ever crossed paths? Jarvis had just left his position as CSO of the JSOC SEALs in 2016, but he'd worked closely with the Israeli version of the Teams for decades . . .

"Iran will leverage this immediately into calls for violence against Israel, but they may also seize the moment to mobilize their proxy terror groups and attack American forces in the region," Trussler said. "Once this news is out, our military personnel are in real danger. I also expect a significant impact to maritime stability and commerce in the Persian Gulf and Arabian Sea."

"I agree," said Admiral Rousselot, the recently promoted Chief of Naval Operations.

"When do we expect this news to break publicly?" Jarvis asked, turning to Buckingham now. He squeezed his hands together as the tremor worsened.

"Any minute, Mr. President," the DNI said.

"We need more time," Jarvis said, feeling a headache coming on. "Time to figure out what's really going on here before the Middle East spirals completely out of control. This has the feel of a false flag operation to me."

"Iran?" the National Security Advisor, James Hittle, suggested.

"It would make sense, Jim, but both we and the Israelis have pretty robust intelligence assets at many levels in Tehran," Buckingham said. "Between us, we would have had some indication of this coming—or of *something* coming—if Iran had run the op. It's true that Khalid has publicly condemned Iran's role in proxy terror group attacks in the region, so there is motive. But I would think access would be very difficult indeed. VEVAK has tentacles in Saudi Arabia, to be sure, but inside the palace? It seems unlikely."

There were nods around the room. Jarvis saw a particularly concerned look on Secretary of State Ted Baker's face.

"I agree with Reggie," Jarvis said. "This doesn't feel like an operation Shamone would green-light. But we need more than just a gut feeling to work from, or this situation will go to hell very, very quickly." He turned to Buckingham. "We need the entire IC on this. And I need Petra read in right away as well. I assume that's in the works already?"

"It is," Buckingham said. "We're putting together a joint interagency task force to work with the Saudis on this to see if we can uncover the truth—"

Jarvis held up a hand and nodded at the coming question. "I'm going to call the King of Saudi Arabia and grease those skids. We need our people inside, but that will require a lot of diplomacy under these circumstances. I'm sure I can make it happen." He turned back to his defense team. "We need to be prepared, gentlemen. We need our presence in the region reinforced for the predictable response from the bad actors. No American in the Middle East gets harmed, or there will be hell to pay. Make that clear, gentlemen."

"Yes, sir," General McMillian, the Chairman of the Joint Chiefs, said. "The *Ford* Strike Group is on station in the Med, but I'd like to augment the Naval presence with a squadron of F-22s out of Langley. We'll stage them in Turkey, if they'll let us, and from Italy, if not."

"Once Saudi King Mohammed announces that the Crown Prince Khalid's murder is tied to Mossad, our allies in the region are going to have a hard choice to make," Hittle said. "Supporting Israel will come at great cost if the region erupts into war, and terror proxies will target nations who openly support Shamone. We should plan for policy changes and loss of access and support."

The Crown Prince in Saudi Arabia was the true governing monarch for international relations, Jarvis knew, but King Mohammed would surely be deeply involved now, right? It would take time for the new Crown Prince, Faisal al-Saud, to get up to speed.

"You're right, which is why we need to mobilize a second strike group to the region. In the meantime, I'll try and buy us some time to work with our allies to prepare for the worst-case scenarios," Jarvis said, hoping it wasn't wishful thinking. He knew little about Prince Faisal, who he assumed would now ascend to Crown Prince duties. So he would start with King Mohammed.

"Yes, Mr. President. We can task our forward-deployed PACOM asset into the Arabian Sea," McMillian replied.

"Very well. Let's reconvene here in four hours," Jarvis said, "or sooner, if events warrant. In the meantime, gentlemen, let's get to work."

With that, the room began to empty. Jarvis rubbed a thumb into his left temple where his brewing headache grew. He looked up and found himself alone with his DNI.

"This is a disaster, Reggie. If we can escape this without going to war, it will be a miracle." Jarvis needed ibuprofen, or coffee. "I want to hear your unfiltered thought on the situation."

"You said that you wanted Petra read in, sir," Buckingham said. "Can I assume that you want the . . . um . . . the denied asset to run this Joint Interagency Task Force?"

Jarvis sighed. He had two good options at his disposal—Ember, or the Tier One's Gold Squadron—either of which could take point. But did he really want Ember down range on this? He didn't need deniability outside his normal chain, and therefore the smart choice was to hold Ember in reserve in case a scenario unfolded where deniability was required. Gold Squadron had certainly proven themselves more than capable during the recent London counterterrorism operation against al Qadar. Maybe JSOC tasking was the logical choice.

"Who are you thinking to run this thing, Reggie?" he asked, curious if the DNI would reach the same conclusion.

"Well, we're mobilizing representatives from FBI, NCTC, and CIA, of course. But as far as taking the lead, I recommend we task the Tier One unit, since they bring another element we might need if things go south quickly. Anticipating maritime conflict and disruption, Group Eight might fit the bill to join surface assets in the region as well, as they have cyber and tech resources that could come in handy."

Jarvis nodded. The rapid advances in the UUVs, the underwater drones, had grown Group Eight's utility for just such a mission. And, combining spooks with SEALs as they had when they merged Groups Three and Ten had been a force multiplier for sure.

"Then it sounds like you and I are of the same mind on this one. Let's mobilize a JSOC element to Bahrain and embed one or two members into the investigation task force. That gives us maximum flexibility." Jarvis had a bias, of course, but he liked the idea of JSOC running the show, giving them pointy-tip-of-the-spear capabilities up front rather than having CIA run the op. "In fact, let's put them in charge of the task force. Who's that intel officer who unmasked the al Qadar operation in London?"

"Whitney Watts," Buckingham answered immediately, the name apparently top of mind already.

"Great," Jarvis said. "I want her and Gold on point."

"Done, Mr. President. It will be the next call I make."

"Good," Jarvis said. He turned to leave, then stopped himself and looked back. "I'm glad it's you running ODNI, Reggie. I don't know if I've ever told you that before, but it's true."

"Thank you, sir," Reggie said with a self-effacing smile. "I'm grateful to serve."

"Do you want to listen in on the call with the King?"

Reggie nodded. "I wouldn't mind being in the room for that one."

Jarvis rose. "Then why don't you get that arranged. Prep notes for me on anything important I need to know about His Majesty and ping me in the Oval when it's set."

"Roger that, sir. On it."

"In the meantime, I'm going to ring Shamone," he said, heading for the door. "This ought to be interesting."

CHAPTER 4

TIER ONE NAVY SEAL COMPOUND
MACDILL AIR FORCE BASE
TAMPA, FLORIDA
0757 LOCAL TIME

Chunk was unlocking his cage in the armory when he felt a hand on his shoulder. He turned, fully expecting it to be Riker, but the face that greeted him belonged to Captain Bowman.

"Mornin', sir," he said, greeting the unit CSO.

"That's debatable," Bowman said, his voice heavy with sarcasm. "Is Watts in yet?"

"I assume so, but I haven't seen her yet."

"Well, find her and both of you meet me in my office," the O6 said.

Chunk pulled the hot cinnamon-flavored toothpick he was chewing from the corner of his mouth. "Is everything all right, sir?"

"We're most definitely getting involved in the mess in Saudi Arabia," Bowman growled. "I just got off the phone with

DNI Buckingham, and he threw me a helluva curveball. Just find Watts and I'll explain everything in my office."

"Roger that, sir," Chunk said. He popped the toothpick back in and set off to find Watts.

En route to the N2 shop, he passed through the antechamber that housed the Operation Crusader Memorial, which honored the tragic mission in which the entire Tier One SEAL team—the very unit that Chunk's Gold Squadron had replaced—had been wiped out in a single act of terrorism. The display presented three rows of gold tridents affixed to a black backdrop and was bookended by an American flag on the left and the US Navy flag on the right. An engraved inscription above the tridents, finished in gold-leaf lettering, read:

REMEMBERING THE MEN OF OPERATION CRUSADER.
BRAVE MEN HAVE FOUGHT AND DIED BUILDING THE
PROUD TRADITION AND FEARED REPUTATION THAT
I AM BOUND TO UPHOLD.

And below the rows of tridents, two lines from the SEAL creed:

"THE LEGACY OF MY TEAMMATES STEADIES
MY RESOLVE AND SILENTLY GUIDES MY EVERY DEED.
I WILL NOT FAIL."

Chunk was surprised to find Saw standing in front of the wall, staring at the inscription himself. Chunk didn't say anything—just stepped up to stand shoulder to shoulder with his brother in a moment of shared remembrance and respect.

"It's crazy that it's been three *years* since Crusader went down," Saw said, breaking the silence.

"I know," Chunk said, tapping his closed right fist to his chest over his heart. "And I still feel it. I knew almost all those guys."

"Me too." Then, after a long pause, Saw said, "Can I ask you something?"

"Anything."

"If everyone who died on Crusader had been given a crystal ball before going to BUD/S and had known this would be their fate, how many of them do you think would have become SEALs anyway?"

Chunk smiled, not because the question was funny—quite the opposite—but because it was the very same question he'd asked himself many times. In his warrior heart, the answer was as clear as day.

"Every single one of them," he said.

Saw nodded.

"Just out of curiosity, why do you ask?" Chunk said, looking at his brother SEAL.

"This wall is the reason I didn't retire." Saw turned to meet Chunk's gaze, and from memory uttered the words engraved on the wall. "*The legacy of my teammates steadies my resolve and silently guides my every deed.* That's the point of it all, right? The legacy of service is what matters, but not legacy in the way most people think about it. Not personal legacy, not how many medals and ribbons we accumulate. It's about the collective legacy of all the missions undertaken by the brotherhood. Imagine how much more terror and death would have happened in the world if fear of fate had prevented every man whose trident is on that wall from becoming a SEAL . . . I'm glad I don't have a crystal ball, Chunk. At least this way, if something were to happen to me tomorrow, I can meet my maker with no regrets."

Chunk let his teammate's words sink in. After a long moment, he said simply, "No regrets."

Feeling strangely emotionally buoyed and exhausted at the same time, Chunk gave his brother a one-armed hug, then continued on his way to the N2 shop. There he found Watts in her office, working at her desk. He rapped on the doorframe beside the open door.

She looked up from her computer. "Hey."

"Hey," he said. He noticed her glasses, which she only seemed to wear while doing computer work. She looked good in glasses.

Dude, you gotta turn that shit off in your brain.

"What's up?" Watts asked, with an *I'm kinda busy* undertone that made him realize he was still staring at her.

"Bowman needs to see us in his office," Chunk said, adopting a detached, all-business tone.

"Now?"

"Yeah," he said. "And to answer your next question: No, I don't have any details."

"Just a sec," she said, turning her attention back to her computer to type something.

Normally, he'd wait for her to finish up, and they'd walk to Bowman's office together. But today he made himself turn and leave without her. It was kind of a dick move, but that *almost* moment at the racetrack between them had done a real number on him, and he needed to do whatever it took to get the pendulum swinging back the other direction. Still, she jogged to catch up to him, and they ended up arriving at Bowman's office at the same time anyway.

"Come in and shut the door behind you," Bowman called before Chunk even had a chance to knock on the doorframe.

Chunk and Watts did as instructed and sat in the two open seats opposite the CSO's desk. Chunk assumed that Bowman had called them in to further brief them on the situation in

Saudi Arabia that had prompted the "possible tasking" text message yesterday afternoon while they'd been at Homestead with the Sawyers. When Chunk had called in, Bowman had told him only that Gold had been put on "hot standby" in preparation for imminent tasking in the Middle East; however, both the catalyst behind the 0300-alert status, and the tasking itself, had not been explained—nor had Chunk seen anything in the news to give any color to the situation.

Which meant whatever bad thing had happened, it was being kept locked down tight.

"I just got off the phone with DNI Buckingham, and Gold Squadron is deploying to Bahrain in two hours," Bowman said, letting that hang in the air a moment before continuing. "Also of note, President Jarvis made a by-name request for Watts to be assigned to a joint interagency investigative task force, which will fall under the JSOC umbrella but will be operating autonomously from the rest of Gold."

"Wait, what? Me?" Watts said, her expression incredulous.

"Yes, you," Bowman said, leaning in to rest his elbows on the desktop.

"Um, okay . . ." she said, clearly taken aback. "When you say joint interagency investigative task force, which agencies are you talking about? And what exactly are we going to be investigating?"

"A fair question, and I'm going to give you the best answer I can with the information that I know," Bowman said. "It would appear that Saudi Arabia is prepared to link the death of Crown Prince Khalid to Israel. They claim to have evidence that Mossad agents were responsible for the killing. Once that gets out, the powder keg of Iranian terror proxies will explode—and the violence will not just be directed at Israel."

"Well, obviously, that's insane," Watts said as soon as

Bowman had finished. "The Israelis would not assassinate the Crown Prince in the middle of a diplomatic campaign to normalize relations between the two countries."

"The President and the DNI are of the exact same opinion, which is why they're standing up the task force. You and agents from DIA, FBI ERT, and the NSA will be going into Riyadh to investigate the assassination claim being made by the Saudis and report your findings back to the White House," Bowman said.

"Of course, sir," Whitney replied, her eyes wide at the news she would be heading up the joint investigation.

Chunk's first reaction to the news was irritation that Whitney, his intel lead, was being poached from Gold for task force work. Yes, the task force fell under the JSOC management umbrella, but it was pretty clear that DIA would be running the show. His second "revised" reaction after he'd swallowed his annoyance was to feel damn proud and happy for Watts. The fact that President Jarvis had made a by-name request to put her on the investigation team meant that she'd developed a reputation that extended beyond the special operations microcosm that was the Tier One. *Hopefully, they tasked Bobby Theobald*, he thought, remembering the badass former operator and agent who'd helped save Gold's bacon in Mingora on their very first op prosecuting Hamza al-Saud in Pakistan.

However, Chunk's happiness for Watts quickly degraded into a third and final feeling: anxiety. Anxiety not only over her safety on the mission but also anxiety that her bright and rising star might mean that one day she'd be poached by DIA, CIA, or possibly even Task Force Ember.

"I'm flattered, but I'm not a crime scene investigator," Watts said. "There are definitely more qualified individuals out there better suited for this job."

"Watts," Bowman said with a chuckle, "I hope what I'm hearing is humility and not you trying to weasel your way out of this assignment."

"Well, the truth is, sir, I'd rather—"

Bowman cut her off with a raised hand. "You're going. It doesn't matter who you are or what your pay grade is. So long as you work here, you don't say no to by-name requests—especially when they come straight from the President."

Chunk saw Whitney's jaw tighten with irritation, but she nodded in defeat.

"Good, it's settled," Bowman said. He turned to Chunk. "As for the rest of the squadron, you'll be deploying to NAS Bahrain. But be ready to deploy anywhere in the CENTCOM AOR at the drop of a hat. When news of Prince Khalid's murder breaks publicly—and it will break—chaos and craziness will quickly ensue. The Security Council's concern is that every terror cell and Iranian proxy group in the region will amplify and capitalize on the narrative that Israel was behind the assassination to launch terror attacks on Israel itself and other locations throughout the Middle East. It goes without saying that POTUS wants America's top counterterrorism unit in-theater ready to go. You'll fall in under CENTCOM but will be paired up with Group Eight and the Israeli special forces. Admiral Miller runs the show in Bahrain, and you'll be coordinating everything via him and his staff."

"Yes, sir," Chunk said simply.

"Any questions?" Bowman asked, looking back and forth between the two of them.

When Watts didn't say anything, Chunk answered for both of them. "No, sir. Do you want to brief the entire team before we ship out, or want me to take care of it on the flight?"

"No time to brief before; you can do it in transit. Besides, it's a rapidly evolving situation, so who knows what will have changed by the time you get there."

"Understood, sir."

"Good luck, and Godspeed to both of you," Bowman said. Chunk noticed he had an *I'm glad I ain't in your shoes* grin spread across his face.

"Thank you, sir," Chunk said.

He led the way out of Bowman's office, waiting until they were halfway down the hall to turn to Watts. "By-name request—don't see that every day. That's impressive, Heels."

Watts shot him a look, but he wasn't sure what that look was supposed to mean. After a beat, her expression softened. "Thanks, I guess . . ."

"You guess? What's wrong? Are you nervous?" he asked, glancing at her as they headed back to the N2 shop.

"I don't know, Chunk," she said, keeping her gaze forward and down the hallway. "For some reason, I've got a bad feeling about this one."

CHAPTER 5

THE OVAL OFFICE
THE WHITE HOUSE
WASHINGTON, DC
0811 LOCAL TIME

Since Warner's death, Jarvis knew he had been reactive. Reasoned, analytical, intentional—but reactive. Since Ember's defeat of the plot in Delhi, he'd been focused on making sure that Warner's legacy was honored, that his initiatives were followed through on, and that his agenda was completed. That, and Jarvis was also focused on the life he intended to begin in just a few more months—a life outside the White House with his new bride and soulmate, Petra.

But in this moment, Jarvis had to remind himself of something vitally important to the office of the presidency and to the nation he loved and served.

Warner was no longer the President.

Kelso Jarvis now served that role.

Jarvis took a moment to sit in silence behind the Resolute

Desk, feeling the weight of the situation and his role in it as President of the United States. This was not the first time he'd been alone in the Oval Office, but it was the first time he'd paused to recognize it. He focused on not allowing this to be a passive experience. He needed to actively ground himself in the place, power, and history of the Oval. To properly serve as President, even for a short time, he needed to weave himself into the office—and to permit the office to weave itself into the very fiber of his being.

That was the tricky thing about the oath he'd taken, something Warner had not had the opportunity to explain to Jarvis before his passing: Serving as President was different from every other leadership role he'd ever accepted. The presidency wasn't a job. It wasn't a title. It was something that transcended those traditional definitions.

I am the voice of the nation.

I am the will of the people.

I am the United States of America: past, present, and future.

As President, the needs, desires, beliefs, and opinions that drove Kelso Jarvis, the man, needed to be constantly assessed, questioned, and kept in check. The nation came first. The office came second. Kelso Jarvis came in third.

His desk phone buzzed, and he took the call on speaker.

"Yes?"

"Mr. Crouch is here for you," Jenna, his Presidential Secretary, said. "And he asked me to inform you that Israeli Prime Minister Shamone is standing by to receive your call."

"Thank you, Jenna. Send Andy in."

A beat later, Andy Crouch, Jarvis's Chief of Staff, entered the Oval Office and made for one of the two open chairs on the other side of the Resolute Desk. He passed Jarvis a printed sheet of bulleted talking points for the call with Shamone.

Jarvis picked up the page, read each of the eight bulleted items, and committed the three he'd not thought of on his own to his mental list. This single-page prep procedure wasn't something the two of them had explicitly discussed. It was something Andy had just started doing—because Andy was smart, efficient, and he understood his boss.

Jarvis set the paper down in front of him. "Anything we need to talk about before?"

Andy didn't need time to ponder the question. He'd come prepared, as had become their standard protocol. "I think we need to get a commitment from Shamone that there will not be retribution for the killing of their operatives. We can't afford a Sword of Gideon event in the middle of whatever brokered peace we negotiate between the new Saudi regime and Tel Aviv."

Jarvis nodded. But if he were in Shamone's shoes, would he make such a promise? His mind flashed back to a conversation he'd had years ago with his late friend Levi Harel, back when Jarvis had been the DNI. The VEVAK Director of Foreign Operations, Amir Modiri, had masterminded an operation to penetrate the upper echelon of Israeli intelligence. Modiri had plans and was poised to use proxies to destabilize the country in an operation that, if not for John Dempsey and Task Force Ember, would have likely succeeded. Now Harel's voice played in Jarvis's mind with as much clarity as if the self-proclaimed cranky old Jew from Tel Aviv were sitting in the room with him: *"Shamone doesn't give a shit about the circus you call the world stage. What he cares about is a future where Iran—emboldened by the brazen execution of Mossad leadership without consequence—escalates its agenda of terrorism, regional destabilization, and anti-Semitism. If we let this stand, if we do nothing, more Jewish blood will flow."*

Jarvis reached up and massaged his temples. The headache was raging now. He did not intend to use the power of his office to bully allied nation leaders to his will. He would give his best advice, but the final authority for how Israel conducted itself lied with the Israeli people and her government. Still, his oath obligated him to the best interest of the United States, just as Shamone's did to the safety of Israel. The task at hand was to try to make those needs intersect in a way that served them both.

That required a relationship. That required a partnership.

Shamone is going to do what he deems necessary, regardless of what I say—and regardless of the fact I'm the President of the United States.

When he lowered his hand, he noticed Andy staring at him—or more specifically, at his trembling right hand. Jarvis clamped the fingers closed into a tight fist.

"You okay, boss?" Andy asked with a furrowed brow.

"Overcaffeinated with a killer headache," Jarvis said with a weary chuckle. "A terrible combo, but apparently it comes with the job. Or so I'm learning."

Crouch smiled. "In that case, I'll start carrying Aleve. Hit me up anytime you need some."

"Roger that," Jarvis said. He nodded at the desk phone. "Let's make the call."

Andy rang the communications watch officer to initiate the call to the Israeli PM at his office in Kiryat Ben-Gurion. Three minutes later, Shamone was on the line with him, the conversation on speaker for Andy to hear.

"Thanks for taking my call, Yossi," Jarvis said, using the Israeli PM's given name for the first time in their relationship—a power move, but one that the new hierarchy demanded.

"Ah, so now we're on a first-name basis, are we, Kelso?" Shamone said, clapping back.

Jarvis flashed Andy a tight smile. In an even, respectful tone, Jarvis replied, "Are we not brothers, forever bonded in blood?"

"That didn't take long. Only a couple of weeks on the job and you're already reminding me of my debt," Shamone said with a cynical-sounding laugh, referencing the assassination attempt on his life that Jarvis had thwarted in the Old Cemetery in Tel Aviv.

Jarvis sighed loud enough for Shamone to hear. "If I offended you, my apologies. If you prefer honorifics, Mr. Prime Minister, I can accommodate."

After a long, uncomfortable pause, the Israeli PM spoke. "I'm sorry, I'm being difficult, Kelso. You caught me on a bad day . . . which is the only kind of day I seem to have lately."

"These are difficult times," Jarvis said in solidarity. "I'm struggling too."

Now it was Shamone's turn to let out a heavy sigh. "I'm going to address the elephant in the room so you don't have to. The answer is no, we did not do this. Assassinating KBA is not in our best interest. Khalid was a reformer, and the most reasonable Saudi royal I've dealt with over the years. We were making good progress toward—how shall I say?—a civil national discourse. I would never have traded KBA for his brother. Faisal is an unknown quantity. His ascension makes me nervous, and I'm not alone, am I, Ari? Ari Cohen is here with me, by the way."

Jarvis pressed the mute button and looked at Andy. "Ari's the new Mossad Chief?"

"Yep," Andy said.

Jarvis unmuted the phone. "Hey, Ari . . ."

"Mr. President," Cohen said, cordially on the line.

"I've got my Chief of Staff, Andy Crouch, listening in on my end," Jarvis added.

"No problem," Shamone replied. Then, in his legendary no-nonsense manner, the Israeli PM said, "Do you want to hear our working theory?"

"Let's hear it."

"Faisal murdered his brother to seize the crown and plans to frame our agents for it. He's going to conduct a sham investigation, announce false findings publicly, and stoke public outrage to shift the spotlight from his administration to mine. He's going to turn the entire Middle East against us and set us back twenty years in diplomacy. It is dictator handbook page one—cover your crimes by starting a war and cement power by seizing control of the military and implicating all your enemies as traitors or collaborators. I'm telling you, Jarvis, it's about to get ugly."

Jarvis looked at Andy. He realized immediately there was nothing to debate. This was the most plausible and likely explanation. Just like Shamone had said, it just didn't pass the commonsense test for the murder to have been a Mossad operation.

"We hear you, and we're inclined to agree with you," Jarvis said, leaning in to put his weight on his forearms on the desk. "Do you think Faisal did this alone, or do you think he had outside help?"

"This is the question that has been racking my brain. Finding internal collaborators, buying them off, planning the murder—these are all things Faisal would certainly be capable of. But piercing the NOCs of our guys"—Shamone let out a whistling breath—"I don't know. Ari has Tzomet going crazy working the problem. We had zero indicators their covers were compromised."

Andy gestured for Jarvis to mute the phone, which he did.

"That's not a bankable data point. We pierce NOCs and don't act on the knowledge for years, sometimes never," Andy said.

Jarvis nodded and unmuted the phone.

"As you might imagine," Shamone continued, "we have other—um—assets inside the Kingdom that we believe would have alerted us, had an Israeli operation inside the country been uncovered. I must ask, though I suppose you may not answer: Do you have similar assets? And if so, what are they telling you?"

Jarvis didn't think Shamone was really looking for corroborating intelligence as much as gauging the American President's trust and commitment.

"We don't have any ongoing operation inside the Saudi government that would have alerted us," he said. "If we did, I would share with you, I promise. This is an escalating event that affects both our nations, and we consider you our strongest ally. That being said, Yossi, it is not uncommon to let a pierced NOC run its course."

"But then you would be implying I am not being honest with you, Kelso," Shamone interrupted to point out. "And I can assure you that you do work in a world different from ours. If an American agent or asset operating under a NOC in the Middle East is exposed, they are arrested and traded for something of value. When ours are blown, they are tortured and murdered. Our enemies wish for the Jewish existence to be annihilated from the earth. You must understand the difference."

A pause followed. When the static on the line disappeared, Jarvis knew that Shamone had muted his own line while he talked with his Mossad Chief.

A few moments later, the PM came back on the line. "Ari and I just had a little disagreement. But given the stakes and the unconditional trust that Levi Harel had in your integrity and judgment, I'm going to tell you. We have a guy well positioned inside the GIP counterespionage division. We know what NOCs they've pierced and which ones they haven't. These guys were intact. It is a measure of our relationship and trust whether you believe me or not."

"Then there's only one explanation. Faisal had outside help," Jarvis said.

"You can't see it, but I'm nodding."

Jarvis's thoughts returned to the theory his National Security Advisor had floated in the Situation Room. "What about your old nemesis, Iran? This has all the hallmarks of a VEVAK influence campaign. This wouldn't be the first time they penetrated a network of yours. A particular recently discovered double agent comes to mind."

"I don't need to be reminded of such things, my friend. MOIS is a daily thorn in my side. But to your point, Iranian involvement is our working theory. But we need time," Shamone said. "If the Saudi government announces that they have Mossad agents who killed the sitting Crown Prince, the truth coming out later won't matter. Israel will be at war on all fronts, and the world will be on fire."

Jarvis gritted his teeth. He did believe that Shamone was being transparent, but even if he wasn't, both leaders knew this last fact was absolute.

"I know, Yossi, and I'm going to try to get both of us that time. My next call is with King Mohammed. I'm going to propose sending a joint agency investigation team to augment the Saudi's own internal investigations. If we can get a team inside the palace, I'm confident we'll not only discover the truth, but we'll also be able to help write the narrative."

Shamone laughed. "That would be wonderful, Kelso, but I won't hold my breath."

If it had been anyone else, he might have bristled at the comment. But not with Shamone. The Israeli PM and his mentor and friend Levi Harel had been friends and colleagues for four decades at the time of Levi's passing. Jarvis had heard countless stories from Levi over the years about Shamone and practically felt like he knew the man. By virtue of Levi's respect and admiration for Shamone, Jarvis was willing to give the Israeli PM plenty of interpersonal leeway.

"I have a few levers I can pull with the King," Jarvis said. "There's reason to be optimistic."

"I hope you're right. Good luck, my friend."

"Before we hang up," Jarvis started. He let the sentiment hang for a moment before continuing, "I have a favor to ask."

"So, I was right. You're calling in my debt," Shamone said, the edge returning to his voice.

"No, think of it as a call for restraint."

"I'm listening."

"We know you lost agents, good men who were murdered in cold blood for nefarious purposes. But now is not the time for retribution. It's within your right to pursue and punish those responsible for the killing, but all I ask is you give us time and a heads-up before you conduct a campaign. Is that fair?"

"So, Israel reports to you now. Is that what I'm hearing?" Shamone came back hard.

Jarvis inhaled deeply through his nose, swallowing the flare of anger in his chest. "Time and notification is all I asked for, Yossi. And it serves the interest of both of our nations to have the truth uncovered to share on the world stage before any escalation. An all-out war in the Middle East brings every proxy nation and terror group to the fight. That will be a genie we can't put back in the bottle."

"Very well," Shamone said. "You have two weeks. Consider this your notification."

Before Jarvis could reply, the line went dead.

"Spicy," Andy said with a chuckle from the other side of the Resolute Desk.

Jarvis fixed him with a half smile. "That's Shamone. Went about as well as we could have hoped. He's stressed."

"And for good reason," Andy said. "But do you think we can trust him to be open and honest with us?"

Jarvis pursed his lips, then nodded. "Right now, he feels trapped in a corner. If we can give him a little breathing room, I think he'll dial it down a notch and we'll be able to tackle this as a team."

"And if not?"

Jarvis blew air through pursed lips. "If not, then Beit Aghion might find itself the epicenter of World War III."

CHAPTER 6

INTERROGATION MONITORING SUITE
BLACK SITE FOR THE MINISTRY OF INTELLIGENCE OF THE IRANIAN REPUBLIC OF IRAN (A.K.A. VEVAK)
TEHRAN, IRAN
1819 LOCAL TIME

Arash Reza picked up the Glock 19.

He turned the gun over in his hands, examining it while the man standing across the table from him shifted his weight nervously from his right leg to his left, undoubtedly wondering what Reza was intending to do with the 9mm pistol. Reza knew exactly what he wanted to do with it. Unfortunately, they both worked for the Ministry of Intelligence, which meant shooting the man was out of the question. On paper, he and Hosseini were on the same team. But org charts rarely represented reality.

In Reza's mind, Hosseini's duties were merely . . . *janitorial.*

While working in his NOC, Reza never carried a firearm. His job at the Ministry did not require one either, but he went to the range at every opportunity to maintain his proficiency. He'd requisitioned the pistol instead of accepting the clunky, heavy, standard-issue PC-9 Zoaf—an Iranian-made clone of the SIG Sauer P226. He liked how the Glock was lightweight. He liked the composite construction. He liked the blocky, no-frills, utilitarian design. But most of all, he liked that it used a striker-fired mechanism with no hammer or thumb safety to fuss with.

Grab a Glock, pull the trigger, and a bullet fires.

Simple.

Predictable.

Streamlined.

It had been a long day, and Reza was tired. His patience had run out an hour ago. He was ready to go home, where a hot meal and an even hotter girlfriend awaited him. But before that could happen, he needed to wrap up this interrogation. He was 100 percent confident that one of the two men currently being held captive by Hosseini was a Mossad agent and that the other was a hapless civilian. Unfortunately, Reza was 0 percent confident which man was which. Both had been interrogated and tortured, and both men had reacted in virtually identical ways: blanket denials at first, then blanket confessions in exchange for a reprieve from the agony.

Reza, for his part, refused to perform torture. Not out of principle, as torture was often effective, but for other reasons that were contradictory and difficult to articulate. Maybe, despite the cold, Machiavellian nature of his job, he harbored some vestigial sense of fairness. Strapped in a chair, no man has a fighting chance. How was that fair? But nature certainly didn't care about fairness. The Ebola virus robotically turns its host into an agonizing pile of bloody goo.

Spiders inject venom, paralyzing their prey before liquefying their insides and consuming them from the inside out. Sharks tear their living prey apart chunk by chunk without remorse or consideration.

But does that mean I must be like such creatures?

He took no pleasure watching torture and took no pleasure performing it. It did not make him feel strong or powerful—quite the opposite. It was for this reason that Arash Reza left torture to the sadists—to hollow, lesser men like Hosseini, who prided himself as an artist, but who in reality was nothing more than a failed field agent with sadistic proclivities.

Reza stared at Hosseini now. The man had been defensive when Reza had pressed him about his failure to extract details that validated either man's confession.

"What are you planning to do with *that*?" Hosseini asked, eyeing the gun.

"If we don't get a verifiable confession soon . . . shoot someone, I suppose," Reza said.

"It's not my fault," Hosseini said with a *don't blame me* tone in his voice. "I can start removing body parts, if you like."

Reza shook his head. "No. I want you to put them in the same room. I will talk to them together."

"But keeping the subjects separated is—"

Reza cut him off. "Do as I say."

Hosseini cleared his throat. "Which room do you want me to put them in?"

"I don't care, Hosseini."

The torturer hurried out of their tiny interrogation monitoring suite, leaving Reza alone with a single laptop computer. The screen had a split-window streaming video of each prisoner from Wi-Fi cameras mounted on the walls. Both men sat hunched in their chairs, heads hanging with blood and drool dripping from their mouths, arms bound behind the chair-backs. Without the plastic ties on the prisoners' wrists, they'd fall out of their chairs.

Hosseini had worked them over hard.

On his screen, Reza watched Hosseini enter the room that housed a man who went by the name of Abdul Mehrab. Mehrab claimed he was Iranian born, and that he worked as a government consultant in Tehran. His birth records and work documents all checked out, but that wasn't proof of anything. The Zionists were the best in the world at hacking databases and creating ironclad NOCs for their agents.

Hosseini shouted at Mehrab to wake up, but the man didn't react. Instantly losing his patience, Hosseini slapped Mehrab in the side of the head, which did the trick. The man looked up with glazed eyes, and Hosseini told him to stand up—all but impossible with Mehrab's wrists still bound behind the chairback. So Hosseini told the battered prisoner to bring his chair with him. With great difficulty, Mehrab leaned forward, bending at the waist, and stood just enough to lift the front feet of the chair off the floor. Stooped, the prisoner shuffled after Hosseini, carrying the chair on his back like a two-legged turtle.

With a weary sigh, Reza got to his feet, shoved the Glock into his waistband, and followed the pair into the other interrogation room, where Naveen Kevah, the other prisoner, was being held. On entering, Reza's nostrils were assaulted by the musky stench of torture, a smell created by the amalgam of excreted biological fluids: sweat, blood, and urine. Neither man had shat himself, thank God—yet. But that was coming. Instead of plugging his nose, Reza inhaled deeply—grounding and connecting himself to the moment.

He needed to connect with the primal predator within him. Beneath his sense of fairness, beneath his humanity, beneath his empathy, the primitive mechanisms of his brain were hardwired to detect weakness. Deep in his biology, powered by his five senses, he possessed the means to discern truth from deception.

"Sit there and face forward," Hosseini said to Mehrab, pointing to a spot next to Kevah.

The prisoner did as ordered.

Hosseini went and stood in the left corner, his back against the wall where he lit a cigarette to enjoy while he watched Reza work. Reza centered himself between the two men. He sighed and looked from Kevah on the left to Mehrab on the right. Both men were awake, lucid with fear and expectation. Reza studied each man for several long seconds, then pulled the Glock from his waistband and aimed the muzzle at the floor, his right index finger inside the guard and on the trigger.

Mehrab's gaze was fixed on the Glock. Reza watched as the man's lips began moving in a silent prayer. In Mehrab's eyes, Reza saw nothing but fear. Reza shifted his gaze to Kevah, who glanced at Mehrab. In that briefest of moments, Reza saw something else flicker in Kevah's eyes. In Kevah's eyes, he saw concern . . .

Concern for his asset.

All doubt erased from his mind, Reza raised the gun and shot Mehrab in the abdomen.

In his peripheral vision, Reza saw a shocked and confused Hosseini turn to glare at him, mouth agape. Reza ignored the torturer and looked at Kevah.

"Why did you do that?" Kevah asked, confirming Reza had made the right choice.

"We can save him. We have good hospitals in Tehran, but only if you cooperate quickly. Right now, blood and other things are leaking into Mehrab's abdominal cavity. If you answer my questions, I will save Mehrab."

Defiance and rage rolled across Kevah's face. Kevah knew he'd just outed himself, and he also knew that Reza had seen it. The Zionist spy shifted his gaze to Mehrab, whose dirty tan-colored shirt now had a growing crimson stain on the belly. After a moment of tortured indecision, Kevah looked back at Reza.

"Save Mehrab's life, and I'll talk," the Zionist said.

Reza shook his head. "Talk, and I'll save his life."

Kevah said nothing for a long moment. Then, in a defeated monotone, he told Reza everything he wanted to know. When Reza was satisfied, he turned to Hosseini.

"Take Mehrab to the hospital."

Hosseini screwed up his face at Reza. "Are you serious?"

In answer, Reza walked over and cut the plastic ties binding Mehrab's wrists. "A deal is a deal."

Mehrab, who Reza had just learned was an Iranian informant run by Kevah, did not look well. His gray pallor, glazed eyes, and listless posture told Reza the man would not survive, even with the best medical treatment available. Reza had shot Mehrab just to the right of the midline, ripping a hole in the largest vein in the body. It would bleed much more slowly than an artery, but nonetheless, time was nearly out for him. When it became clear that Hosseini would be unable to walk Mehrab out alone, Reza went to the man's other side. With Hosseini, they half carried, half dragged the Zionist collaborator out of the room. Reza kicked the door shut behind him, leaving Kevah alone.

Once they were halfway down the hall and out of earshot,

Reza ducked out from under Mehrab's limp arm, leaving the dying man for Hosseini to manage. Hosseini looked at Reza with a confused expression.

"What are you doing?"

"I'm going home."

"What about *him*?"

"What *about* him?" Reza echoed, annoyed.

"Do you really want me to take him to the hospital, or was that just acting?"

Reza shook his head at the stupidity of the question. "I don't care what you do with Mehrab, so long as Kevah believes he's been taken to the hospital. As for the Zionist, no more torture for tonight. Give him water, meat, and bread. I might have more questions for him tomorrow."

Hosseini looked angry, but he nodded and struggled to drag the traitor away to wherever it was people like Hosseini disposed of bodies. Janitorial wasn't Reza's department.

Reza walked to the bathroom and checked himself for bloodstains. "Shit," he said, noticing blood on his left shirt-sleeve and cuff. Irritated, he took off the shirt, balled it up, and threw it in the trash can. Then, shirtless, he grabbed his messenger bag, stuffed the Glock into the hidden compartment inside, and walked out the back door of the safe house. Using the key fob, he unlocked his Peugeot 508 sedan and popped the rear hatch for the boot where he always kept a change of clothes. After shrugging on a clean shirt, he put his bag inside and closed the lid.

His girlfriend, Aliyah Amani, had no idea what he did for a living, and he had hoped to keep it that way.

As he pulled out of the lot, his mobile phone chimed with a text message. He grabbed the phone from the center console and looked at the message. His boss, Director of Foreign

Operations Hassan Golzar, wanted him to come in. Reza exhaled with exasperation, pulled the car over to the side of the road, and called the office.

Golzar's secretary, Jelah, answered.

"This is Reza. I just got a text to come in. Is it urgent, or can it wait until tomorrow?"

"It's urgent," Jelah said, "but I can't say more on the phone."

"Understood. Let him know I'm on my way."

"Yes, Mr. Reza," she said.

The line went dead, leaving Reza wondering the reason for his summons. His mind automatically went to Hosseini. If the worm had somehow already informed Golzar about Reza shooting Mehrab . . .

No, that can't be it.

He blew air through pursed lips at the prospect of being late, again. Like most beautiful women, his girlfriend was high-maintenance and expensive. But she was also, surprisingly, quite self-reliant and adept at handling change. The thought had occurred to him on more than one occasion that she'd make a capable agent. But unfortunately, Aliyah, like Faisal, was an assignment.

Instead of calling, he decided to text her the bad news. Hopefully, she wouldn't get upset.

I'm going to be late my
love. A thousand apologies

Her reply came swiftly:

Thanks for letting me know
Should I eat without you?

If you wait, I'll take you out
Somewhere nice. And after . . .

I like the sound of that, kiss

Twenty-eight minutes later, Reza pulled the 508 into his reserved parking slip at the Ministry of Intelligence and Security building in Tehran, feeling both uncertain and curious as to the purpose of the impromptu meeting.

He made his way through the warren of staircases and narrow hallways to the third floor, where Director Golzar's homely but dutiful secretary, Jelah, sat behind a tiny desk in an alcove outside his corner office. Outwardly, Jelah presented as completely immune to Reza's charms. But try as she might to hide her sexual frustration with a mask of indifference, Reza knew she'd sleep with him in an instant if he pursued her. Reza was acutely aware of how attractive he was, and he exploited his looks at every opportunity. Even now, in his late thirties, he drew glances and gazes from women—and men—of all ages. Without his looks, he would have never been recruited by VEVAK or accepted into Oxford.

He would never have befriended Faisal.

"You can go in," Jelah said, looking up at him over the top rim of her eyeglasses. "He's ready for you."

Reza nodded and fixed her with a cordial smile before letting himself into the Director's office.

Golzar sat behind an ancient and worn wooden desk. He looked up to greet Reza with a weary but professional closed-lipped smile. He wore a short-sleeve oxford-style shirt, open at the collar with no necktie, and a gold watch on his right wrist. Golzar was balding but kept what little hair he had trimmed neat and short. The man was gaunt, but somehow had good color to his skin despite working past sundown every day. Reza would be hard-pressed to find any manager or director in VEVAK who worked longer and harder than Golzar. This, like so many other aspects of his boss's personality, was a double-edged sword for Reza.

"Have a seat, Arash."

"Thank you," Reza said. He lowered himself into the narrow wooden armchair on the left, facing his boss, because the armchair on the right was currently occupied by a stack of folders. In fact, piles of folders took up most horizontal surfaces in the cramped office, which Reza realized had slowly become a file vault. Golzar had a habit of never returning the files he requisitioned.

"I have something important to talk to you about, but before I do," the Director said, eyes blinking behind his round spectacles, "tell me about the interrogation."

Reza swallowed his annoyance at having to wait to hear the important news and dutifully read Golzar in on the events of the day.

"So Kevah is Mossad, just as you predicted."

Reza nodded. He hadn't *actually* predicted Kevah to be the Zionist and Mehrab the asset, but there was no value in pointing this out.

"Are you sure we can't save Mehrab? Otherwise, it's a missed opportunity to find out exactly what he's leaked."

Reza felt his face flush. Why hadn't he thought of that before he'd so callously left Mehrab's fate in Hosseini's hands? Kaveh would resist revealing the intelligence he'd collected because that information was already banked, and doing so would put other Mossad agents and active operations at risk. Kaveh had broken, but only to save his asset's life. When the lives of other colleagues and sources were on the line, he'd resist.

"I don't think he's going to make it," Reza said at last.

"Pity, it will be harder to extract those details from Kevah," Golzar said, echoing Reza's thoughts. "Okay, well, see what else you can get tomorrow. Good job getting the confession."

Reza nodded.

The Director removed his eyeglasses and began to clean them with a square lens cloth. At fifty-nine years old, Golzar had reached the pinnacle of his career. A lifelong bureaucrat, he would never be promoted to Minister—not because he wasn't smart enough or capable of fulfilling the job, but because he lacked the drive and political machinations to even be considered for it. Golzar was diligent and meticulous. He was a rule follower, who kept the rank and file organized and in line. As far as Reza was concerned, Golzar was the polar opposite of his predecessor, Amir Modiri—a cunning, ambitious risk-taker with designs on becoming the Minister of Intelligence. Reza was convinced that was why Mahmoud Safavid, the current Minister of Intelligence, had picked Golzar to take Modiri's place after Modiri and his wife were assassinated at the Grand Bazaar nearly three years ago: Minister Safavid did not perceive Golzar as a threat.

But that didn't mean Golzar wasn't good at his job. Golzar's organized, methodical, low-risk approach to spy craft, Reza reasoned now, might in fact be the superior strategy in a world where drawing unwanted attention was a death knell.

Espionage, after all, was supposed to happen quietly and in the dark.

After a long beat, Golzar returned his eyeglasses to their perch on his nose.

"Khalid bin Ahmed al-Saud was murdered."

Reza blinked. He felt his consciousness experience a seismic shift. In his life, he'd only experienced this phenomenon one other time—when the Twin Towers had fallen in New York City on 9/11. At the time, he'd been a twelve-year-old boy, but the impact had been profound and irreversible. One moment, the world was one way, and the next it was different, like someone abruptly shifting the tracks ahead of a train barreling at high speed. The momentum is too powerful to stop, but the direction has been changed. The passengers have no choice but to travel to the new destination, looking back helplessly and wistfully at the path they were once on, now disappearing in the distance.

A smile curled the Director's lips. "It's a remarkable turn of events, wouldn't you say?"

"Faisal is now the Crown Prince?" was all Reza managed to get out.

Golzar nodded. There was a look of veneration on his face.

He did it, Reza thought, leaning back. He smiled with wonderment. *I can't believe he actually did it.*

"This was your doing, wasn't it?" the Director said.

"I can't believe it. Yes, I planted the seed and have been watering it for years, but Faisal—" he started to laugh. "I mean—I provided every tool he needed and recently gave him . . . assets . . . that could make it happen. But after so many times so close to the prize, I never really thought he had the balls to follow through."

"Congratulations, Arash," Golzar said. "From what I understand, you have invested many years in this campaign."

This was both true and also an understatement. In fact, he'd invested his entire adult life into this mission. The plan, which had been the brainchild of Amir Modiri, was beautiful in its simplicity and beyond audacious: Turn the al-Saud royal family from a wary adversary to a partner and ally in the Middle East. Why should Shia and Sunni brothers undermine each other to the benefit of their true adversaries? For too long, the Americans and the Zionists stoked the fires of animosity and mistrust between the two most powerful nations in the Middle East—Iran and Saudi Arabia. Modiri's powerful, hopeful words—words he'd used to recruit Reza—still echoed in Reza's mind all these years later: *"Imagine what we could accomplish if we were united?"*

Reza's influence campaign had been slow and methodical, with Modiri coaching him throughout it all. It had required Reza to become someone else—a man whose skin he'd lived in for so long he wasn't sure which Reza was the real Reza anymore. Like two trees whose trunks are woven together as saplings and then grow together to become one organism, the two parts of Reza had become indistinguishable and impossible to separate.

Reza remembered the day he'd first planted the seed in Faisal's mind, years ago on the deck of the superyacht *Tranquility* while anchored off the coast of Santorini: *"I know he is your brother, but it seems he cares more about appeasing the Americans and the Jews than in the future of the region. The Kingdom of al-Saud could raise the entire region, with the Kingdom at the head of the table. If only you were Crown Prince . . ."*

Reza snapped back to the present, his mind and body invigorated by ambition and possibility. "Did he frame the Zionists?"

"Details are scant, but that is the rumor."

Reza pumped his fist in the air. "Yes, this was my plan. And by God, Faisal did it."

"Then you deserve to be congratulated. It was a stroke of genius."

"Thank you, sir," Reza said, his mind already charging ahead at light speed. "We must capitalize on the chaos to turn world opinion against Israel and the Americans. We can't squander this opportunity."

Golzar chuckled. "We don't intend to."

"I want to be reassigned," Reza blurted.

Golzar's eyebrows went up.

"Not reassigned," Reza corrected himself. "What I mean is repositioned. It's time for the Oxford-educated Iranian playboy to get a government job. We need to trade my nonofficial cover for an official one. I need to be able to interface with Faisal in both a personal and political capacity. He is going to be dealing with heads of state on a daily basis. Starting now, he will shed his playboy persona to become a Prince and politician. For him to respect me, and for me to retain access and influence, I need to do the same."

"Yes, I agree. It's why I summoned you."

Reza tried not to smile. If the man had an ego, he never fed it. Reza rarely reverted to honorifics, but now he couldn't help himself. "Thank you, sir."

Golzar put his eyeglasses back on. "What about Aliyah? How do you think she'd react to you taking a government job?"

"Oh, I think she'd be an asset in my role."

Aliyah's father was wealthy Emirati. Reza was convinced the only reason the man had tolerated his daughter's relationship with an Iranian playboy was because of Reza's friendship with Faisal and his connection to the al-Saud family.

Golzar screwed up his face. "You think Aliyah Amani aspires to be a politician's wife? Honestly, Arash, I'm surprised you convinced her to move to Tehran at all. How much longer do you think she'll tolerate the restrictions on her freedoms living here under this regime? She's an Emirati.

Wearing the hijab. Living as a homemaker. This is not the life she aspires to."

Reza nodded. Golzar was right. Aliyah would consider him taking a government job as a step in the wrong direction. *Unless it served her father's interests . . .*

"Make me the Ambassador to Saudi Arabia," Reza blurted.

"If only I had that kind of power," Golzar said through a laugh.

Inside, Reza bristled but kept his expression neutral. "But you think the idea has merit."

"It definitely has merit. You would have a reason to meet and talk with the Crown Prince regularly. If not the Ambassador, maybe there's a role for you as his deputy. Let me think on this. I will request a meeting with Minister Safavid tomorrow. I will discuss it with him, but as you know, Ambassador Salahi is a friend of President Esfahani. It will be difficult to displace him."

A vulpine grin curled Reza's lips. "But less difficult if there were a by-name request from the new Crown Prince for him to be replaced."

Golzar laughed. "Your mind works like your mentor's did."

"I'll take that as a compliment."

"As you should. My predecessor set many great plans in motion. I am a fortunate man to have inherited his . . . investments in Iran's future, shall we say," Golzar said.

The look in Golzar's eyes told Reza that the Director considered Reza himself to be a position in that investment portfolio. Reza nodded at the compliment.

"It's getting late. I have a lot of work to do," Golzar said, leaning forward in his chair. "I have many operations to plan in the coming weeks to challenge the Americans and Zionists and create chaos in the region. And you need to talk to your friend in Riyadh . . ."

"Yes, sir. I'm on it."

Reza stood and took his leave. As he made his way toward the door, Golzar called out behind him.

"And don't forget to pleasure your woman tonight. Her life is about to get turned upside down."

Reza turned and shot the old man a wry smile.

"Don't worry, sir. Pleasuring women is the one other thing I'm very good at."

CHAPTER 7

THE SITUATION ROOM
THE WHITE HOUSE
WASHINGTON, DC
1214 LOCAL TIME

Jarvis had the DNI, the NSA, SecState Baker, SecDef Trussler, Vice President Margaret Whalen, and the First Lady, his wife, Petra, assembled in the Situation Room for the call with Saudi King Abdul Rahman Mohammed al-Saud. Unlike the private call he'd had with the Israeli PM, Yossi Shamone, earlier that morning, this conversation was best suited for an audience. The team he had assembled were functionally the "head shed" for the United States of America—the best and brightest men and women in government, and people Jarvis trusted implicitly.

"The King is on the line and ready for you, Mr. President," Andy said, trotting into the room and closing the door behind him. He pulled up a chair to sit at an angle beside Jarvis, who took a seat at the head of the conference table.

Jarvis glanced down at the single page of notes Andy had prepped for him, then leaned forward and pressed the button to connect the voice-only call.

"Your Majesty, King Mohammed, this is President Jarvis speaking. Let me begin by offering my most sincere condolences on the loss of your son, Khalid. As Vice President, I interacted with him on several occasions and found him to be an insightful man and leader," Jarvis said.

"Thank you for those kind words," a male voice replied.

Jarvis ticked his gaze to Baker, who was shaking his head. The Secretary of State mouthed, "*Not the King.*"

"For the sake of clarity, Mr. President, you're speaking with Faisal bin Ahmed al-Saud. My father, the King, offers his most sincere apologies for being unable to attend this meeting as arranged. He's grief-stricken beyond words and feeling unwell. As you can imagine, this entire situation has caused tremendous stress for the King. But rest assured, as Crown Prince, I have his full confidence and authority to speak in his stead."

Jarvis pressed his lips together in a hard line and looked at Petra. She gave him a little eye roll that summed up this wrinkle perfectly: typical, annoying, and to be expected.

And unfortunate . . .

Negotiating with Faisal out of the gate was precisely what Jarvis had hoped to circumvent with this call.

"I'm sorry to hear that. I certainly hope that, despite his grief, the King is in otherwise good health."

"Well, as you know, my father is no longer a young man. I probably shouldn't be sharing this, but I've noticed recently that he can become easily confused and absent-minded. But the doctors tell me that's not uncommon with early-stage dementia. Like I said, I have His Majesty's full confidence and authority to negotiate on behalf of the Kingdom," Faisal said with the air of newly minted power.

Jarvis pressed the mute button. "Is the King suffering from dementia?"

"Not to my knowledge," Baker said. "Last time I spoke with him, he was as sharp as a tack."

Jarvis unmuted the phone. "That's an interesting thing to say. I didn't realize we were negotiating, Your Highness. I am simply offering my nation's help and support in this difficult time."

Faisal took a moment before reacting. "A figure of speech, Mr. President. English is a second language for me."

"*Innahu lee aydan*," Jarvis joked in Arabic, saying the same was true for him. He knew from Andy's notes that Faisal was Oxford-educated, and he wasn't going to let the new Crown Prince hide behind his English as an excuse.

The comment earned a laugh from Prince Faisal on the phone, and from Petra, but no one else laughed. The rest of the Cabinet did not speak Arabic.

"Since we've not had occasion to speak before," Jarvis continued, switching back to English, "I'm grateful for this opportunity, Crown Prince Faisal. I hope you and I can develop a strong working relationship, similar to the one I had with your brother, Crown Prince Khalid. It is my hope—and the hope of Secretary of State Baker and the State Department—that you will continue your brother's legacy of reform, diplomacy, and economic development."

"That is my hope as well, Mr. President. But unfortunately, my brother's assassination requires that I press the pause button on all his initiatives and partnerships. You see, President Jarvis, my brother was murdered inside the palace by an enemy of the Crown—by an enemy of state. My first and foremost priority as Crown Prince is to discover who is responsible for this savage and brutal attack on my family and on the Kingdom and bring that party to justice."

As soon as the final syllable left Faisal's mouth, Jarvis pounced.

"I completely understand the importance of conducting a comprehensive investigation of this tragedy, which is why my administration would like to offer assistance in this matter. I've taken the liberty of dispatching a small elite team of analysts and investigators to assist your own experts in investigating the murder. They bring decades of experience in examining crime scenes of the highest importance—including the office that investigated 9/11 and the recent attacks in London. I want you to know, Your Highness, that all of FBI and DOD's investigative resources are available and at your disposal."

"Thank you, Mr. President, for this generous offer of assistance, but I must graciously decline. Ri'asat al-Amn al-Dawlah is already conducting a detailed investigation . . ."

While Faisal talked, Andy slid a piece of paper in front of Jarvis with a hand-scribbled note:

A.K.A. the Presidency of State Security. Agency formed in 2017. Merger of General Intelligence Presidency and General Investigation Directorate.

". . . and I have every faith in their capabilities. But don't worry. As soon as the investigation concludes, I will make the findings public. The world deserves to know the truth about who is responsible for this cowardly, heinous attack on the Kingdom and House al-Saud."

Baker turned his notepad to Jarvis: *Offer him something to stall.*

Jarvis pursed his lips in aggravation. The SEAL in him

despised political horse trading. As an operator, he was a direct-action guy and never one to try to bribe, buy, or cajole his way out of a jam.

No, he decided. *I'm doing this my way.*

Jarvis leaned toward the speakerphone. "So, if I'm hearing you correctly, Prince Faisal, you're refusing my nation's offer of support and solidarity on this matter? You'd prefer to keep the United States at arm's length as a partner as you weather this storm? You'd prefer to begin your tenure as Crown Prince in isolation? I must tell you that surprises me. As a newly minted President myself, offers of support and public affirmation from my fellow world leaders were critical to helping me find my footing during the early days of my presidency. It's a shame—I would have loved to have given you a resounding public endorsement as the Kingdom's new functional head of state."

A long pause followed. Finally, Faisal spoke.

"I will take your words under advisement. If I decide that outside assistance might be beneficial, I will direct Ambassador Noor to contact Secretary of State Baker's office," Faisal said.

"Our team will be standing by in Bahrain waiting for that call," Jarvis said. "Just out of curiosity: Does Your Highness intend to release an official statement confirming the death of Crown Prince Khalid before or after the official investigation is complete?"

"I have not decided. Why do you ask? Do you have an official request, or any diplomatic concerns that I and my staff should be aware of, Mr. President?"

The smug, self-important undertone in Prince Faisal's voice annoyed Jarvis, but he was in control enough not to let it show in his reply.

"Speaking frankly, we're concerned about regional stability. One could certainly imagine a scenario where an official statement from the Crown that prematurely implicated another government or group in the death without proper due diligence might lead to an inflammatory situation where violence and civil unrest result. We would hate to see a conflagration erupt in the Mideast. Your brother was a beloved and respected man. We want to avoid any . . . misunderstandings."

"Thank you for that sage counsel, President Jarvis. I will give your advice full consideration."

Jarvis didn't detect any arrogance or subtext in the comment, but he didn't know the man well enough to be certain. Jarvis concluded the call, and when the line was dead, he turned to Baker.

"I want a list of every trade deal, defense contract, and FDI in place or being negotiated with the Kingdom over five hundred million dollars, and I want it on my desk in thirty minutes. I need to know what levers I have available to pull. If I have to put the screws to this guy to control the narrative, I will."

Baker's face flashed with dismay, which Jarvis suspected meant aggregating that much information that quickly was likely impossible. To the Secretary's credit, he simply said, "Yes, Mr. President."

Jarvis next turned to the DNI. "Reggie, I want a dossier on Faisal—everything we know, suspect, and don't know about the new Crown Prince. A personality profile, his spending habits, offices and positions held in government, his allies, his enemies, his friends, his lovers . . . everything."

"Yes, sir. Already in progress," Buckingham said.

He nodded and looked at Petra with a *what am I forgetting?* stare.

"Would it be valuable," she offered, "to have Secretary Baker attempt to schedule a follow-up call with the Crown

Prince in, say, twenty-four hours? If Prince Faisal knew he had a ticking clock to make a decision, he might be more inclined to accept our offer of cooperation."

Jarvis nodded, silently loving his wife for her tactical mind. "Great idea. Ted, what do you think?"

"I think the First Lady is, as always, diplomatically insightful. Do you like the twenty-four-hour time horizon, or do you want to be more or less aggressive?" Baker asked.

"Let's shoot for 0900 our time tomorrow."

"Yes, sir, Mr. President."

"Before we break, does anyone have any observations, insights, or opinions gleaned during that call that you'd like to share?" Jarvis asked. He looked square at Reggie. He knew the DNI well enough to read Reggie's mind.

"This is purely conjecture," Buckingham said, taking the cue, "but I suspect the new Crown Prince wasn't entirely honest with us about the King. I question whether His Majesty was informed of this call. Seems unlikely to me that the King would voluntarily sit this one out."

"I second that sentiment," Baker said. "And I have reason to question the veracity of the dementia comment Faisal made. During my last several interactions, King Mohammed was mentally sharp."

"It would be a mistake to underestimate Faisal," Jarvis said. "We could be witnessing a well-organized internal coup. Reggie, do we have any assets in the King's inner circle or inside the Royal Palace?"

Buckingham shook his head. "Unfortunately, we do not, Mr. President."

Jarvis blew air through pursed lips. "All right. That means getting a team of our investigators into the palace is our top priority. Time is of the essence, so get them moving. That will be all."

Instead of lingering in the room, as was his normal practice, Jarvis departed with Petra to let the post-meeting conversations between his Cabinet members and their deputies take place without him. As he walked back to the Oval with Petra at his side, he found himself having to concentrate harder than usual to take long strides and maintain an even gait.

Petra noticed, drawing closer to him. "Is everything all right? You seem . . . tense."

"I'm having a flare today," he said, his voice a near whisper, using the term they both understood to refer to his Parkinson's. "Andy *definitely* noticed."

She took his hand. "I think it's time we read him in on the truth. It will make things easier for you and, I think, lower your stress."

Jarvis had been thinking the same thing for several weeks now, but expanding the circle of people who knew about his diagnosis was a risk.

He grinned at her. "You know what Benjamin Franklin said about secrets?"

"I don't believe I do," she said.

"Three may keep a secret only if two of them are dead."

She smiled wryly. "Well, for your sake, let's hope old Ben is wrong about the math on this one."

CHAPTER 8

KING'S ROYAL CONFERENCE ROOM
AL-YAMAMAH PALACE
RIYADH, SAUDI ARABIA
1929 LOCAL TIME

The moment Faisal terminated the call with the American President, he knew he was in over his head . . .

Way over his head.

But he didn't dare let on. If he'd learned one lesson in his privileged life, it was to never show weakness. A Prince could be misinformed, but he was never wrong. A Prince could be misled, but he was never fooled. And most importantly of all, a Prince could feel uncertain, but he must never be in doubt. Surrounded by his senior staff and advisors, Faisal knew this moment demanded strength. He could feel their eyes on him. They were all waiting for him to say something.

So, he straightened up in his chair and said, "I have the American President exactly where I want him, begging for access and information."

The statement was met with a concord of nods—some genuine, some oozing with obligation. This annoyed Faisal. He did not want to be the type of leader under whom fear of reprisal turned advisors into sycophants and sandal-lickers. He did not want those beneath him to be so afraid that they withheld critical information or hid the truth from him.

And yet they must remember their place . . .

No one in his regime was irreplaceable. When the time was right, he would demonstrate this by removing one of the men in this room from power. The question was who.

I'll know when I know, he reassured himself.

As Crown Prince, Faisal was now the de facto executive leader of the Kingdom of Saudi Arabia. His father, the eighty-year-old King Abdul Rahman Mohammed, was monarch and head of the Cabinet of Ministers. But the Crown Prince ran the country.

In addition to becoming Crown Prince, Faisal had assumed the other titles that came with the job. He was now the Deputy Prime Minister and the Defense Minister. Unfortunately, unlike his dead brother, Khalid, Faisal had limited experience with politics, economics, defense, or matters of state. In fact, he'd only recently been appointed to his first position in government. The King had chosen Khalid as his successor over a decade ago, and as such, Khalid had been groomed for the job. Khalid had served in multiple noteworthy positions—including Prince of the Court, Special Advisor to the King, Head of the Saudi Economic Development Council, Deputy Foreign Affairs Minister, and Deputy Defense Minister—before being named Crown Prince. Ten years of service had educated and prepared Khalid for leadership and allowed him to build a web of allies and trusted advisors.

Conversely, Faisal had spent nearly all his years since graduating Oxford living the life of a playboy.

But why shouldn't he have? Unlike European monarchies, where the eldest son inherited the throne with each generation, the House of al-Saud followed a succession plan in which the monarch's younger brothers were the preferred heirs to the monarch's sons. King Mohammed had broken this agnatic principle, appointing his eldest son, Khalid, as Crown Prince, which should have made Faisal next in line. But after being named Crown Prince, Khalid had told Faisal that he intended to groom his eldest son, Majid, to succeed him as Crown Prince when he ascended to King. By following in their father's footsteps and embracing primogeniture instead of Saudi tradition, Khalid erased all possibility of Faisal's accession. For years, Faisal had accepted his fate—it was a relief, in fact. All the luxury and privilege with none of the responsibility or work? Why not?

Over time, however, Faisal had changed his mind.

And he had Arash Reza to thank for that.

Two years ago, Faisal had started plotting and planning. At that time, his nephew Majid had been fourteen, which meant the window for Faisal to act had become limited. The deed needed to be done while Majid was a teenager, before he formed alliances and relationships of his own. In addition to assembling the team to assassinate his brother and frame the Israelis, Faisal had also devoted time to deepening his relationship with his father, the King. That effort had finally paid off when the King appointed Faisal as Prince of the Court. As Prince of the Court, Faisal oversaw the Royal Court's operations; managed the King's schedule; and acted as a key advisor to the King on domestic affairs, policies, and issues concerning the royal family and the sovereign wealth fund. More importantly, he functioned as the King's gatekeeper, controlling access to the King for other royals, state officials, and persons seeking an audience with His Majesty. This role had been invaluable in helping Faisal learn and understand the power brokers in the Kingdom.

The position had also given him the opportunity to earn his father's trust and poison the King's opinion of Khalid as too liberal and too receptive to Western influence. With a slow, methodical effort, Faisal had painted a picture of the Crown Prince as a man driven by a grandiose vision of a reformed Saudi Arabia that did not honor the customs, traditions, and Islamic principles the King held dear. Faisal could not be certain, but after the shock of the murder had worn off, he thought he'd sensed relief from the King when Faisal had promised that as Crown Prince he would slow down, halt, and in some cases reverse the changes Khalid had made. He'd used this same promise—of "returning to traditional values"—as part of a charm campaign he'd launched eight weeks ago in a series of meetings with hard-liners and power brokers who'd lost influence and wealth under Khalid's reign. These men had pledged fealty to Faisal within hours of learning of Khalid's death.

Three such loyalists were now sitting at the conference table with him. He'd bought their allegiance with the promise of power, prestige, and position in the new regime. He'd also swelled their bank accounts. The rest of the Ministers and advisors seated around the table were Khalid's men, and not read in on the coup. This was a major problem and liability for Faisal, and something he had no choice but to manage over time. They'd either fall in line or he'd have them replaced.

Anyone is replaceable.

"Your Highness, I don't understand why we would not

accept the American President's offer of investigative assistance," said Princess Ramia Bint Noor, the Ambassador to the United States. Ramia was the first female Saudi diplomat to serve as Ambassador to any country, and she'd been appointed by the former Crown Prince, who was, in fact, her father. She was a reformer and fiercely loyal to Khalid for the opportunity and prestige her appointment had given her.

This bitch should probably be the first to go, Faisal thought, forcing a tolerant smile onto his face.

"Because, Ambassador Noor, we do not need their help. I was there when the Israeli assassins murdered my brother, along with two other witnesses. What investigative prowess do you think the Americans can possibly offer that our own specialists don't already possess?"

"It's not a question of investigation; it's a matter of confirmation. We need them to publicly back your claim," Ambassador Noor said.

"My *claim*?" he said, shooting her an offended, incredulous look. "Are you implying the events I bore witness to did not happen as documented?"

"Your Highness, I'm not implying anything of the sort. What I'm telling you is that the moment you release an official statement—that the agents of the Israeli government murdered Crown Prince Khalid—you are asking the world powers to pick a side. As a matter of precedent, the United States historically sides with Israel. By refusing President Jarvis's offer, you have eliminated a possible path where the US investigators agree with our findings and back your statement—as opposed to the blanket denial that will surely be issued by Prime Minister Shamone."

The way this woman spoke to him like an equal was so brazen. Faisal wanted to put her in her place, to fire her on the spot, and it took every fiber of his being to resist reprimanding her. But to do so now would be both impulsive and imprudent. He'd not had time to interview her replacement, plus Ramia supposedly had a strong working relationship with the US State Department, Secretary of State Baker, as well as her counterpart, the American Ambassador to Saudi Arabia. She was also the person in the room with the most functional knowledge about current trade, investment, security, and other policy-related matters between America and the Kingdom. As much as he hated to admit it, for the immediate future, he needed Princess Ramia.

Also, what she said rang true. He had not thought it through as she had.

"While I agree with your proposed strategy of winning the White House's backing on our findings, allowing a US investigation team into the palace is incredibly naive, Princess Ramia," said Sayed al-Salma, the Director of the Presidency of State Security (PSS). "They do not want to send an investigation team. They want to send spies into the Royal Palace. Who knows what espionage technology they would install in our walls, ceilings, and onto our computer networks. And after they complete their real mission, which is to compromise palace security, there is still no guarantee they will back us over the Zionists."

Faisal was grateful to not be the one to rein in Princess Ramia, but he also had not considered this possibility. He nodded vigorously. Sayed was one of *his* men, and the most important member of Faisal's inner circle. Without Sayed's backing, the coup would have been impossible. Buying Sayed's loyalty had cost Faisal a quarter of a billion, but it had been worth every riyal.

"Maybe there is a way we can split the difference," said

the Saudi Minister of Foreign Affairs. "Can we give the Americans limited access in exchange for a promise of support? We can confiscate all their equipment on arrival and require them to function as observers. Besides, it's not a risk—we know the evidence is irrefutable. The Crown Prince himself witnessed the murder. I think there is value to preserving ties with Washington. Can you imagine the impact of President Jarvis siding with the Crown Prince over the Jews? The blow to Israel would be immeasurable."

"Why would the Israelis do this? I have no love for the Zionists, but it makes no sense," said Abdulaziz al-Rabiah, the Saudi Interior Minister. "Crown Prince Khalid was the first Crown Prince to engage in frequent and regular communications with Prime Minister Shamone. They had a good working relationship. Would you not agree, Ambassador Noor?"

"I agree. It does not make sense to me . . ." Princess Ramia said.

It looked to Faisal like she was about to say more, but she suddenly thought better and held her tongue. He looked back and forth between Abdulaziz and Ramia, and he thought he saw a flicker of something between them. Faisal knew that rumors were already circulating that he had orchestrated his brother's murder, but this was to be expected. So long as those who spread the lies were identified and punished, and as long as the drumbeat of the official narrative drowned out all other noise, then everything would be fine. All Faisal needed to do was survive the next several weeks, control the flow of information to and from the King, and stave off any would-be challenges from other princes. Then the Kingdom would be his.

History is written by the victors.

"I will think on this and consider whether we give the Americans access," Faisal said, standing abruptly to signal the meeting was over. "Right now, I need to check on His Majesty and update him on the call with President Jarvis. We'll reconvene first thing in the morning, and I'll give you my decision."

As he turned to walk out of the room, he realized how desperately he wanted to talk to his Iranian friend, Arash Reza. He needed someone he could trust unconditionally to help him formulate the next round of chess moves. Reza was good at strategy. The truth was that Faisal hadn't planned much beyond the false flag assassination of his brother, because in his heart of hearts, he'd not truly believed he'd get away with it.

A self-satisfied smile spread across his face.

Yes, I'm in over my head, he thought. *But dear God, it's a rush to be Crown Prince.*

CHAPTER 9

LESAGE APARTMENT COMPLEX

TEHRAN, IRAN

2039 LOCAL TIME

Reza stopped kissing Aliyah's neck long enough to look at the vibrating mobile phone on the nightstand beside the bed.

"Don't answer it," she said, naked and a little breathless beneath him.

He didn't dare do what she asked. Not with everything going on.

"I'm sorry, I can't," he said, scooting off her so he could reach the phone.

The exasperated sigh she responded with told him everything he needed to know about the choice he'd just made. He checked the caller ID: *Unknown*. Curiosity piqued, he accepted the call and pressed the mobile phone to his ear.

"Reza . . ." he said.

"Please confirm I'm speaking to Arash Reza?" a serious male voice asked in Saudi-accented Arabic.

"Yes, this is Arash Reza," he said, glancing over at Aliyah, who was staring at him with a wounded, annoyed stare.

"Standby to speak with Crown Prince Faisal bin Ahmed," the voice said.

Aliyah, who had very good hearing, perked up at this and propped herself up on her elbows, her expression morphing from dejected to intrigued.

The line clicked. Faisal's voice was the next thing Reza heard.

"My good friend, I have some terrible news I need to share with you. But before I do, I must insist that you swear to secrecy regarding what I'm about to tell you," Faisal said.

"You and I have been friends for many years. Have I ever once betrayed your trust?" Reza said, looking at Aliyah.

"Never once, but I need to hear you say the words. The words are our pact."

"I understand. Consider this my oath—I will keep private and secret what you are about to tell me," he said, standing to walk out of earshot from his girlfriend. He knew she would not be able to honor such a pledge.

"The rumors are true: My brother, Khalid, is dead. As of today, I have succeeded him as the Crown Prince of Saudi Arabia."

"I'm not sure whether I should be offering you my condolences or congratulations," Reza said, turning his back on Aliyah so she couldn't see his grin.

"Both, my friend," Faisal said. "Both."

"In that case, my condolences and congratulations, Your Highness."

"Thank you, my friend," the Crown Prince said. After a pause, he added, "I owe you a debt of gratitude, because you always believed in me. And for many years, you were the only one who did. Now, I would like to—how shall I say it?—express my gratitude for your friendship and counsel over the years. What, my brother, can the Crown Prince of Saudi Arabia do for you?"

"I want for nothing, except maybe an opportunity to dialogue and visit with you more frequently than we've been able to these last three years," Reza said, the words flowing smoothly from his mouth. He'd rehearsed this line a half dozen times during his drive home from VEVAK HQ to his apartment.

"I suspect that will be an easy request to grant," Faisal said with a little laugh.

"Not necessarily. You're head of state now, and I am not. You'll be interacting with dignitaries, ambassadors, and other heads of state. You won't have the time or occasion to lounge and visit with me. And that's okay. It's life. I'm just your mate from Oxford," he said, dangling the lure.

"Then we need to rectify that situation. Tell me what to do, and I'll do it."

Reza hesitated for effect. "I would imagine that a by-name request for a new Deputy Iranian Ambassador to Saudi Arabia might solve the problem, especially one coming directly from the Crown Prince."

"It's brilliant, but why *Deputy* Ambassador? I want to deal with *you.* Arash Reza should be the eyes, ears, and mouth of Iran in the Kingdom of Saudi Arabia. I want *you* to be the Ambassador," Faisal said with the definitive finality of a god.

Reza chuckled. "Maybe we start with the Deputy and go from there."

"Are you sure? I can make it happen."

"I know you can, but it is probably best to be methodical, and to take things one step at a time."

Faisal laughed. "That's always been your problem, my friend. You're too humble. You deserve so much more than you're willing to take. If only you'd been born a Saudi, I would have promoted you to Prince of the Court and have you rule at my side."

"Thank you, Your Highness. That is what I'm supposed to call you now, correct?"

"Only in public. In private, we will always be Faisal and Arash."

"I like the sound of that," he said. Choosing his very words carefully, he added, "And I've got to tell you, I'm impressed, Faisal. So very, very impressed with . . . your ascension."

"Thank you, my friend. I think back often and fondly to the time we spent together as young, idealistic men. You told me that we could change the world together. Let's make it happen," the Crown Prince said.

Before Reza could reply, the call disconnected.

He'd not drank any alcohol, but his head was buzzing with endorphins that made it feel like he had. It had taken many years, but finally the puzzle pieces were clicking into place. Everything that he'd imagined and worked to orchestrate was happening. Faisal would make the call, and he wouldn't take no for an answer.

I will be the Ambassador to Saudi Arabia, and the Crown Prince will do whatever I whisper in his ear.

Grinning, he turned to look back at Aliyah. She was now sitting up in bed, her back resting against the headboard and her naked torso a vision of perfection in the dim light of their darkened bedroom.

"How much did you hear?"

"Enough to piece it all together," she said. Instead of being angry or annoyed, she was gazing at him with desire and anticipation.

"So, will you and your father be disappointed if you were to marry a lowly diplomat?" he said with a coy smile.

"A lowly diplomat who happens to be best friends with the richest, most powerful man in all the Middle East? Let me think about that . . ." she said, tapping her chin with a bemused expression. "I suppose we could live with that."

He swelled with anticipation as she beckoned him back to bed with a curled index finger.

"Listen to me, Aliyah, because this is important," he said as he climbed onto the foot of the bed and crawled toward her. "You cannot say anything to anyone about what you heard or what you learned tonight. From now on, our life will be one of secrets and manipulations. We will be interacting with heads of state, royalty, and the most powerful and dangerous people in the world. One slip of the tongue could start a war or topple governments."

He saw her shudder with arousal—not from his body nearing hers but from his words. He'd always known what she craved most, and now he was in a position to give it to her.

She reached up and pressed her right palm to his left cheek. "Don't worry. I've kept all your secrets. Kept them from everyone, including my father. And I always will." Then she kissed his mouth, long, slow, and tenderly.

Her pronouncement caused Reza's heart to skip a beat. What did she mean she'd kept his secrets? Did she know he was a spy for VEVAK? Had she worked out that she herself was only in a relationship with him because he'd been on an assignment to get to her father? He tried to make his face a mask and hide his surprise.

"My secrets?" he asked, as innocently as he could muster.

She shook her head with pitying bemusement. "Yes," she said, reclining naked for him.

He wondered if his cover was blown, and if so, how she'd managed it. Maybe she was a shrewder woman than he'd given her credit for. Did it matter? Looking at her lying there, waiting for him, he decided that maybe it didn't.

"Because you love me?" he asked, steering away from the subject.

"And because you're handsome, and intelligent, and very good in bed . . ."

"Naturally," he said playfully.

"But most importantly," she said, spreading her legs, "because you're the only man who's capable of getting me what I want."

"And what is that, my love?" he asked, relaxing now as he resumed doing what he was doing before Faisal's unexpected phone call had interrupted them.

Breath trembling, she answered with a whisper in his ear. "Power."

CHAPTER 10

THE NEXT DAY
US NAVAL FORCES CENTRAL COMMAND (NAVCENT)
NAVAL SUPPORT ACTIVITY BAHRAIN (NSA BAHRAIN)
MANAMA, BAHRAIN
1422 LOCAL TIME

Whitney Watts stepped out of the air-conditioned SUV that had driven them from the Bahrain airport to the base, and into the harsh morning sun. Immediately, a wave of heat hit her, like opening an oven door.

"My God, it's hot," she muttered.

"But it's a dry heat," Chunk said with a frat-boy grin as he stepped up beside her. He pulled a pair of wraparound sunglasses from his chest pocket, snapped his wrist, and popped them on his face in one smooth maneuver. Even dressed casually in gray cargo pants, Merrell camp shoes, and a black T-shirt, Chunk couldn't avoid looking like the Tier One US Navy SEAL he was. "I hope you didn't forget to bring shades . . ."

Technically, she hadn't *forgotten*—because you can't forget something you didn't think of in the first place. And now that Chunk had brought to her attention how insanely bright it was outside, she realized she was squinting so hard that her face was scrunched up like a shar-pei.

"That's a big fat negative," Watts said, holding a hand above her right eye and closing her left.

Chunk shrugged his backpack off his shoulder, dug into a hidden zipper pocket, and retrieved a second set of what she now saw were Wiley X shades. He handed them to her. "These are my spares. Don't lose 'em, Heels."

"Thanks," she said, accepting the shades, annoyed that he'd taken to calling her Heels of late.

She understood his coolness. After their talk at the London Eye, they'd made a mutual decision to put some distance between them—to maintain their professional relationship, for the good of the team. It was a decision she agreed with. But Chunk was taking it too far, she thought. Before they had both started to feel something more, they had already been friends and teammates. It felt now like Chunk was taking them further back than needed—and frankly, she missed his friendship, particularly now, when she needed it the most. Chunk had always been her support system, and after all she'd been through during her captivity by al Qadar, she needed that now more than ever. Why should she be punished for something they both felt, and that they *both* agreed to nip in the bud?

"Heels forgot her glasses, didn't she?" Riker said, ambling up beside Chunk wearing a pair of full-wrap, oversized sunglasses with a bright orange mirror-reflective finish and heavy black frames.

"And what the hell kind of sunglasses are those?" she said, dishing it back to Riker. "Did you steal those from an old lady who just had her eyes dilated?"

"These," the SEAL breacher said, gesturing to his face with an expression that was equal parts disbelief and indignation, "are the best damn fishin' sunglasses ever made."

"Smith Boomtowns?" Chunk asked with a knowing nod.

Riker grinned and stuck out his fist for a bump. "Brother knows quality when he sees it."

Watts rolled her eyes behind her borrowed shades.

Whitney had never been to Bahrain. The island nation known as the Kingdom of Bahrain was located in the Persian Gulf, nestled between Saudi Arabia and Qatar. At around three hundred square miles, Bahrain was about a third of the size of Rhode Island, the smallest US state, but with 1.5 times the population at 1.5 million people. She'd looked it up during the flight over. The other interesting factoid she'd learned was that while the ruling monarchy was Sunni, the majority of the population of Bahrain were Shia Muslims. While not well-versed in the history, she knew that the two main branches of Islam had split in the ancient past, and that ideological and political differences between the sects had resulted in tension and conflict over the years that continued to this day—especially between the two most powerful Muslim countries in the region, Saudi Arabia and Iran.

Sort of like the Catholics and Protestants in Ireland, she thought, pondering the accuracy of that comparison.

Yet somehow the Kingdom of Bahrain not only made it work, they flourished. She had no doubt that religious and ideological differences flared here, but it didn't end with killing and sectarian violence. It turned out, she believed, that prosperity removed a lot of tension. When people were safe, secure, well-fed, and happy, religious and philosophical differences rarely led to bloodshed. There was probably an important lesson there.

A Lieutenant Commander dressed in digital cammies came out to greet them. She immediately noticed the embroidered black trident insignia he wore above his name tape.

"What's up, brother?" Chunk said, wrapping the taller man up in a bear hug. "You're a pencil pusher these days, eh? How the hell did that happen, bro?"

The SEAL officer, who was clean-shaven and sported a regulation haircut—unlike the shaggy crew Chunk led—laughed. "Just checking the box. Don't worry. I'll be back in the suck when this shore tour is over, assuming God still loves me."

"Hear that," Saw said, walking up to say hello.

"Good to see you, Saw," the officer said, shaking Saw's hand. "How's the family?"

"Five by," Saw said, and Whitney saw a little flash of pride in his eyes.

"This is our intel lead, Watts," Chunk said, gesturing to her.

"Heard you're a helluva analyst. Lieutenant?" the SEAL said, guessing.

"Actually, I'm not Navy," she said, shaking his proffered hand.

"Oh, sorry. I assumed you were Naval Intelligence."

"We poached her from NCTC, who poached her from Langley," Chunk said.

"I'm Commander Ruzecki, by the way, aide to Admiral Miller," the SEAL said, releasing her hand from his own thick paw. "But you can call me Joe."

"Nice to meet you, Joe. I'm Whitney."

"Great to meet you," Ruzecki said. "And welcome to Naval Support Activity Bahrain. If you guys would like to follow me, I can show you inside where you can use the facilities before we meet with the Admiral."

Spence caught up with the four of them as they stepped inside the NAVCENT HQ building, which was just as big of a thermal shock as stepping off the SUV into the Bahrain heat, only in reverse. The superpowered air conditioners they had running instantly made Whitney shiver now that she had a layer of sweat on her body. After clearing security, Commander Ruzecki showed their contingent the bathrooms and the briefing SCIF, where everyone was given bottled water.

They weren't made to wait long; the Admiral joined them not five minutes later. The room stood when he entered, but the Admiral quickly waved for Chunk, Riker, Saw, Whitney, and Spence to take their seats. Admiral Miller was a tall, thin, handsome man with dark brown hair and a face that reminded Whitney of the late-night host Jimmy Fallon. In his current billet, Miller had multiple titles: Commander of United States Naval Forces Central Command, Commander of United States Fifth Fleet, and Commander of Combined Maritime Forces. The three-star wore a Surface Warfare Officer, or SWO, insignia on his chest.

"Welcome to Bahrain," the Admiral said. "For those of you not familiar with our facility, NSA Bahrain is the only permanent frontline Navy base in the Middle East. We serve as a logistical and C2 node for all ships deployed to US Fifth Fleet, as well as coalition forces operating in the CENTCOM AOR. This facility may have a compact footprint at 268 acres, but we service and support a community of eighty-five hundred personnel. This community has a positive relationship with our host nation, and it is my job to keep it that way."

Whitney glanced at Chunk, who leaned back in his chair. Three stars were different in the big Navy, she guessed, and Miller had found an interesting way to kick things off. The opening bit was obviously his standard command-greeting spiel, the same one he probably had used a hundred times with VIPs, but she was curious to see where this was going.

"I want everyone in this room to always keep top of mind that Bahrain is connected to Saudi Arabia by the King Fahd Causeway. That fifteen miles of cement and steel is not just a road. It is an umbilicus. Despite what anybody tells you, these two nations *are* tethered—economically, strategically, and politically. It would be a mistake for anyone in this room to presume otherwise. I say this because when the news of Khalid's death breaks, the impact will be felt here first."

She nodded, now dialed into his headspace. From a leadership perspective, Miller was operating on a metaphorical island, in the middle of an actual island, in the middle of the larger metaphorical island of Saudi Arabia's sphere of influence, which extended to the entire Middle East. Any decision he made had to factor in the geopolitical ramifications to his host nation and the eight-hundred-pound gorilla fifteen miles to the west.

"But," he continued, "it's not only these two relationships that matter. CENTCOM is a strategic hub for an entire region. This command manages and interfaces daily with a thirty-eight-nation coalition to maintain maritime stability in arguably the most challenging and dynamic region on the planet. You're talking about roughly four thousand miles of nautical travel from the Suez through the Red Sea, through the Arabian Sea around the peninsula, to the top of the Persian Gulf. We have to manage choke points, heavy traffic, pirates, rebel ships, and terrorists. On top of that, we have the Iranian Navy and their proxies to contend with.

"The point I'm trying to make is that, even on a good day, executing our charter is a challenge. But when this bombshell news hits, I anticipate maritime chaos will quickly follow. Managing that chaos is my job, not contributing to it is yours."

He paused long enough that it felt like he was waiting for someone to acknowledge his words on behalf of the group.

"We hear you and understand your concerns, Admiral," Chunk said, taking the cue. "We're here to provide support and be a pointy-tip resource to mitigate negative activities from bad actors who might try to capitalize on that chaos in the Fifth Fleet AOR."

The Admiral seemed to like Chunk's response. He nodded, and that was that. Then he rose.

"My N2 shop has secured a workspace for your task force, including your own TOC and SCIF. But it goes without saying that I expect to be kept in the loop on anything that affects this AOR tactically or strategically." He leaned in, his hands flat on the table, staring at Chunk. "I understand the covert nature of your work and that of your team, Commander Redman, but there are thousands of men and women operating aboard a myriad of platforms in this AOR. Keeping their commanders informed of the threats keeps them prepared but also safe. Are we clear?"

"We are, sir," Chunk promised, rising and offering his hand. "That's why the White House put Navy in charge, sir," he joked, with the charismatic grin that always won the day.

"Joe will get your team settled and will function as liaison between your task force and this command. In the meantime, let's hope the rumors coming out of Riyadh are not true," the Admiral said.

With that, the three-star excused himself to head to his next meeting.

Ruzecki pressed to his feet. "I'll give you a quick tour of the building, and after that let you get settled in. As far as lodging, I booked rooms for everyone at the Navy Gateway Inns and Suites. Hope that works for you guys."

"It's perfect, Joe. Thank you," Chunk said, rising along with the rest of the leadership team.

It was not lost on Whitney that neither Admiral Miller nor Commander Ruzecki had mentioned anything about the joint investigation task force team that Whitney was supposed to be participating in. The uncertainty around her tasking, her team, and the timeline was starting to needle her. The clock was ticking, and she didn't like being unprepared. As they followed the Admiral's aide out of the conference room, she sidled up beside Chunk.

"When and where do I meet the other investigation team members? The Admiral didn't say anything about my mission in the brief."

"He was a little light on those details, wasn't he?" he said as he pulled out a tin of snuff, which he started packing with his bear paw of a hand. "Well, I guess all I can say is they'll get here when they get here."

They'll get here when they get here, she thought with a mental eye roll. *Classic Chunk . . . that man's pants could be on fire, and he'd still take the time to pack a dip and crack a joke before he put it out.*

CHAPTER 11

OFFICE OF THE DIRECTOR OF FOREIGN OPERATIONS
IRANIAN MINISTRY OF INTELLIGENCE AND SECURITY
(MOIS A.K.A. VEVAK)
HIRMAND STREET
PASDARAN, TEHRAN, REPUBLIC OF IRAN
0615 LOCAL TIME

Despite the predawn hour, when Reza arrived at the Ministry, he found the office buzzing with activity. The news of the Crown Prince's death had still not hit the internet or the major media outlets, but the boast Golzar had made during their last meeting about big plans in the works was clearly more than lip service. Whenever the big news did break, Reza suspected that VEVAK's proxies would be primed and ready to unleash hell on the Zionists.

His mind remembering last night's sex with Aliyah, he climbed the stairs to the third level and made his way to Golzar's office.

"Good morning, Jelah," he said to Golzar's secretary.

"Good morning, Arash," she said with a furtive but reserved smile. "You may go in; he's expecting you."

Reza went in and found Golzar, as usual, sitting behind his desk and polishing his glasses. His boss looked up, his face showing more excitement and purpose than Reza had seen before.

"Have a seat," Golzar said, skipping a greeting and gesturing to the chair opposite his desk.

Reza did as he was told. While he did, Golzar turned his computer monitor so that Reza could see it. The Director was on video conference call, and on-screen Reza saw a man sitting in a spartan room with a porthole window behind him. The picture was grainy, and the lighting was bad, but Reza recognized the man on-screen. It took Reza a beat to recall his name, but when he did, he greeted his fellow operative, Jahan Heydari, with feigned warmth.

"It's been a while, Jahan. How are you? How's the family?" Reza said, shifting in his chair so that his own face shared the webcam frame with Golzar.

"Good to see you, Arash," the deep-cover operative said. "The family is doing fine. At least, so they tell me on the few occasions when I'm able to see them."

The not-so-subtle comment was meant for Golzar, not for him, but Reza gave the man an empathetic nod. "This is the life we've chosen, yes? One of hardship and sacrifice."

"For some more than others," Heydari replied.

Reza knew *that* barb was meant for him. It had been at least two years since Reza had last seen the man. On paper, Reza and Heydari held the same rank and title in the Foreign Operations directorate, and both men had been creations of Amir Modiri; however, while Reza enjoyed a life of privilege and luxury in his NOC, Heydari had been dispatched to the trenches. Like all the "Unknown Soldiers of Imam Zama," by working for the Ministry of Intelligence, Reza and Heydari had both agreed to live double—or, in Heydari's case, sometimes triple—lives. It was one thing to agree to the harsh reality of their trade as a young new recruit. It was entirely another to be forced to live it. As the months turned into years, and the years turned into decades, some men in the shadow service became resentful. Once the novelty and excitement of secrets, travel, and tradecraft wore off, he'd noticed that a bitterness often crept in to fill the void.

Which is why I never want to get old.

Heydari was the directorate's top proxy development field agent. His job was to inform, fund, and arm fighters in Yemen and the West Bank, which often required him to embed with these groups for prolonged periods. Not only was Heydari experienced, but he was crafty and meticulous. He'd survived countless Israeli and American dragnets and somehow managed to remain below the radar and preserve his numerous legends for nearly two decades. Heydari was the perfect agent to begin mobilizing the resources they would need to topple the Zionists.

"I wanted to read both of you in on each other's operations," Golzar said, getting straight to business. "Jahan is currently at sea, aboard the vessel *Dakar*, in the Mediterranean Sea en route to rendezvous with the merchant ship *Earabat Albahr* in preparation for a top secret mission with Sayf Allah."

Sayf Allah, or Allah's Sword, was a small but well-funded and capable terror cell. Populated mostly with disenfranchised terrorists from other organizations that had been destroyed, such as al Qadar, Sayf Allah's leadership maintained close ties to Hamas, Hezbollah, and the Houthis. The group was passionate about striking the American and the Zionist devils at any opportunity, and so it was no surprise that Golzar had chosen them to be the vanguard in the coming onslaught against Israel.

What was a surprise, however, were Golzar's next words, which practically knocked Reza out of his chair.

"That mission is to smuggle a nuclear weapon into Gaza and, using the Hamas tunnel system, sneak it into Israel and strike Tel Aviv," the spymaster said.

"A nuclear weapon?" Reza said, choking on the words. "You can't be serious."

"I'm dead serious," Golzar said, his expression as immutable as granite. "Assuming you can get agreement from the new Crown Prince, this strike will wipe the Zionists from the face of the earth once and for all."

Reza knew that the Islamic Republic—with secret help from the Russians—had successfully built a low-yield nuclear weapon, but he'd never imagined they'd actually use it in a first-strike scenario.

He said as much. "A nuclear first strike? Isn't that a bit extreme?"

"Ridding the Middle East of the scourge of a Zionist state has always been our charter from the Supreme Leader, has it not?" Golzar said, seemingly unperturbed.

"Yes, but using a nuclear weapon to do this will start World War III," Reza said, his mind already contemplating the Israeli and American counterstrikes. *I need to get Aliyah out of Tehran*, he realized. The relationship might have started for strategic reasons, but he realized he cared for her now.

"Our strategists do not believe there will be a nuclear retaliation. With Saudi Arabia and Iran united, and with the world against them for murdering Crown Prince Khalid, and with

Tel Aviv destroyed, the Zionists will surrender. It will be like Japan in World War II. They will not risk Jerusalem. And they will not risk total annihilation."

Reza looked from Golzar to Heydari to see if his counterpart had concerns. The seasoned field operator simply stared at the screen.

"Don't worry, Arash. Like I promised Jahan, we will make arrangements to keep both your loved ones out of harm's way. I've already had my secretary book a ticket for Aliyah to Abu Dhabi," Golzar said to Reza. To Heydari, he added, "Same goes for your wife and sons. Tell me where you want to send them, and I will see it done."

Powerless to change anything about the decision, all Reza could do was nod. His stomach felt queasy. He thought the idea of nuking Tel Aviv was both outrageous and imprudent. Having squared off against the Mossad for years, he knew the Israeli mindset. They would not roll over. They would not surrender.

"As far as your assignment," Golzar said, smiling at Reza, "I'm pleased to report you were right. One call from the Crown Prince was all it took. Congratulations—you are now officially the Deputy Ambassador to Saudi Arabia for the Islamic Republic of Iran. The Ambassador has been informed, the official website has been updated, and your presence in person at the Royal Palace in Riyadh has been requested. From what I understand, His Royal Highness has even extended your position a permanent office and residential apartment in the palace. Lucky for us, it appears His Highness highly values your counsel. Your flight leaves in an hour. Don't be late."

Hearing this, feelings of pride and accomplishment momentarily usurped the dread he'd been feeling. A permanent office? A residential apartment in the palace? He couldn't believe it was really happening. All the seeds he'd meticulously sewed over all those years *had* taken root after all. With Faisal in his pocket, and the power of the Saudi purse at his disposal, there was virtually no limit to what Reza could accomplish.

Still, Reza had trouble concentrating while Golzar finished the brief and discussed the communications protocols that both Reza and Heydari would use to route encrypted messages and updates. Golzar alone would act as the communications hub between his two best field agents. Assuming Heydari successfully smuggled the weapon into Gaza, Golzar would not initiate stage two without Reza first winning and communicating the Crown Prince's blessing. For the alliance between the Islamic Republic and the Kingdom to grow strong and change the world, there had to be trust, alignment of strategic goals, and agreement on the tactical means and methods to achieve those goals. For the two nations to become powerful allies, they had to be on the same page and have each other's backs. Together they were powerful enough to rule the region, but independently they risked devastating retaliation.

This first operation would be a trial by fire.

"Good luck, Arash," the Director said, standing and handing Reza a new mobile phone with the new and tailor-made encryption hardware for his new assignment. "And may Allah's will be done."

Apparently dismissed, Reza nodded, accepted the phone, and turned to Heydari on-screen.

"*Khodâhâfez*," he said, wishing the operative God's protection in Farsi—acutely aware that his counterpart's tasking was infinitely more dangerous than his own.

Heydari reacted with a little snort through his nose and a smile that showed off his stained and crooked teeth. "*Mîbînamet*, Reza," Heydari said, choosing the most casual of all goodbyes—a statement in and of itself by not wishing Reza luck or God's protection in return.

No matter . . . Reza thought as he turned to leave Golzar's office. *There are generals and foot soldiers. Today I am a general.*

CHAPTER 12

NAVY GATEWAY INNS AND SUITES (NGIS)
NAVAL SUPPORT ACTIVITY BAHRAIN (NSA BAHRAIN)
MANAMA, BAHRAIN
0628 LOCAL TIME

In the dream, Whitney was on a life raft. Alone, freezing, and adrift.

Sometimes, MI6 Agent Runner Lucy Kim was in the raft with her. Sometimes not. Sometimes Whitney made it to the L5 deepwater autonomous data collection ocean buoy before the raft sank. Sometimes she didn't. But regardless of which version of the PTS-induced nightmare her subconscious decided to torture her with, Chunk was never there.

And this disturbed her.

Because he was supposed to be there.

As far as she was concerned, he *had* been there with her.

Air hissed and sputtered from a pin-size hole in the donut-shaped inner tube. Cursing, she searched everywhere for the patch kit that had come with the raft's emergency supplies but couldn't find it. It had been there when she'd inventoried the Pelican box, but now it was gone. Raindrops began to pelt her exposed arms, her back, and the top of her head. She screwed up her face, wondering what had happened to the life raft's cover tent. The drops came harder and faster, each one stinging on impact and stealing her warmth. The shower quickly became a deluge, filling the inside of the raft with water and causing it to sink deeper into the waves.

"No!" she screamed as she searched for the hand bailer, which was now also missing.

But before she could find it, a rogue wave slammed into the raft, capsizing it and driving her deep into the black, frigid, depths. As she desperately kicked and pulled toward the surface, her brain screamed: *This is not the way it's supposed to happen!*

A banging sound woke her with a start.

She sat up, disoriented and shivering in bed. Only then did she realize her phone alarm was going off. Her circadian rhythm was so out of whack from the flight and time zone changes that she'd been out cold and slept through her alarm.

A second knock sounded as the cobwebs in her mind began to clear.

I'm in Bahrain, not the English Channel, she told herself as she swung her legs off the side of the bed and the room came into focus. She silenced her phone alarm and checked the time.

Shit, I'm going to be late.

"Coming," she called, quickly throwing on a sweatshirt as she trotted to the door.

She undid the safety latch, jerked the lever-style handle, and opened the door, fully expecting to see Chunk standing there.

But the face that greeted her belonged to Robert Theobald. Grinning, he looked down at her pajama pants. "Well, good morning, sleepyhead."

"Bobby? Oh my God, what the hell are you doing here?" she said.

The middle-aged DIA agent smiled and opened his arms to her for a hug, which she happily stepped into. She had a level of trust with Theobald similar to that with the guys at Gold. He'd saved her life in Pakistan on her very first deployment with the Tier One. Waves of memories and emotion swept over her—from escaping a terrorist death squad at the hotel in Mingora to the horrifying al Qadar drone attack on Kandahar Airfield that they had barely survived.

She stepped back to look at him. This morning, he was dressed in cargo pants and a gray sports shirt. His face—handsome, for a guy in his early fifties—looked a little gaunt. And he'd felt thinner than she remembered when she'd hugged him.

"To answer your question," the DIA man said with a knowing smile, "I'm the task force lead."

"Seriously?" she said, beyond relieved to be working with at least one person she knew and trusted.

"Yep, we're both working under the ADMA."

ADMA stood for the Associate Director for Military Affairs—a three-star billet at CIA, a position typically held by someone with a trident on their chest. The ADMA's principal role was coordinating between CIA and DOD when the Navy JSOC elements were needed for special operations. With Bobby showing up at her door, one nagging puzzle piece clicked into place.

"I'm really glad it's you running the show," she said.

"Well, we'll see how you feel about that in twelve hours," Theobald said with a laugh, then glanced at his watch. "How much time do you need? I figured we could ride together to the airport."

"I packed last night—just need to change and quickly brush my teeth. Meet you out front and we can be on the road in ten?"

"Roger that. See you down there."

As promised, ten minutes later, she was climbing into the front passenger seat of Theobald's car. It wouldn't be a long drive to the airport, but hopefully long enough for her to get answers to at least a few of her questions.

"Still working with Commander Redman?" Theobald asked, kicking off the conversation as she clicked her seat belt.

"Yep, essentially the same crew you met in Mingora," she said, realizing with a small measure of guilt that she'd actually not said goodbye to Chunk last night after the team dinner out in town. He'd been a little standoffish during the entire evening, so she'd spent most the time talking with Saw about Ellie and the kids.

Oh well, not my fault.

"I saw that you guys took down al Qadar," he said. "Strong work."

"Thanks," she said with a nod. "Bobby, I'm going to be honest with you. The brief I got from my CSO about this task force and our objectives was extremely limited. I know that the Crown Prince is dead, and the Saudis claim he was assassinated by Mossad, but that's about it. Any chance you can give me a primer on both our charter here and on Saudi politics?"

"Absolutely," he said. "Let's start with our charter. It's pretty simple, really. POTUS worked a deal with the new Crown Prince—Faisal bin Ahmed al-Saud—not to release a public statement about the murder of his brother, Khalid, until the US had a chance to validate the findings of the Saudi investigation. Obviously, if the Saudis hold Israel responsible, then we're facing a shitstorm of epic proportions in the Middle East."

"Obviously," she echoed, "but that still doesn't entirely fill in the blanks for me. What exactly is our mission objective? If I didn't know better, I'd almost say the DNI has chartered us to solve a murder case."

"That's *exactly* what he's asked us to do."

"But we're not homicide detectives, Bobby. I'm a counterterrorism analyst, and you're a field operations officer who collects intel and runs foreign assets."

"I know, and that's why the DNI teamed us with one of the FBI's best crime scene investigators. Her job is to analyze the evidence. Our other team member is one of NSA's top cybersleuths, who is going to try to hack into their network and pirate their video surveillance data. Our tasking is to use any and all methods necessary to find out if the Mossad assassinated the Crown Prince—and if not, to determine who did. The Saudis are only allowing a team of four, so each team member has a very specific role to play."

"I still don't see what *I* bring to the table."

"You bring that giant analytical brain that deconstructed the al Qadar terror network and outsmarted Qasim Nadar, the world's most dangerous terrorist mastermind. Your job is to do what you always do—pick through the data, find the pattern, and separate fact from fiction."

"I guess," she muttered.

They drove in silence for a little while before Theobald said, "How much do you know about the Saudi royal family and politics?"

She bobbed her head from side to side, then said, "Assume I know nothing."

"We both know that's not true, but I get you. It's not something you've done a deep dive on lately," he said with a chuckle. "Not a problem. The first thing you need to know is that Prince Khalid was not like his father, King Mohammed. Make no mistake—Khalid was a rich, self-absorbed, power-hungry narcissist, but he was also a forward-thinking, shrewd capitalist. The days of a pure-play, petrol-driven economy that defined his father's reign are over. Technological innovation and climate change are real, and the movement away from fossil fuels is inevitable. It's not a matter of if; it's a matter of when. Khalid understood this, and he watched with envy while his neighbors to the east turned Dubai and Abu Dhabi into meccas—no pun intended—of finance, real estate, banking, and tourism. The Emirates figured out that a closed, insular, and politically hard-line Muslim nation without a functional and diversified economy would not weather the coming storm. When the world decides to turn its back on oil in the coming decades, it will also turn its back on the Arab oil states. So, they took steps to prevent that from happening—and look at Dubai today. It's thriving, and not because of oil, or Islam, or because it embraced Western politics. Dubai is thriving because it transformed itself into a hub of commerce, investment, and tourism."

Whitney nodded.

"Khalid realized that if the Kingdom didn't do something similar, it would be left behind. So, the first thing he did was relax the mandate that all women had to wear head coverings in public and suspend the ban on women driving to promote tourism. The second thing he did was implement reforms to encourage foreign direct investment in Saudi Arabia. Third, he launched a multibillion-dollar international rebranding and infrastructure development campaign called Vision 2030."

"I've heard of that," she said. "Isn't there some plan for a giant, hundred-mile-long city?"

"Yes, it's all part of NEOM, a massive nationally funded development project. But it's not the social reforms or mega development projects that got him killed. Any theories on what might have?"

"His willingness to participate in talks to normalize relations with Israel?" she said, taking a guess.

"Bingo," he said. "A tentative date had been set for two weeks from yesterday to sit down with the Israeli PM face-to-face in Tel Aviv. As you can imagine, this is the holy grail of Middle East foreign policy for Secretary of State Baker, and it was a legacy priority for President Warner. I can only assume it bears the same weight for the new President. But for many hard-liners in the Kingdom, normalizing relations with Israel is a line they are simply unwilling to cross, no matter the long-term economic value."

"What about Faisal? Where does he stand on all this? Was he aligned with his brother or with the hard-liners?"

"That's the million-dollar question, and one I don't have an answer for. According to our sources, Faisal's only aspiration is, and always has been, to lead the life of a royal playboy. Yachts, fast cars, Western women, and decadence—those things seem to have been Faisal's priority over the years."

"So, you don't think he has designs on the throne?"

"I didn't say that," Theobald said, shooting her a sideways look. "I imagine that kind of power must be pretty intoxicating."

She nodded. "Do you think we'll get to interview him as part of the investigation?"

He chuckled. "I *think* the answer to that question will tell us a lot."

"When do I get to meet the other members of the team?"

"At the airport."

"Have you ever worked with them before?"

"Nope," Theobald said. "But I hear they're good."

"With where we're going, and what we're expected to do," she said with a healthy dose of fatalism, "I sure hope so."

CHAPTER 13

AL-YAMAMAH PALACE
AL-HADA DISTRICT
RIYADH, SAUDI ARABIA
0755

Faisal looked at the phone ringing on the ornate mahogany desk. He'd been expecting this call.

"Yes?" he said, forcing a nervous and harried sound into his voice.

"Your Highness, it is Bashar al-Hadi," said the King's senior Royal Court Advisor. "King Abdul needs to see you. It is urgent."

"I desperately need to see him as well," Faisal said, his voice strained. "Between us, Bashar, I am feeling overwhelmed and ill-prepared for the role that has been thrust upon me. The American contingent will be arriving soon, and I am in desperate need of my father's wise counsel. Can you ask the King to meet me in the Shadhavar conference room?"

Named for a mythological creature from medieval Arabian

lore, the Shadhavar conference room was a secure meeting space, one without cameras or microphones. It had only two access points: the primary entry and the access from the Crown Prince's private office, located directly next door.

A long pause hung in the air, and Faisal could picture Bashar al-Hadi making a sour face.

"Why don't you come to His Majesty's chambers instead?"

"I have sensitive documents for His Majesty's eyes only. Everything is prepped and ready to be viewed in Shadhavar. It would be difficult and time-consuming to move it all."

"Very well. I will explain this to him."

"Thank you," Faisal said with mock deference. "At His Majesty's convenience. I will be waiting."

He replaced the phone. His smile widened as he glanced behind him at the two *professionals* now waiting in his office—new members of his security team with particular and specialized skills. He gave a curt nod, and the two men moved into their hidden ready positions—one in the ornate private office bathroom, the other in the corner behind the office door. Faisal rose and walked next door into the Shadhavar conference room. He closed the door behind him and took a seat at the head of the conference table, where he had prestaged papers and other documents. He knew without a doubt that the King would acquiesce and come to him here.

His father's desire to mentor was his greatest weakness.

Only minutes later, the large secure door swung open. Bashar led King Abdul Rahman Mohammed al-Saud into the room, the King's face drawn and his posture heavy with grief. Yet despite the burden he carried, the King could not help telegraphing his annoyance at being summoned with a chastising glare at his son. At eighty years old, his father was well past his prime, but a team of cosmetic surgeons and professional stylists did a respectable job disguising it. His long-gone gray beard was dyed a shiny ebony weekly, and the combination of regular Botox injections, facial peels, and the liberal application of bronzer made him look—at least from a distance—two decades younger than he was. Dental implants gave him a bright, too-perfect smile, and hair transplants had kept his hairline forward and full.

This morning, however, his father's chronological age seemed to ooze through the facade, and this almost gave Faisal pause to reconsider what he was about to do.

No, he told himself. *Do not pity him. An old viper is still a viper.*

"Thank Allah," Faisal said, looking up from the papers in front of him. "Politics is more complicated than I imagined. I had no idea how much work it was to be Crown Prince. Khalid made it look so easy. I feel overwhelmed and underprepared for the arrival of the Americans."

King Abdul's expression softened. "The loss of Khalid is one we will all feel for years to come, Faisal," he said. "How can I help you?"

"If I might suggest, Your Majesty," Bashar said, interrupting, "that we begin by addressing the issue of the intercepted call?" The King's most trusted advisor shot Faisal a look full of venom. "How dare you usurp a call between the American President and the King without His Majesty's consent—or even his knowledge!"

The King's posture stiffened. "Bashar is right. Explain yourself, Faisal."

"What in Allah's name are you talking about?" Faisal summoned the shocked look he had practiced in the bathroom mirror, working to keep surprise and confusion in his voice instead of the anger he actually felt.

"How can you claim ignorance?" Bashar demanded.

"Do not forget your place, Bashar," Faisal said, standing. He permitted just the proper measure of anger to creep into his voice. "I will not be addressed with disrespect, and most certainly will not be spoken to like a child. I am the Crown Prince of Saudi Arabia, and I represent the King, the Council, and the Kingdom." He leaned in. "You will speak to me with the respect and deference that I and my position demand."

Faisal thought, with some pleasure, that he saw fear flash in Bashar's eyes. The man had been around long enough to witness the Machiavellian methods that House al-Saud used to exact retribution and punishment against those who defied it. Bashar glanced at the King for reassurance but got only a stern look. The King raised a hand, preempting the advisor from arguing.

Faisal knew a rebuke was coming from his father, so he spoke quickly. "I *did* take a call with President Jarvis, but my intention was not to usurp. To the contrary, my intention was to function as your shield, Father. To collect information about the Americans' position so you and I would have time to confer and strategize before you were forced to confront President Jarvis. Is that not the role of the Crown Prince, to function as a political intermediary? This is what Khalid would have done, is it not?"

The King nodded approvingly. Faisal's explanation was not only respectful but also followed the precedent set by his father's most beloved, deceased son. Faisal ticked his gaze to Bashar, whose nervous eyes confirmed what Faisal already sensed. *I control the narrative now, you worm.*

"Your intentions were noble, Faisal, but next time you should notify me in advance," the King said. "It is more valuable to strategize before *and* after such important political calls."

"Wise words, Father," Faisal said with a supplicating bow. "I'm still learning, and this is why I rely on your mentorship."

"Of course you are," King Abdul said. "You have been thrown into the arena with lions and gladiators, Faisal. But don't worry. I've survived many battles and vanquished many foes over my thirty-year reign. I will teach you everything you need to know."

Faisal resisted the urge to grin. He could not have scripted this interaction better had he tried.

"Your Majesty, perhaps we can speak in my office in private? I wish to discuss my call with the President Jarvis but also strategize how best to handle the arriving American investigators."

"American spies, no doubt," the King said with a sour look.

"Crown Prince Faisal, I meant no disrespect," Bashar said. "I am happy to share my own insights and counsel on these matters. The King has trusted me for—"

"Prince Faisal is right, Bashar," Abdul said, giving his advisor a soft smile. "I need to speak with my son in private—King to Crown Prince. Wait outside. I will summon you if and when I need you."

"Yes, Your Majesty," Bashar said. He gave a deep and deferential bow. "I am your humble servant."

"Thank you, Father," Faisal said.

Faisal opened the door to the private office, leading his father inside without giving Bashar so much as another glance. He crossed quickly toward the desk, which was angled just slightly off to the right, keeping his father's eyes away from where Faisal's security man stood in the corner, poised to strike.

As the door closed behind the King, the man—an experienced soldier and assassin—did just that. Faisal kept his back to the scene unfolding behind him, not wishing to see his father's eyes in the moment of betrayal. He did, after all, love his father very much. There was only the slightest of sounds—the slipping of his father's expensive Italian shoes on the marble floor, he thought—as the assassin plunged a needle into his father's neck. After a moment, it grew quiet. Faisal turned in time to see his father being very gently lowered to the floor and placed on his back.

"Is he . . . *okay*?" Faisal asked. His voice cracked slightly with real emotion as he looked down at his father on the marble floor. The King's eyes were closed, but he was breathing slowly, like a man in a deep sleep.

"He is, Your Highness," the man said.

The other operative came from the bathroom with a compact black zipper case in his hands. The operative bent beside the King and unzipped the case, revealing several prefilled syringes.

"I have administered only a deep sedative," the first operative said. "The drug we used has enormous amnestic effects as well, so he will have no memory of the several minutes before it was administered. He is safe and comfortable, I assure you."

The second professional was tapping a syringe, perhaps to ensure it was free of air. But instead of a needle, the vial ended in a large tube.

"What is *that*?" Faisal asked.

"Bupropion. With the MAO inhibitors your father is on, it should give him a seizure. I will administer it intranasally so there will be no needle marks to arouse suspicion. One injection site is enough. But before giving it, I need to apply an eye drop," the operative said.

He set the applicator down beside the King's sleeping body, removed a bottle with a dropper on the end from his case, and placed several drops of the liquid into the King's left eye.

"This compound will dilate one pupil, making it look like His Majesty has had a stroke, completing the illusion to fool the King's doctors."

"He must not die," Faisal cautioned. "It is imperative that my father be disabled but recover."

Faisal was proud of the plan he'd devised to keep the King from meddling, while simultaneously preserving the hierarchy and line of succession that gave him the power he needed. Should his father die, and he became King, that power would fall on the new Crown Prince. Faisal had to remain Crown Prince for as long as possible, the position from which he had the most power and control over the daily operations of government. With Israel painted as a common enemy, and the West's predictable support for their Zionist ally, he could forge an alliance between the Kingdom and Iran—an alliance that his father would never have condoned after decades of mistrust and bad blood between the two nations.

"He will not die," the operative said, then shined a light in the King's left eye. "But we will need to have access to him during his medical care to administer drugs as necessary to maintain the illusion."

"Leave that to me," Faisal said as the agent sprayed the insidious compound into his father's nose.

"Any moment now," the agent said. He zipped the case shut and handed it to his partner.

"Leave now," Faisal commanded. "And let the charade begin."

As the two operatives exited the office through the door to the Prince's private chambers, Faisal ran to the opposite door to the conference room and flung it open. As Faisal had predicted, Bashar had busied himself studying the documents spread out on the table, taking full advantage of the opportunity to be left alone with confidential information.

"Bashar! Help!" Faisal screamed in panic. "My father . . . something's wrong."

"What?" a shocked Bashar said, looking up. "What happened?"

"I . . . I don't know. He just . . . I don't know . . . he fainted. I think he's having a heart attack."

Faisal dashed back into the office with Bashar in tow. Then, as if ordained by Allah himself, they watched as King Abdul began to seize where he lay on the floor.

"I think he's having a seizure," Faisal said as the King began to shake and shudder. His expensive gray trousers turned dark in the crotch as he soiled himself.

"Your Majesty?" Bashar said, taking a knee beside his King. His eyes were wide. "Your Majesty, can you hear me?"

"What are you doing? Call the King's doctor!" Faisal screamed at Bashar.

Bashar looked up, stunned and glassy-eyed with confusion.

"Now, you fool!" Faisal screamed at Bashar.

Bashar, frozen with indecision, didn't react.

"Fine, I'll do it. Stay with him," Faisal barked. He sprinted out of the room, allowing himself the slightest of grins as he turned his back to the King's advisor.

He crossed through the conference room and tore the door open, shouting out into the hallway, "We need help! Someone, please . . . the King is having a seizure. We need a doctor!"

He heard shouts and shoes pounding on the marble floors outside as the alarm was sounded. He was pretty sure that this, his second performance, was even better than his first.

Moments later, Security Chief Saad, along with two paramedics and the King's personal physician carrying a blue bag, stormed down the hallway toward him.

"This way," Faisal said to them, panic and anguish still in his voice as he led them through the conference room to the office. "I think he had a seizure. Or maybe a heart attack. I don't know. One minute he was talking, the next he collapsed."

The doctor and paramedics rushed to his father's side and immediately got to work checking his pulse, breathing, and pupil dilation. One paramedic opened his shirt while the other charged a portable defibrillator in preparation for CPR. Faisal leaned in, peppering them with questions about the King's status—playing up his frantic concern.

"Let them do their work, Your Highness," Bashar said, tugging Faisal by the sleeve. "His Majesty is in good hands now."

Faisal let the King's advisor lead him away to give the doctor and EMTs space to work. Once they were out of earshot from the others, he spoke.

"Bashar, we must not let anyone know this has happened. My father is strong; he will surely recover from whatever this malady is. But, if we really are at the brink of war, we cannot let our enemies suspect that King Abdul is ill. Do you understand?"

Bashar stared at him, his compassion replaced for an instant with something else.

"You are right, of course, Your Highness," Bashar said. "We will not let this go beyond those who know already."

"I need to know I can trust you, Bashar," Faisal said, his voice now calm and even, staring into the man's eyes. "Do you understand?"

Bashar, perhaps too afraid to speak, gave a curt nod and looked down at his feet.

"Good," Faisal said, then gripped Bashar by the shoulders.

"Do not leave my father's side. I am putting you in charge of his recovery. If anything happens to him, it will be your fault. But don't worry, my friend. I will fly in the best doctors in the world if I must. There is no price I would not pay to safeguard my father's life."

CHAPTER 14

NSA BUILDING 3
BAHRAIN INTERNATIONAL AIRPORT
BAHRAIN
0724 LOCAL TIME

Whitney stood in front of the tinted glass wall of windows in the preflight lounge watching the heat mirages outside. Entranced, she watched as the tarmac appeared to ripple and dance like a reflecting pool. In reality, the concrete was dry as a bone and so hot you could fry an egg on it, but to her, the water mirage looked real.

In her peripheral vision, she noticed Theobald step up beside her. "You're awfully quiet this morning," he said. "Is everything all right?"

She turned and flashed him a closed-lip smile. "Everything's fine."

He held her gaze for a moment. "I'm a pretty good listener—or so I've been told—if you need someone to talk to."

She liked Theobald. On her very first mission with the Tier

One, he'd been there for her as both a mentor and a guardian. When she'd needed a rock, he'd been a boulder.

"I had a difficult thing happen on a recent op," she said. "I'm still working through it."

"Something that happened *to* you or *because* of you?"

"A little bit of both, but mostly the former."

He nodded and shifted his gaze out the window. "Been there a few times myself . . ."

They stood in silence watching a large commercial jet taxiing for takeoff. This wasn't the time or place for soul-baring, but to her surprise, she heard herself say, "Her name was Lucy Kim, and she was my friend. We got taken, and bad things happened. Thanks to her courage, we managed to get free. But during the escape, she was shot, and she died a little while later."

Theobald nodded slowly but didn't say anything.

"I almost didn't make it myself. To be honest, I'm surprised I did," she said and blew air through pursed lips. "I can still picture her face on the life raft . . ."

"I'm sorry that happened to you," he said. "And I'm sorry Lucy didn't make it."

"You would have liked her, Bobby. She was a total badass—taking all the abuse and protecting me," she said, smiling before a dark cloud of survivor's guilt consumed her. "It's not fair how it ended. She's the one who deserved to live."

Theobald put his arm around her shoulder and gave her a gentle one-armed hug. With anyone else, she might have been put off by the gesture, but it was exactly what she needed. With tears pressing, she boxed up the memory and forced Lucy's angelic, pale visage from her mind.

"Anyway, I'm not looking for therapy, but I appreciate you listening."

He let go of her shoulder and took a step back. "I'm going

to go check with the pilot—see how the preflight is going. The others should be here any minute."

"I'll wait here for them," she said, collecting herself.

He nodded and disappeared out the west-side door, which led to the hangar. Moments later, the east door to the lounge opened and a blast of hot air flowed into the room, followed by the two remaining members of the investigation team: a man and a woman, both carrying duffels. Whitney forced a professional smile onto her face and walked over to greet the duo.

"Hi," Whitney said, extending her hand to the very tall, broad-shouldered African American man who, according to Theobald, worked undercover as a cyberspook from the NSA's supersecret S328 unit.

"Hi, I'm Sam—Sam Octavius," the man said, gripping her hand with thick fingers that she imagined could break every bone in her hand if he wanted to.

"Whitney Watts," she said. "Nice to meet you."

"Likewise," Sam said, releasing her hand.

"I understand you work for State?" she said, giving a nod to his official cover.

"Yeah, I'm something of a pinch hitter. They move me around when and where I'm needed. Just recently transferred to Ambassador Harley's staff," he said, referring to the American Ambassador to Saudi Arabia. "If things get dicey, I'll be the team's point man on all diplomatic comms with the Secretary of State during the investigation."

In this innocuous-sounding reply, Sam Octavius had managed to convey plenty. Unless she was reading too much into things, it sounded like he'd just confirmed two critical details: First, he was an experienced field agent with diverse situational experience; second, if the Saudis tried to restrict or sever the team's comms, he would make sure they had a secure channel with DC. He'd specifically mentioned comms with the Secretary of State, not the American Embassy.

"It puts my mind at ease to know we'll have a direct line to the very top, if need be," Whitney said, holding eye contact. "As far as delicate situations go, this one certainly ranks near the top."

He flashed her a broad smile. "*Delicate* just so happens to be my middle name."

"Oh really? I would have guessed linebacker."

This earned her a laugh from both Octavius and his teammate. Whitney turned to the woman standing next to him and stuck out her hand.

"Jenn Mullican. Nice to meet you, Whitney." Mullican was a fit, attractive, fortyish woman who was dressed in a pantsuit and wore her mousey brown hair straight and shoulder length.

"Nice to meet you too, Jenn," Whitney said, shaking hands.

A second blast of hot air flooded the room as Theobald returned from the hangar. "What did I miss?" he asked, shaking hands with Jenn and Sam. He seemed to have already met them. From the look on his face, Whitney could tell he was feeling good about the team dynamic.

"I was just about to tell Whitney that I spent most of my career working out of the Dallas Field office, where I specialized in crime scene investigations as part of the Evidence Response Team," Mullican said. "But three months ago, the Bureau threw me a curveball and I got transferred to DC. Apparently, the joint world is making by-name requests these days."

"Called up to the majors, huh?" Octavius said.

"Or maybe sent down to the minors." Mullican grinned. "Some days I'm not so sure."

"Oh, it was definitely a demotion," Theobald said. "Trust me, I'm speaking from experience."

They all laughed. Each of them understood the double-edged sword that was interagency task force work.

"What about you, Whitney? What's your pedigree?" Mullican asked.

In Whitney's case, her cover was simple: She didn't have one. From a paperwork and records standpoint, she'd never technically left her position as a counterterrorism analyst at NCTC. Outside the Tier One SEAL community, nobody knew she worked at the JSOC element. The government had even maintained her lease on her old apartment to support the narrative that she was still home-based in Northern Virginia. Whether Sam and Jenn had been read in on her current billet was not something she knew or had any control over. It was also irrelevant because it didn't impact how she would perform her role on the investigation team.

"I've been in counterterror my entire career—analysis and investigation for NCTC," she said, keeping it simple and to the point.

"Cool," Octavius said. He looked at Theobald, then added, "Looks like we got all our bases covered."

"It's the right team for the assignment," Theobald said, shifting his gaze to Sam and Jenn's bags, which they'd both set down on the ground beside them. "Fair warning: I would not be surprised if the Saudis take custody of any weapons and gear they deem potentially problematic. Are either of you carrying?"

Both Sam and Jenn nodded.

"All right, well, if your piece is something fancy, expensive, or has sentimental value, I'd recommend leaving it locked up here at the hangar. There's a chance you might not get it back if you bring it with."

"I'm willing to roll the dice," Mullican said. "Just a Glock 19."

"Not me," Octavius said. "Mine's a Wilson EDC X9, fully customized."

"Oh yeah, you'll definitely want to lock that bad boy up here," Theobald said, then looked back at Mullican. "What about CSI-type stuff? Any high-tech gear you can't afford to lose?"

The FBI agent pursed her lips. "Well, everything I brought, I need. It's all replaceable, but not cheap."

"Uncle Sam will foot the bill if it gets confiscated. What about you, Sam?"

A wry smile curled the corner of the cyberspook's mouth. "Just my work laptop and satphone. Both of which they can inspect and scan, but I hope would be permitted to remain with me so I can do my email and make calls," he said innocently.

"Excellent. Jenn, you can lock up your weapon in the gun locker. I'll grab some bottled water from the fridge, and then why don't we head into the hangar and get settled on the jet. It's only one hour fifteen to Riyadh, so a quick hop. My contact at the embassy has arranged transportation for us from the airport to Al-Yamamah Palace."

"Al-Yamamah Palace is the King's residence, correct?" Whitney asked.

"Yes," Theobald said, "but in the same way that the White House is the residence of the President. It's also the seat of the monarchy, functioning as the administrative center of the government."

"And it's the supposed location of the murder," Mullican added. She rolled her eyes. "The most heavily guarded complex in the country, and we're supposed to believe the Crown Prince was left unguarded? Yeah, right . . ."

"So, you're a skeptic?" Whitney said.

"Aren't you?" the FBI investigator said.

Whitney nodded. "Yeah, but I'm trying to keep an open mind nonetheless."

"We'll talk more about it on the plane," Theobald said and gestured for them to get going.

Whitney grabbed her roller bag by the extended handle, then followed her new teammates out of the lounge and into the hangar, where a Gulfstream G500 was fueled up and ready to whisk her into the heart of the Kingdom of Saudi Arabia.

CHAPTER 15

JSOTF SCIF
US NAVAL FORCES CENTRAL COMMAND (NAVCENT)
NAVAL SUPPORT ACTIVITY BAHRAIN (NSA BAHRAIN)
MANAMA, BAHRAIN
0745 LOCAL TIME

Chunk leaned back from the laptop computer where he scoured the high-side feeds for any chatter coming in that he might need to be concerned about. He needed to start thinking strategically and proactively, not just prepare to be reactive.

Unless Heels and Theobald perform some miracle in Riyadh, a shitstorm of epic proportions is coming soon . . .

It also kept his mind distracted from thinking about Watts. He'd kind of ignored her last night at the team dinner, and he wasn't exactly sure why. They had agreed to keep things professional and not allow what they had both been feeling to become a distraction or something that would fracture the team. But he also knew he was taking it further than he needed. They were still supposed to be friends, and after everything that had happened to her on that yacht, she probably needed someone to talk to. He'd also not had an opportunity to say goodbye to her before she left this morning for the airport. Theobald had apparently driven her.

Something I should have offered to do.

Chunk trusted Theobald beyond almost anyone he knew outside of the team—a trust built on the brotherhood born in fire and blood in Mingora and Afghanistan—but he had to be creeping up on fifty years old, and he was not a Tier One SEAL. And Watts, despite her recent push for a higher level of fitness and firearms proficiency, was an analyst, not an operator.

She's a teammate, and by definition that makes her safety my responsibility . . .

A paper clip smacked Chunk in the side of his head, and he turned to see Saw, who was looking at his own computer screen to his left around the conference table.

"You okay, boss?" the SEAL sniper asked.

"Oh, I'm better than okay. When I wake up in the morning, Shipmate, I piss excellence," Chunk said with a crooked grin, adapting one of Saw's favorite lines from the movie *Talladega Nights*. They'd traded so many one-liners from the cult classic film at the Homestead NASCAR race that at one point Ellie had playfully threatened to take the kids and leave if they didn't shut up.

"Is that so? Because I don't see it," Saw said through a laugh, then fired back one of Chunk's favorites: "In fact, with all due respect, sir, I didn't realize you'd gotten experimental surgery to have your balls removed."

"Shake 'n Bake, baby," Chunk said and held a fist to his teammate, who bumped it. "In all seriousness, I'm good, dude. Why do you ask?"

"You just seem stressed out this morning. Which I get, given world events, but that ain't you."

Chunk nodded. "Just trying to anticipate fires and think a step ahead."

"And worrying about Heels," Saw said. It was a statement, not a question, but one without any judgment.

"That too."

"I don't like her in the lion's den without one of us, boss," Saw said, echoing Chunk's own private thoughts. "If the Crown Prince assassination is a false flag set up by this Faisal cat, then she's in the eye of the storm, with none of us to bail her out."

"I hear ya, but she's smart, capable, and in good hands with Theobald," Chunk said, feeling his teammates' eyes on him. He wondered if Saw knew that he and Whitney had flirted with crossing a line that simply couldn't be crossed. "Orders are orders. POTUS wants us to be here and ready when the shit does hit the fan."

"I guess," Saw conceded, his face clouding.

"How's the family, bro?" Chunk asked. "Sorry we had to cut the NASCAR weekend short."

"It's all good, man," Saw said. "They had a great time. Hell, I had a great time. Thanks for the opportunity."

Chunk nodded. "Easy day."

He knew it had been a tough choice for Saw to stay in the unit after the attack on his family in Tampa by an al Qadar assassin nearly a year ago. But the conversation they'd had at the memorial wall before they'd deployed had given Chunk insight into his teammate's motivations. After the decision, Saw had been back to his old self—better, in fact. He'd risen to the challenge of taking on more leadership responsibility. But he also checked in with Ellie at home more frequently than before, which sometimes could be a worrying sign that all might not be well at home. For a guy like Saw, a real family man, the stress of his family being unhappy could be a distraction that proved deadly.

"It was tough for Ellie, at first. I think the idea of the family being out of harm's way filled her with hope, but she's the wife of a frogman and stepped up. You saw her at Homestead. She's leaned into the challenge and is doing awesome now."

Chunk nodded with admiration. Saw and Ellie were a team—a model for marriage in a business where the divorce rate was high and the life grueling—and being a team meant hard work, honesty, and sacrifice. A mental picture of Watts popped into his head just then. He saw her looking at him like she did when they'd had that intense moment together riding the London Eye—strong in her vulnerability, honest in the aftermath of adversity.

Could she have been my Ellie?

He shooed the disruptive thought away. That ship had sailed.

Then there was a metallic click, and Chunk felt the air pressure change in the room. He turned over his shoulder, expecting to see Spence enter the room with their new partners from Jerusalem, but Captain Bowman strode in instead. His face was clean-shaven and serious beneath his close-cropped hair. Bowman closed the door behind him, then folded his arms across his generous chest beneath the subdued trident on his digital cammies.

"Sir, I didn't realize you were joining us in-theater," Chunk said, rising to his feet.

"Sorry for the lack of heads-up, Keith," Bowman said with unusual gentleness. "I've been on a nonstop loop of conference calls the whole way over. Pentagon chiefs, the White House, ODNI, NCTC—you name it."

"We're watching the feeds closely, sir, but nothing actionable yet. Anything we should know?"

Bowman gestured for Chunk to take a seat. Bowman collapsed into the chair beside him.

"Just an assload of conjecture," Bowman said. "Consensus is that the Crown Prince's death is a false flag meant to either rise this Faisal dude to power or cause, at minimum, a proxy war in the region—if not an all-out war against Israel. Everyone's going round and round about who the puppet master is: Faisal and a cabal from inside the Kingdom, Iran's VEVAK, or players in any of a variety of terror organizations in the region. One thing we learned from al Qadar is that even smaller terror groups can mastermind sophisticated operations."

Bowman leaned in now, folding his hands on the table. "In another few days, it won't make a damn bit of difference. Because if the Saudis announce that they believe Mossad assassinated a sitting head of state, this war happens no matter where it started or what the truth is. Every terror organization and Iranian proxy group will be pointing everything from pistols to cruise missiles at Jerusalem. Then America makes a tough choice."

"Sir," Saw said quietly. "There is no scenario in which letting Israel fall to terrorists is something the United States can let happen."

"I agree," Bowman said. "But we're warriors, not politicians. That's a call for the Commander in Chief."

"Well," Chunk said, "thank God the White House is occupied by a former frogman."

"Definitely," Bowman said. "But I imagine the world gets a lot less black and white in that seat. We need to be ready to be the tool that Jarvis needs when he needs it. Right now, that means letting the spooks work while we prepare for direct intervention."

"To that end," Chunk said, "I think we need to operate under the premise that the Saudi accusation will leak out sooner rather than later."

"Agreed," Bowman continued, "but when that happens, I believe Jarvis will be able to use political pressure to keep Saudi Arabia from all-out war. But that won't stop the proxies from reacting immediately."

"Hamas and Hezbollah are looking for any excuse to attack Israel," Saw said. "I would expect rocket attacks within minutes of the news breaking."

"Agreed," Chunk said. "The biggest risk, in my opinion, is Iran. They have the most to gain from a full-scale assault on Israel. They will mobilize all their proxies in the region, not just Hamas and Hezbollah. And America is still the Great Satan, so our forces and personnel in the region are also at risk."

"Which is why we'll need to focus on maritime operations along the coast," Bowman said. "The various players out there have missiles, rockets, suicide boats targeting our fleet throughout the AOR. We are the in-theater QRF to take down threats as they pop up. Expect a serious game of Whac-a-Mole."

"Sounds like Iraq and Afghanistan in 2005," Chunk said.

"It'll be worse," Bowman replied. "That's why your guest partners"—he checked his Suunto watch—"who should be here any moment, need to be both supported and utilized. That means being highly relational in this collaboration, Chunk."

A smile spread across Chunk's face. "Sir, I hope you're telling me the intelligence specialists will be working with from Israel are Shayetet 13?"

Bowman gave him a wink. "I'm not *not* saying that."

"Perfect," Chunk said. "Having Israeli frogmen to round out the team will give us real insights and direct-action support."

As if on cue, there was another click and a rush of air as the heavy door opened. Spence came through, grinning, along with two operators in unmarked khakis and sport shirts.

"Captain Bowman, sir," Spence said, his face suggesting he was surprised to see the CSO. Then to Chunk and Saw, "Boss, Senior, I want to introduce you to a couple of guys."

The older of the two new arrivals stepped forward, hand extended. "I am Sgan Aluf Ami Galant, Operations Officer of this contingent."

Chunk shook hands with the man who's rank of *Sgan Aluf* in 13 was equivalent to a Commander in the US Navy. "Keith Redman, Gold Squadron Commander," Chunk said and nodded at Saw. "My teammate is Senior Chief Nick Sawyer."

"Saw," the sniper said.

Galant nodded, then turned to Bowman and addressed him by name. "Eric, it's been too long, my friend."

To Chunk's surprise, Bowman stepped up and embraced Galant. "How are Rachel and the girls?"

"Terrified but strong, as Israeli women are," Galant said with a resigned smile.

"Ami and I served together at the Tier One in our JO days," Bowman said, filling in the blanks for Chunk. "Before Operation Crusader."

"Such a tragedy. We grieved your loss," Galant said softly. Then, getting back to the business of introductions, he gestured to his Israeli companion. "This is Seren Ze'ev Mirashi. He commands one of our best Haposhtim assault platoons."

Mirashi, who's IDF officer rank of *Seren* was equivalent to a Navy Lieutenant, nodded to the group of them and said, "Hopefully, your government has authorized full cooperation so we can partner effectively. I fear the time is short before the shooting starts."

"We have full authority for joint operations and covert interventions to safeguard either nation's security," Bowman said.

"Excellent. And our government has authorized assets from our underwater units and Land Forces Egoz Unit under the command's umbrella," Galant said. "So, we're prepared for various scenarios."

Mirashi glanced at his commander and received a nod. "We already have a lot of intelligence to discuss with you. We will brief you on all the bad players in the region we are concerned with and where we think they are most likely to strike. Mossad has provided details we're authorized to share so we may all be on the same page."

"Let's get to work," Chunk said, taking a seat at the conference table.

Finally—something concrete they could act on.

CHAPTER 16

KING KHALID INTERNATIONAL AIRPORT BAHRAIN
THIRTY-FIVE KILOMETERS NORTH OF RIYADH, SAUDI ARABIA
0817 LOCAL TIME

Whitney looked out the window on the port side of the Gulfstream as it taxied toward an area of tarmac at King Khalid International Airport, where a dozen other private jets were parked. She couldn't help but notice three black Range Rovers parked in a line, waiting with an all-male security force standing at the ready beside the vehicles.

"Hey, Sam," Theobald said from the seat behind her. "Looks like they might be throwing us a curveball. We might be going directly to the palace."

"Roger that," the cyberspook said from his seat across the aisle from Whitney.

She watched Sam unzip his backpack and quickly make gear adjustments, although she couldn't tell exactly what he was doing. Despite all the time she'd spent in Tactical Operations Centers and her familiarity with high-tech gear at the

Tier One, Whitney had limited practical knowledge when it came to cyberwarfare. Like most analysts, she was a competent technology user, but she had no training in either optimizing or compromising hardware or software. The circuitry and code that ran inside the various black boxes that ruled the cybersphere was an enigma to her.

Still, she was curious.

Just like she'd grudgingly become an adopter and user of the weapons of war that her SEAL brothers used as the tools of their trade, she could imagine a future where she learned how to do what Sam did. Complexity didn't intimidate her. Unraveling it was her superpower.

She glanced at the trefoil knot tattoo inked on the inside of her left wrist. Did knot theory have any applications in cyberwarfare?

When things calm down, I'll have to ask Sam about it.

The Gulfstream jerked to a halt, announcing their arrival. A heartbeat later, the plane's captain did the same over the cabin speakers. She stood, along with her teammates—except for Sam, who was so tall he had to hunch even in the center aisle—and followed Theobald toward the cabin airstair door.

On stepping outside, a blast of hot air and bright sunlight hit her. Squinting, she descended the steps and joined Theobald at the bottom on the tarmac. Despite the early hour, heat was already radiating from the concrete. A security guard opened the rear passenger door of the middle Range Rover in the three-vehicle convoy, and a smartly dressed woman wearing heels and a white headscarf stepped out. Whitney recognized her instantly as Princess Ramia Bint Noor, the Saudi Arabian Ambassador to the United States.

A spike of panic hit her. She turned to Jenn. "Did you bring a headscarf?"

"Don't worry. It's not required for foreigners and tourists anymore," Mullican whispered back. "I looked it up yesterday."

"Oh, thank God," she said.

Princess Ramia smiled broadly as she walked up, escorted by a male bodyguard, to greet them. "Welcome to the Kingdom of Saudi Arabia. I'm Ambassador Noor."

"Thank you, I'm Robert Theobald, the lead investigator on our team," Theobald said, stepping up to shake the Princess's extended hand. "On behalf of the team, let me offer our heartfelt condolences for the loss of Crown Prince Khalid. I know he was a man of great vision, implementing tremendous reforms in your country."

The Princess's smile disappeared, and her expression went solemn. "His death is a terrible loss for the Kingdom. Thank you for traveling all this way and offering your support and expertise to augment our investigation. Discovering the truth and sharing it with the world is imperative; otherwise, we risk unleashing chaos and enmity in the region. These are fraught times in the Middle East. Our neighbors look to Saudi Arabia and our relationship with the United States for guidance."

Listening intently, Whitney was quick to notice the Princess's thoughtful and elevated speech. She spoke like a diplomat, and her English had no discernible accent. Watts knew that Noor had lived in the US for several multiyear stints during her childhood and had attended Georgetown University, Whitney's alma mater, though she'd graduated nearly two decades earlier. Whitney thought it was no coincidence that Noor had been appointed to the same role held by her father during the late eighties and nineties: Ambassador to the United States. Noor stood straight, with her shoulders back and bright espresso-colored eyes looking straight and unblinking while she spoke with Theobald. She exuded confidence, power, intelligence, and, well, wealth.

The Princess sidestepped to greet Whitney next. "And you are?"

"Whitney Watts," she said, taking the woman's soft hand in her own. The Ambassador's caramel-colored skin and slightly plump fingers made Whitney's pale, thin digits look wraithlike by comparison. "I'm a senior counterterrorism analyst at the National Counterterrorism Center in Virginia."

"A pleasure to meet you, Ms. Watts. Your expertise and insights are welcome here."

Something in the woman's dark eyes told Whitney that the Ambassador was speaking truthfully. Maybe it was a stretch, but Whitney couldn't help but sense that Princess Ramia was glad they were here.

"For obvious reasons, time is of the essence," the Princess said, speaking to them all now. "Crown Prince Faisal has directed that we transport you directly from King Khalid airport to Al-Yamamah Palace to expedite completing the investigation. I hope this is not a problem for you."

"Not a problem at all," Theobald said without hesitation. "We came to work. So, let's get to it."

"Excellent," the Ambassador said. She turned to Whitney. "I would be honored if you would ride with me, Whitney."

Whitney glanced at Theobald, shocked. He responded with a subtle, wordless nod.

"Happily. Thank you, Madam Ambassador," Whitney said, not sure which title Noor preferred: Princess or Ambassador.

Whitney turned to follow the Saudi Princess to the idling Range Rover and climbed into the passenger compartment. The luxury SUV had two captain's chairs trimmed in buttery-soft, cream-colored leather. Whitney settled into the obscenely comfortable seat and crossed her legs at the knee.

"I understand you're partial to bulldogs?" Whitney said, flashing the Princess a wry smile.

"Bulldogs?" Noor echoed, smiling but confused.

"Georgetown. You're a Hoya, right?" Whitney said. She started to sing the first line of the Georgetown fight song: "It's been so long since last we met—"

"—Lie down forever, lie down," the Princess sang back, catching on now and laughing. "You're a Hoya too?"

"I graduated six—hold on—make that seven years ago."

"Wow," the Princess said, her expression taking on a nostalgic tone. "My time at university feels like another lifetime ago. I'm coming up on my twenty-year reunion. Can you believe that? God, how the time slips away."

"Well, I think you look great, Madam Ambassador. Or should I be saying Your Highness? You're the first royal I've met."

Noor chuckled graciously. "When it's just the two of us, please call me Ramia. When we're working, I prefer Madam Ambassador."

"I can do that," she said.

"Is this your first visit to the Kingdom of Saudi Arabia?" Ramia asked.

"It is."

"But you've been to the Middle East before?"

"I have," she said, stopping short of providing any details.

She knew this one-on-one time with Noor was an opportunity she couldn't afford to squander. The Princess had invited Whitney as her private companion for the commute for a reason, and Whitney intended to find out why. The most likely reason was that once they arrived at the palace, Ramia would be forced to cede control of the narrative to Prince Faisal.

Now's my chance to get her unfiltered thoughts.

"I'm curious," Whitney said quickly, before the Princess could reply, "is there any family history or important details that might be helpful to me and my team to understand before we arrive at the palace?"

She wasn't sure if Ramia would pick up on the subtext in her question or answer her literally.

Ramia picked up her bottle of water, unscrewed the top, and took a sip. While she drank, Whitney saw her gaze tick to the two suited men in the front seats—the driver and her bodyguard—as if to signal concern. Both men were looking straight ahead, sitting in silence. There was no soundproof divider between the front seats and passenger cabin, like in a limousine, which meant the two men could hear everything she and Ramia talked about.

And the radio is off.

Ramia returned the cap to the bottle and, like a prima ballerina, used a ballet of words to answer Whitney's query.

"When the former Crown Prince appointed me to this job, I became the first female ambassador in the history of the Kingdom, not just to the United States but to any country. His decision upset the conservative factions in both the government and the religious establishment, but here I am, five years later, as an agent of change and reform. I'm also a member of the International Olympic Committee Women in Sports Commission and chairwoman of Saudi Geneco—a nonprofit whose mission is to foster gender equality and economic inclusion for women in the Middle East. Also, did you know my office was the first to offer Rosh Hashanah greetings to Jews in the United States, wishing them a happy Jewish New Year?"

"I did not know that," Whitney said. "But I'm glad you're sharing these kinds of details with me."

The Princess met her eyes. "There are some who will look at Crown Prince Khalid's death as an opportunity to turn back the clock—to reverse the progress that has been made. Not only for women's rights in the Kingdom but also in diplomacy. I believe an ambassador must think multilaterally. My job is not simply to manage diplomacy between the Kingdom of Saudi Arabia and the United States but to think about the Kingdom's relationships and standing in the global community of nations."

"Have you had an opportunity to discuss these concerns with Crown Prince Faisal?" she asked, treading into what was definitely uncharted territory for the conversation. Finding out where Faisal stood politically compared to his brother was a huge priority.

"Not yet. He is very much focused on the assassination investigation," Noor said.

Whitney noticed she used the word *assassination* for the first time. Whitney's brain was spinning a mile a minute, trying to figure out exactly what Ramia wanted or needed. She made a quick mental list:

She's worried she will be replaced as Ambassador.

That the reforms and progress made inside the Kingdom and abroad will be unmade.

That Crown Prince Faisal plans to use the murder of his brother as the catalyst for upending the geopolitics and balance of power in the Middle East.

Whitney inhaled deeply, while her mind followed the thread to the logical conclusion.

She thinks our findings and the subsequent international statement by the Jarvis Administration is critical to stop everything she's worked for from unraveling, and that's what she's signaling now.

"I understand," Whitney said, holding Ramia's eyes. "Well, when you next speak with him, please assure the Crown Prince that helping the Kingdom ascertain the truth, even if that truth is difficult to accept, is our one and only goal."

The tension in the Ambassador's face seemed to ease, which Whitney took as a sign that the dance of nonverbal cues and subtext had worked. But did the two brutes in the front seats also understand what had transpired? And if so, would they report it to the new Crown Prince? A wave of uncertainty washed over her, and with it, she became suddenly and acutely aware of how vulnerable Princess Ramia—despite her pedigree and position—was in this moment.

And of how vulnerable I am without my team . . .

A flash memory of her abduction in London—being black-bagged, thrown in the back of a van, and injected with a sedative—filled her mind. She fought the urge to cross her arms and hug her chest, but she lost the battle.

"Are you cold, Whitney?" Ramia asked, taking note. "I can have the driver adjust air-conditioning."

"I'm always cold, but don't worry about me," she said, forcing a smile. "I'll be fine."

PART II

"Only virtuous people are capable of freedom. As nations become corrupt and vicious, they have more need of masters."

—Benjamin Franklin

CHAPTER 17

JSOTF SCIF
US NAVAL FORCES CENTRAL COMMAND (NAVCENT)
NAVAL SUPPORT ACTIVITY BAHRAIN (NSA BAHRAIN)
MANAMA, BAHRAIN
0905 LOCAL TIME

Chunk looked up from the table to see Riker heading toward him with a speed that told him that he wasn't going to be able to finish this breakfast. He sat beside Ze'ev Mirashi, who had a fork at the ready to dig into the steaming plate of cheesy eggs and sausage. Chunk shoveled two big bites into his own mouth in rapid succession.

Should have got it in a to-go container . . .

Mirashi noticed Riker now, too, and let out his own sigh.

"What's up, Riker?" Chunk asked.

"Need you guys in the SCIF ASAFP," Riker said, hands on his hips.

Riker was too fit to be out of breath, but it was clear to Chunk he had jogged over here.

"What is happening?" Mirashi asked, rising immediately and tossing his napkin on his tray.

"New actionable intelligence is all I know," Riker said. "Both our bosses are looking it over and sent me to get you."

"Let's roll," Chunk said, pushing back from the table, snagging one last sausage link to consume on the go.

Minutes later, as Riker keyed in the code for the magnetic door to the SCIF, Chunk looked down the hall, where he noticed Saw on the team satphone.

"You good, bro?" Chunk called out.

Saw nodded with a finger up, turned away from them, and leaned his head in to finish his call, no doubt to home.

"Sorry," Saw said sheepishly after he'd hung up. "I promised I'd try and talk with the kids before we got busy. Ellie has her hands full, now that Connor is doing T-ball. I keep telling her Maggie is old enough for preschool so she can have a breather, but Ellie's not ready for that, I guess."

"All good, man," Chunk said. He had no idea how that juggling act worked, but it seemed impossible. Lots of SEALs failed at it; however, Saw and Ellie seemed to have something special.

They should teach a class on it or some shit. I'd take that class.

Chunk and Saw followed Riker through the metal door. Chunk saw Trip and Antman leaned over laptops, and Saw hustled over to join them in the bustling SCIF. Intelligence Specialist and Navy Chief Petty Officer Michelle Yi stood beside her own computer terminal in the corner, deep in conversation with an Israeli counterpart. The man was in uniform, but Chunk could tell just from his build and how he stood that he was an analyst, not an operator.

"Sorry to break up the breakfast, Keith," Bowman's voice boomed from where he stood beside Ami Galant.

"All good, sir," Chunk said. Mirashi took a seat next to the two Shayetet operators, who were sitting across from Chunk's teammates at the large oval table. "What's going on?"

"Israeli intelligence has confirmed that an Egyptian-flagged cargo vessel, the *Earabat Albahr*, which recently transited from the Red Sea through the Suez Canal into the Med, appears to be carrying Chinese-made CJ-10 cruise missiles," Galant said, his tone controlled and almost casual for having delivered such grim news.

"Well, that seems like bad news," Riker said, crossing his arms beside Chunk.

"Yes, this is an eyebrow-raising concern," the Shayetet 13 commander said. "But not the entire story. The CJ-10 is capable of carrying a five-hundred-kilogram conventional warhead. Or," he paused, "a nuclear payload. The missile has a range of fifteen hundred kilometers, which is nearly a thousand miles, which means it could target Israel from a great distance. And last, human intelligence combined with satellite imagery indicates the ship is carrying mobile launchers concealed inside shipping containers."

"That's a problem," Bowman said. "So, who do we think these missiles are being delivered to?"

"This is the worst news of all," Galant said with a nod to the Israeli Intelligence Officer Seren Becker, who was seated beside Michelle Yi. "Seren, you're up."

Becker stood and addressed the group.

"We have validated intelligence that a Houthi terrorist contingent boarded the *Earabat Albahr* two days ago with the ship docked in the port of Mukalla, Yemen," the Israeli intelligence officer said. "In other words, it appears the missiles might not need to be delivered at all to be used against us."

Chunk pursed his lips, then spoke up. "Let me get this straight: This ship has the missiles, launchers, and the terrorists on board to fire the weapons from virtually anywhere in the Mediterranean Sea. Sounds like we'd better do something about these damn things ASAP."

"How immediate is the threat? I mean, it's complicated programming and shooting missiles at sea, so maybe they're en route to deliver them to a land-based operation," Spence said, playing devil's advocate. "But even if these Houthi jackasses actually know what they're doing and could get off the shots from a ship, won't the Iron Dome destroy the missiles before they reach their targets?"

"The Iron Dome is very, very effective," Galant said, "but it is not one hundred percent. The CJ-10 is a land-attack cruise missile, not some low-tech rocket. Even a single CJ-10 getting through with a conventional warhead would be devastating. But imagine the destruction if it was armed with a nuclear warhead."

"Do you have any reason to suspect that the Houthi's could somehow have gotten access to a nuclear weapon?" Chunk asked dubiously. That was a reach, in his mind. Even if the Chinese sold them the CJ-10 missiles and launchers, they certainly weren't stupid enough to sell terrorists nukes with them.

He watched Becker's gaze shift again to his boss, Ami Galant, his look a question.

"This team is a joint task force," Galant said to the intelligence specialist. "Here we are all warriors. We keep nothing from one another. I have served beside Captain Bowman, and I assure you they can be trusted."

"Very well, sir," Becker said, then let out a long, slow breath. "Mossad has reason to believe that the Iranians have succeeded in producing a small stockpile of weapons-grade enriched uranium. The intelligence is conflicting, but there is a report they've completed work on two operational warheads."

"Wait . . . what?" Yi exclaimed, speaking for the first time. She looked at Becker in shock. "Why is this the first time we're hearing this?"

"More to the point, why would your government not share that information?" Chunk asked, incredulous.

"Because we have no hard proof. This has not yet been confirmed," Galant said, stepping in. "Our asset inside Iran only shared this new information in the last seventy-two hours, and it is still being vetted. It is possible, considering all that is happening in the Kingdom of Saudi Arabia, that it was felt that loyalties between the United States and Israel might be"—the Israeli officer seemed to consider the best words to use, then caught Chunk's eyes—"tested."

"I would have thought that our presence here, on this task force, would have mitigated any such concerns," Chunk said, his anger rising. "Our President has sent us here, risking American blood in combat for our shared cause."

"I agree with Commander Redman," Bowman said, looking at Galant with disappointment. "Our commitment to Israel's safety and security is as important to us as our own interests and assets in the region. Not knowing about this potential nuclear development is a huge deal. It changes the threat level in the CENTCOM AOR and means our forces are not properly prepared for that danger. We will be routing this intelligence to POTUS immediately."

"I would react the same if I was in your place. But understand: These are not my decisions to make. Israel is fighting for our very life, our right to exist. The fact that *we* shared this information with you now is proof of our faith in your allegiance," Galant said, his expression contrite.

Bowman gave a curt, tight-lipped nod, apparently accepting the situation for what it was. "Where is this ship now?"

Yi tapped her laptop and brought up a satellite image on the large monitor behind her. The Mediterranean Sea filled the screen, with the southern coast of Turkey at the top, the Israeli coast to the right, and the northern coast of Egypt at the bottom. Chunk saw a red square halfway between Egypt and Cypress with a dashed red line traced back to the south, toward the Suez Canal and Red Sea.

"This is the *Earabat Albahr*," Yi said, highlighting the square with an arrow from her laptop. "According to the published record, her next scheduled stop is Limassol, Cypress. As you can see, she is currently headed due north toward Cypress and is about ninety-seven miles off the coast of Israel."

"Is she on time, per her track and the scheduled docking?" Spence asked.

"Debatable," Yi replied. "According to my calculations, they're running behind, but they are following the shipping lanes and on a legitimate track toward Cyprus. That said, assuming the Israeli intelligence is correct and there are missiles on board, the ship is perfectly positioned right now to launch a strike on Israel."

"They wouldn't dare launch until *after* an announcement from Saudi Arabia blaming Israel for the Crown Prince's death," Riker said. "If that happens tomorrow, they'll be out of position."

Chunk considered this. It brought up the bigger question of just who the hell was pulling the strings here. Because if this ship really had nukes, and if it really intended to use them, then the plan was in motion already. Meaning *someone* knew the assassination would occur and that it would be blamed on Israel. And that someone was likely the one who had arranged the killing in the first place. Iran seemed the most likely suspect. Not that it mattered in the short term, unless you were the President of the United States or the Prime Minister of Israel.

For this team, all that mattered was denying the enemy the opportunity.

"With the range of those missiles, they could be anywhere in the Med and still be in range of Israel. It's just the closer they are, the faster the missile is on target and the less time the IDF has to react," Yi said.

"It would be very helpful to know when we thought that announcement might occur," Becker pointed out.

"We have a team in the Kingdom right now working that very issue," Chunk replied.

"I think we should consider the possibility, based on this ship's track and current position, that there could be coordination happening between the Saudis and the terrorists in control of this boat. And if that's the case, then we have little time to waste," Galant chimed in.

"Then it's a no-brainer. I say we hit the ship ASAFP," Riker said, fire in his eyes at the thought of getting in the fight.

Chunk stared at the map closely and pursed his lips. "Maybe," he said and looked at Yi. "You said the *Earabat Albahr* is staying in the shipping lanes at present, correct?"

"That's right," Yi said. Chunk could see the light bulb snap on for her too. "You want me to run archived imagery and see which, if any, other ships might be trailing her movements or converging on her position."

"Yes. Do it now," Chunk said. Then he turned to Galant. "Sir, we're going to search imagery from the last forty-eight hours or so to see if there are any other vessels shadowing or vectoring to join the *Earabat Albahr*. We should consider the possibility that this is more than a single ship trafficking arms. What if instead of port-to-port transit this repositioning is part of a coordinated evolution?"

Galant nodded, a look of respect in his eyes. "You're proposing the *Earabat Albahr* might not be working alone."

"Exactly. And if that's the case, whoever is pulling these strings might have a command-and-control vessel in the region to coordinate a planned attack with other ships or even aircraft and ground units. We've seen this before."

"Very good insight, Commander," Galant said, then instructed Becker to integrate Yi's data.

The Israeli intelligence specialist tapped away on his computer and brought up two new red triangles with historical tracks that converged on the *Earabat Albahr* from different directions.

"We had considered this as well and have identified these two vessels as candidates for command-and-control vessels, or additional terrorist ships carrying weapons. Both are vectoring toward our primary target, but we are particularly interested in this one." Becker moved a pointer over the triangle to the southeast. "This vessel, the *Dakar*, is flagged in the database because it's been in the vicinity of three previous Houthi attacks conducted in the Gulf of Aden and the Red Sea. Also noteworthy, Jahan Heydari was photographed by a Mossad asset embarking on this vessel in Bandar Abbas, Iran, two weeks ago."

"Why is that relevant?" Riker asked. "Is the dude important?"

"Yes, I'm sorry, let me explain," Galant said. "Heydari is a MOIS agent—has been for over a decade. He is an operative of particular interest, flagged and watched closely by our intelligence apparatus. Instead of bringing him in, we monitor his activities closely, because his area of specialty has been mobilization of proxy groups in Yemen and more recently in Gaza and the West Bank . . ."

As Galant spoke, Becker popped an image in the upper-right corner of the large screen: a passport-style photo of a rough-looking man with dark eyes and a graying beard.

"He has been identified visiting with Hezbollah leadership both in and out of the country," Galant continued. "He has been linked to Houthi rebel terror attacks, and most recently has been the conduit for intelligence and funding for the new radical group Sayf Allah."

"So, you think this Heydari dude is currently on the *Dakar* and is tasked to meet up with the ship carrying the missiles?" Riker asked.

Becker raised his eyebrows. "I do find it curious that the *Dakar* rounded the Arabian Peninsula, passed through the Suez Canal into the Med, and is steaming on what appears to be a rendezvous course with the *Earabat Albahr*."

Riker nodded and turned to the Israeli commander to ask the question weighing on Chunk's mind as well. "If the *Dakar* has a history of being a bad actor, and Heydari is on it, then I'd say we just found our HVT."

"Agreed," Chunk said. "Time to start working up a mission package."

"Joint task force means joint operations," Bowman said, his voice a pissed-off growl. "Chunk, while we're operating with the Israelis, I want you and the boys in unmarked slicks. No patches, no personal items, no morale identifiers. We are one team with the Israelis."

"I agree," Galant said. "The unmarked protocol is in the best interest of both our nations. We will use covert air and sea assets for transportation as well."

Chunk knew that Shayetet 13 had a big stable of air and

sea platforms from a dozen countries to choose from, just like CIA's ground branch did. On this mission, their combined team would look like whatever they wanted and would give credit after the win to whatever overt military unit the head shed chose.

Just like we do in the Tier One.

"I've greased the skids for staging in Amman, Jordan," Bowman said to the group. "Get packed and loaded out. We're on the clock, people. Plane leaves in two hours. Break."

As the assembled operators took their leave to prep, Bowman waved Chunk over for a sidebar.

"What's up, boss?" Chunk said.

Bowman waited until nearly everyone had cleared out before answering. "Expect relations to get chilly for us in Jordan if the Saudis leak the news of the assassination and the Jordanians know we're partnering with Shayetet 13. We need to keep the joint nature of our current task force locked down tight, if you know what I mean."

"Roger that," Chunk said.

Bowman leaned in close. "We need to let President Jarvis know what's going on. If Mossad is right, and Iran is nuclear capable *and* arming their proxies with nukes, this is an entirely different mission than the one we were sent here to do. The stakes just went up . . . exponentially."

CHAPTER 18

LEAD VEHICLE OF A SECURE CARAVAN FROM THE AIRPORT
RIYADH, SAUDI ARABIA
0850 LOCAL TIME

Whitney listened intently as Ambassador Noor gave her a brief history of Riyadh, the capital of Saudi Arabia and the most populous city on the Arabian Peninsula. According to Ramia, the name *Riyadh* meant "the Meadows," but looking at the barren, brown desert all around them, Whitney couldn't imagine why.

"How do you supply water to seven million people in a city located in the middle of the Nafud desert?" Whitney asked.

"An excellent question. Historically, from underground aquafers, but those have been mostly depleted, so now our water comes primarily from desalination plants located along the Persian Gulf. The water must be pumped over four hundred kilometers and up two thousand feet in elevation to get here. It's a problem, that's for sure."

"Madam Ambassador, we're arriving at Al-Yamamah Palace," the driver said from the front.

While their IDs were in-processed at the main gate, Ramia explained that the massive walled complex—in addition to being the King's private residence—housed the Royal Court, the Shura Council, the royal mosque, and numerous government administration buildings. After clearing this first checkpoint, the Range Rover caravan drove down a palm tree–lined road past an impressive garden courtyard with a large fountain in the center—an ostentatious display in the middle of a water-starved desert.

Unlike the marble pillars and neoclassical design of the White House or Capitol Building in Washington, DC, here Arabian architecture dominated. Tall, pointed window arches, crisscrossing geometric lines, and intricate tile work gave the buildings a proud, exotic feel. After looping around the grounds, the Range Rover caravan parked under a covered side entrance that Ramia explained was used for staff and non-VIP guests.

Apparently, our little task force doesn't rate the red-carpet treatment, Whitney thought as she climbed out of the air-conditioned luxury SUV to reunite with her colleagues. Before she could get in a word with Theobald, though, an Arab man dressed in a black suit flanked by two other men in suits walked up to greet the American contingent.

"Greetings. My name is Asim Saad, and I am the Head of Security for Al-Yamamah Palace. The Crown Prince welcomes you to Saudi Arabia and thanks you for your offer of assistance with our investigation. Before I give you access to the crime scene, however, you must complete a security screening. Leave your luggage in the vehicles and follow me inside," Saad said.

He motioned for them to follow. One of the two guards flanking Saad approached Whitney and handed her a black headscarf.

Confused, she accepted it and watched as the same guard walked to Mullican and thrust an identical headscarf at her.

"Put this on," the man said with a stern, humorless expression.

Whitney glanced at Jenn, who shrugged.

"What is the meaning of this?" Ambassador Noor said, intervening. "These are not Muslim women. There is no requirement for them to cover."

"This is a new policy implemented by Crown Prince Faisal this morning," Saad said. "All women, regardless of nationality or religion, are required to wear a head covering while on palace grounds."

Whitney looked at Ramia and saw the Ambassador performing a silent calculation in her head: whether to challenge this edict or not. She got her answer a beat later when Ramia, jaw set, walked over to help Whitney.

"Here, let me show you how to wear one of these," Ramia said, her voice tight.

"Thank you," Whitney said, letting the Ambassador wrap the headscarf over her scalp and sweep it around her neck and shoulders.

They both turned to Mullican, who was doing a decent enough job of arranging her own scarf. "How does mine look?"

"It looks fine," Ramia said.

Theobald had been silent during the exchange. The DIA operative's expression was inscrutable, but Whitney could see the unspoken message in his eyes: *Buckle up, boys and girls. This is only the beginning . . .*

"This way," Saad said, his voice commanding and stern.

Despite the instruction to leave all their luggage in the SUVs, Sam and Jenn both carried backpacks. As team leader, Theobald had decided they were going to try to push the envelope at every friction point and see what they could get away with. Passive-aggressive was their modus operandi while they were here. They would only get one shot at this, so they needed to make it count.

Once inside, they were directed to a security checkpoint similar to airport TSA, with an x-ray belt scanner for personal items and a millimeter wave scanner for people. Theobald gestured for Sam and Jenn to go first with their bags, which were predictably flagged upon being scanned.

"You're not allowed to bring mobile phones, weapons, computers, or unsanctioned electronics into the palace," Chief Saad said, from where he now stood on the other side of the scanner, clutching Jenn and Sam's bags with a disapproving glare. "You will have to leave these items in a locker here and retrieve them upon your departure."

"How are we supposed to do our job without the tools and equipment necessary to conduct our investigation?" Octavius protested.

"Very simple, we will provide you with any photographs or instruments you need," Saad said. His expression indicated this was nonnegotiable.

"All right, pack it up, team," Theobald said, rotating his index finger in a circle in the air over his head. "I told the Secretary of State this was going to be a waste of time; it looks like I was right."

"Wait, stop," Ramia said. "You're leaving?"

"Yes, ma'am," Theobald said. "We were promised cooperation, but confiscating our equipment and controlling what we can and can't photograph and analyze compromises both the legitimacy and the validity of our independent assessment. It's not *independent* if your head of security dictates what we can and can't do. Let's go, people."

Playing along, Whitney performed an about-face and started walking toward the exit. Mullican and Octavius followed suit.

"Mr. Theobald, please," Ramia called after them. "Give me a moment please to try to rectify this situation."

Whitney turned, crossed her arms, and stood next to Theobald. She watched as the Ambassador, fire in her eyes, walked over to Chief Saad out of earshot from the rest of the group.

"Anything interesting come up during your drive with the Ambassador?" Theobald asked in a quiet voice while they waited.

"She's definitely worried."

"Go on."

"About Faisal using this as an opportunity to turn back the clock and unravel all the reforms and progress made during Khalid's rule."

He nodded. "What about the regional reaction?"

"That too, obviously. I feel like she needs us as much as we need her."

"Looks like things are getting a little heated between those two."

Whitney and Theobald watched a fiery Ramia locked in conversation with an increasingly angry Saad.

"Oh yeah, he's pissed."

As quickly as it started, the conversation ended with Ramia jamming her index finger into Saad's chest, getting the final word, before Saad turned on a heel and stormed off. With a satisfied expression on her face, Ramia walked back to stand with the four Americans, who were still waiting by the door outside the scanner.

"I told him this is not how the Kingdom treats important guests such as yourselves," the Ambassador said with a shake of her head. "I told him to either fix this with the Crown Prince personally, or I will be taking you directly to the American Embassy to discuss this matter with Ambassador Harley and the White House."

"Thank you, Madam Ambassador," Theobald said. "We appreciate you standing up for us."

"It's my duty," Noor said. Whitney watched as the woman held her teammate's eyes. "And I hope that when and if the time comes in which our situations are reversed, you will do the same for me."

CHAPTER 19

GRAND FOYER
AL-YAMAMAH PALACE

Arash Reza, the newly appointed Iranian Deputy Ambassador to Saudi Arabia, was delivered from the airport to the palace in a black Range Rover. On arrival, he was escorted by two security guards into the Grand Foyer, the entrance reserved for world leaders, dignitaries of import, and celebrities. The opulence of the hall struck him like a physical force, which was entirely the point, he imagined. The polished Italian marble floor, the towering white columns gilded in golden geometric patterns, the crystal chandelier the size of an automobile hanging from the center of a multitiered vaulted ceiling—all worked together in breathtaking effect. And standing under the chandelier, bathed in fractured crystalline light, stood the Crown Prince. Dressed in the traditional white thawb and red-checkered ghutrah of his house, Faisal looked . . . regal.

And powerful, his inner voice noted.

"You are a most welcome sight, my brother," Faisal said, opening his arms wide in a warm, beckoning gesture.

Reza walked up to greet him, and to his surprise, was immediately wrapped up in an unexpected bear hug. Reza awkwardly hugged Faisal back, acutely aware of the watchful eyes of the dark-suited bodyguards standing off to the side, hands clasped in front of them. Sensing his discomfort, Faisal broke the embrace and followed Reza's wary gaze to the two men. A smile spread across his face.

"These men are my most trusted agents," Faisal said with an easy laugh. "They are more than mere bodyguards, Arash. They are the men I trust to take care of things that must be done in secret. They have been part of everything I've accomplished from the beginning."

"Everything?" Reza asked.

"Don't worry. They've pledged their lives in my service," Faisal said, wrapping a reassuring arm around Reza's shoulders. "Besides, we're all bonded in our mutual knowledge of the truth. There is no going back for them—or any of us—now."

Reza gave a respectful nod but received nothing in return. If these two were party to the murder of Crown Prince Khalid, then it would mean Reza was now tied to these men as well. Faisal had just confirmed for them that Reza, too, was read into the Crown's deepest and most damning secrets.

"You did what needed to be done," Reza said. "For the Kingdom and for the Crown. Nothing more, nothing less."

"I did my duty. But it was not easy, my friend," Faisal said, looking down.

"What about your father, the King?" Reza asked, treading into a potential minefield with the question—but a minefield that unfortunately had to be crossed.

Faisal exhaled and looked down at his hands while he

spoke. "My father's reaction was what you would expect—shock, anger, and despair at the murder of his son by the Israelis . . ."

"I hate to have to ask this question, but does he accept the fiction, or does he suspect you had a hand in this?"

Faisal shook his head. "Unfortunately, I can't answer that question, my friend. And it is a question we might never learn the answer to. Early this morning, the King suffered a neurological event. The doctors say his aged body was so overwhelmed with grief and stress that he appears to have suffered a stroke. He's currently unconscious in a coma-like state. The doctors are unsure when he will come out of it."

His friend's remorse sounded hollow to Reza, but then again, Crown Prince Faisal bin Ahmed al-Saud had been raised in a family known for its ruthlessly cunning means and methods. One does not amass the greatest fortune on earth with *pleases* and *thank-yous*. Obviously, the King's illness was no coincidence, but for some reason, Faisal did not feel either ready or obligated to read Reza in on the truth.

Let him have this fiction for his dignity, the spy in Reza's head instructed. *You're exactly where you need to be.*

"I cannot claim to know the burden you must be carrying, but because of your strength and selfless sacrifice, the Kingdom will flourish," Reza said, looking Faisal in the eyes. "And so will all Muslims. For the first time in centuries, a true alliance between the Kingdom and Iran is possible. I am honored to be a part of this new beginning that, I know in my heart, will benefit the whole world."

"I have always loved your idealism, Arash," Faisal said through a laugh. He turned with a wave. "Follow me. We have much to discuss."

Reza followed his friend, now one of the most powerful

men in the world, through the palace to a sitting room in the Crown Prince's royal apartment. He gestured with a hand for Reza to take a seat in an opulent gold-and-white chair, separated from an identical one by a small table with a tea service already arranged. Faisal then dismissed his minders. For the first time, Reza and Faisal were alone.

Relaxing, Reza took a seat, and so did Faisal.

"Chai?" Faisal said, gesturing to the tea service on the table between them.

"Don't mind if I do," Reza said and poured himself a cup. "Would you like some, Your Highness?"

Faisal swatted away the comment. "Knock it off. We're alone now," he said. "If the time ever comes when I can't pour my own damn tea, then you have to promise to smack me."

Reza laughed at the comment, lifted the expensive teacup to his lips, and sipped. The steaming hot chai was, without a doubt, the best he'd ever tasted.

"I'm glad you're here, Arash. I need someone who I can really talk to. I'm under immense pressure," Faisal said, his stiff posture seeming to relax as he spoke this truth.

"That's why I came. Talk to me."

At first Reza thought Faisal might confess the truth about whatever it was he'd ordered done to the King, but instead the Prince recounted his call with the American President yesterday. Faisal seemed disappointed in himself that he'd pledged to President Jarvis to stall releasing a public statement until after the investigation had been completed by the American task force. The prince went on to confess his fear that the Americans would see through the assassination cover story he'd created.

"Why do you care so much about the Americans or whether they embrace the fiction?" Reza asked when Faisal had finished. "You're charting a new path forward, without them—a united Middle East with the Islamic Republic as your partner."

"Arash, the world you envision is beautiful and admirable. But building it requires great power. Before his death, my brother linked the Kingdom's future and fortune to the West. He believed he could grow the Kingdom by bolstering commerce with America and the Zionists. And his plan was working—we have thrived economically. Severing ties with the West is not so simple a matter. Pretending that America does not have power and influence in the region is naive. But you are also right that we need a partner who not only shares but prioritizes our interests. Iran is that perfect partner, but this change must be done delicately—a gradual process as the alliance gains strength throughout the region. The Americans must still see us as *their* partner until it is too late. You must recognize this?"

Now it was time for Reza to earn his pay. An alliance between Saudi Arabia and Iran could never flourish with the wedge of the Jewish state in the region, especially when that wedge was supplied with American military hardware and aid. And in any case, orders were orders. Golzar had given him very specific tasking to complete, tasking that now felt even less certain than when he'd boarded the plane in Tehran this morning. He needed to get Faisal on board with a massive proxy attack on Israel and the use of the nuclear weapons now at their disposal. He was surprised by the authority with which Faisal commanded this conversation. This Faisal, the one dressed as a true Saudi Prince, had evolved from playboy and Reza's unwitting pawn into a real power player. Reza had expected to be the lead in this conversation, but that was not exactly how this moment was unfolding.

I need to connect with the carefree Faisal of our university days.

Reza leaned in, forearms on his knees.

"Faisal, accept this counsel as what it is, the humble opinion of a friend and fellow visionary. And now, I suppose, the counsel of the new Iranian Deputy Ambassador to the Kingdom."

Faisal looked amused and set his cup on the table. "I would hope that you would never ever feel uncomfortable sharing your counsel and opinions with me, Arash," the Crown Prince said. "We are friends first and allies always. I need you and your counsel. You have inspired all that has happened with your vision. You should always speak freely—openly and without any fear of my reaction. These are private conversations."

Reza returned the smile. The experienced operative buried just beneath the surface knew that, while the Crown Prince might even believe what he was saying, it was unlikely to be true for long. Perhaps there was some merit in Reza's moving pieces on this chessboard more quickly, while Reza's counsel was still heard and his influence still meaningful.

"The truth is, I don't want to overstep. You are the Crown Prince now."

"You cannot overstep, my friend," Faisal said, shooing away the very idea.

"Well," Reza said, choosing his words carefully. "I am not naive. I know that the Kingdom has diplomatic, economic, and military agreements with the United States. President Jarvis has levers he can pull to try to punish the Kingdom if you don't cooperate. But have you considered the possibility that those levers become obsolete in a Middle East without a Jewish state? What if we have a once-in-a-lifetime opportunity to completely change the rules of the game . . ."

"I'm listening," Faisal said, picking up his tea.

"America has long been Israel's strongest supporter, but is this alliance absolute? Is America willing to forfeit all economic and diplomatic ties to a united Middle East for the sake of propping up a failed Zionist state? What if we could snap our fingers and *poof*, there was no Zionist state? In that world, Saudi Arabia would become the most powerful and influential nation in the region. Without Israel, America loses its anchor."

Faisal was already shaking his head.

"If you are suggesting what I think you're suggesting, I assure you it is not possible, Arash. Our military is formidable, but I am not prepared to declare war on Israel. It is a war that Saudi Arabia is unlikely to win and could not win if the Americans sided with the Jews. No, once the evidence of Mossad murdering my brother is released, we will call for world condemnation of the Zionists. From there, it must then be a slow, strangling political and economic death for the Jews."

Arash's smile now turned genuine. This was the answer he had expected—and the one he agreed with, because it was true. The combined military might of Israel and the United States was a juggernaut that even a unified Saudi Arabia and Iran had zero chance of defeating.

"I agree with you," Reza said, his voice taking on a conspiratorial tone. "But in preparation for my arrival here, I was given top secret clearance and briefed by the Ministry of Intelligence and Security."

"Have you been recruited to spy on me, Arash?" the prince said through a laugh. "The very thought—"

"Not at all," Reza replied quickly, showing appropriate—and partially real—concern. "I am not a spy."

"No," Faisal said, sipping his tea and shaking his head. He appeared to find the idea as absurd as it was amusing. "Of course you are not."

"These briefings have opened my eyes to *possibilities*, Faisal. I know that our intelligence community has long been involved in operations against the Americans and the Zionists, but as an outsider, I had assumed that much of the proxy-war rhetoric on both sides was exaggerated propaganda. I never believed that these proxies could really be a major military asset to combat the Zionists and the West."

"And what do you believe now?" Faisal asked, setting his cup down again, clearly intrigued.

"The proxy wars and false flag operations, the assets at the disposal of MOIS—assets now at *our* disposal—far exceed anything I had ever imagined. The Americans don't even know the half of our capabilities. Iran has shown restraint until now, hidden our true capabilities and the true capabilities of our partners."

"What are you proposing, exactly?" Faisal asked. From his face, Reza suspected he knew full well.

"Faisal, with your approval, Iranian MOIS will orchestrate a massive false flag attack on Israel, unleashing multiple terrorist proxy groups without constraining their tactics, weaponry, and targets, as Iran has done in the past. Using the catalyst of your brother's assassination, a terrible blow could be landed, with absolutely no trail leading to the Kingdom of Saudi Arabia."

Faisal pursed his lips in thought for a moment. Once again, Reza was struck by the changes in the man. He was cautious, deliberate, logical, and analytical. He had come a long way from the woman-chasing playboy he had befriended more than a decade ago. He had a confidence and authority Reza had not expected.

And that was likely a little dangerous for Reza and his plan.

"It is tempting," Faisal said finally, "but I fear it would have the opposite effect from what you imagine." Reza opened his mouth to protest, but Faisal cut him off. "You should not feel bad about this. Geopolitics is new to you, Arash, and you do not think like a politician—something I love about you. But you will learn. A major proxy attack against Israel will *hurt* our cause, not help it. By giving an even larger terrorist threat for the Americans to focus their attention on, we likely only increase their likelihood of intervening in the area. They will bring in their carrier strike groups, bolster their troop presence, reestablish the Iraq and Afghanistan war footing. No, I fear the type of operation you propose would give them an enemy to defend the Zionists against and would refocus the world's attention away from the murder of the Crown Prince. We cannot shift the story to make Israel the victim of this story. Israel must be the villain, and Saudi Arabia the victim. To achieve the outcome we desire, we must maintain control of the narrative from beginning to end. Do you understand?"

"I do. Controlling the narrative is important," Reza said, ignoring the obvious condescension. He stroked his chin as if in deep thought. "But the narrative becomes irrelevant if the damage to the Zionists is catastrophic—perhaps even mortal."

Faisal raised an eyebrow in surprise.

"Well, you have my attention now, my friend. But how could the Houthis or Hamas or Hezbollah—or even all three working in a cooperation—possibly execute an attack of such magnitude? The Iron Dome is very effective; even a massive salvo of advanced weapons would not penetrate enough to do such damage."

"Unless the attack came from below instead of above," Reza said, now giving his own knowing grin. "And if the attackers did so with weapons of much greater destructive power. You see, my friend, in my new position, I have been briefed on secret aspects of my country's nuclear capabilities. Secret from the whole world—except, now, for you and I."

For a long moment, Faisal simply stared at him in stunned silence. "You are full of surprises, Arash, aren't you?"

Reza now reached for his own tea, feigning a slight tremor in his hand even as he swelled with pride at how perfectly he had just baited his friend.

"Elimination of the Jewish state . . ." Faisal said, his voice curious, as if trying on the idea for size like a fine suit. "And you believe your proxies are capable of executing such a mission?"

"Iranian covert operations personnel would be embedded with the terrorists to oversee the mission cradle to grave."

"And no trails would lead to Saudi Arabia?"

"How could they?" Reza said. "It's not your intelligence service, not your field agents, not your bomb. The only one taking a risk here is Iran. But we will not proceed without your agreement and blessing. If you say no, I will report your dissent to the Ministry, and the mission will be canceled."

Golzar had been clear on this point. This mission of opportunity was one too good to pass up, but it was Reza's responsibility to get Faisal on board. The alliance between Saudi Arabia and Iran was the core mission because it was an alliance that would permanently shift the balance of power not just in the Middle East but across the globe. But removing the Israeli threat and fomenting proxy wars in the region could accelerate the timeline of the two nations taking their leadership position in the region.

Faisal let out a long, slow breath, then began to nod slowly, a grin curling up in the corners of his mouth.

"A Middle East without Israel—I never thought it possible until now. Imagine our nations' united purpose, without an adversary dividing us. Total Islamic control of the region," he said. "And we will control this narrative as well. Together Saudi Arabia and the Islamic Republic will loudly condemn the attack and then hunt down and punish the proxy terrorists responsible for the attack. We will condemn all terrorism, and in doing so rule with an iron grip."

Reza allowed his mouth to drop open as if in awe. "That is brilliant, Faisal. You are every bit the visionary leader I have always known you would be. And so, do I have your agreement? Shall I inform my superiors to proceed with the plan?"

Before Faisal could answer, the door opened to the sitting room, and one of Faisal's operatives entered, approached the prince, and whispered into his ear. Reza saw Faisal's face twist with anger.

"Is there a problem?" Reza asked.

Faisal stood and clasped a hand on Reza's shoulder. "The American investigation task force is here. Chief Saad is reporting difficulties. They haven't even stepped foot inside the palace and already they are refusing to cooperate. Ambassador Noor, a most difficult woman, is causing trouble again. Apparently, my intervention is required. I will answer your question, but first I have the Americans to deal with."

"I understand," Reza said, hiding his irritation with the ill-timed interruption.

Faisal turned to one of his bodyguards. "Escort Deputy Ambassador Reza to my office. He can wait for me there."

The man nodded.

"It is everything we ever dreamed of, my brother," Reza said, injecting his voice with youthful enthusiasm. "It is all coming true."

"It is," Faisal said, turning to leave. "Together we will be unstoppable."

CHAPTER 20

EAST ENTRANCE
SECURITY CHECKPOINT
AL-YAMAMAH PALACE

To Whitney's surprise, when Security Chief Saad returned, he brought Crown Prince Faisal with him. Faisal was dressed in a traditional thawb—an immaculate and pressed white robe that stretched to his ankles. In stark color contrast, on his head, the prince wore the iconic red-and-white-checkered keffiyeh and black agal, which not only distinguished Saudi Arabian men from other Muslims in the region but was also a symbol of nationalistic pride. *The Saudi Arabian equivalent of a proud New Yorker sporting a Yankee's cap*, she thought.

Something about Crown Prince Faisal seemed familiar and stirred a negative visceral reaction in her, but she couldn't quite articulate what it was.

Faisal vectored with intention and military bearing toward Ramia. They exchanged words privately in Arabic, and the prince's expression held firm and self-important the entire time. After what looked to Whitney like a dressing down, Faisal turned his back to the Ambassador and walked to greet Theobald.

"Welcome, my friends. I'm Crown Prince Faisal." The prince's lips stretched into a warm, brotherly smile as he extended his hand to Bobby. "Thank you for coming. We are very grateful for your assistance and expertise."

"It is an honor to meet you, Your Highness," Theobald said, shaking the prince's hand. "This is Sam Octavius, from the State Department."

"A pleasure to meet you, Your Highness. I'm sorry about your brother. I also have an older brother, so I can only imagine what you must be going through," Octavius said, his voice empathetic.

Faisal nodded but stared at Sam with silent judgment.

"Your Highness, I'm Special Agent Mullican, an FBI forensic investigator," Jenn said, shaking Faisal's hand.

"We welcome both of your contributions," Faisal said.

Whitney thought she saw Faisal's eyes narrow ever so slightly on hearing Jenn's title, but the smile plastered on the Prince's face never wavered.

Finally, it was Whitney's turn to greet the most powerful man in Saudi Arabia. Still smiling, Faisal extended his hand to her, but when she clasped his palm, a powerful revulsion snaked through her. The world in her peripheral vision seemed to melt away until only the two of them were present in the security screening room. An intrusive vision of Din Faraj, the terrorist who'd imprisoned and tormented her on the *Dauphine*, flashed through her consciousness, superimposing itself like a ghostly transparency over the Crown Prince's features. The similarities were uncanny—identical piercing stares, matching cruel smiles, the same condescending attitude, dripping with contempt for women. Her entire being recoiled in primal warning, every instinct screaming at her to escape, to get as far away as possible from this malevolent presence.

In the time since her kidnapping in London, she'd had two panic attacks—both of which she'd hid from Chunk and the rest of the team. This moment felt like it was ramping up to be the third. Faisal's bright white teeth flashed between the dense curls of his heavy black beard. He was speaking to her, but her pulse was pounding so loud in her ears she couldn't make out what he was saying. She watched his lips until they stopped moving. A heartbeat later, his eyebrows arched in what seemed like equal parts perplexity and amusement as he waited for her reply.

"I'm Whitney Watts from the National Counterterrorism Center in McLean, Virginia, where I work as a counterterrorism analyst," she said robotically, the autopilot in her brain taking over.

He chuckled at her response while still clutching her hand in his uncalloused, possessive fingers.

"Very nice to meet you, Ms. Watts," Faisal said. For an instant, she thought he was going to raise her hand to his lips to kiss it, but he didn't. Finally, he released her and turned to Theobald. "Chief Saad tells me you have objections to our security protocols?"

Whitney took an involuntary step backward to open the space between herself and the Crown Prince. *He's the Crown Prince, not Din Faraj. You're safe. He's not going to kidnap and torture you*, she told herself while shifting to a quiet four-count tactical breathing pattern to stave off hyperventilation. Gradually the pounding drum in her ears resolved, and Whitney felt herself returning to the moment—her consciousness no longer rebounding inside her skull like a panicked bird trapped inside a glass house.

She focused, listening intently as Faisal and Theobald talked.

"That's correct, Your Highness," Theobald replied. "We're not going to be able to do our jobs and augment your investigation if your security protocols strip us of the tools of our trade—"

"There appears to be some confusion on your part. We're not saying you can't use the tools of your trade. If you want to take a picture, then you tell Saad, and we will take a picture. If you want a hundred pictures, we will take a hundred pictures," Faisal said. "If you want to look for and take a fingerprint, our technicians will do this for you. Whatever information you want, with whatever instrument you need, we will provide it. Is this sufficient for you?"

Theobald did not let Faisal's *why are you being so unreasonable?* subtext rattle him. "Unfortunately, it's not sufficient. That would be like you telling my team to drive in a Formula One race but prohibiting them from driving their own race car."

A clever metaphor, Whitney thought, remembering that before becoming Crown Prince, Faisal had been a playboy prince who harbored aspirations of becoming a Formula One race-car driver. The Crown Prince's expression hardened, as he appeared to realize he'd underestimated Theobald's resolve. He said nothing for several seconds, then turned to his Chief of Security.

"Saad, they are permitted to bring their cameras and forensic instruments into the palace. But no weapons, and no mobile phones."

"Yes, My Prince," Saad said with a dutiful bow of the head.

"This is the extent of my compromise," Faisal said, turning

back to Theobald. "Accept it or leave—it makes no difference to me."

"Thank you, Your Highness," Theobald said without a trace of victory in his voice. He turned to the team. "You heard the Crown Prince—personal mobile phones and firearms will remain here in a locker."

The team nodded in unison and walked as a group to a locker stand along the back wall of the sterile, modern security processing room to secure their phones and pistols, the latter of which Whitney wasn't packing anyway.

"I trust you will report your results to Chief Saad as soon as you've completed your analysis?" Faisal said, addressing Theobald.

"You have my word," Theobald said.

"And I will hold you to that."

With a humorless expression, Faisal turned and departed with his security detail in tow.

Theobald nodded toward the security scanners. "Y'all go ahead through," he said to Jenn and Sam, the unspoken message that he and Whitney needed to caucus.

Once everyone was out of earshot, Theobald turned to her. "Everything okay? You kinda went *deer in the headlights* back there for a minute."

She forced a smile. "Everything's fine."

"You sure?"

"Yep."

He held her gaze a second. "If you had a read on something, you'd tell me, right?"

"Absolutely," she said. She noticed Ramia, who'd remained silent for the entirety of their interaction with Faisal, waiting and watching off to the side. "I'm going to see if the Ambassador would like to join us, if you don't mind?"

"Good idea," Theobald said, letting her take the lead.

Whitney turned to the Ambassador, whose lips were so tightly pursed Whitney imagined they were holding back a scream of frustration.

"Thank you, Ambassador Noor, for your support in this matter. Would you like to join us while we do our work?"

Ramia shook her head. "I have phone calls to return and emails to write. I have an office here in the palace. When you've finished for the day, Chief Saad will notify me. I would be happy to escort you to your hotel."

"Sounds like a plan," Whitney said. She looked at Theobald.

"Agreed. We'll meet you after, Madam Ambassador," he said.

Minutes later, on the other side of security, Chief of Security Saad was walking them through the palace. Each room they entered was more impressive than the last. Whitney considered herself well-traveled—she'd visited many beautiful buildings, including the Louvre in Paris, Westminster Abbey in London, the Biltmore Estate in North Carolina—but nothing she'd seen came close to the opulence on display in Al-Yamamah Palace. She couldn't help but wonder how many billions of dollars had been spent to build, decorate, and furnish the palace.

"How big is the palace?" she asked Chief Saad, who was leading from the front, his two suited underlings trailing at the rear.

"Four million square feet," Saad said without looking at her. "Over one thousand rooms in total."

Theobald whistled. "Damn . . ."

"What did you expect?" Saad said with a snort. "House al-Saud is twenty times wealthier than the British Crown."

Theobald looked at Whitney, his eyes wide with shock at the obscene wealth of the Arab monarchy.

Their final destination was a grand reception room, the

likes of which Whitney had never seen before. A polished Italian marble floor the color of fresh cream covered an area the size of a hotel lobby. The regular tiles were interlaced with sweeping mosaic designs made of thousands of individual cut pieces. In the center of the room, her gaze was drawn upward to a domed ceiling, where a massive bubble-glass chandelier, at least fifteen feet in diameter, hung. The walls, panels, pillars, and ceiling were decorated with geometric designs of azure, gold, and white. But most breathtaking of all were the four bronze statues of Arabian stallions positioned in four corners and facing inward to the center of the room. Each horse was life-size and reared up on its hind legs, head thrown back, mane and tail wild in the wind.

Mullican, on the other hand, ignored the architecture, mosaics, and sculpture work and walked straight to an area that was cordoned off with yellow tape strung between portable stanchions. Inside the barrier stood a dais, elevated above the rest of the room by three marble steps, which featured a beautiful desk and gilded chair. Also up on the dais, positioned opposite and facing the desk, sat a pair of ornate armchairs, presumably for guests or officials in conversation with the Crown Prince. Whitney noted what appeared to be a bullet hole in the upholstered back of the chair on the right. There was dried blood spatter still present and shell casings on the floor, but no weapons were on the scene.

"This is where the Zionist assassins murdered Crown Prince Khalid," Saad said.

"Is this some sort of joke?" Mullican snapped, hands on hips as she surveyed the scene.

"Excuse me, is there a problem?" Saad asked, sounding put out.

"Yes, there's a problem," the FBI investigator fired back,

then with a sweeping gesture said, "You call this a crime scene? Where are the bodies? Where are the murder weapons?"

"Obviously, we couldn't leave them. The bodies have all been taken to the morgue for autopsy. The weapons were bagged and collected for fingerprint and DNA analysis, of course."

"Uh-huh," she said and used a finger to tug on the flimsy yellow tape. "And you think this secured the perimeter? I can only imagine how many pairs of feet have trampled this scene."

He bristled. "We are in the heart of the Royal Palace, one of the most secure places on the planet. I assure you, Agent Mullican, this crime scene has not been tampered with."

"If it's so secure, then how did three supposed assassins waltz in here and murder the Crown Prince?" Mullican said, holding the man's gaze. She clearly was trying to ruffle the man into exposing something.

Theobald walked up and put a hand on her arm. "Dial it down a notch, please, Jenn. We've got one shot at this, and this is it."

She nodded, then turned to Saad. "We're going to need a list of all personnel who have entered this room from the time of the incident to present. We also need pictures of the room prior to the incident, but more importantly copies of any and all photographs of the scene after the murder but prior to the bodies and evidence being removed. I assume your forensics team took photographs?"

Whitney watched as Saad's jaw tightened. Clearly, he did not like being talked to this way, especially by a woman. "Of course we took photographs," he said, but stopped short of agreeing to provide her with copies.

From her backpack, Mullican removed two Tyvek suits,

shoe covers, nitrile gloves, and a hair cover for herself. She handed one set of PPE to Sam and donned the other herself. After dressing out, she lifted the yellow barrier tape to duck under it.

"May I?" she asked.

Saad nodded.

"Sam, are you coming?" she asked with a look at Octavius.

"Hells yes," he said and ducked under the barrier tape she was holding up. "I'll be shooting lots of pics, but if you want something specific, let me know."

She nodded and looked back at Theobald. "A scene like this, even with a team of ten agents, would take all day if not longer to adequately process. But I guess I'll try to work a miracle with the limited resources we have and compressed time window."

Whitney guessed at the real audience for the comment: Chief Saad.

Apparently, so did Theobald, because he just smiled. "I believe in you, Jenn. You too, Sam."

"Let's start with a panorama of the room," Mullican said, turning her attention back to Sam and the task at hand. "Then get shots of every entrance and exit, as well as lines of travel to the dais. After that, we'll place the exhibit markers methodically and get pics of the bloodstains and spatter and arrangement of shell casings on the floor."

"Copy that," Sam said and started taking photographs.

As Sam initiated the perimeter photographs of the room, Whitney watched Mullican remove a special flashlight from a sheath on her belt before fully zipping up the Tyvek suit. The FBI investigator adjusted the light mode setting on the device to what looked like very bright white light and slowly walked around the taped perimeter, occasionally crouching down to aim the light low and almost parallel across the polished marble floor. Whitney observed Jenn close her eyes and let out several deep sighs and shake her head as she traversed the scene.

"There's been so much foot traffic through the crime scene it's completely contaminated. Based on what I'm seeing, conducing a shoe-tread print collection and comparison to determine the movements of relevant players during the incident will be impossible," Mullican said, standing up. She glared at Saad, but the Saudi Security Chief said nothing and crossed his arms.

Whitney, who'd never participated in a crime scene investigation, walked up to the tape barrier and stopped beside Mullican, who was now looking up at the massive chandelier, brow furrowed.

"What's the issue?" she asked, curiosity piqued.

"This lighting is problematic. The crystals act like prisms refracting and scattering the light all over the place. The only thing that would be worse was if they had a disco ball hanging here," Mullican said.

Whitney couldn't help but laugh at the comment. "So what are you going to do?"

"There's not much I can do," she said and adjusted the settings on her fancy flashlight. "I'm going to switch to UV spectrum and see what I can find."

For the next half hour, Mullican and Octavius whispered to each other as Mullican placed evidence markers throughout the scene and Sam captured corresponding photographs. Mullican retrieved a laser distance meter and began taking measurements of significant evidence items within the crime scene in relation to the dais, and a single measurement from the dais to a fixed point in the room. As she obtained each measurement, Mullican entered the distances on a rough drawing on a clipboard.

At one point, she held up her sketch to Theobald. "Archaic, huh? This is best I can do without a team and instruments."

"You're doing a great job, Picasso. Keep up the good work," Theobald said and shot Whitney a crooked smile.

During the flight from Bahrain to Riyadh, the four of them had war-gamed out how they could all help each other execute their individual objectives while appearing to function as an investigative team. Sam's job was to penetrate the palace's computer network without looking like he was engaging in cyberactivity. During the evidence-collection phase, he would act as Jenn's photographer. The fancy digital Nikon camera he carried *did* take pictures, but it also did much more. Sam said if he could get the hardware-packed device through security and into the building, he should be able to do his thing. Whitney hadn't probed him for details, figuring the less she knew about the classified black hat hardware, the better.

After the photographs were taken, Jenn removed her soiled black nitrile gloves and pulled a fresh pair from her backpack and slipped them on with a double snap. If this case had happened Stateside, Whitney knew the FBI would have a mobile forensic vehicle loaded with top-of-the-line forensic equipment at the crime scene. Mullican had made it clear to Theobald on the flight from Bahrain that her capabilities would be highly limited, with only the makeshift evidence-collection kit she had to work with. Nonetheless, she was a pro and took her time collecting and assessing the evidence that was available to her.

Whitney watched the FBI ERT veteran inspect the bloodstains and shell casings marked with numbered yellow plastic pyramids—each about four inches tall—that she and Sam had positioned as evidence markers on the floor. With Chief Saad's permission, Mullican carefully used forceps to collect the shell casings, which she then individually placed in small white boxes, each box labeled with the corresponding number of the evidence marker. Then Mullican utilized individually wrapped sterile Q-tips to collect samples from the many pools of dried blood within the crime scene. The Q-tips were then carefully placed in suspended swab boxes, also labeled with the corresponding place marker number.

As Mullican worked, Whitney noticed how she regularly exchanged her soiled gloves for a fresh set, jotting notes in her flip pad as she did. At one point, Mullican told Chief Saad that she would need clothing samples from the suspected killers to analyze for gunpowder residue—a request that the Saudi security lead immediately balked at, surprising no one.

After finishing with the blood spatter, Mullican moved on to inspecting the three chairs—two in front of the desk, and the Crown Prince's throne-like chair. As she worked, Mullican talked, reminding Whitney of a sports broadcaster giving a play-by-play. Her commentary, while informative, had another motive: to rattle Saad.

". . . No latent finger or palm prints observed on the armrests of the chairs, which is odd. If there had indeed been a meeting in the hall, latent prints and other fibers and fluids from the victims would likely have been transferred to the furniture . . ."

"This bullet hole seems out of place based on the supposed location of the shooter. Bullet trajectory analysis needed to be performed . . ."

". . . the Crown Prince's chair does not appear to be saturated with blood, as one would expect from such a heinous act of violence . . ."

Whitney, for her part, realized she was just standing around in supervisor mode, watching her teammates work but not doing any herself. Her panicked memory of Din Faraj when she shook Faisal's hand had knocked her off-balance, but it was time to box that incident and wake up the slumbering analyst in her mind. She was very good at unraveling mysteries and reconstructing events, and this murder scene was no different. She started scanning the layout and geometry of the reception hall, noting the entrance and exit locations and the distances from each to the central dais. She tried to imagine the mechanics of a plausible scenario in which Mossad assassins could successfully infiltrate the palace, dupe security, and defeat Khalid's personal detail to murder him in this room. The proposition defied logic.

Whitney found Security Chief Saad with his arms crossed, glaring at Jenn and Sam as they worked. He glanced at Whitney, then quickly looked back.

"Excuse me, Chief Saad," Whitney said. "While my colleagues are evaluating the murder scene, I'd like to take a look at the video surveillance recording of the event."

She saw the Security Chief's jaw tense ever so slightly before he responded. "There is no video recording of the event."

"What? You can't be serious." The incredulity in her voice was unfiltered.

Saad turned to glare at her now, his arms still crossed. "I'm completely serious. This space is the private reception quarters of the Crown Prince. There are no cameras in this room."

"Hmm," she said, not believing him.

"You don't believe me?" Saad asked, offended.

"Of course I believe you," she said.

She scanned the ceiling corners behind him for contradictory evidence. She didn't see any overtly obvious cameras, but that didn't mean anything. The miniaturization of camera lenses and the wide-scale adoption of mobile phones made them readily available and easy to hide. There could be a thousand hidden camera lenses in the reception hall, and she'd be lucky to spy a single one without specialized detection hardware.

"What about photographs of the scene *before* the bodies were removed?" Theobald asked, stepping up beside her.

"Yes, we have these types of photographs," Saad said.

"Can we see them?" Whitney asked.

"Now, or after your colleagues are finished with their information collection?"

"After," Theobald said quickly, presumably not wanting to give Saad an excuse to rush or prematurely shut down Jenn and Sam's work.

Saad nodded. They all returned their attention back to the dais, where their teammates were now inspecting and photographing the Crown Prince's desk and throne-chair.

The events of the morning had all but confirmed everything Whitney and her teammates suspected. There was no way the Mossad assassinated Crown Prince Khalid. Her gut told her this was an inside job, most likely a coup by Faisal to seize power and frame the Israelis. She'd have to wait, of course, for Jenn's assessment, but the "investigation" they were participating in sure felt like theater—the crime scene a carefully prepared stage fashioned for them by the play's director, Security Chief Saad. Whitney looked at Theobald. He pursed his lips and shook his head, and she suspected they were of the same opinion.

We're being railroaded, and there's nothing we can do or say to change it.

CHAPTER 21

ZENOBIA CONFERENCE ROOM

AL-YAMAMAH PALACE

It took every fiber of Whitney's willpower not to laugh at the answers the Crown Prince's head of security was giving to their questions.

Chief Saad was delivering bullshit by the truckload. She could see from the expression on Jenn's face that her FBI investigator colleague was equally exasperated. While she and Mullican were pressing Saad, Theobald had slipped into the role of peacemaker, occasionally taking the Security Chief's side. This was good intuition on Theobald's part. Otherwise, the Security Chief might already have stormed out of the room as they systematically poked holes in the cover story the Saudis had concocted to explain Crown Prince Khalid's murder.

"So, you're telling us the Israeli assassins moved so quickly they were able to slit Crown Prince Khalid's throat with knives *before* the prince's security detail could draw their pistols and fire?" Whitney said, paraphrasing Saad's explanation.

Saad stared daggers at her. "Is it really so difficult to understand? The assassins were sitting in audience on the dais with the Crown Prince, whereas his two bodyguards had been ordered to stand off to the side."

"And why would the Crown Prince have done this? Wouldn't he want his bodyguards nearby?"

Saad chuckled.

"I don't understand what is funny about my question?" Whitney said, reaching up to adjust her headscarf. It kept slipping toward the back of her scalp.

"Obviously, you never met Prince Khalid. He was not a man who feared for his life. He was Crown Prince for nine years, and never once was there an attack on his life. He hated his bodyguards hovering around him. He didn't like the message that it sent. In the Royal Palace, he had no reason to fear for his life."

"But clearly he should have had a reason," Mullican said.

"Clearly," Saad replied, shifting his eyes to Jenn.

"Just to be clear, you were in charge of security when the assassination occurred?"

Saad visibly stiffened. "That is not true. I was appointed to Chief of Security by Crown Prince Faisal. I was not a member of Crown Prince Khalid's detail."

"I didn't realize that." Mullican made a note. "It would be helpful to speak with your predecessor. Can you summon him to this meeting?"

"Impossible," Saad said, "because he is deceased. Killed by the same assassins who murdered the Crown Prince."

"So he must be in one of these pictures of the victims?" she said. "Will you show me, please?"

"This is him here," Saad said. He pointed to a picture of an Arab man in a dark suit on the ground, his neck sliced open.

"I've investigated a lot of crime scenes over the years, and I've never seen so many slit throats," Mullican said.

"Apparently, these assassins were *really* good with knives," Sam said, looking up from where he sat in the corner, tipped back in his chair, shoulders against the wall.

For the past fifteen minutes, Sam had supposedly been indexing and cropping all the photographs he'd taken of the crime scene. In reality, Whitney knew that wasn't what Sam was really doing. He was using the camera's interface to try to hack into the palace's security network before Saad's patience expired and he kicked them out.

"Everyone knows the Mossad has the best assassins in the world," Saad said, his tone measured and matter-of-fact.

"How did these three Israelis manage to get weapons through security? Did they not have to go through the same security checkpoint that we did?" Mullican asked.

"Of course they did, but the weapons they used were specially designed to avoid detection. They carried ceramic blades hidden inside special sheaths that disguised the geometry and avoided setting off the metal detector. The backscatter x-ray scanner was a change I implemented after taking over as Chief of Security."

"It's my understanding that these three men were living and working inside the Kingdom," Whitney said. She was curious how Saad would react to the new tack she was about to take.

"That is my understanding as well," he said.

"So, if your government had concerns about these men, why would they be granted a private audience with the Crown Prince?"

Saad scoffed. "You're presuming our intelligence apparatus had pierced the Israelis' legends. Obviously, that was not the case, or their request for an audience would have been denied. I'm growing tired of these questions, which feel more like accusations than inquiries."

Looks like I hit a nerve, Whitney thought.

"That is certainly not our intention, Chief Saad," Theobald said. "I think my colleagues are simply trying to understand how these three men could have pulled off the unthinkable."

Saad sighed. "This incident is terribly frustrating for me. If *I* had been Chief of Security instead of my predecessor, Crown Prince Khalid would still be alive."

Whitney scrutinized the man's face and posture for tells of insincerity and found plenty. The way Saad angled his body away from her and toward the scene; the way he didn't make eye contact while he spoke; his boasting statements about how things would have been different had he been in control; the puffing up of his chest.

He's lying . . .

"We understand how difficult this must be for you," Theobald said, assuaging rather than antagonizing.

"Is there any additional information you require to complete your investigation?" Saad said, his demeanor shifting from thoughtful back to agitated.

"Plenty more. Sam and I need to re-create where the bodies fell in relation to—"

Before she could finish, Theobald stopped her, placing his hand on her forearm. "Jenn, a word in private, please?"

Jaw tight, Mullican let Theobald pull her aside.

"Listen, I get it. I really do," Theobald whispered. "But you do understand what we're up against here, right?"

"Yes, but without the re-creation and without clothing samples from all decedents—including the Crown Prince—my analysis will be severely hampered."

Theobald cleared his throat. "It's not going to happen."

"Then at a minimum, I need to exam the bodies of the deceased," Mullican fired back, loud enough for everyone, including Saad, to hear.

Whitney saw Saad instantly bristle and glare at Theobald with an expression that Whitney interpreted as *control your women, or I will.* But Theobald only nodded in concurrence with Mullican's request and held the security chief's gaze.

"Which bodies do you want to examine?" Saad asked, visibly displeased.

"All of them, of course," Mullican said.

"Impossible. Crown Prince Khalid's body is being prepared for the funeral. The photographs tell the tale of what happened."

"If not the Crown Prince, then at a minimum I must be permitted to evaluate the Israeli assassins, the two dead guards from Prince Khalid's detail, and the former Chief of Security," Mullican said.

Saad didn't respond for a long moment. Finally, he said, "I will need to confer with the Crown Prince. The bodies have been transferred to a hospital morgue. Arrangements will need to be made."

"We expected as much. Not a problem."

"Since the hospital is outside the palace grounds, we should make sure Sam got all the photos he needed before we depart," Theobald said. He glanced from Mullican to Octavius in the corner.

"Good point. Sam, did you get all the photos you need, or do you need more time?" Mullican asked.

Sam flashed her a wide smile, answering the real question she was asking. "I shot every angle you asked for, as well as capturing images of each glossy on this table," he said, gesturing to the conference table, where the Saudis had supplied photos of the crime scene. "But I sure would love to have copies of those raw image files. Also, I'm sure there were more pictures taken than what was printed here on the table. Can we get copies of those as well?"

"Chief Saad," Mullican said, turning to their host, "are the photographs you've shared with us here the full library of images taken of the crime scene before the bodies were moved?"

Saad nodded. "That is correct."

"There are no other photographs?"

"No."

Jenn's mouth twisted into a disapproving pout. "I find that difficult to believe, but okay. In that case, can we get the raw digital originals from your archives?"

"Impossible, because as you see, these photographs were taken with a conventional camera using film."

"Seriously?"

"You keep challenging my integrity, Agent Mullican. It is disrespectful, and you have exhausted my patience. Do they not teach women in America that it's rude to disrespect a man in his own house?"

"Excuse me, I didn't realize—"

"Hey, Jenn," Whitney cut her off. "I have a question about one of these photos." She gave the FBI agent's sleeve a tug.

At first Mullican looked annoyed. Then her teammate smiled and turned away from Saad toward the conference table. "Sure, Whitney. Which one?"

"We'll wait here while you make the arrangements with the hospital morgue for our visit. Thank you, Chief Saad," Theobald said to Saad behind them.

"Thanks for that," Mullican said in a low voice. "I was about to lay into the guy."

"I get it," Whitney said. "The man's infuriating."

Once Saad had left the room, Theobald walked over to join them. "I hope you didn't mind me playing good cop," he said, "but I felt like it was needed."

"I'm glad you did," Mullican said, "or we probably would have been booted off the premises a half hour ago. I assumed it would be helpful to draw attention away from Sam, but I probably went a little overboard. But damn it, what's the point of any of this if I'm not permitted to do my job?"

Theobald nodded. He looked tired. "It's all good. And I know the crime scene was a joke. And know for a proper investigation you'd need two days, but did you get what you needed? If not, I can try to push for more time."

"I got everything worth getting. To be honest, I'm surprised Saad let me take DNA samples of the blood spatter," Mullican said, tapping the packed-up sample kit she wore across her chest like a purse.

"Me too," Theobald said.

"Do you really think they'll let us examine the bodies?" Whitney asked.

"I doubt it, but if they don't, I'll ask ODNI to make a fuss until they acquiesce." Theobald turned to Mullican. "Do you have any preliminary conclusions or observations you want to share?"

"Yes, but not here."

"Roger that."

As the team talked shop about the positions of the shell casings and angles of blood spatter, Whitney contented herself to moving in a slow circle, taking in the big picture of the room. She tried to imagine the killer or killers entering and attacking the Crown Prince, and tried to imagine where the Israelis blamed for the attack would have been standing when they were gunned down. Of course, all of it could easily have been staged to feed the narrative the Saudis wanted delivered, right? She allowed various versions of the events to unfold in her head while they waited. Finally, ten or fifteen minutes later, Saad returned.

"Arrangements have been made at the hospital for you to inspect the bodies. You will be given fifteen minutes. A second autopsy or any desecration of the bodies will not be permitted, for religious reasons," Chief Saad said, his voice a hard line.

"Understood," Theobald said.

"The Crown Prince thanks you for your cooperation and asks that you submit your findings to his office prior to making any official statements or releasing any documents to the media. His Highness has—at the behest of your American President—delayed reporting our findings. As a good and reliable partner, the Crown's expectation is that you will show us the same courtesy. We are partners in this investigation, and it is our expectation that any press releases or media briefings will be handled in a joint manner."

"That is our expectation as well," Theobald said, sticking his hand out to Saad.

The security chief shook it. "I have other matters to attend to now. My men will show you out."

Theobald nodded. He started toward the door himself, but then stopped and turned back.

"Speaking of the Crown, Chief Saad, how is the King? We've not heard from him since the Crown Prince's death."

Whitney could have sworn she saw Saad flinch.

"His Majesty is, understandably, distraught with grief. He is mourning the loss of his eldest son. What he needs most is privacy and time to grieve."

"Of course," Theobald said.

"When can we expect your report, Mr. Theobald?" Saad asked.

"Hopefully, by the end of the day. If not, no later than tomorrow."

Saad nodded but said nothing.

As Saad escorted them back to the security checkpoint to retrieve their phones and personal items, Theobald's parting question about the King had sent Whitney's mind spinning. She'd not expected to meet the King as part of this visit to the palace, but it was noteworthy that no one had mentioned the monarch since the murder. If Faisal was the mastermind behind his own brother's death, was King Abdul complicit as well? And if not, how did the usurper prince intend to handle his own father's wrath at him conducting fratricide?

She decided to put a pin in that one until later, when they were able to speak freely. In the meantime, she'd hold her tongue and wait to see what clues the bodies of the dead were willing to give up.

CHAPTER 22

KING ABDUL HOSPITAL

RIYADH, SAUDI ARABIA

Whitney hugged herself against the chill of the morgue, which was located in the basement of the ultramodern and state-of-the-art King Abdul Hospital. She watched with morbid curiosity as the mortician pulled a cadaver storage rack out of the mortuary refrigerator. The cadaver, one of the three Israeli "assassins," was uncovered and naked.

In the movies, they're always covered by sheets. Where's the damn sheet? she thought, trying desperately not to look at the dead man's genitals.

This wasn't too hard, as Whitney's eyes were instead drawn to the large Y-shaped cut on the dead man's chest that stood out in strong contrast to the gray pallor of the skin. Whitney felt a small twinge in her own chest as she followed the incision with her eyes from the shoulders down to the belly button and below. She could only imagine the nightmares Mullican must get from looking at this stuff day in and day out.

The mortician guided the stainless-steel tray on rollers onto a wheeled transport cart that he'd aligned with the chiller rack. He performed the body's transfer with practiced ease and precision, so much so that she wondered how many corpses this man had processed over the span of his career.

This dead Israeli's face was deformed from gunshot wounds.

And his eyes were open.

Why are his eyes still open? Isn't protocol to close dead people's eyelids? she thought.

Once the transfer was complete, the mortician wheeled the cart to the middle of the room and positioned the cadaver under a large overhead examination light. Dramatically illuminated, the body looked more ghastly, not less. She hated the pasty gray of dead flesh. An involuntary shudder rippled through her, traveling from head to toe. This was her first time in a morgue, and she was a little surprised how much it was bothering her. She'd seen some disturbing shit during her time with the Tier One. Hell, she'd spent hours talking to Lucy's corpse on the raft. A clinical setting like this should have been no sweat for her, but she found it disturbing nonetheless.

A wrapper crinkled behind her, and she turned to find Sam munching on a protein bar.

"Seriously?" she said. She felt like she might vomit into her mouth.

"What?" the big man said with an exaggerated grin. "I'm starving. I haven't eaten anything all day."

"Excuse me, excuse me," the mortician said. "There is no eating or drinking in the mortuary laboratory."

Sam quickly shoved the rest of the protein bar into his mouth and pocketed the wrapper. Then, mouth full, he said, "Sorry, won't happen again."

The mortician tsked and shook his head. Then, irritated,

he turned to Mullican. "You're allowed to visually examine the body, but nothing more."

"Understood," Mullican said, defiantly snapping on a fresh pair of black nitrile exam gloves. She checked the toe tag. "First victim is male, mid-twenties or early thirties, identified as Peter Abeln, which we'll need to validate. Whitney, can you make a note?"

"Check," she said. Whitney had offered to be Jenn's scribe during this part of the evolution. She turned to a clean page in the notepad and wrote the dead man's name on the top line of the page.

"I count four gunshot wounds: two to the face, one to the right shoulder at the junction of the clavicle, and one in the sternum. Sam, can you get pictures of these, please?"

"On it," Octavius said, swallowing the last of his protein bar. Completely unfazed by the corpse, he walked up to the cadaver cart and began snapping digital photos of the dead man's wounds.

Mullican turned the cadaver's head to the side. Something in the dead body popped, followed by a squishing sound. Whitney gagged and looked away, her gaze going to the armed Saudi escort from the palace who was standing by the door watching them like a hawk. Chief Saad had whispered something in the man's ears before they'd departed, and Whitney wondered what the instruction had been.

In her peripheral vision, Whitney saw Mullican adjust the head again.

"Stop that!" the mortician said, rushing over. "I told you this is a visual examination only. You do not have permission to touch the body."

"I heard you, but I need to evaluate the exit wounds, which I cannot *see* unless the head is repositioned," she fired back.

"Then ask me, and I will do it."

Mullican pursed her lips at him, then turned to Whitney. "The victim appears to have been shot at an angle offset on the victim's right side at close range, based on wound presentation—"

"Why do you say *the victim*?" the mortician asked. "This man was no victim. He was a murderer."

"How do you know that?" Mullican said, her eyes snapping to him. "This is a confidential investigation. Were you briefed on the incident by Security Chief Saad or a palace representative prior to performing the autopsy? Were you pressured by the palace to reach *predetermined* conclusions?"

"No . . . of course not. I just assumed . . ." the mortician said, sputtering.

"You just assumed *what*?" Theobald asked, joining Mullican in applying pressure on the man.

The man crossed his arms. "Uh, nothing. Never mind."

Mullican glared at the mortician for a moment, before returning her attention to the corpse. After studying the bullet wounds, she worked from the head down on the right side of the table. When she got to the dead man's right wrist, she paused, pulled a flashlight from her pocket, and clicked it on for a closer look. She took the cadaver's hand and rotated it into supination.

"Stop. You're not allowed to touch the corpse," the mortician said, practically shouting this time.

"Did you find something?" Theobald said, stepping in front to block the man.

"Ligature marks," she said, her tone ripe with condemnation as she used a square of gauze to wipe repeatedly at the cadaver's wrist.

"What are you doing? Stop that immediately!" the mortician said, trying to get around Theobald.

"This man's hands were bound," she said and walked with purpose around the exam cart to the other side to inspect the left wrist. "And the proof of this appears to have been concealed with flesh-colored makeup."

The mortician lunged around the cart, desperate to block Mullican, but Octavius's iron grip locked on to his arm. In a heartbeat, Saad's security guard whipped out his weapon, leveling it at Sam. But Theobald was faster. Before anyone could blink, his concealed pistol materialized, aimed dead center at the guard's forehead, his situational awareness and combat-honed instincts trumping everyone in the room.

"Everyone, let's take a deep breath, lower our weapons, and de-escalate this situation," Theobald said, his voice cool, calm, and collected.

Only on hearing this did the security guard realize that Theobald had a gun and was covering him. The guard shifted his aim from Octavius to Theobald. "You lower your weapon first," he shouted.

"Sure, sure," Theobald said. He smoothly lowered his weapon and angled the muzzle at the floor. It was not lost on Whitney, however, that he kept his index finger on the trigger while rotating his wrist to make it difficult to see from the guard's point of view.

"Set your weapon on the ground," the guard said. "Now."

"If you lower your weapon, I'll put mine on the floor."

The guard shook his head.

"Listen to me, boss," Theobold said. "We're all professionals here, just trying to do our jobs. You shooting me, and my colleagues killing you, isn't going to work out great for either of us. So how about we both holster our weapons and get back to the business we came here to do, which is evaluating these corpses."

The guard's gaze ticked from Theobald first to Octavius, whose right hand was now in position to pull his own weapon from the holster in the small of his back, then to Mullican, whose right hand was inside the flap of her suit coat. The Saudi guard did the math and lowered his weapon. When Theobald holstered his, the guard did as well.

"That's better," Theobald said and smiled.

"This autopsy inspection is over," the guard said. He thrust his hand toward the mortuary's exit. "If you agree to leave now, I will not report that you pulled your weapons and threatened my life."

Whitney could practically see the turning in Theobald's head as he weighed the options, which at this point, were extremely limited. After a moment, he said, "I reckon we've seen everything we need to see here. What do you think, team? Ready to pack it up?"

As if to put a big fat exclamation point on the comment, Octavius raised his camera, focused on the ligature marks on the dead Israeli's wrists, and snapped a parting picture. The digital camera clicked loudly. Despite the massive tension in the room, Whitney had to stifle a laugh at the brashness of it.

Mullican looked disappointed, but she understood the unspoken reality of the situation. The team had caught the Saudis doctoring evidence and called them out. The posturing, the pretending that both sides would reach the same conclusion about the events surrounding Crown Prince Khalid's murder—all of that was over. The gambit was up. What happened next was the fresh unknown they needed to war-game out. And to do that, they needed to divorce themselves from their Saudi minders as soon as possible so that Jenn could speak freely about her findings.

"You're right. We've seen everything we need to see,"

Mullican said, removing her gloves. Whitney noticed she stuffed this pair into her pocket instead of throwing them in the trash.

They left the morgue, escorted by the still-agitated guard. Whitney savored a brief respite of heat when they stepped out of the icy, air-conditioned hospital and walked the fifteen yards to an idling black Range Rover. Nobody talked as they were driven in the luxury SUV to the Ritz-Carlton Riyadh, which was located a mere block away from Al-Yamamah Palace. There, two porters from the hotel staff unloaded their bags and stacked them on a rolling luggage trolley. Theobald instructed the porters to meet them in the lobby. Then he gathered the team in a tight huddle outside under the portico, out of earshot from anyone.

"All right, listen up," he said, finally rid of their palace minders but keeping his voice low. "As tempting and nice as it would be, we can't let our guard down inside this hotel. This property is practically connected to the palace. We need to assume that our rooms are bugged and that we are under surveillance. I'll contact the US Embassy and arrange a pickup. Once we're in a SCIF, Jenn can debrief her findings, and we'll review any cyberdata Sam harvested."

Whitney, Sam, and Jenn nodded their agreement.

"That said, I do want to make sure we're all on the same page. Jenn, true or false: What we just witnessed was a well-orchestrated cover-up and charade by the Saudis to hide the truth about Prince Khalid's murder?"

Jenn chuckled. "Correct, but I wouldn't go so far as to call it well-orchestrated. Something nefarious happened in that reception hall, but the Saudis didn't provide us with any conclusive evidence to prove their narrative that Mossad assassins murdered Prince Khalid at his desk."

"Agreed," Whitney said, "but unfortunately, the converse is also true. We don't have any hard evidence to prove the Israelis *didn't* do it. Without witnesses or video surveillance footage, we can't prove Faisal or some other rogue element inside the palace murdered the Crown Prince. All we can do is say that our findings don't match the Saudi report."

In her heart, she knew it was Faisal. It was the only reasonable explanation. Not just because he was now running the Kingdom—motive enough, for sure—but because who else would have the clout inside the Kingdom to pull this off and cover it up?

"Now hold on. I don't hear any fat lady singing," Sam said, grinning wide. "I haven't had a chance to do my thing yet. This ain't over. If there's a smoking gun, I'll find it."

"I was hoping you'd say something like that," Theobald said and clapped a hand on Sam's shoulder. "In the meantime, everyone take thirty to get cleaned up. Then we'll head to the embassy."

Whitney followed her teammates into the lobby of Riyadh's most opulent and exclusive hotel. As she did, her thoughts drifted to Chunk—and to whatever tasking he and the boys would be given when her damning report of the Saudi cover-up reached the President's desk.

CHAPTER 23

CROWN PRINCE'S PRIVATE OFFICE RECEPTION AREA

AL-YAMAMAH PALACE

Reza's head bobbed with microsleep.

He'd been up for the past twenty-four hours, and the lack of sleep was catching up with him. Faisal had instructed Reza to wait in his private office reception area while he met with the American investigation task force. Unlike the expansive and opulent royal reception room, where Faisal had most certainly murdered his brother, Khalid, this reception area was no bigger than a typical office. It housed Faisal's personal assistant—a man whose name Reza could not remember—and a pair of armchairs. Reza had chosen the seat positioned in the corner across from the PA's desk, angled toward the door. He pinched the skin on the outside of his thigh, trying to keep himself awake, but the jolt of pain only shocked him from his stupor for a few seconds at a time before drowsiness prevailed and his head bobbed again.

The door slammed open, and pounding footsteps woke

Reza with a start. He jerked upright in his armchair, eyelids popping open to see a furious Faisal storming into the waiting area with his two black-suited enforcers in tow.

"You were sleeping?" Faisal asked, his tone angry and expression incredulous.

"I'm sorry, Your Highness," he said, using the honorific automatically, which was both strangely subservient and surprising. "I haven't slept in two days, and I—"

"Forget it. Come with me. I require your counsel," Faisal said, cutting him off. Before Reza could respond, the Crown Prince shifted his attention to his hired guns. "You two, wait here. I will speak to Deputy Ambassador Reza alone."

The two men looked at each other in silent communion and nodded.

As Faisal marched past his assistant's desk, he barked, "We are not to be disturbed."

"Yes, Your Highness," the assistant said with a bow of his head.

Reza popped to his feet and trotted to catch up with Faisal. The Crown Prince didn't stop in his office, though, but kept on going into a connected conference room and slammed the door behind them.

Before Reza could even ask what was wrong, Faisal started thundering.

"It's an absolute disaster. The Americans weren't fooled. I should have never trusted Saad with something so important," Faisal said, shaking his fist as he paced around the table. "I told him that it was too risky. I told him they would want to inspect the bodies, but he assured me that he would take care of all the details. Well, he didn't. And now we're fucked."

Reza had already concluded that the odds of the cover story fooling the American investigators were extremely low. If

Faisal had brought Reza in during the planning stages, perhaps Reza could have helped orchestrate something cleaner and more convincing. No matter: His friend had forced regime change, and that alone was a huge victory. And now Reza was alone with Faisal, with none of the Prince's minders or manipulators to undermine or challenge his guidance.

"Tell me exactly what happened. Maybe I can help," Reza said, massaging a terrible crick in his neck from sleeping in the chair.

Faisal threw up his hands in exasperation. Like a dam opening the floodgates, he told Reza everything that had transpired while Reza had been asleep.

". . . So, as you can see," the Prince concluded, "there is no way this investigation team is going to issue a report to President Jarvis that validates or matches the Crown's findings."

Reza nodded, keeping his expression measured, but inside he felt a swell of anxiety and pressure, because now they were officially on the clock. The next few hours were critical. They were now in a race with the Americans to determine who would control the narrative. Without casting Israel as the villain, and without the manufactured outrage that followed, the proxy attack to wipe out the Jewish state would not happen. *Could not happen.* Their last conversation had been interrupted before he'd gotten Faisal's agreement on using terrorist proxies to deliver a nuclear strike on Tel Aviv. It was now or never.

I will use his desperation to my advantage . . .

"You're right," Reza said. "They've seen through the deception, and they will share their conclusions with the Israelis—"

"Perhaps I can negotiate with President Jarvis a different message," Faisal interrupted, his face desperate. "A compromise. Something less damning."

"Why should the Americans get to control the narrative?

What if we're looking at this entire situation backward? What if instead of viewing what happened with the investigation team as a problem, we see it for what it really is—*an opportunity*?" Reza said, baiting the trap.

"Go on," Faisal said. He stopped pacing and looked intently at Reza.

"Let's preempt the Jarvis White House. We have the King's office release an official statement about Khalid's assassination, and we do it now, before the American team has even had a chance to report their findings. We show the smoking gun in Israel's hand and force the United States to contradict our statement. We put the onus on President Jarvis to call the King a liar."

"But the King is—"

"I know, but the world doesn't know that. We release that news tomorrow and blame his failing health on everything that has happened. It will only garner more empathy and support for the cause."

"Yes, I like this plan," Faisal said, nodding enthusiastically. "We force them to contradict our findings, blame the Zionists' plot for my father's decline, and let the world react."

Now, for the next domino . . . Reza thought to himself.

"Yes, precisely. And there is one more matter we must decide—" Reza began to say but cut himself off.

"What? What were you going to say?"

"No, it's not a decision to make under stress and time pressure," Reza said, shaking his head.

"Let me be the judge of that. Tell me, Arash, what were you going to say?"

Reza looked down at his hands for a moment, then up at the Crown Prince's eyes, which were shining with anticipation.

"Well, I was going to say that we were interrupted before

we could finish our earlier conversation. I told you about the covert mission using proxies to deliver a nuclear strike to the heart of the Jewish state."

"Yes. My answer is yes," Faisal said, eyes burning with emotion.

"A difficult but wise decision, my brother," Reza said with a deferential nod. "We have this one small window to capitalize on to change the world. Shall I inform my superiors now?"

"Not yet. We need to see how the world and our allies react to the press release," Faisal said, waffling. "We also need to deal with the urgent matter at hand."

Reza nodded. "Where is the American team now?"

"At the US Embassy. They've summoned Ambassador Noor, I presume, to present their findings to her before submitting them to the White House, but that is not guaranteed. They could transmit their report at any time."

"Then don't let them. Cut power to the embassy. Block their internet, cellular, and satellite communications. Don't let them leave the country. Make the White House blind, deaf, and mute while we spread the word of the Zionists' treachery. By the time the Americans try to change the narrative, it will be too late. The wildfire will have spread out of control, and no one will be listening."

And the war to wipe the Zionists from the face of the earth will already be underway.

Before Faisal could reply, the phone on the conference room table buzzed.

"Damn it, I told him no interruptions," the Prince said. With a clenched jaw, he leaned into the middle of the table and pressed the button to answer the call on speaker. "Were my instructions not clear? What do you want?"

"Your Highness," the Crown Prince's personal assistant

said. "I apologize for the interruption, but Security Chief Saad is here. He says it's urgent that he speak with you. May I send him in?"

Faisal groaned. "Fine, send him."

A moment later, Chief Saad entered the secure conference room. He looked nervous.

"Your Highness . . ." he said.

"Don't just stand there with your mouth open—speak," Faisal snapped.

"Um, yes, Your Highness," Saad stammered. "The cyber-security team leader has just informed me that he believes the palace's security servers have been infiltrated."

"I was assured that was impossible."

"As was I, Your Highness, but it appears whoever did this used an exploit that our cyberteam was not aware was even possible. I am not a cyberexpert, so I did not understand the technical explanation."

"It was the Americans," Reza said, speaking up before Faisal could ask another question. "The investigation team was probably responsible for this."

"But that is impossible," Saad said. "I was with them the entire time. I didn't give them access to our control room. I made them leave their phones in lockers at the security screening center, and none of them were using a computer."

"You're saying they didn't bring *any* electronic devices with them into the palace?" Reza asked.

"No," Saad said, quickly.

"Nothing? Not even a digital camera?" Reza asked, pressing.

"Well, one member of the team did have a camera. But it was a real camera. I saw it taking pictures."

Reza looked at Faisal. "I'm not a cyberexpert either, but think about how much technology is packed into an iPhone.

The American NSA could probably hide a lot of hardware in a digital camera."

"Let's assume for a moment you're right, and the camera had technology to hack into our security network. What would be the purpose?" Faisal asked.

"I could think of a dozen reasons," Reza responded, "but given their assignment, I would imagine they were trying to access the security camera footage of the event. I assume you have video surveillance in the royal reception room?"

"Of course, but we denied the existence of the footage to the Americans."

"If I were the team leader of the American task force, I would not believe such a statement. Hacking the security servers and trying to obtain the actual footage would be the exact evidence the Americans would want to provide President Jarvis. With this footage, Jarvis will gain the upper hand over you. Unless you submit to his demands, he will threaten to release it to the media. We're talking about blackmail in perpetuity. He will use this recording to lord over you as long as you are in power. You will become his dog on a leash."

"Then I have no choice but to stop the American team at all costs," Faisal said, red-faced. "But we can't stop electrons once they press send."

"That's true, which is why I proposed the drastic measures of locking down all communications in and out of the American Embassy," Reza said. "But we must act quickly."

"Can we do this, Chief Saad?" Faisal asked.

"I don't know, Your Highness. I will need to check with al-Salma. It is my understanding that we have assets working inside the American Embassy who might be able to facilitate, but this is far outside my purview. As you know, Your

Highness, my authority only extends to within the walls of the palace," Saad said.

"Fine, I'll call al-Salma myself," Faisal barked. "I want you to focus on working with the cyberteam to secure the palace data servers. Find out if the Americans obtained the surveillance footage of the event or not."

"Yes, My Prince," Saad said. He bowed and hurried out of the room.

Faisal turned to Reza. "Arash, I want you to work on drafting the press release while I meet with Director al-Salma. You've always been skilled and persuasive with words. Now is the chance to put that skill to work doing the very thing you've talked about for all these years. Will you do that for me?"

"It would be my great honor," Reza said, grinning on the inside at how quickly he'd been able to manipulate Faisal to accelerate the timeline of the announcement, convincing him how important it was that they get this done before the Americans made an effort to refute their story. "I'll begin work on it immediately."

As Reza headed toward the door to retrieve his bag and computer, Faisal stopped him. "Brother . . ."

Reza turned to his friend, the Crown Prince. "Yes, Brother?"

"You're very good at strategy. If I didn't know better, I would have thought you'd been doing this your whole life."

Reza smiled and bowed to his friend. "Thank you. Coming from you, I'll take that as the ultimate compliment."

CHAPTER 24

US EMBASSY

SENSITIVE COMPARTMENTALIZED INFORMATION FACILITY (SCIF)

"Your lips are literally purple, Whitney. Are you okay?" Jenn asked with a concerned look on her face.

"Yeah, well, that's because I'm freezing. I think this SCIF is actually colder than the morgue in the basement of the King Abdul Hospital," she said, resisting the compulsion to blow warm breath into her cupped fingers like it was winter. "I packed for the desert, not the arctic."

Her teammate laughed. "It's hot as hell outside, so I think the engineers oversized all the AC units."

"And they put men in charge of setting the thermostat," Whitney said. "How are you not cold?"

"My metabolism runs pretty hot. I'm like a guy in that respect, I guess. Probably one of the reasons I get along so well at the FBI," Jenn said with a grin.

"Not me. If I could travel with a space heater, I would."

At the moment, they were taking a break waiting for

Princess Ramia to arrive so they could brief her on Jenn's findings. In addition to Whitney, Jenn, and Theobald, US Ambassador Lucas Harley, his Chief of Staff, and the Deputy Chief of Mission were all present in the SCIF. Sam Octavius, however, was conspicuously absent; he was presently working with the NSA remotely to comb through the Saudi's palace security servers, which Sam had managed to gain access to during their palace visit. Whether they'd be able to find any surveillance footage or secret files pertaining to the murder was anybody's guess, but Whitney desperately hoped they would. By assessing the evidence they'd been allowed to collect, Mullican had competently and confidently concluded that the crime scene in the palace had been staged, and the corpses of the Israeli Mossad agents had been doctored postmortem. Unfortunately, without hard proof, however, Crown Prince Faisal and Chief Saad could still deny their conclusions as conjecture.

"Ambassador Noor has just arrived," the Ambassador's Chief of Staff announced as he returned the desk phone handset to its cradle. "She'll be joining us after she's screened by security."

"Good, because the clock is ticking and the President is waiting," Ambassador Harley said, verbalizing the same thought no doubt on everyone's mind.

At Whitney's urging and Ambassador Harley's concordance, Ambassador Noor had been invited to hear their conclusions *before* submitting the findings to the ODNI, SecState, and President Jarvis in the White House. Not only was this a courtesy to a woman they all viewed as an important ally in Riyadh, but they also were interested in hearing Noor's thoughts on how Crown Prince Faisal would react to the team contradicting his story. Moments later, the magnetic lock on the door to the SCIF shifted, the door opened, and a smartly dressed Princess

Ramia entered alone and unaccompanied. The moment the door closed behind her, she removed her headscarf and greeted Ambassador Harley and his staff. The Deputy Chief of Mission escorted her to a seat at the table, which she took before turning her attention to Whitney, Theobald, and Jenn.

"It looks like we are missing one member of your team . . . Sam, I believe?" Ramia said as she scanned the room.

Like anyone could miss Sam.

"Sam is working on a special project for us at the moment," Theobald said. "Hopefully, he'll be able to join us and contribute in short order."

"Very well," the Princess said. "Shall we begin?"

Whitney cued up the visual presentation they'd prepared while Jenn walked to the projector screen to lead the discussion. They'd kept the number of slides to a minimum and focused only on elements that contradicted the cover story that Saad and Prince Faisal had cooked up. With seasoned efficiency, Jenn led Ambassador Noor through their findings, starting with the numerous oddities in the case: the lack of video surveillance, the assassins readily clearing security, the use of knives to kill the Crown Prince and his three bodyguards while meeting virtually zero resistance, and so on. Soon Mullican shifted to the evidence and crime scene assessment.

"On this slide, we've created a bird's-eye map of the royal reception room. The orange triangles represent the locations where the bodies of the alleged Israeli assassins fell after being shot. Pictures of the bodies were taken in these locations, and we were permitted to view and photograph these images, which were taken using conventional film photography. Based on dried blood-spatter patterns at the scene, the position of the bodies in the photographs, and the angles of the entrance and exit wounds, in my professional opinion, there is less than a ten percent chance that the alleged assassins were shot in the documented locations," Mullican said.

"What are you proposing, Agent Mullican? That the bodies were moved?" Princess Ramia asked.

"Not moved, Your Highness—*staged*. Evidence suggests the bodies were staged in locations and documented as such to support the assassination narrative developed by Security Chief Saad and Crown Prince Faisal."

Ramia pursed her lips on hearing this. She nodded for Mullican to continue.

On that cue, Whitney advanced the slide to a photograph taken in the morgue depicting the Mossad agent's wrists.

"What you're looking at here, Ambassador Noor, are ligature marks on the wrists of the alleged assassin that we discovered inspecting the body in the morgue," Mullican continued. "The marring is consistent with the type of trauma associated from the forced application of handcuffs or plastic restraints. More damning, however, was that makeup had been applied to the corpse to conceal the bruises. On our arrival at the morgue, I was prohibited from touching the cadavers or reperforming any autopsy procedures. Visual inspection only. I violated that mandate when I noticed the bronzer on the cadaver's wrists. After discovering the ligature marks, we were immediately escorted out of the morgue by Saad's security team and not given the opportunity to evaluate any of the other corpses."

The inside of the SCIF fell so quiet that Whitney could actually hear the pulse in her ears. Everyone waited for Ambassador Noor to react. Finally, Ramia spoke, her complexion losing much of its warmth and color as she did.

"What you have discovered appears to confirm my worst fears." She took a deep breath and shifted her gaze to Whitney.

"Agent Watts, as the counterterrorism analyst on the task force, based on the evidence collected and observed, do you believe that Crown Prince Khalid's death was an act of terrorism?"

"No," Whitney said.

"Do you believe that Crown Prince Khalid was assassinated by a foreign power?"

"No, ma'am, I do not."

Ramia shifted her gaze to Jenn. "Agent Mullican, as the FBI crime scene investigator, did you collect any irrefutable evidence that Security Chief Saad or members of his staff were responsible for the murder of Crown Prince Khalid?"

Mullican shook her head. "No. There's nothing that we observed or collected that proves who *actually* murdered Crown Prince Khalid. Any reasonable person, when presented with our findings, would have cause to doubt the veracity of Chief Saad's narrative. But we cannot irrefutably disprove it either."

"Have you confirmed the real identities of the three alleged assassins?"

Mullican looked at Theobald, who nodded. "Yes, Your Highness, we have."

"And?"

"They are Israeli nationals who work for Israel's Mossad."

"So that part of Faisal's narrative is true?"

"Yes, Madam Ambassador," Theobald said, jumping in, "but they were in-country to collect intelligence, not murder the Crown Prince. Think about it: Such an assignment would not have been in Israel's best interest. Crown Prince Khalid was taking steps to normalize relations with Israel."

"I'm well aware," Ramia said and exhaled through pursed lips. "So, what do you plan to do next?"

"We'll route our findings up the chain—" Theobald began

to say but stopped when the light above the SCIF door turned red and the magnetic lock clicked.

All eyes shifted to the door. Sam Octavius entered like a man on a mission. "We got it, Bobby," he said, a little breathless.

"Got what?"

"Proof," the cyberspook said. He tossed a USB memory stick to Whitney, which she caught in her right hand. "Saad lied. There *is* video surveillance in the reception hall."

Fingers trembling with anticipation, Whitney plugged the thumb drive into the notebook computer's USB port, opened the first of two video files, and clicked play.

The silent scene that unfolded before everyone's eyes confirmed everything the investigation team had theorized and filled in all the remaining gaps. Princess Ramia gasped when a pair of men—men she clearly recognized—murdered Khalid, ambushing him at his desk and stabbing him multiple times in the chest before slitting the Crown Prince's throat so violently and deeply it was practically a decapitation. The murder did not happen in the reception hall, but rather in an office that Whitney had not visited during the tour. The video clip ended with a third man—who Whitney instantly recognized as Security Chief Saad—entering and talking heatedly with the killers.

"Is there audio?" Theobald asked.

"Not for this recording. The other one has it," Octavius answered.

Whitney clicked on the second video file. A new window opened, and it began to play. In this clip, which was significantly longer, the dead Crown Prince was carried into the reception hall and placed into his throne-chair behind the desk. Three more dead bodies, which Whitney took to be the former Chief of Security and Khalid's two primary bodyguards, were also carried into the room and staged around the dais.

"Skip ahead to the eleven-minute mark," Octavius said. "They just fiddle around moving the bodies for the next ten minutes."

Whitney did as he asked. A huge commotion erupted as multiple Saudi guards dragged the three Israeli spies, wrists bound behind their backs, into the room. The men were forced to their knees in front of the dais. A moment later, Faisal walked into the frame. He talked for a moment with Saad, who handed him a pistol with a suppressor, then everyone except for Faisal ran out of the room and off camera. Next, Prince Faisal began screaming. He opened fire on the closest of the Israelis to him as his guards came running back into the reception hall and opened fire on the other Israelis, executing them at point-blank range.

Whitney pressed pause.

Nobody said anything for a long moment.

Octavius broke the silence. "After that, they reposition the dead shooters and set up the crime scene. Then they summon the King . . ."

Whitney turned to Ramia, who looked like she was about to be ill.

"As difficult as this video was to watch, at least now we know the truth," American Ambassador Harley said. "And we have proof."

"How did you obtain these videos?" Ramia asked, her expression deadly serious as she fixed her gaze on Sam.

"I think you know," Octavius said.

Ramia reached up and began to massage her temples. "It is a catastrophe. Not only for Saudi Arabia but for the Middle East and the world. Faisal has very different aspirations for Saudi Arabia than his brother. I suspect my days as Ambassador are numbered."

"If you need protection, we can help you," Whitney heard herself say, speaking way above her pay grade.

"Miss Watts is correct. If you fear for your life, I can offer you sanctuary here at the embassy and begin the paperwork process for actual asylum in the United States," Ambassador Harley added, making Whitney's impromptu offer official.

"Thank you. That is very kind, but this is not a problem I can run away from. So long as I have breath in my lungs, I will do what I can to protect the progress made over the past eight years for my country and my countrymen," Ramia said. "We must contemplate our next steps very carefully. I do not think it would be wise to release this video publicly."

"Nor do I," Harley said quickly, "but we are obligated to include it in our report. The President must know the truth, and he will decide how and when to use the information."

"What do we tell the Crown Prince?" Theobald said, posing the question to the group. "He's expecting a copy of our findings. The expectation was we would be releasing a joint statement. Obviously, that can't happen now."

"We have to stall, until President Jarvis has time to digest this report and decide on a course of action," Harley said. He looked to Ambassador Noor. "Can you help us with that?"

Before she could respond, the conference room telephone rang. Harley's Chief of Staff immediately answered the call, and everyone waited while he listened.

"Thank you for bringing this to my immediate attention. I'll brief the Ambassador and the others."

The Chief of Staff hung up the phone and turned to his boss, grim-faced.

"I'm afraid I have some bad news—Crown Prince Faisal preempted us and released a statement."

"And what did it say?" Harley said, sitting up straight in his chair and leaning in.

"He's announced that his brother was assassinated, and that the Crown has proof the hit was ordered by Prime Minister Shamone and carried out by the Israeli Mossad . . ."

CHAPTER 25

REMOTE STAGING AREA
INSIDE THE KING ABDULLAH SPECIAL OPERATIONS
TRAINING CENTER (KASOTC)
NORTHERN OUTSKIRTS OF AMMAN, JORDAN
1212 LOCAL TIME

Chunk followed Ze'ev Mirashi across the dusty desert airfield, moving from the full-size mock-up of an airline terminal and control tower toward the double hangars just a hundred yards north, their doors partially open. He glanced fondly at the Airbus 300 and Boeing 737 on the sand-covered ramp to his right. He'd trained here with Gold Squadron shortly after they'd taken down what they'd believed at the time to be the al Qadar mastermind in Pakistan. The training opportunity had been invaluable—with multiple run-throughs of aircraft hostage rescues on the different planes, which not only had fully operational cockpits and galleys but had been equipped with pop-up targets in the seats simulating both terrorists and hostages. Gold Squadron had been like kids in a candy store inside the world's most advanced combat simulation training base. Nearly a hundred training buildings stretched across the complex, from Third World–style compounds to apartment buildings and embassies, K-9 ranges, and urban combat driving courses, all the way to this full-scale airport. There was almost always an American special operations team training here, which seemed fair since the United States had funded the project.

"You've been here before, it seems," Mirashi said, stepping up beside Chunk. The Israeli operator grinned at him. "I can tell from your face you were on what you call memory lane."

Chunk laughed. "Yeah, well, I've done a few trips here over my career. It's the best training facility in the world, especially for operations in this theater."

"Perhaps," Mirashi said, glancing around the sprawling complex before winking at Chunk. "We have some secrets still in Israel, you know."

"I do indeed," Chunk said. "And I've been in battle with exchange operators from Shayetet 13 more than once, my friend. You are truly the elite."

"You're too kind," Mirashi said humbly as he passed through the hangar doors. "But we were able to arrange for this."

The Israeli gestured at four foreign helicopters staged inside the hangar. Not only were they marked with the exact scheme of the Syrian Air Force, but they were actual Kamov KA-28s—the Russian export version of the KA-27 that the Syrian Air Force was using as a combat transport. With its counterrotating overhead rotors and twin vertical stabilizers instead of a tail rotor, it was an easily recognizable helo.

"Holy shit," Chunk said, slapping Mirashi on the back. "Bowman said he had arranged for your guys to transport some special birds for the op, but I didn't expect this. How the hell did you get them decked out so quickly?"

"We have these units standing by at all times," Mirashi said, running a hand down the side of the bulky, awkward-looking bird. "And don't worry. They work way better than the actual Syrian aircraft—especially in the hands of our pilots."

Chunk peered inside. "Good. I would hate to end up in the drink a couple of hundred miles offshore. This will make the approach a little less hairy, I should think."

"Yes," Mirashi said and pointed to the weapon suspension stations with gun pods. "With firepower, just in case."

"What's our range and speed?" Chunk asked. While he knew Russia produced multiple variations of the airframe for everything from attack missions to submarine hunting, he wasn't intimately familiar with its specs like he was American birds.

"The published range is just under a thousand kilometers—about six hundred miles. We've modified these aircraft with additional fuel pods—see them there, inboard of the gun pods—which extends that range to nearly double, but at the cost of payload. These will hold twelve operators per aircraft, and we've also modified the powerplant to give us a little more speed over the 130-knot cruise they were designed for."

"One sixty?" Chunk asked hopefully, thinking how much he'd miss the performance and speed of the MH-60M Blackhawk. The special version they used in JSOC gave them nearly a 190-knot cruise, plus an assload of weaponry.

Mirashi shrugged. "One hundred and fifty, depending on the payload. We'll be able to deliver the assault team efficiently, have some loiter time, and enough fuel to fly home, as long as the target ship is located within a radius of four hundred kilometers from this base—which according to intelligence, it is."

Chunk patted the bulbous nose of the modified KA-28. "That'll do, donkey . . . that'll do," he said.

Mirashi just looked at him quizzically.

Chunk gestured toward the hangar doors and led Mirashi across the tarmac to the small terminal building they had commandeered as their planning space. The Jordanians had arranged for their "CIA" guests to have a secure SCIF-level TOC inside. Chunk entered through the double glass doors, Mirashi in tow, and was greeted by two American Ground Branch operators dressed in blue jeans but full battle rattle up top. They checked their CAC cards, which identified them as "Special Joint CT Task Force 99." The bearded operator gave them a nod and unlocked the heavy door.

Instead of the normal, giddy, and animated atmosphere ahead of a mission, inside the TOC, he was greeted with a hushed and grim vibe.

"What's happened?" Chunk asked immediately as the door shut behind him.

Bowman looked up from where he stood talking to Saw. Behind him stood Ami Galant, arms crossed, the Israeli commander's eyes burning.

"The Saudis have made an announcement blaming Israel for the assassination of the Crown Prince and vowing retaliation," Bowman said, his voice hard.

"There's been an explosion of chatter from every crazy terror group on the planet calling for the annihilation of Israel," Becker, the Israeli intelligence officer, added, his voice taut with emotion. "A cry for a worldwide intifada against Israel and against any who support her is all over the internet."

"Death to Israel, and death to America," Michelle Yi said.

Chunk felt his chest tighten and gritted his teeth. The match had been thrown into the powder keg, and the coming explosion was going to leave a lot of people dead on both sides.

"Where is our task force investigation team right now?" he asked, his thoughts immediately going to Watts and Theobald.

"They're inside the United States Embassy in Riyadh," Bowman said. "This is happening right now, in real time."

"Then we need to get them the hell out of there," Chunk said, his chest suddenly tight.

"The Marines at the embassy are on high alert, and I have Blue squadron on standby if they need an extraction. I got it covered, Chunk. They're going to be okay," Bowman said and clapped a hand on Chunk's shoulder. "*Our* priority right now is to take control of the *Earabat Albahr* before the terrorists on board can fire missiles, possibly armed with nukes, at Israel. That is priority one from the President. We've got the green light."

"Roger that, sir," Chunk said, compartmentalizing all thoughts of Watts so he could get his mind locked and loaded for battle.

"Get those birds rolled out of the hangar and gassed up," Bowman said to Mirashi. Then, turning to Chunk, added, "Assemble the team. We brief in five minutes, then it's showtime."

CHAPTER 26

US EMBASSY
SENSITIVE COMPARTMENTALIZED INFORMATION FACILITY (SCIF)
RIYADH, SAUDI ARABIA

Whitney had barely processed the shocking news of the Saudi press release when the lights went out in the SCIF.

"What just happened, David?" Ambassador Harley said in the pitch black, addressing his Chief of Staff.

"It appears . . . we've lost power, sir," David said.

Whitney picked up her mobile phone and turned on the flashlight. Others followed her lead, and soon the room was illuminated by a patchwork of white LED phone lights.

"Strange—the emergency backup generator should have come on by now," Harley said, his voice tinged with both irritation and concern.

Theobald lifted the conference room table phone handset and put it to his ear. "The hard-line is dead."

"Wi-Fi is down as well," Octavius said and made for the

door. “Mag locks are supposed to fail open on loss of power. Assuming it does, we should exit and get a SITREP.”

“Agreed,” Theobald said, rising from his seat.

On cue, Whitney heard the click of the magnetic locks disabling, and Theobald pushed open the door. With Sam holding the slab, Whitney grabbed her backpack and followed everyone else out of the SCIF to the hallway outside, which was also dark. Now outside the EMF-shielded space, she checked her phone display: no service.

She rotated her phone screen to show Theobald. “Should we be worried?”

“Maybe,” he said, checking his own phone for service and shaking his head. “Probably.”

Whitney’s brain began war-gaming out a scenario that was both improbable and too terrible to contemplate. But then, since she’d joined Gold Squadron at the Tier One, her professional life seemed to be nothing but one impossible scenario after another.

“Sam, has any of the evidence we collected at the palace been transmitted to ODNI yet?” she asked, looking up at the cyberspook in the dark.

“No. I didn’t want to jump the shark. I was waiting until we’d finalized our report and briefed Ambassador Harley,” he said.

“And that includes the video surveillance recording of the murder you found on the Royal Palace servers?”

He nodded. “Correct.”

“Is it possible that the Saudis could have detected you breaching their network security?”

“Unlikely, but I’ll never say never.”

“Would they be able to tell which file you hacked?”

“We made a copy and left the original in place. I’m very good at covering my tracks. But again, anything is possible.”

Whitney turned to Theobald and, in a low voice, said, "Since I took this job, Bobby, I've come to believe there's no such thing as coincidence. We saw through the Crown Prince's deception, and he knows it. The gambit is up. We need to exfil."

"Agreed," he said. He turned to Ambassador Harley. "Mr. Ambassador, I think you might want to consider evacuating the embassy."

If Harley heard Theobald, he didn't let on. Instead, he addressed his Chief of Staff. "David, find out why the backup generators aren't running. Get the power back on ASAP. And find me Diggs, while you're at it."

"Yes, sir," David said and took off running down the dimly lit hallway.

Theobald tried again. "Mr. Ambassador, we have concerns about your safety and the safety of your staff. I recommend—"

Harley cut him off. "I heard you the first time, Mr. Theobald, but that's a decision I'm going to make in consultation with my security lead, Byron Diggs, and my boss, the Secretary of State. Evacuating the embassy comes with both political and logistical challenges," Harley said. "That said, you and your team are under no obligation to stay. In fact, your departure might help stabilize the situation here."

Theobald nodded and stuck out his hand to Harley, who shook it. "Understood, sir," Theobald said. "Thanks for the hospitality and support."

Harley cracked a fatalistic smile. "And thank you for showing up out of the blue and making my life difficult."

At that very moment, a trio of bearded operator types—men who Whitney pegged as CIA GRS—jogged up to confer with Ambassador Harley. While two of the guys fell into conversation with Harley, Whitney saw a flicker of recognition in the third shooters' eyes as he spied Theobald.

"Well, well, well, look what the cat dragged in?" the man said to Theobald.

"Mick O'Malley?! Oh my God. How is it they haven't fired you yet?" Theobald said, pulling the operator into a bro-hug. "You're living proof that miracles really do happen."

Both men laughed and then stepped back to take a measure of each other.

"How you doin', Bobby?"

"Same old, same old. You?" Theobald said.

"Little balder, a little fatter, and a little poorer than the last time we saw each other."

Theobald chuckled. "Amen to that, brother."

"I assume your presence is the spark for whatever shit-storm has apparently just hit the embassy?" Mick asked. He turned to look at Whitney. "In case nobody's told you, trouble and this guy go together like white on rice."

"My friends have been known to say the same thing about me," she said with a grin.

"Well, shit, then the two of you are perfect for each other," Mick said and pulled out a tin of Skoal to pack himself a lip. "In all seriousness, I assume y'all heard the announcement? Talk about kickin' the hornet's nest."

Theobald pursed his lips. "Yep, we were here to try to head that off, but unfortunately that didn't happen."

"So, what now? You buggin' out?"

Theobald nodded.

"Airport?"

"Yep."

"Do you need an armed escort? There are mobs gathering in protest everywhere. The news reports that the same thing is going on throughout the Middle East."

"Are you asking or offering?"

Mick snorted a laugh. "Both, of course."

"Then the answer is yes. Assuming the Ambassador can spare you, it certainly might expedite things."

"Let me talk to the boss man, and I'll see what we can do. Cool?"

"Cool," Theobald said and bumped fists with the man.

While Mick caucused with his teammates and the Ambassador, Theobald turned back to the investigation team, who were gathered in a semicircle listening and waiting for instructions.

"Did any of you leave anything behind at the Ritz that you're unwilling to part with?"

Whitney, Sam, and Jenn all shook their heads.

"Good. Everyone pack up, hit the head if you need to, and meet in the garage. Wheels up in five minutes," Theobald said.

Whitney turned her attention to Princess Ramia, who'd been standing silently off to the side, listening and watching the controlled chaos in the hallway around her with her arms folded. Ramia wore the expression of a woman whose life had just been turned upside down—the same look Whitney had seen on the faces of survivors of natural disasters who'd lived but lost everything.

"Ambassador Noor, thank you for your support today," Whitney said, stepping up to say goodbye to the woman whose life was in unquestionable danger. "I know we're leaving you in quite a difficult position . . ."

Ramia fixed Whitney with a wan smile. "As a Saudi woman, I'm no stranger to difficult positions. But I will forge ahead, because this is the only path I know."

Whitney nodded and extended her hand, and was surprised when the Princess opened her arms and stepped in to offer her a cheek-to-cheek embrace.

"You're smart to run," Ramia whispered. "I fear we have seen only a glimpse of what my cousin is capable of."

On those chilling words, Whitney broke the embrace and took a step back. She locked eyes with the Princess but couldn't find the syllables to construct a suitable response. Sometimes there simply wasn't anything else to say.

Mick, the operator, returned a heartbeat later with fire in his eyes. "I got the green light. You've got me and Jackson as your driver and escort, but we've gotta go now."

"Roger that," Theobald said and looked to Whitney. "You ready?"

"Yeah, let's get the hell out of here," she said.

As she set off down the hall, Whitney cast a final backward glance at the Princess. She was overcome by the unshakable feeling that she would never see the woman again.

CHAPTER 27

CROWN PRINCE'S PRIVATE OFFICES
AL-YAMAMAH PALACE
RIYADH, SAUDI ARABIA

Reza watched as Faisal paced back and forth inside the Crown Prince's secure conference room.

The announcement that Israel had assassinated Crown Prince Khalid sparked the exact explosive result they had predicted. The outrage had already inspired mobs of protesters against the Jewish state and the West throughout the Kingdom and beyond. Faisal had ordered Saudi operatives to act as instigators and incite an angry mob outside the American Embassy. And now they had received word that the Americans were attempting to leave the embassy. The plan had been that the mobs staged around the American Embassy would keep them in place.

"How is this possible?" Faisal slammed a fist on the conference table. "You must stop them from leaving. Kill them! Whatever it takes, Saad."

"We will find them," Saad said, avoiding the Crown Prince's gaze.

"What do you mean you'll find them? If they're leaving the embassy, they're headed to the airport, you idiot. If we can't contain them at the embassy, then stop them before they take off and ruin everything. Call airport security and deny them access to their plane. Prevent them from taking off and seize their jet."

"Your Highness, if I may . . ." Reza said before Saad could answer.

Faisal whirled toward him, eyes flashing with anger—and maybe, Reza thought, fear.

"Speak," the Prince commanded.

"Might I suggest we send a hit team disguised as protesters to the airport? They can dispatch the Americans, but it will give us a cover story for their demise."

Faisal nodded and turned to Saad. "Saad, dispatch a security team of trusted men from the palace detail to the airport to stop them. Lethal force is authorized. Kill them all."

"Yes, My Prince," Saad said. "Do you want me to do as Deputy Ambassador Reza suggests and direct the men to disguise themselves as rioters?"

"There's no time for games. Send them armed and in uniform."

"Four Americans shot dead at the airport will not go unnoticed," Reza jumped in. "That's why I suggested a cover story."

The prince fixed his angry gaze on Reza but addressed his security lead. "Chief Saad, make sure your men recover the bodies and bring them back. We'll claim the Americans were shot leaving the embassy and stage the bodies in the street."

"As you command, Your Highness," Chief Saad said, bowing and leaving the room.

"We'll claim the Americans were CIA operatives aiding the Israelis," Faisal said, his anger cooling as he reined in his emotions. "That will help bolster the narrative."

"Brilliant," Reza said.

Faisal has certainly filled the shoes of his new role quickly. The man he looked at now bore little resemblance to the party boy of their college years or the billionaire playboy Faisal had seemed quite content to be in the shadow of his brother. Reza had predicted he could step up, and he had. *If he maintains this resolve, the alliance between the Kingdom and the Republic of Iran will be formidable indeed.*

Reza's mobile phone chimed in his pocket with a text message notification. He could predict who it was and what the message was about. He fished the encrypted phone from his pocket, checked the screen, and read the coded message routed from Director Golzar:

> Business materials are packed
> and ready to ship. Provide
> shipping instructions.

Reza looked up from the screen to find the Crown Prince's gaze fixed intently on him. Now that they were alone, it was time to press Faisal on authorizing the terrorist strike on Tel Aviv.

"I've been informed that preparations have been made for the special operation we discussed earlier. The weapon is ready to be moved into Gaza . . . with your agreement and authorization."

Faisal didn't answer immediately, his face a portrait of uncertainty. "If I authorize this, there's no going back. I cannot ignore the fact that Israel has nuclear weapons they could use to retaliate. Can you guarantee that Israel will not be able to trace this back to the Kingdom?"

"How could they? The weapon, the proxy fighters, and every piece of this operation was coordinated by Iran."

Reza watched the cloud of uncertainty on Faisal's face morph slowly into resolve. He had made his decision, and Reza knew it.

"Do it," the Crown Prince said.

"Yes, Your Highness," Reza said, intentionally using the honorific.

A surreal feeling washed over him as he typed his coded response giving the green light for the attack that would change the world:

Authorization obtained

Ship materials to address on file

Understood

Sending

And just like that, it was done.

Two college mates, aspiring Muslim men who'd waxed poetic about changing the world from the deck of a yacht sipping drinks in the sun, had schemed and maneuvered their way into positions of power to actually make good on that dream. From a text message sent by Reza's own fingers, Jahan Heydari would now be given the order to execute the most audacious false flag operation in history.

And the Zionists would suffer an attack that would bring the Jewish state to its knees.

CHAPTER 28

CHEVROLET SUBURBAN DEPARTING THE US EMBASSY

RIYADH, SAUDI ARABIA

The sharp crack from a bottle hitting the window beside Whitney's head made her duck and cover reflexively in her seat. How the angry crowd of Saudi protesters had assembled so quickly outside the US Embassy defied logic, but here they were. They were many, and they were angry.

Whitney looked up and saw a spiderweb of cracks spiraling out from the impact point.

"That window's compromised. Trade seats with me," Octavius said.

The old Whitney would have done as instructed automatically, but she wasn't that person anymore. She'd been abducted, beaten, and nearly drowned. She'd fought a terrorist who was almost twice her size and won—albeit with Lucy Kim's help—by plunging a knife into the man's neck, abdomen, and femoral artery until he bled out. She'd faced down Qasim Nadar at gunpoint in a London city tunnel and walked away the victor, saving herself and Nadar's pregnant wife in the process.

The words that came out of her mouth took her a little by surprise. "That's very chivalrous of you, Sam, but I don't see how your safety is any less important than mine."

A big grin spread across Sam's face. "Okay, Watts, you do you."

"Hey, Mick, that ballistic glass is compromised," Theobald said from where he sat in the back bench seat beside Jenn.

"It's not ballistic glass," Mick said, turning in the front passenger seat to look back at Theobald. "This ute ain't up armored."

"What! You've gotta be friggin' kidding me," Mullican said.

"Only the Ambassador's ride is armored. In case you hadn't noticed, he ain't with us," Mick fired back.

"The threat level in Riyadh has never warranted an armored fleet," the driver, an operator who'd introduced himself as Thatch, piped up as he struggled to maintain forward progress without running people over. "Jesus, this is nuts. I've never seen anything like this before."

A second bottle smacked into the front windshield and bounced off, leaving a contact divot but not cracking the glass. Whitney felt her heart rate ramp up to match the rising aggression of the crowd outside. The crowd—mostly men in their twenties and thirties—shouted, spittle flying from their open mouths, angry eyes fixed on the SUV, fists pumping in the air. As their numbers swelled, so did their courage, and they closed in completely around the Suburban. Someone slammed a flat palm against the driver's-side window, a smack so loud Whitney flinched. Then, as if of one mind, the entire throng of agitators began pounding on the windows, door panels, and hood of the big Chevy SUV. Whitney had once driven through a hailstorm and thought that was loud, but the racket from the collective pounding was practically deafening inside the cabin.

A skinny young man climbed up onto the hood and began jumping up and down, collapsing the sheet metal over the Suburban's engine compartment. Then he started kicking the windshield repeatedly in front of Thatch.

"Fuck this guy," Thatch said.

He goosed the accelerator just enough that the man on the hood lost his balance and fell, landing on the hood with a resounding thud before toppling off the left-side fender onto the pavement below. This momentarily silenced the crowd as it processed what had happened, then incited a wave of fresh outrage.

"The situation is deteriorating," Theobald hollered from the back seat.

"No shit," Mick shouted back.

Someone slammed a pipe into the back window, shattering the glass into a million shards and breaching the cabin. A crazed protester immediately tried to climb into the back of the SUV. Theobald reacted instantly, yanking his pistol, swiveling in his seat, and pointing the muzzle at the forehead of the invader, who'd already gotten half his torso into the cargo compartment.

"Back . . . get back!" Theobald barked, using his command voice so the message transcended the language barrier.

Whitney watched the young man's eyes go wide with surprise and fear. He flung himself backward out of the gaping hole that was once the rear window.

The pipe wielder, however, seemed only emboldened by his accomplishment and raised the pipe to strike again. Before she could see what happened, the window beside her exploded, raining chunks of glass down over her torso and lap. She looked left to see an Arab standing just outside the window, holding a cricket bat over his head, raised in jubilant victory. Another man beside him bared his teeth, screamed like an animal, and lunged for her with both hands through the gap. Whitney shrieked as he grabbed a fistful of her hair with one hand and her right forearm with the other. He jerked her—with surprising strength and ferocity—toward him, trying to pull her out the window. She tried resisting, but he'd won control of her momentum, and she felt herself lifting off the seat.

A horrific image—of the frenzied crowd literally ripping her apart limb by limb—filled her mind's eye.

She screamed and tried frantically to brace her palms against the doorframe. Just when it seemed she was about to go out the window, she felt a powerful force jerk her back by the waistband of her pants. In her peripheral vision, a massive brown fist flew past her right cheek and slammed squarely into the middle of her attacker's face. Despite the chaos, she heard the man's nose shatter with a sickening crunch. He released his grip, and she instantly fell backward, crashing into Sam's broad chest.

"I gotcha, Watts," Octavius said, catching her in his lap.

"I changed my mind about trading seats," she said, in between heavy breaths.

She might have heard his laugh, but it was drowned out by the roar of Theobald's pistol, which she saw kick and flash to her left as he squeezed off a warning shot over the head of the pipe-wielding attacker. The gunshot instantly froze and silenced the crowd.

"Keep shooting!" Thatch shouted from the driver's seat. "Try to scatter them so I can get us the hell out of here."

Theobald angled his gun skyward and fired twice.

Whitney watched a wave of panic ripple through the agitators. A moment later, people began to shout and run chaotically, scattering in different directions. Thatch laid on the horn, but the path ahead was still blocked by people.

Cursing like a sailor, O'Malley opened the sunroof and fired his pistol repeatedly until, like Moses parting the Red Sea, the crowd in front of the SUV split into two masses. Not hesitating a second, Thatch mashed the accelerator, and Whitney felt the big SUV surge forward. The Suburban's V-8 engine roared as the big ute shot through the gap and quickly put the mob in the rearview mirror. Whitney, who was still sitting on Sam's lap, exhaled through pursed lips.

"Damn, that was close. That bastard almost got me out the window." She turned to look at Sam. "Thanks for that."

"Easy day," he said. "Besides, I've been jonesing to punch somebody since I got here. You just gave me an excuse."

"Okay, seriously, what the hell was that?" Jenn said.

"That was the power of manufactured public outrage," Mick replied. "Their Crown Prince was murdered, and they need someone to blame."

"Yeah, but the Crown's statement pointed the finger at Israel, not the US."

"And we're Israel's biggest ally and supporter, which makes us complicit . . . or something to that effect," Theobald said. "You can bet that's the messaging being used by the protest instigators."

"By instigators, I assume you mean Crown Prince Faisal's own men?" Mick said.

Theobald traded a worried look with Whitney. "Wouldn't surprise me in the least."

"Do you think they're going to let us fly out?" Jenn asked.

"I give it coin-flip odds," Theobald said.

"If there's even a chance we're going to get detained, we need to transmit everything we've got. President Jarvis needs to know exactly what we found." Whitney bent at the waist to retrieve her mobile phone from the backpack at her feet and checked her screen. "Damn it, still no service. Sam, didn't you say you brought a satphone with you?"

Sam nodded and lifted his backpack onto his lap. After a second of rooting around, he found it and tried the power button. "It won't turn on," he said, his voice a growl.

"They made us leave all our phones in lockers when we were in the palace," Whitney said. "I bet Chief Saad's guys did something to it."

Sam nodded. "Blocking our mobile phones from accessing the Saudi cellular networks is easy when you control the cellular providers, but blocking satellite traffic is a different matter altogether. Looks like they solved that problem by sabotaging my hardware."

"Shit. What do we do?" Jenn said.

"We just have to get to the jet," Theobald said. "It's got radio and satellite internet access."

"Do the pilots know you're coming?" Mick asked, swiveling to look back at them.

"Nope, because we haven't been able to call them."

The GRS shooter pressed his lips into a hard line and shook his head. "Well, if they ain't there, then I'll fly you to Bahrain my damn self."

"I didn't know you were a pilot?" Theobald said as his lips split into a wide grin.

"Yeah, well, we do a lot of crazy shit in JSOC, as you know. They sent me to Flight Safety for flight training when I was at Delta."

"Does that mean you're licensed?"

Mick shrugged, grinned, and said, "Qualified, licensed—potato, patato . . . I haven't crashed yet. That's all that really matters in situations like this."

"Works for me," Theobald said.

Whitney tilted her head and looked skyward. "God help me," she murmured.

CHAPTER 29

FISHING TRAWLER

TWENTY-FIVE NAUTICAL MILES OFF THE COAST OF GAZA

Lying on his back on the bare mattress, Jahan Heydari watched the black fly buzz around the lone porthole window in the filthy bunk room. The stupid insect had no idea that it was on a boat. No idea that the invisible force field standing between it and freedom was a simple piece of glass. No idea that no matter how many times the fly smashed its stupid face into that pane, the invisible barrier would not move. Would not break. Would not yield.

"We are not so different, you and I," Heydari said to the pathetic insect.

Except instead of a pane of glass, Heydari was imprisoned by professional obligation.

His encrypted mobile phone chimed with an incoming text message. He looked at the screen and read the single-word order from Golzar:

Execute

He texted back:

Acknowledged

As a fourteen-year covert operations veteran, he knew his adversary better than the princes and politicians in their palaces and luxury office suites. More intimately than the bureaucrats in their safe, comfortable offices in their self-important capital cities. He'd survived in the trenches of the shadow war against the Zionists and the Americans because he never made the mistake of underestimating their intelligence-collection prowess, their tactical capabilities, and their will to win. He'd avoided capture and assassination by moving early and moving often, by anticipating their interventions, and by sacrificing the fools in the jihadi ranks to feed the hunters so that he might slip away.

He knew that the order to execute the operation would come too late from Golzar.

Just as he knew that the Americans and Israelis would identify and raid the *Earabat Albahr* and the *Dakar*.

Which is why he'd acted immediately after the early-morning video conference call with Golzar and Reza. As soon as he'd been read in on the Saudi royal coup and that Reza had been appointed Deputy Ambassador and was flying to Riyadh, his tactician's mind anticipated the day's events. His jealousy and contempt for the handsome golden boy of the MOIS did not cloud his judgment about his colleague's capabilities. Just as Heydari was a master of manipulating the martyrs and lieutenants of jihad, Arash Reza was equally masterful at manipulating the elite power brokers in his orbit. He knew

Reza would win the new Crown Prince's agreement to attack the Zionists, and so Heydari had moved the nuclear warhead just after dawn.

He'd summoned a fishing trawler—whose captain he'd paid handsomely to loiter in the area—and transferred the weapon off the *Earabat Albahr*. The fishing vessel had then transited inland, inconspicuously with the rest of the daily fishing trawler fleet, and anchored offshore. The trawler captain, of course, had no idea what was inside the massive wooden crate on his middeck, and he never would. Even if the man was arrested and interrogated by the Jews, he could not compromise the mission.

With a weary sigh, Heydari rolled out of the squeaky rack, stretched his back, and went to find the ship captain. It was time to tell him to head into the harbor at Gaza City, where they would unload the package and transport it by UNRWA truck to Beit Hanoun, where the Sayf Allah terrorists were waiting. After that, the only thing left for Heydari to figure out was how to complete the mission and slip away into the night like he always did.

Because unlike the attacks he'd orchestrated in the past, this payload was almost guaranteed to make him a martyr—whether he wished it or not.

CHAPTER 30

KING KHALID INTERNATIONAL AIRPORT
RIYADH, SAUDI ARABIA
1342 LOCAL TIME

Whitney, who'd been cold the entire time in Saudi Arabia, was sweating profusely.

With the side and back windows of the Suburban blown out, the stiflingly hot desert air flooded the cabin and completely overpowered the SUV's air-conditioning. Comfort was the least of her worries now. Getting out of the country without dying was the only thing she cared about at the moment.

"You guys arrived via the royal terminal, yes?" Mick said from the front passenger seat as they approached King Khalid International Airport.

"Yes, but Ambassador Noor met us on the ramp, circumventing all the ordinary crap. We didn't have to clear customs or enter the terminal building," Theobald said.

"Hmm," Mick said and scratched at his beard. "Did you happen to note where they parked?"

Theobald nodded. "Our jet is in slip 4A in the south parking area. Unless, of course, they moved it. It's a white Gulfstream G500 with navy-blue accents," Theobald said, then rattled off the tail number from memory.

Whitney was impressed and made a mental note that she needed to pay closer attention to such things in the field. She was, by nature, an attention to details kind of girl, but she tended to leave the logistics to others on her team who were responsible for planning and executing it.

When she was little, her dad once chastised her that if she didn't stop watching TV all the time, she'd fill up her brain with so much useless information she wouldn't have any memory left for the important stuff. For some weird reason, the comment—which she later realized was sarcasm—made an impact on her regardless. It made sense that the human brain, just like a computer, had a finite capacity. There was only so much data she had time to focus on and commit to memory, so she'd taken her dad's "advice" to heart and only worried about the important stuff and ignored the rest. As an analyst, the approach had served her well, allowing her to more efficiently separate the wheat from the chaff. But now that she was doing more and more fieldwork, she'd have to make a change.

In the field, remembering as many details as possible could be the difference between life and death.

Thatch eased off the gas, and the Suburban slowed as they approached the airport. With a sideways glance at Mick, he said, "Hey, boss, decision time: Terminal or tarmac?"

"Tarmac," Mick said. Then, louder and addressing the group, he added, "Listen up, guys, we're going to try to drive to the plane directly. The south ramp is fenced off with a dedicated security checkpoint. If a flight plan hasn't been filed, it's unlikely you'll make any headway clearing security in the royal terminal anyway. Our best bet is to play the diplomatic privilege angle and hope the gate guard clears us. Hopefully, the flight crew is dialed in on current events and is waiting with the jet or hanging out in the pilot's lounge. If not, I'll call NAS Bahrain from the cockpit and get things rolling while Mick finds them."

"And if they don't let us through?" Jenn asked.

"We'll cross that bridge when we come to it," Mick said, an answer that Whitney hated but didn't see any value in challenging.

They arrived at the security checkpoint for tarmac and runways a few minutes later. Thatch lowered all the windows prior to pulling up—in an attempt, Whitney guessed, to make the Suburban look less noticeably damaged and conspicuous. Tarmac access was controlled by a simple guard shack with a retractable gate arm located on an access road to the south of the terminal building. To Whitney's surprise and relief, the guard who came up to greet them smiled and his eyes flashed with recognition on seeing Thatch.

"Hey, Nadim, how's it going, brother?" Thatch said, leaning his elbow on the driver's door windowsill.

"It's hot as hell today, but okay. Did you hear the crazy news?" Nadim said with perfect English, his gaze ticking from Thatch to scan the faces in the passenger seats. When his gaze settled on Whitney, she smiled at him. He didn't reciprocate before his attention turned back to Thatch.

"Yeah, I did. I'm so sorry, man. I've only been here a year, but Crown Prince Khalid was good people. I know everybody liked him," Thatch said.

Whitney watched Nadim's expression harden. "You work at the American Embassy. You hear things. Tell me the truth: Did the Mossad really do this terrible thing?"'

Thatch blew a raspberry with his lips. "That's intel way

above my pay grade, brother. I drive the VIPs where and when they say, but nobody tells me shit."

Whitney thought the answer would irritate the guard, but it had the opposite effect. Nadim nodded and said, "Guys like us are expected to do the protection work, but they love to keep us in the dark."

"Amen to that." Thatch held out his fist to Nadim, who bumped it with a black-gloved knuckle.

"Are you dropping off?" Nadim said, scanning Whitney and her teammates a second time.

"Yeah, these guys flew in this morning, and they're heading out before things heat up."

Nadim lifted the tablet computer in a black rubber case he wore hanging from a shoulder strap. "I don't see anything scheduled . . ."

"No, you wouldn't. This is an emergent departure."

Nadim nodded at the comment. "What's the tail number?"

Thatch rattled it off from memory.

"Okay. I see it here . . . jet arrived this morning. Looks like it's been refueled and on ready status. Do you want me to notify Ground Control that the passengers have arrived and you'll be filing a flight plan?"

Thatch turned to Mick, who said, "Nah, we'll let the flight crew take care of that. Not even sure which airport they're heading to yet."

"Okay, you can enter," Nadim said. He turned and gestured to an unseen partner in the guard shack to open the swing arm.

"Thanks, brother. Catch you on the way out," Thatch said with a two-finger salute to Nadim. He eased the SUV forward past the checkpoint and onto the access road.

"Well, that was easy," Sam said with a laugh of disbelief once they'd passed through the gate.

"Nadim's good people," Thatch said with a grin in the rearview mirror.

That Thatch had taken the time to get to know Nadim by name reminded Whitney of how Chunk carried himself. Making friends and being nice to people—regardless of their race, gender, social class, nationality, or profession—was not only a good way to live but also smart tradecraft. Thatch's effort had certainly paid dividends today.

Whitney checked her mobile phone for connectivity, but the "NO SVC" indicator was still showing. She felt Sam's eyes on her, and she looked over and said, "Still no service."

"Me too," he said.

"That's our jet," Theobald said, scooting up between the middle-row captain's chair and pointing through the windshield at the Gulfstream that was parked in the exact location where they'd disembarked. With everything that had transpired, their arrival felt like a lifetime ago.

"The airstair is down," Mick said. "Maybe the flight crew came back on their own."

"Or maybe there's a Saudi security team on board who've commandeered the aircraft waiting for us to show up?" Jenn said.

"Maybe . . ."

Whitney scanned for parked vehicles and didn't see any. Still, instead of pulling in and parking immediately by the airstair, Thatch looped around the starboard side and front of the jet, giving them an opportunity to complete a security scan and park nose out for an easy exfil.

"How 'bout y'all stay in the vehicle and I'll check things out," Mick said as Thatch brought the big SUV to a halt, leaving the transmission in drive.

Theobald nodded.

Mick jumped out of the front passenger seat and jogged

over to the jet. Whitney noted that he left his sidearm holstered as he quickstepped up the airstair and disappeared inside the jet. Thirty seconds later, he popped his head out the open hatch—located forward on the port side just behind the cockpit—and gave them a thumbs-up.

"Let's go," Theobald said.

Thatch stayed put in the driver's seat while the rest of them grabbed their backpacks and exited the Suburban. Whitney followed Theobald up the airstair steps into the business jet, which had to be over a hundred degrees inside. Standing next to Mick, just behind the cockpit door, was the male cabin attendant who'd accompanied them and the two CIA pilots from Bahrain.

"Jet's open because Richards here was being proactive and prepping for a possible early departure," Mick said.

"When we saw the news break, we tried to call you guys, but the calls wouldn't go through," Richards said. "I volunteered to cab it over to the terminal and prep in case y'all needed a quick exfil. Then I lost cell service, and I was like, shit, I can't call the pilots or you guys. I was just about to walk back to the terminal when you pulled up."

"So, the pilots are where?" Theobald asked.

"Standing by at the Airport Marriott. You can literally see it out the starboard side. It's a straight shot, two miles down Airport Road, or 539, or whatever it is."

"All right, listen," Mick said. "Bobby, you go tell Thatch to haul ass to the Marriott and pick up the pilots. In the meantime, I'm going to fire up the APU, power the instruments, comms, and get some air moving in here. Richards can help me with preflight while I try to get NAS Bahrain on the horn and file a flight plan with RUH ATC. Hopefully, by the time Thatch gets back with the pilots, we're ready to rock and roll."

"Sounds like a plan," Theobald said with a nod.

"What can we do?" Whitney asked, gesturing to the trio of herself, Sam, and Jenn.

"Take a seat, cross your fingers, and sweat your ass off until we're airborne," Theobald said with a chuckle and disappeared out the hatch to give Thatch his marching orders.

CHAPTER 31

ISRAELI SPECIAL OPERATIONS "SYRIAN" KAMOV KA-28 HELICOPTER
EIGHT HUNDRED FEET OVER THE MEDITERRANEAN SEA
1402 LOCAL TIME

Sucking on a toothpick, Chunk sat on the canvas bench in the cargo hold of the Israeli-acquired, Syrian-flagged, Russian-made helicopter. The bird was vibrating so badly he was grateful the last meal he'd eaten had been breakfast. The last time he'd flown in a "repurposed" Russian helicopter had been years ago in the Iraqi desert on a covert operation augmenting Task Force Ember's John Dempsey.

That helicopter had crashed.

Awesome.

But that hunk of junk had been an Mi-17, not a KA-28 maintained or upgraded by the IDF's secret Skunk Works. And also important to note: John Dempsey wasn't on this op, which meant Chunk had none of that dude's dark mission mojo to worry about. Chunk loved Dempsey like a brother, but whenever he augmented one of Dempsey's missions, the situation always seemed to go to hell regardless of the amount of preparation.

So, we have that going for us, he thought with a chuckle, which prompted him to perform one final check of his gear.

As much as Chunk loved maritime operations, he despised swimming in the open ocean. From above, the deep, blue Mediterranean Sea looked inviting. Calm, peaceful . . . harmless, even. But Chunk knew better. Every ocean had sharks—tons of them—lurking below and out of sight, ready to make a meal of him.

Thankfully, if everything went according to plan, he wouldn't be getting wet today. The plan was to fast-rope directly onto a pair of RK Tir II "Zolfaghar" missile craft—a Syrian fast boat imported from Iran based on the Iranian IPS-18—which somehow the Israelis had obtained. The boats were brand new to the Syrians and were equipped with two North Korean "Noor" anti-ship missiles each, also built in Iran under license from the DPRK. When he'd asked whether the Israelis had stolen the boats and missiles or simply reverse engineered them, Mirashi had simply smiled and shrugged.

Chunk scanned the eleven badass operators from the elite Shayetet unit as they performed the same gear and buddy checks that he—the lone American on the stick—had just completed in preparation for the infil. He and Ze'ev Mirashi, who commanded Haposhtim Unit, had agreed that they would not create blended squads of American and Israeli operators for this critical, short-fuse op. To maintain their maximum lethality and effectiveness, it was best not to introduce unnecessary variables.

Israeli intelligence had intercepted—though not yet decrypted—numerous communications between the *Dakar* and the *Earabat Albahr*, information that had given weight to Chunk's command-and-control ship theory. Fearing that other yet-to-be-identified vessels could also be part of the operation targeting Israel, Bowman had ordered Chunk be present on the stick that hit the Senegalese-flagged *Dakar* command-and-control ship while the rest of Gold Squadron took on the primary target, the *Earabat Albahr*. Chunk understood the CSO's reasoning, but being separated from his guys gave him serious heartburn. He'd lobbied to lead the *Earabat Albahr* hit, but Bowman had held firm that American leadership be present when taking the *Dakar*. That left Spence and Saw to lead two sticks of Gold Squadron SEALs for the assault on the Egyptian-flagged cargo vessel.

"Two minutes," came the voice of the pilot in his headset.

Subconsciously, Chunk cinched his rifle sling tight and refastened the straps on his gloves in preparation.

"Are you ready?" Mirashi asked, catching his eye.

"Hooyah," Chunk said and spit the toothpick out of the corner of his mouth.

A moment later, he felt the helicopter descend and flare into a hover, and the pilot reported they were on station. The rope master opened the clamshell-style cargo door on the port side and kicked out the rope bag.

"*Acha . . . acha . . . acha*," he said, which Chunk guessed meant "go"—or something like it—because the Israeli operators began to disappear out the side. After the sixth man, the rope master halted the line and radioed the helo pilot to reposition over the second fast boat.

Chunk felt the helo tilt and drift, then steady back into a hover.

The "Syrian" Zolfaghar fast boats were not big vessels. The square footage of the LZ—which, in this case, was the aft deck behind the pilothouse—was barely big enough to accommodate six. The boats had been pre-positioned by the Israeli Navy twenty-five nautical miles away and out of sight from the *Dakar* for safety; otherwise, they never would have conducted a helo fast-rope infil in broad daylight. Chunk shuffled aft, second to last, and gripped the thick, heavy rope between the insoles of his boots and with his gloves. A grin curled up the corners of his mouth as the wind buffeted him on the cargo platform. He looked down, verified the rope was dangling over the stern of the sleek-looking missile boat, and began his descent, using the friction that rapidly warmed his hands through the gloves to control his speed. He hit the deck hard but absorbed the impact with his legs working as twin shock absorbers.

He stepped clear and took a knee as Mirashi landed behind him. The Israeli team leader looked skyward and waved off the helo, which jettisoned the rope and turned east to head back to base. With everyone aboard, the Navy boat pilot, concealed from view inside the cockpit cabin, brought the boat's three twelve-hundred-horsepower engines to life. With a roar, the fast boat made a hard turn to starboard.

Chunk steadied himself on the rail as he stood up. Off to his left, he saw the second Tir II accelerating in formation with them. Chunk shuffled forward, ducking around the Israeli crewman manning the large 12.7mm machine gun on the port gunwale, and following Mirashi through the large gray oval hatch into the fully enclosed cockpit. The boat pilot, who was dressed in the old-style woodland cammies of a Syrian Navy sailor, gave Chunk a nod. Chunk nodded back and descended the three-step ladder into the large forward enclosed cabin of the seventy-foot-long missile boat. The rest of the team was already shedding their uniforms and gear into neat piles on benches that ran along the starboard hull. Ahead, a single door led to an equipment room, from which another sailor was handing out Syrian uniforms for the operators to change into. Chunk accepted his bundle and donned the Syrian Navy uniform, which was a little tight, but would suffice. He secured his personal kit, slipped a smaller green vest and kit over his head, and accepted a Russian AK-74M assault rifle that was handed to him.

He glanced at his watch. They were on schedule.

Spence and Riker would be aboard their respective Syrian Kamarov KA-28s already, with the rest of the Gold Squad shooters heading toward the *Earabat Albahr*. There would be no direct comms between the American assault force headed toward the Egyptian ship, armed with its deadly missiles, and Chunk's all-Israeli team en route to intercept the *Dakar*. Nonetheless, perfect timing would be required between the two assaults for the mission to succeed.

That was where Michelle Yi and Becker came in, back at the TOC in Jordan.

"Center, this is Sword," Chunk called after checking the frequency on his compact radio, which would send his signal back to the TOC via satellite. "Sword is India."

"Roger, Sword," said Seren Becker, the coordinator for Sword. Chief Yi would be running comms for Gold Squadron, call sign Knife. It had been agreed that Chunk, as the senior ranking officer, was in command of the overall assault, but Mirashi would lead his men in battle. "Center shows you India. Report, Juliet."

"Copy," he said and glanced at Mirashi—call sign Sword Two—and the Israeli officer shot Chunk a confident look.

"Let's keep the guys down here," Chunk said. "But you and I should head up to the bridge."

"Copy that," Mirashi said, then gave an order in Hebrew

to his men. Together they climbed the three steps back up to the cockpit, Chunk keeping his Russian-made rifle in a combat carry on his chest. They would be on target in less than an hour.

"Fingers crossed we're right and this ruse will work," he said to Mirashi as he dogged the latches on the door.

"Yes," Mirashi agreed, then gave him a wry grin. "But if everything goes to hell, we do have four anti-ship missiles at our disposal."

"Damn right," Chunk said.

But if it came to that, the mission was probably already fucked.

CHAPTER 32

KING KHALID INTERNATIONAL AIRPORT

RIYADH, SAUDI ARABIA

While Whitney waited for Thatch to return with the pilots, she couldn't stop thinking about Princess Ramia. If the Princess decided to challenge Faisal's narrative in her role as Saudi Ambassador to the US, she would certainly pay a price. If she didn't die in a tragic car accident or plane crash, then Whitney imagined Ramia's fate would probably mirror that of other wealthy women who made trouble in the Arab world: She'd be publicly shamed, stripped of her title and position and financial assets, and locked up. Whether she ended up in an actual prison or became a prisoner in her own home was of little distinction; Ramia would disappear from public life, robbed of her voice and power to influence policy and opinion.

"What's on your mind, Whit?" Theobald said, dropping into the seat across the aisle.

Theobald didn't call her Heels like Chunk and the rest of the guys. Using her dad's pet name for her, "Whit," was something new, but it didn't bother her. Bobby felt like the big brother she'd never had. She felt comfortable and at ease around him; he'd earned her implicit trust, and he never overstepped.

"I can't stop thinking about Ambassador Noor," she said, answering his question after a beat.

"She'll be safe at the embassy. Those protesters are not going to breach the embassy."

"I'm not worried about that. What I'm worried about is what's going to happen to her when she goes back to the palace. God only knows what Crown Prince Faisal will accuse her of, especially after we submit our report and the White House responds publicly."

Theobald nodded. "Yeah, it could get bad for her. But we offered her protection, and she turned it down."

Subconsciously tracing the trefoil knot tattoo on her wrist, a fresh thought came to her. "What I don't understand is, what is the King's position on all of this? Surely the King didn't authorize fratricide in his house. He named Khalid as Crown Prince and let his eldest son run the government for nearly a decade. Why would he change course now? Faisal was never groomed to lead. It doesn't make sense to me that he'd go along with Khalid's murder."

"Those are all excellent points."

Gooseflesh stood up on her forearms as an epiphany struck.

"What if King Abdul *didn't* go along with it at all? What if he's been duped from the beginning about the murder? The press release stated it was issued from the King's office, but was it really? Or was that Crown Prince Faisal's doing? Come to think of it, why a press release? For something this big, the King would have called a press conference. But we haven't seen or heard from him since the news broke. I assumed that was because he was waiting for the investigation to be completed. But what if Faisal sold the King the same bullshit assassination story he sold us? I mean, of course he did. He can't tell his father the truth."

Theobald scrubbed his face with his hands and let out a heavy exhale she could tell meant he agreed with her. He frowned and met her eyes.

"Now I'm starting to wonder if Faisal didn't just kill his brother. What if this was a twofer?" he said.

"Oh God, what if you're right? It certainly would be one way to cement his power . . ." Whitney said as her mind kept working the problem. The pieces didn't all fit. "But if so, then why wouldn't Faisal have killed them both at the same time? It would have been cleaner and simpler. He could have blamed the Israelis for both murders and have only one cover-up to manage."

"Because he doesn't want to be King," Jenn said, walking up along with Sam to join the conversation from where they'd been sitting two rows back. "He wants to be Crown Prince because that makes him the functional head of government. The King's just a figurehead."

"You're right," Theobald said. "Crown Prince is where the power is."

The sound of pounding footsteps on the airstair interrupted their conversation and drew their collective gaze to the cabin door, where their pilots were entering the jet.

"We're up to speed on everything," the pilot said to Theobald. "Thatch briefed us on the ride over. Don't worry. We're going to get you guys out of here ASAP."

"Hooah," Theobald said and gave the pilot a two-finger salute.

"We've got to go back," Whitney blurted.

Theobald screwed up his face at her. "Go back *where*?"

"To the embassy. We've got to get to Ramia before she confronts Faisal," she said, practically tripping over the words she was talking so fast.

"Whoa, whoa, whoa—we aren't going back to the embassy," Theobald said. "Our job was to investigate the assassination, collect and analyze the evidence, and report our findings to the Director of National Intelligence and the White House. We completed two of our three mission objectives. To complete the third, we need to get airborne before they ground stop this plane so we can transmit our data."

"Sam and Jenn can do that. They should definitely exfil, but you and I need to go back," she said, imploring Theobald with her eyes.

"Look, I admire your dedication or whatever to Ambassador Noor. She's a brave and impressive woman, but protecting her is not our tasking. You've got to let it go."

Feeling the crush of time, she grabbed Theobald's wrist and squeezed. "Listen to me, Bobby, my gut tells me we have a microscopic window to stop this bullshit train *before* it leaves the station and runs away down the tracks forever."

"How?" he said, the exasperated look on his face telling her that he'd yet to connect the dots.

"By telling the King the truth . . ."

Her words hit Theobald like a slap to the face. Immediately, Whitney could see he got it. "And Ramia's the key. If she can get us access to the King, and we can show him the video, then he'll have Faisal arrested."

"Exactly!"

"Provided the King's not already dead," he said.

"Yes."

"And provided Ramia can get us into the palace, past Chief

Saad and all of Faisal's security, without us getting arrested or shot . . ." he continued.

"Yeah, that too."

"*And* provided we don't get yanked out of the Suburban by a mob of angry protesters and bludgeoned to death in the streets of Riyadh."

She pressed her lips into a hard line but nodded.

"I'm really not liking this plan, Whit," Theobald said and shook his head.

"What are you guys talking about?" Mick said, walking up to them from where he'd been relieved by the pilots in the cockpit. She heard the slow, crescendo whine of the first of the two jet engines spooling up and lighting off. Her sense of urgency rose to a fever pitch.

"Mick, we need a ride back to the embassy," Whitney said, her voice pleading.

The GRS man chuckled. "That's a good one."

She winced and flashed him her best *I'm sorry* face.

"Hold on—you're actually serious?" Mick looked from Whitney to Theobald, seemingly hoping the latter would be the voice of reason. When Theobald didn't contradict her, the operator said, "Ah shit, we're really doing this?"

Theobald nodded. "Afraid so. We'll brief you and Thatch in on the ride back."

"Are you guys sure about this?" Sam said, speaking up for the first time.

Whitney rose and turned to the big guy. "You're a rock star, Sam." She shifted her gaze to Mullican. "And so are you, Jenn. Thank you both for everything. So long as you guys transmit our findings, the mission objectives are complete. Which is why we have to split up. If there's a chance to stop Faisal and have the King tell the world the truth about what happened, then it's worth the risk. It's not just Ramia's life hanging in the balance. Millions of lives are potentially at risk if the Middle East goes to war. We have to try."

"So, I guess the rumors I heard about you are true," Jenn said, narrowing her eyes at Whitney.

"What rumors?"

Jenn clapped her hand on Whitney's shoulder. "That you're a hell of an analyst who's got balls of steel."

CHAPTER 33

SYRIAN-FLAGGED TIR II MISSILE BOAT
POSITIONED TWENTY-TWO HUNDRED YARDS FROM THE *DAKAR*
NINETY-SEVEN MILES WEST OF HAIFA, ISRAEL
MEDITERRANEAN SEA
1509 LOCAL TIME

From inside the small bridge of the missile boat, Chunk used the range-finding binoculars to study the merchant ship *Dakar* through the small square windows of the pilothouse. So far, the target ship had made no moves or given any indication that it was aware of their presence.

Unless they're nothing more than a cargo vessel after all . . .

"They must know we're here by now," Chunk mumbled to Mirashi as he scanned the empty foredeck of the ship.

Their sleek, low-profile fast boat had a tiny radar signature, but it was broad daylight and the middle of the afternoon. From the elevated pilothouse of the *Dakar*, their missile boat would be easily visible with binoculars at this range.

If I'm looking at them, then they can be looking at me.

"How sure are we of the intel regarding that Iranian MOIS operative Heydari?" Chunk said. "Are we positive he's on board?"

"High degree of confidence," Mirashi said. "I can't remember receiving bad intelligence from the task force within Shin Bet that provided this information. If they said Heydari boarded this vessel, then he boarded it."

"Look, I believe that Heydari boarded this ship when y'all said he did. But that was two weeks ago. Two weeks is a long time, and I assume you guys haven't had eyes on this ship twenty-four seven since then. For all we know, Heydari could have gotten off in a different port . . ." Chunk said, his thoughts running ahead.

"Maybe."

"And even if Heydari is still on board, it doesn't necessarily tell us what *Dakar* and the *Earabat Albahr* are up to, does it?"

Chunk's question was rhetorical, but he imagined Mirashi got the sentiment. It was entirely possible that the *Dakar* was *not* a command-and-control ship, and they were wasting time and resources on a red herring. He lifted the glasses to his eyes again and scanned the ship, looking for shooters at least.

"Maybe it is a little late to be questioning such things, my friend. We're here. We've committed to this op," the Israeli said with a hint of annoyance.

"I know. I'm sorry. Sometimes I can't help myself. Something just feels off to me," he said, still scanning. "I don't see any activity topside. Not even a roving watch."

"It is not unusual to see little visible activity topside on a merchant vessel, especially during transit," Mirashi reassured him. "Also, keep in mind, if *Dakar* is also serving as command and control, all the important people and activity will be in ship's communications suite."

"Mm-hmm," Chunk said as he continued his scan of the

vessel. "Weren't there two CONEX boxes on the deck on the satellite imagery Yi showed us when we briefed in Amman?"

"I think so. Why?" Mirashi said.

"Looks like there's only one now," Chunk replied, then keyed the radio on his kit. "Center, Sword One."

"Sword, Center—go ahead," Michelle Yi's voice answered immediately.

"Center, confirm you have eyes on the *Dakar*," Chunk said.

"Affirmative," Yi replied.

"How many CONEX boxes do you see on the main deck?"

She came back after a brief pause. "I see one."

"Sword Two and I seem to remember two on the imagery of the ship when we briefed in Amman, pre-op."

"Let me check. Standby . . . Looks like your memory is spot-on; there were two."

"What happened to the other one?"

"I don't know," she said, her tone almost a question. "They have a deck crane. Maybe they moved it to a cargo hold below-decks."

"How long have you had continuous eyes on *Dakar*?"

"Since 1330 local. A little over ninety minutes. Is there a problem? I can look back through the satellite history and see what I can see, if you want?"

Chunk hesitated. Yi didn't have time for that, and it probably didn't matter anyway. The rest of Gold should be on final approach to raid the *Earabat Albahr* in two of the Israeli-modified Syrian-flagged Kamarov KA-28s. Yi supporting that op was the priority.

"SITREP on Knife?" Chunk asked, asking for an update on his teammates.

"Less than ten miles to Beneteau," Yi replied, using the code for the final position point for the assault on the other ship. Once they had control of the vessel, they would call, "Jackpot."

"Roger that. Don't worry about the CONEX box for now," Chunk said.

"It's okay. I'll try to find a resource here who can help out and look into it, Sword," she said, not dismissing his weird hunch like so many other people might.

Which is why I love having Chief Yi on my team.

The Israeli boat driver tapped Mirashi, who was standing next to Chunk, on the shoulder.

"We're being hailed on channel sixteen by the *Dakar*, sir," the soldier said.

"Put it on the speaker, Tevie," Mirashi replied, and the boat pilot flipped a switch.

Chunk heard the hail but could not make out what the caller was saying. The conversation was in Arabic, and his vocabulary was limited.

"They are asking for us to identify ourselves and if there is a problem," the Shayetet 13 operator named Tevie said.

Mirashi looked at Chunk, who gave an affirmative nod. They had anticipated this and war-gamed out their response. Every minute stalling would help improve the odds of mission success.

"Tell them we've been dispatched as a security escort, to keep them safe on their important journey. Tell them our presence is to serve as a deterrent to the Jews and the American Navy, who may be operating in the area."

Tevie gave Mirashi a thumbs-up, then reached for the microphone and repeated the message in Arabic.

A pause followed, long enough to make Chunk's pulse pick up, but when the radio talker on *Dakar* responded, his voice sounded calm.

"They said they are grateful for the protection," Tevie translated.

"Let them know our two ships will be taking positions on the port and starboard sides of *Dakar* amidships, with five hundred meters of separation to defend them from any threats," Chunk said, and Tevie spoke the message into the radio.

"Dani," Mirashi said to one of the two operators sitting at a weapons control panel on the port side of the pilothouse. "You are comfortable with the firing controls on the missiles?"

"Yes, Seren," the man answered, using Mirashi's rank.

"Plot a firing solution on the *Dakar* and have our teammates on the other boat do the same. Understand that if and when the time comes, the objective is to disable—not sink the *Dakar*, but disable."

"Yes, sir," came the curt reply.

Mirashi slipped past Chunk and stuck his head out of the hatch onto the deck, where two Shayetet 13 operators stood, both clad in Syrian Navy uniforms. He shouted in Hebrew for them to man the 12.7mm machine guns port and starboard. "We can look and be prepared at the same time," Mirashi said with a crooked grin to Chunk.

"Agree completely," Chunk said, reflexively tightening his grip on the Russian-made assault rifle slung across his chest.

The question whether the *Dakar* was a command-and-control ship would be answered very soon. When the rest of Gold squad hit the *Earabat Albahr*, how the *Dakar* reacted would tell Chunk everything he needed to know.

CHAPTER 34

AIRPORT ROAD

KING KHALID INTERNATIONAL AIRPORT

1412 LOCAL TIME

At Theobald's insistence, Whitney grudgingly agreed to sit in the seat behind Mick on the passenger side—the side without the busted-out window—while Theobald took her original seat. She wasn't thrilled about the prospect of having to navigate the gauntlet of protesters outside the American Embassy a second time. The first time had almost been game over for her, and that time the SUV had had all its windows. But Theobald was right—they needed Noor if they were to have any hope of getting into the palace.

As soon as they exited the tarmac security checkpoint and turned east on Airport Road, she broached the topic of how exactly they were going to do things differently this time around.

"I'm just sayin', if I keep enough speed on, they're going to move out of the way," Thatch said.

"In theory, I agree with you, but what if they don't? Are you just going to run them over?" Mick fired back.

Thatch let out an exasperated exhale, then, with chilling sobriety, said, "Hopefully, we can avoid them completely. But if not, I can promise you one thing, dude: I ain't letting them take us."

Their mobile phones still had no service, which meant no comms with Post One at the embassy. But Mick had radioed ahead from the cockpit to let the Ambassador and American Embassy security know that Whitney and Theobald were returning. At the time of the call, the mob of angry protesters was still outside the front gate and gaining in numbers.

With protesters blocking the main entrance, they needed another way in. The perimeter of the embassy compound was secured by a ten-foot concrete wall, but there was a secondary access point on the west side of the compound to service foot traffic. Under Ambassador Harley's tenure, that entrance had been closed, but Mick and Theobald's infil plan was to use that entrance anyway and avoid the front altogether. The head of security at the embassy had concurred and promised the gate would be manned and ready to receive the team on arrival.

"Well, let's hope we can make it to the west gate without them seeing us," Theobald said from the back, trying to ease the tension between Mick and Thatch.

"Hope ain't a strategy, bro," Mick said.

Theobald was about to reply, when something caught his attention. He pointed out the front windshield. "We've got incoming . . ."

Whitney squinted and saw a caravan of three black SUVs inbound on Airport Road about a half mile ahead.

"Get low," Mick barked as he dropped down in the front passenger seat so that his head was below the dashboard.

Whitney and Theobald did as instructed, both crouching in the footwell between the front captain's chairs and the middle row. She saw Theobald wince as he repositioned.

"You all right?" she asked.

"Yeah, just cut my knee kneeling on a shard of glass," he said. They'd brushed off the seats, but the floor inside the SUV was still littered with pieces of the window.

"Do you think they're coming for us?" she asked him.

"Yes, but I doubt they know that we split up and half our party didn't board."

"That airport security guard Nadim knows."

"True, but I'm hoping whoever these guys are, they haven't talked to Nadim yet."

She nodded at Theobald and prayed he was right. If not, the massive gamble they'd taken would be all for nothing. Heart pounding like a bass drum in her chest, she waited, knees and quads complaining as she crouched in between the seats.

"Here they come . . ." Thatch said, his voice a tight cord. "Man, they're really hauling ass."

A beat later, Whitney heard the roar of a dozen tires on pavement as the inbound Saudi convoy screamed past them at speed to their left-hand side. Nobody spoke. Whitney felt Thatch accelerating.

"I think we're good . . ." Thatch said. "They didn't even look at me as they went by."

"Let's keep low until we're on the highway heading back. Just to be sure," Mick said.

"Roger that," Theobald said from his crouch.

When another thirty seconds passed by without incident, Whitney exhaled with relief and traded glances with Theobald. He flashed her an *easy-day* grin, which made her wonder how Chunk and the boys were doing on their tasking. Hell, did they even have tasking? She'd been so completely immersed in her own mission that she had no idea what the rest of Gold was up to. And without comms and cell service, she was completely disconnected from the world outside the Kingdom. But if the mob outside the embassy in Riyadh was any indicator, the Middle East was likely in chaos following the "King's" announcement about the Mossad assassinating Crown Prince Khalid. If Gold wasn't engaged already, things were about to get very busy for America's most lethal and capable special operations unit. She knew with near-absolute certainty that Iran would capitalize on the opportunity and give its proxies the green light to unleash hell on Israel.

Which was why her latest self-imposed emergent tasking had to succeed.

"All right, I think it's safe for you guys to sit up," Thatch said.

Whitney wormed her way out of the tight spot between the seats she'd been crouching in and back into the captain's chair. Her lower legs and feet immediately tingled with pins and needles as blood flow was restored. Then something happened to her that had never happened before: She found herself wanting to be armed. In her role at the Tier One, she had no need to carry, concealed or otherwise. She didn't mind her colleagues carrying—in fact, she preferred it so she didn't have to—but despite forcing herself to spend time at the range and become increasingly proficient with firearms, she didn't like them.

Right now, though, as they sped toward what was increasingly feeling like the lion's den, Whitney desperately wanted a pistol.

"Can I get a weapon?" she said, tapping Mick on the shoulder.

"Yep." He bent forward to retrieve one from a lockbox. He handed her a coyote-brown Glock 19 in a universal IWB holster with a belt clip. "This is the only holster I got."

"It'll do," she said, pulling the pistol from the holster. She pulled the slide back to check the chamber and found it empty. With comfortable efficiency, she ejected the mag and checked it. This pistol was equipped with the 19's standard-issue fifteen-round double-stack magazine and was topped off with what appeared to be 9mm hollow points. Satisfied, she drove the mag home and racked the slide to ready the weapon for action. She returned it to the holster, which she slid inside her pants above her right hip, affixing the clip to her waistband before letting her blouse drape over the top of it.

Now, packing heat, she felt better.

She looked out the windshield to check their progress, then turned to Theobald.

"Do you think they made it airborne before the security squad arrived?" she asked him. It was a pointless question, because obviously he was with her in the same information vacuum, but it was also the kind of question people ask each other anyway. Sometimes the heart needed a little hope and reassurance, even if it was false hope and reassurance . . .

Theobald pressed his lips together into a tight line, then nodded. "Yeah, my gut tells me they did."

"Mine too," she said. That was a lie—her gut was decidedly noncommittal on the matter—but regardless, she did feel a little better.

"I think you should carry this," Theobald said.

She turned to look at him. Theobald was offering the USB thumb drive with a copy of security footage of Crown Prince Khalid's murder that Sam had hacked from the palace servers.

"Why?" she asked, hesitating.

"I don't know . . . just a feeling it will be safer with you."

"All right," she said, accepting the little device with the stored pixels that could change the course of history.

It seemed highly unlikely Chief Saad would let her and Theobald reenter the palace. Most likely they'd be arrested on sight. Which was why they were going to the embassy first—so they could war-game out a plan with Noor to get access to the King. She reached under her blouse and deposited the USB drive inside the bra cup cradling her left breast. This particular bra had little pouches to hold gel inserts to make her look bigger if the outfit demanded, and the bottom of the empty pouch was a perfect spot to hide the memory stick. She looked up to find Theobald watching with a bemused look on his face.

"You just wanted to see where I'd hide it, didn't you?" she said, narrowing her eyes at him.

"The thought never crossed my mind."

"Yeah, right," she said, a smile breaking through.

"Three minutes out," Mick said, interrupting the banter. "Get ready."

"Approaching from the west," Thatch said, talking loudly to be heard over the road and wind noise. "I'm not going anywhere near the main gate, so hopefully the protesters won't spot us."

"Agreed," Theobald said. "What's the abort criteria?"

"If both gates are mobbed, we bail," Thatch said. "But technically, the US Embassy is American soil. If y'all want to shoot our way in, I'm game."

"Not an option," Mick said. "We're not engaging Saudi civilians under any circumstance."

Thatch grumbled under his breath.

Whitney, of course, agreed with Mick, but Thatch made

an interesting point: If they could just get onto embassy property, they were within their rights to defend themselves.

Thatch made a right turn, and Mick jumped on him for it.

"Bro, al-Idrisi does not go straight through. They got barriers up at the intersection with al-Bouzjani. You gotta go around."

"Dude, this is not my first rodeo," Thatch fired back. "I'm doing a flyby to surveil the west gate on the other side of the barriers. If it's clear, then I'll cut over on S street. But once we get in there, it ain't easy to turn around, so I want to know what we're dealing with."

"Good idea," Mick said, relaxing. "I didn't know jarheads could think two steps ahead."

"We have to. Otherwise, how else can we rescue Army when you get lost?"

Whitney couldn't help but grin. The exchange reminded her of Saw and Riker busting each other's chops at every opportunity.

"Shit . . . that's not good," Mick said as the Suburban drove past a row of concrete barriers on the right.

Whitney gazed out the passenger-side window at the throng of protesters gathered in front of what she surmised was the west security gate of the embassy. The crowd was smaller than what they'd encountered at the front gate but numbered in the dozens—enough people that getting out of the SUV and clearing the checkpoint would be impossible without a physical confrontation. Her stomach sank as Thatch continued around the bend, putting the gate behind them as the Suburban looped around to the west.

"What do you guys want to do?" Thatch said, glancing at them in the rearview mirror.

"I have an idea," Theobald said. "If memory serves, there's a ten-foot gap between the compound wall and the exterior walls of the embassy buildings. It's like a buffer with palm trees and shrubs, right?"

"More like fifteen feet wide, but yes, that's right," Mick said.

"Well, how about if Thatch drives us to the north side and pulls the Suburban alongside the wall. The roof is every bit of six and a half feet tall, but if we climb out the sunroof, we can reach the top of the wall and go up and over. Once on the other side, we can walk around to the west gate and meet the security team there, and they can let us into the building."

"I'm all in. Mick?" Thatch said.

Mick didn't respond for a beat, then nodded. "Let's do it. But, Thatch, you'll need to exfil in the vehicle. We can't leave this thing parked there, or the protesters will follow our lead."

"Obviously."

Whitney chuckled. *These guys bicker like brothers.*

Three minutes later, Thatch had navigated inside the barriers to the perimeter road around the embassy and was heading northeast on al-Idrisi Street.

"That's good," Mick said, pointing to an empty stretch of road along the wall just ahead. "Pull along here. Get as close as you can."

Thatch braked to a stop less than a foot from the wall. "Close enough for you?"

Mick opened the sunroof with the button on the cabin ceiling. "All right, you guys first," he said to Whitney and Theobald.

Whitney stepped up on the center console armrest and stood up. She rotated so that her upper torso was out of the sunroof facing backward, then, with a grunt, pressed up, with her palms on the sides of the sunroof, and climbed out onto the roof panel.

"Yikes, the roof's friggin' hot," she said, scrambling to get to her feet as the red-hot sheet metal burned her hands and knees.

Once standing, she turned to face the embassy perimeter wall. The Suburban's roof was tall, but the top of the wall was about even with her armpits. Getting up there would still be tricky. To her left, she could see Theobald climbing up to join her.

"Uh-oh," Theobald said as he rose to standing height beside her on the roof.

"Uh-oh, what?" she said.

"We've got company," he said. He nodded toward where his gaze was focused in the distance behind her.

She turned to see a pair of male Arab protesters—who had apparently made their way around the corner of the perimeter wall—pointing and talking animatedly.

"They must have seen us drive by," she said.

Mick, whose torso was sticking out of the sunroof, cursed as one of the men turned and yelled in the direction of the west gate.

He's calling the mob, Whitney realized, her heart rate spiking.

"We gotta scoot," Theobald said and planted the sole of his right foot against the vertical surface of the concrete wall to brace himself in a sort of leaning tripod. Next, he knitted his fingers together to make a U-shaped foot sling and held it at waist level. "Step here. I'll give you a boost."

Not hesitating a second, Whitney placed her hand on her partner's shoulder, grabbed the top of the wall with her other, and stepped into Theobald's hands.

"Ready," she said.

He boosted her up onto the wall with the perfect momentum for her to swing her lead leg over and straddle the top but not fall off. The second she stabilized she looked south toward the corner of the perimeter wall. Where there had just been two guys, now there were a dozen angry protesters, several of whom were holding cricket bats. Once they had sufficient numbers, she thought, they'd charge. *Funny how courage works.* The analyst in her wondered if there was a mathematical function that could describe it.

"Hurry up, guys. They're coming," Whitney said, glancing back to her teammates.

That's when one of the protesters yelled an angry, indiscernible battle cry, and the mob began to charge. Theobald lunged and—with annoyingly little effort—hoisted himself atop the wall to sit across from her. At the same time, Mick scrambled to climb out of the sunroof and turned to face the sprinting crowd. She watched him reflexively reach for his weapon, then reconsider. Instead, he grabbed the top of the wall and did a press-up, getting up on one knee the same way Whitney climbed out of swimming pools.

The leading edge of the charging pack reached the Suburban a heartbeat later, and rioters started smashing, shouting, and climbing.

"Go!" Mick shouted.

The Suburban's engine roared, and the big SUV's tires squealed as Thatch exfiltrated with extreme prejudice. Whitney watched a duo of protesters—one who was climbing onto the roof and a second already standing on the rear bumper—go flying. This seemed to enrage the crowd even more, and they immediately turned their attention on the three people sitting on the top of the wall.

"Hang and drop," Theobald said, just as a rock sailed through the air right between his and Whitney's foreheads.

Not wasting a second, Whitney swung her right leg over to the embassy side of the wall and tried to twist and lower herself while hanging on. Her grip slipped, and she hit the ground hard but rolled out of the fall as best she could, ending up on her side on the packed sandy earth. Theobald landed with a thud three feet beside her, but he managed to stay on his feet. Mick dropped next, landing on both feet before rolling like she had.

"Sonuvabitch, I should have shot that fucker," Mick growled as he got to a knee and pulled up his pant leg.

Whitney sat up and winced as her ankle barked with pain.

"What happened?" Theobald asked.

"Dude jumped and hit me in the shin with a cricket bat before I could get my leg over," Mick said.

A rock sailed over the top of the fence and hit the side of the closest building ten feet away.

"Whit, you all right?" Theobald asked, walking over to her.

"I tweaked my ankle on the landing, but I think so," she said.

Theobald extended a hand to her. She grabbed his wrist, and he pulled her to her feet.

"Can you put weight on it?" he asked.

She took a tentative step. It hurt, but the pain was manageable. "Yeah, I'm good."

"What about you, Mick?"

"I'm five by," the GRS operator said and got to his feet.

"US Marines. Put your hands up and don't move!" a baritone male voice barked from the gap between the wall and the building behind Mick.

WW"Didn't realize you were LALO-ing in, Mick," the older of the two Marines said with a grin.

"Yeah, well, I had to change tactics when we saw that welcome party you had waiting for us at the west gate," Mick said.

A rock flew over the wall and landed a foot away from Whitney's left heel. The Marine shook his head, chuckled, then waved a hand for them to follow.

"C'mon, let's get you three inside before you get stoned to death. We've reestablished comms, and there's somebody waiting to talk to you."

CHAPTER 35

LEAD SYRIAN KAMAROV KA-28 IN FLIGHT OF TWO

CALL SIGN THUNDER ONE

122 NAUTICAL MILES WEST-NORTHWEST OF HAIFA, ISRAEL

EIGHT HUNDRED FEET AGL

1520 LOCAL TIME

Sitting in the crew compartment of the very strange-looking twin-rotor Russian helicopter, Nick Sawyer tapped the pocket on his kit that held his favorite family picture. Saw carried it on every op, safely tucked inside a Velcro closure positioned on his center-left chest, directly over his heart. Memories of the weekend trip with the family and Chunk and Heels to Universal Studios and the Homestead NASCAR race swirled around in his mind like a merry-go-round. It had been a great bonding weekend, and he was grateful to Chunk, and the generous sponsor, for gifting the opportunity. He could never afford something like that on his own, and the memories they'd banked were priceless.

He was also grateful for Chunk's patience and counsel over the past year as he wrestled with the decision about whether to stay active duty with Gold or retire from the unit. For Saw, and other guys with families, being a SEAL often felt like a schizophrenic battle between duty and guilt. His brothers on the pointy tip needed him, but so did his family. When he was serving one obligation, he couldn't help but feel guilty about not supporting the other. If he retired, anything that happened to his brothers in Gold because he wasn't there with them would haunt Saw forever and make a damaged husband and father. But if he stayed and something happened to him on a mission, he knew it would crush Ellie and the kids. At the end of the day, he realized, there was no ideal choice for his family.

That was the curse of being a family man on the Teams.

But despite the twin demons of obligation and guilt, he never let himself forget that he lived a blessed life.

If I had to do it over again, I wouldn't change a thing.

He felt the oddly-shaped helicopter flare her nose upward to slow their forward progress, a maneuver that snapped him back to the present. He forced an adorable memory of Maggie "finger painting" with nacho cheese at the NASCAR race out of his mind. He needed his headspace clear, quiet, and fully focused on the mission.

It was almost go time.

After Saw had chosen *not* to retire, Chunk had challenged him to take on a greater leadership role on the team. That was why he had volunteered to lead this stick and fast-rope onto the stern of a target ship with Riker, Trip, Antman, and Edwards instead of staying aboard the KA-28 to provide sniper overwatch from the door of the helo. Mike Rossing, the lead sniper from Bravo platoon, was aboard the other bird and would take that role on for today's mission. Meanwhile, Spence would lead four SEALs from Bravo and land on the bow of the *Earabat Albahr* at the exact same time.

"Two minutes," came the accented voice of the Israeli helicopter pilot in his ear.

It was time for Saw to get his game face on. He removed his fingers from the pocket over his heart and let his hands fly over his kit in a final ceremonial check. The clamshell port cargo doors were now open, and the aircrewman, another Israeli from Shayetet 13, put both feet on the coil of rope, ready to push it out.

"The *Earabat Albahr*'s bridge is hailing us on Guard," the pilot said, now in his ear, referring to the universal emergency frequency for aircraft of 121.5. "The ship's captain is warning us off."

Saw clenched his teeth, knowing Spence would be receiving the same information.

"Tell them we're here for a routine security inspection or something," Saw said. "Say whatever. Just buy time."

"Check," the pilot said and started talking in Arabic on the radio.

Staring out the open cargo hatch, Saw watched armed fighters begin to pour out of the superstructure onto the deck, where a dozen or more CONEX boxes—believed to house land-attack missiles and launchers—were chained down. The fact these fighters were taking cover behind deck machinery and anything but the CONEX boxes confirmed—in Saw's mind, at least—that the shipping containers held the weapons of war that Israeli intelligence had reported.

"Knife Two, this is One," said Spence's voice in Saw's headset.

"Two, go," Saw replied.

"I think we should assume they radioed the Syrian Navy, and they know we're impostors. I say we go in hot." Spence could have given it as an order, but he wanted Saw's read on things.

Saw clenched his jaw, looking down at the handful of

fighters lined up on the rail, pointing Iranian-made assault weapons up at them.

An order would have been easier to handle . . .

But he was pretty sure Spence was right. These guys sure as shit no longer thought of them as allies, or they wouldn't be pointing rifles at them, right?

"Let's do it," he said, then keyed the mic for internal comms with the aircrew. "Gun run ahead of the insertion?"

"Agreed," Spence said. "Guns instead of rockets. I don't wanna blow up anything sensitive on the deck."

"Roger," was all he could think to say. He knew that nuclear weapons—if there were nukes—shouldn't detonate by getting shot at. But what if the terrorist shitheads had rigged some sort of booby trap that detonated the missile propellant or the set charges inside the containers? It wasn't unusual for zealots from outfits like Sayf Allah to send themselves to paradise when things got rough—so long as they sent some infidels to hell on the way, it was mission accomplished.

"Gents, looks like a hot infil. Guns will clear the deck," he said to his stick, though he knew they would have heard in their own earpieces. "Be wicked fast on and off the rope."

Saw got thumbs-up all around and felt the tension grow inside the helicopter. He listened to the chatter between the pilots of the two birds after Spence gave the order as they worked out their respective gun runs and insertions. Saw's left hand migrated, seemingly with a will of its own, back to the pocket on his chest where he kept the family picture.

"Thirty seconds," the pilot said.

Rifle cinched tight against his chest, Saw moved aft to the edge of the door and gripped the rope hanging from the mount above him. He trained on breaching and hot infils all the time, so he shouldn't have felt naked without his sniper rifle.

But he did.

The helicopter banked hard left as the helo came up to the starboard side of the cargo ship, pulling the nose-mounted twin 7.62mm machine guns onto the target. Saw leaned out the door for a better look as the pilot dragged the nose across the ship, squeezing off four separate bursts of the machine guns as he did and tearing apart the terrorists who never even had a chance to return fire.

Spence's bird on the other side would not have that luxury when it repeated the maneuver. All illusions about the true identity of the "Syrian" helicopters were now gone.

The nose dipped, the helo dropped, and Saw's feet felt light on the deck, then instantly heavy as the pilot leveled them off and spun the nose over the fantail for a perfectly positioned hover.

"Go, go, go!" the Israeli rope master hollered and kicked the rope out of the helo.

The heavy black coils dropped and hit the ship's deck just fifteen feet below. Saw was first out, boots locked on the rope and both hands gripping tightly through thick assault gloves. During the fast descent, he scanned for threats and saw two enemy shooters emerge from a door on the superstructure.

Saw landed hard, took two steps left to clear the LZ, and brought his rifle up. Taking a knee, he sighted on the tangos who were running full tilt toward him, rifles up. He positioned his red targeting dot onto the face of the closer threat, the image magnified for him by the VMX-3T he had installed behind the Vortex red dot holographic sight. He squeezed the trigger, and the target pitched backward. At the same moment, Riker fast-roped in from above and landed beside Saw with a thud. Saw shifted his aim left and placed his red dot center mass on the second tango, who had stopped and was taking aim.

Saw squeezed twice in rapid succession, dropping the fighter before he got off a shot.

Saw rose and angled left in a combat crouch. On his right, Riker fell in beside him, scanning over his assault rifle as they moved as a pair forward along the port rail toward the superstructure. He was just about to call, "Beneteau," and let the TOC know they had breached the ship, when something caught his eye.

A sudden glint of light, high up on the superstructure . . .

His breath stuck in his chest as he saw the flicker, high up on the starboard side of the towering pilothouse. His brain identified the glint of light as sunlight reflected off a sniper scope. A split second later, he saw the puff of smoke and the muzzle flash.

The bullet tore through Saw's throat, but to his astonishment, it didn't hurt.

He stumbled but didn't fall.

His hands went reflexively to his throat, where he now felt a burning pain, but his eyes stayed locked on the 05-level flying bridge where the shooter was in cover. Saw's sniper-trained brain reflexively worked the firing solution—elevation and wind compensations—for the return shot he would never get to take. One of the KA-28s streaked past in his peripheral vision, fire and smoke trailing from the nose as the pilot annihilated the flying bridge with his 30mm cannon, completely evaporating the balcony and sniper in one salvo.

Riker turned to Saw, wearing the victorious, shit-eating grin that Saw loved so much.

"Holy shit, I am untouchable, bro," Riker bellowed. "I swear I could hear that round as it zipped past my—"

But the SEAL breacher stopped short, his eyes went wide, and all the color drained from his face as his gaze went to Saw's neck.

Saw felt his legs give out.

He sensed himself falling and braced for the pain of impacting the deck, but it never came because Riker caught him. His brother SEAL was talking to him. Telling something important, he knew, but Saw couldn't hear the words.

Darkness crept across his field of view, like an eclipse blotting out the sun.

And as his fingers fumbled for the picture he kept in the pocket over his heart, he thought, *Oh God, Ellie's going to be so mad at me . . .*

CHAPTER 36

SYRIAN-FLAGGED TIR II MISSILE BOAT
ESCORTING THE SENEGALESE-FLAGGED *DAKAR*
MEDITERRANEAN SEA
1531 LOCAL TIME

Chunk shifted his stance wide and bent his knees deep to keep his balance as the fast boat rolled with the waves. His body felt like a compressed spring—loaded with potential energy ready to explode into kinetic action. Thankfully, he didn't have to wait long.

"Sword, Center—be advised Knife is Beneteau," reported the voice of the Israeli intelligence officer named Becker in Chunk's ear.

"Center, Sword One copies," Chunk said and turned to Mirashi. "It's go time."

The Israeli gave him a confident smile. "We are set. The ascension gear is in place, and the assault team are in harnesses."

Chunk clenched his teeth. Mirashi's men would make the initial breach of the vessel, with the two officers following when the deck was secure. Chunk was a SEAL, and in the Teams—most especially in the Tier One—he was accustomed to leading from the front. But he'd also taken Bowman's advice to heart that Chunk begin to think like a staff officer. If he was shot and killed on the initial assault, there were a ton of life-and-death decisions that would have to be made by someone else . . .

"Seren Mirashi," the boat driver named Tevie said, his voice an urgent and tight cord. "The captain of the *Dakar* is hailing us on channel sixteen again. He has demanded that we stand off immediately."

"Ze'ev," came a voice from outside as the hatch to the aft deck was jerked open. "Sir, personnel on the *Dakar* are manning weapons on the rails."

Chunk knew exactly what that meant. The assault on the *Earabat Albahr* a hundred miles away had already been reported, leading the crew here on the *Dakar* to radio the Syrian Navy to find out the truth about the legitimacy of their two missile boat "escorts."

"Sword One, Center," came Becker's equally urgent voice. "Be advised there is activity on the deck. They are opening the CONEX box on the deck. We don't know what's inside that container . . . but if it *is* a CJ-10 cruise missile . . ."

"This is supposed to be the command-and-control ship," Chunk said, turning to Mirashi. "The *Earabat Albahr* was the vessel your intelligence team identified as the missile threat."

"Yes, but if they are working together, maybe this vessel is carrying weapons too."

"If they do have a CJ-10, how long to set up and fire?" Chunk barked.

"They can be set up to fire in less than fifteen minutes, if the box indeed has a launcher and has missiles loaded already," Becker said. "Perhaps thirty minutes or more, if not."

"Shit," Chunk said. He turned to Mirashi. "I say we disable the ship and assault now."

"I agree," Mirashi said. He turned to the boat pilot. "Reposition and open range in preparation to fire missiles and disable the ship," he said. "Notify the pilot on Sword Three to do the same."

"Yes, sir," the boat driver said and initiated a sweeping starboard turn, maneuvering them around in what Chunk guessed would be a 270-degree arc to get into missile-firing position.

"What are my targeting instructions, Ze'ev?" the missile operator asked, worry on his face.

"We fire above the waterline. We don't want to sink the ship; we want to commandeer it," Mirashi said.

"What about the CONEX box on the main deck? I could try to target it and destroy whatever weapon they're accessing," the operator said.

Mirashi pursed his lips and turned to Chunk. "Intelligence put the missiles with possible nuke warheads on the *Earabat Albahr*. But what if we're wrong? This ship embarked with Heydari from the Iranian port of Bandar Abbas. The Iranians could have loaded the nuclear weapon on this ship and the conventional missiles on the other. It could explain why Heydari is on this ship."

"All the more reason to blow that container to hell," Chunk said, pretty confident that if antiballistic missile systems like the Patriot could shoot down incoming ICBMs without detonating the nuclear warheads, the same principle should hold true here.

"Agreed," Mirashi said and turned to his Shayetet 13 teammate manning the missile control console. "Target the CONEX container on the main deck with missile one and the stern above the waterline with missile two."

The operator repeated the order just as incoming rifle fire began to ping off the pilothouse of their fast boat. The ballistic glass in the square windows held, despite starring pretty badly, but they would not hold indefinitely.

"Gunners, return fire."

A heartbeat later, the Israeli machine gunners on the Tir II began strafing the deck and pilothouse of the *Dakar*. The twin deck-mounted machine guns continued to belch out deadly rounds toward the target ship as they swept through the turn.

"Breachers, check gear," Chunk ordered. "We're boarding immediately after ship-to-ship missiles are fired." And with a hard, confident stare, he added, "And, Mirashi, we're leading this assault from the front."

CHAPTER 37

KING KHALID INTERNATIONAL AIRPORT
RIYADH, SAUDI ARABIA
1527 LOCAL TIME

Sam Octavius felt more than a little guilty fleeing to safety while Watts and Theobald headed back into the lion's den. He glanced at Jenn Mullican and could see from the expression on her face that she wasn't happy about it either. The team had only been together briefly, but they'd bonded. More than that, they'd succeeded. The combination of Jenn's forensic badassery, his mad cyberskills, Watts's ability to befriend and leverage Ambassador Noor, and Theobald's leadership had made them one of the most effective investigation teams he'd ever been a part of.

He chuckled to himself.

Never mind that it was the *only* murder investigation task force he'd ever been a part of.

"I hate splitting up like this," Jenn said, her mental antenna tuned to the same frequency as his own. "I feel like

I'm sneaking away with my tail between my legs while they put their lives on the line."

"Me too." He blew air through his pursed lips. "I just tell myself that if we don't leave and complete the mission by transmitting our findings, the mission will fail. They're counting on us to do that. We'd be letting them down if we didn't."

"Yeah, I guess," she said.

He turned to see if the airstair was still down. The pilot had gone outside to double-check something before takeoff. Through the porthole window on his left, he detected movement that drew his eye and made him swivel in his seat for a better look.

Three black SUVs were hauling ass toward the plane.

"Oh shit," he said.

"What?" Jenn said, her eyes going wide.

"We've got company," he said.

Supercharged with adrenaline, Sam popped to his feet, ducked through the tiny hatch, and leaped off the top step of the airstair. He landed with a thud on the ground and was greeted with a blast of reflected heat from the tarmac. Not seeing the pilot on the port side anywhere, he took a knee and scanned under the fuselage for a pair of legs. There was the pilot, standing on the exact opposite side of the plane near the starboard aft quarter. He glanced back at the inbound Saudi security convoy and guessed he had less than a minute until they were surrounded.

He glanced up and saw Jenn standing at the top of the airstair, her body just inside the hatch. She was looking out at him.

"Tell the copilot to start the starboard engine and turn us around!" he shouted.

She nodded and disappeared.

Heart pounding, Sam ran in a crouch to the nose of the plane, pulled the bright yellow chocks on either side of the front landing gear, and threw them clear with all his strength. Then, arms pumping and legs churning like pistons, he sprinted around the plane to get the pilot.

"Dude, Saudi security is inbound. We gotta friggin' go!" he said.

To the pilot's credit, he didn't argue, question, or hesitate. He just took off in a full run to get back to the cockpit. Sam checked the port and starboard rear landing gear for chocks, and by the time he got to the airstair, the pilot was aboard and the plane was starting to turn, with the starboard engine spooling up. Sam leaped up onto the airstair. At the top, he whirled and saw that the Saudi SUVs were fanning out to encircle and blockade the jet.

Shit, shit, shit, he cursed, his mind seeing that it was game over.

But even though the rational part of his brain had conceded defeat, his body seemed to have a different opinion on the matter. As if acting of its own free will, his right hand reached back and found the pistol grip of the Smith & Wesson MP9 Shield in his SOB holster. His right hand brought the pistol around and sighted on the front right tire of the lead Range Rover. His index finger, also acting of its own accord, squeezed the trigger—once, twice, three times.

The tire popped out, and the SUV swerved hard right, colliding with the vehicle next to it and causing both the vehicles to brake to hard stops. Before he could line up his shot at the third vehicle, the plane swung hard to starboard in a power turn, nearly launching him out of the hatch.

"Close the airstair," someone yelled behind him.

Gunshots echoed from the tarmac, and a round slammed into the aluminum frame—mere inches from Sam's head—as the Saudis returned fire.

"You sonuvabitch, I was only shooting at your tires," Sam said.

Anger flared in his chest, and he scanned for someone or something to shoot, but the plane was turning, and the target SUV had drifted into their aft port quarter.

He felt a hand on his shoulder.

"Sam, pull up the airstair," Jenn said as the engines roared.

He shoved his pistol into his waistband and flipped the silver toggle switch to raise and close the airstair. He watched the chrome articulating handrail fold inward and the clamshell-shaped steps seal against the fuselage.

"Everyone, take a seat and buckle up," the pilot yelled back through the open cockpit door. "Shit's about to get crazy."

Sam dropped into the front-row, portside seat and buckled in. Jenn did the same on the starboard side. Plenty of action movies had chase scenes with cars versus plane on a runway, but this was the first real one Sam had participated in. A flashbulb memory of Tom Cruise leaping off a motorcycle and onto the side of a heavy-haul transport popped into his mind as he looked out the window to look for the last Saudi Range Rover that was trying to stop them. The plane yawed violently, throwing Sam's shoulder into the cabin wall as the pilot made a ninety-degree turn to the right.

Holy shit, I didn't know that planes could do that on the ground, he thought as the fuselage shuddered and the engines roared.

No sooner had they executed that turn than they made another equally hard and sharp turn to the right. The maneuver must have taken the Saudis by surprise because he saw them making a U-turn to pursue. According to Sam's mental map, the pilot must have exited the parking area using a little side road on the east side of the ramp intended for service vehicles, not jets.

Through the open cabin door, he could hear the pilot and copilot arguing.

"Dude, what are you doing—that's the taxiway."

"Yeah, and we're using it as a runway."

"That's fucking nuts."

"It's the same length as the runway, it's clear now, and I know for damn certain nobody's gonna be landing on it."

"Dear God, I pray you're right . . ."

Looking out the opposite side windows, Sam saw the Range Rover attempting to overtake them on the starboard side. He was pretty sure that planes did not have rearview or side mirrors, so he shouted toward the cockpit.

"They're coming up on the right side—they're gonna try to cut us off!"

On hearing that, the pilot dropped the hammer. Sam wasn't sure what the quarter-mile time was for a Gulfstream, but it had to be damn fast because the acceleration pressed him back into his seat. The Range Rover, which had been gaining ground, seemed to stall, then began to drift backward.

Jenn crossed herself, then clutched the armrests as the jet shook and the nose tilted skyward. Sam felt the wheels break contact with the tarmac, and soon they were airborne, climbing at the steepest ascent angle he'd ever experienced in an aircraft—and that included his time on active duty. The jet abruptly banked hard right, rolling nearly onto its side. For a terrifying moment, Sam thought something was wrong with the plane—that the pilot had lost control, and they were crashing—but they soon rolled back to level and kept powering skyward.

Sam swallowed and looked at Jenn, who had her eyes squeezed shut and was mumbling a prayer—a Hail Mary, he thought.

"I know that was pretty dicey," the pilot said over the cabin speakers, "but we're crossing ten thousand feet, and, uh, they can't catch us now. This bad boy has a top speed of .92 Mach, so we'll be out of Saudi airspace in twenty minutes."

Sam exhaled with relief. Jenn reached out her hand to him across the aisle. He took it and gave her palm a brief congratulatory squeeze before letting go.

"We did it," she said, flashing him a *thank God it's over* smile.

"Almost," he said with a grin, then unbuckled his seat belt.

"Where are you going?"

"To get my computer. We've got a murder video to transmit."

CHAPTER 38

FANTAIL OF THE CARGO SHIP *EARABAT ALBAHR*

MEDITERRANEAN SEA

Riker knelt beside the motionless body of his fallen teammate, his Wilson Protector Elite Maritime carbine up and searching, his left knee pressing hard into the base of Saw's neck to stanch the bright red blood that had been spraying into the air. Tears streamed down his cheeks, he felt a sob growing in his chest, and he fought it off as a bearded face appeared at the corner of the superstructure to his left. Riker dropped the red dot onto the man's face and squeezed twice, watching with satisfaction as the head evaporated in a puff of gore from his 300 HAM'R round. The body fell out of sight.

"Center, Sword Three—Sword requests immediate CASEVAC for urgent surgical," he was able to choke out.

He continued his scan, pressing his knee into Saw's neck and feeling the hot blood soak into his cammies. Every fiber of his soul wanted to glance down—to see if the bleeding was slowing, to see if Saw's eyes had taken on that lifeless, cloudy gaze he'd seen in other soldiers he'd watched die on the battlefield—but the first law of combat medicine was that to save a teammate, you had to first win the fight.

A burst of fire from beside and slightly behind him told him that Antman had his back. The suppressed rifle fire further away over on the starboard side suggested Trip and Edwards were similarly engaged.

"I got ya, bro," Antman said.

Riker looked down and immediately could tell that however it turned out for Saw, the image that burned into his brain would be with him forever, sneaking into his dreams late at night.

Riker kept his rifle up and ready, and with his left hand, he pulled the blowout kit from his left thigh cargo pocket, tearing it open with his teeth and dumping the contents on the deck beside him. He looked into Saw's glazed-over eyes but was encouraged by a slow blink and a gurgling cough that brought blood to the SEAL sniper's lips.

"Thunder One, Two—I'm making a gun run across the stern to clear you in for CASEVAC," came an accented voice in Riker's ear.

He used his teeth again, this time to pull out long strands of gauze coated in a medicine that was supposed to help the blood form clots.

"Thunder One, roger," he heard, the pilots now sharing their comms to keep the assaulters in the loop. "Knife Three—we'll be in a hover at the stern rail in sixty seconds for CASEVAC exfil."

"Knife Three," Riker choked out, acknowledging the call.

He made one more quick scan, saw an enemy shooter on the 03 ladder well, but Antman shot the tango in the face before he could react. Riker looked down, the loops of procoagulation gauze in his gloved left hand, and removed his knee. Immediately, a geyser of arterial blood shot out of the base of Saw's neck, spraying across Riker's chest and face, then dripping off the front edge of his helmet, until he began to stuff loop after loop of the gauze into the massive wound on Saw's neck and left shoulder. The sniper round must have been high caliber, but it came across at an angle, tearing an enormous hole, but perhaps not going deep enough to sever his spine or open his trachea and esophagus.

It had sure as shit torn open the artery in Saw's neck, though, and even through his blood-slicked gloves, he felt the warm blood soaking into the gauze. He packed a big trauma dressing into place over the gauze and then put his knee back in place to hold pressure, swinging his rifle across the superstructure forward of them just in time to see a man sprint out of the portside hatchway, heading for the cover of a mechanical box between them.

Riker shot him twice in the chest and watched the terrorist squirm a moment on the deck. Then spent casings rained down on them from above as he heard the long burp of the KA-28 raking deadly fire across the superstructure again. The other KA-28 hovered off the starboard side of the ship, a tongue of fire licking toward the fighters on the deck. Then the bird swung the nose clockwise to let the Bravo team sniper inside the helo go to work with precision.

Riker fired blindly toward the port hatch to keep any fighters from joining the fight while they guarded his wounded brother in preparation for evacuation. A hurricane of wind whipped all around him as the helicopter dropped into hover behind him. A beat later, he felt a hand on his left shoulder.

"We take him now," a voice shouted in accented English.

Riker turned to see two Israeli soldiers he'd infilled with on the helicopter—the rope master and the copilot. Handing over his fallen brother to these men was one of the most difficult things he'd ever had to do.

"Let us take over," the copilot said, his gaze both urgent and empathetic.

Riker nodded as the rope master pushed Riker's knee away from Saw's neck and swapped a hand to hold pressure. Unable to help himself, Riker looked into the glassy eyes of his dying teammate. He thought about how Saw's wife, Ellie, and the kids would react when they got the call and something inside him broke.

Seconds later, the two Israeli operators had moved Saw to the floor of the Iranian-made helicopter, hovering just feet away. When they had him secure, the KA-28 leaped skyward and aft, retreating over the wake of the ship.

Hot, uncontained fury erupted inside Riker—the need to punish and destroy and mete vengeance not just on the enemy but the world itself for what had been done to Saw. He would make them pay.

Every last one of them.

"Let's go," Riker barked, heading forward in a fast, combat shuffle. His rifle wasn't an extension of him anymore; he was now an extension of it. "Six, you're on me," he said to Antman. "Eight and Ten, surge forward toward the starboard hatch."

His teammates acknowledged the order in turn.

"Four, One—forward deck is still unsecure," Spence said in his ear, a much-needed update from wherever the SEAL officer was on the forward end of the ship. "We are engaged with fighters within the CONEX boxes."

"Roger Two," Riker replied. "We'll secure the bridge."

Riker reached the portside hatch in the aft of the superstructure, clearing the ladder wells and decks above them as he approached. Approaching the external hatch that led to the bridge, he reached for a flash-bang in his kit with his left hand, then stopped, changed his mind, and yanked a lethal M67 grenade instead. He pulled the pin and spit it to the ground as he fired a burst of 300 HAM'R into the hatchway.

"Frag out!" he hollered and tossed the grenade upward into the stairwell through the hatch.

He heard a clang as it landed on the riser one level up, followed by a terrified scream. Then he pulled in tight beside Antman, shielding his body against the metal wall next to the hatchway. The *whump* of the explosion was followed by acrid smoke, and a moment later by a different kind of screaming.

Riker was already up and through the hatch, clearing left down the passageway into the superstructure beside the stairs. He saw two shooters backpedaling toward a corner and dropped them both with three shots. Antman squeezed his right shoulder, and he moved up the stairs through the black smoke. He could hear gunfire through the walls off to his right, where Trip and Edwards were now breaching the starboard hatch, and searched for targets as he ascended, stepping over a blackened and bloodied leg. Moments later, he stepped over the mess of what was left of the man it had once belonged to. He fired through the smoke down the passageway of the 0-2 level without being able to see. On the other side of the haze, he took a knee as Antman maneuvered around behind him to continue the ascent, covering at the corner and firing again when he heard the pounding of feet further down the passageway.

In under two minutes, they were at the 0-6 level and ready to move into the passageway. Antman crouched on a knee beneath him at the corner, his own rifle searching for targets. Riker pressed in beside him.

"Knife Eight, Three—we're at the 06 ready to move when you are," he said into the boom mic beside his mouth.

"Ten seconds," came the grunting reply, then more distant gunfire.

A man peered around the corner from the first crossing hallway, and Riker shot him dead center in the face.

A few seconds later, Trip's voice came back in his ear. "Eight and Ten at the O6 landing—call it."

"Move," was all Riker said, squeezing Antman's shoulder as he did.

Instantly the SEAL was up and surging forward ahead of Riker, shifting to the left side of the passageway to clear around the corner and opening a lane for Riker to fire on any targets that popped up ahead of them. At the end of the passageway, he spied the wooden door to the bridge. Every bridge he'd ever seen had multiple access points, and based on this geometry, he assumed there would be a matching door on the starboard side. Trip and Edwards would probably be taking their own places there.

Antman took a knee across from the corner of the crossing passage, firing once, then holding his position. He shouted, "Clear," so Riker surged forward toward the wooden door, fresh adrenaline and rage bubbling up inside him. An image of Saw's glazed eyes flashed into his head, but he forced it out as he took a knee beside the door to the bridge.

"Three—Eight and Ten in position at starboard bridge access," came the call from Trip, matching Riker's mental prediction.

"Eight and Ten, hold at the door, well clear," he said, pulling another M67 from his kit with great satisfaction. "Frag out."

"Eight, check," came Trip's reply.

Riker pulled the pin, kicked the door open, and tossed

the grenade into the forward section of the bridge. He turned, sprinted back down the corridor, and pressed against the wall in front of Antman in a position he hoped was well clear of the frag zone.

The grenade detonated, and he self-assessed. Injury-free, he chopped a hand forward. With Antman a half pace behind him, they kicked through the now-splintered wooden door into the bridge.

On crossing the threshold, he found the pilothouse to be a chaos of broken consoles, blood, and writhing bodies on the floor. A severed arm was resting on the ledge at the base of the angled row of bridge glass—half the panes blown out by the explosion, the other half fractured. He glanced right to see Trip and Edwards breaching in parallel. Trip lowered his rifle and fired twice at someone on the ground. The captain's chair held a squirming bloody body, so Riker fired two rounds into the head below a white ball cap that sat strangely unmarred. In the background of his mind, Riker heard the pop-pop as his teammates fired rounds to finish off the dying terrorist crew.

He moved robotically to the front of the bridge to gaze down at the battlefield that was the main cargo deck below. Bodies littered the deck beside several oversized crates, one of which had been opened to reveal a truck painted dark green—an enormous 8 x 8 he immediately recognized as the mobile launcher truck that the Israelis feared was aboard the ship. The other boxes were surrounded by dead terrorists, but there was one fighter crouched on the aft side of the launcher, hidden from Spence's assault team. The terrorists had managed to raise the missile, and Riker knew he was going to try to fire it.

"One, Three—you have a tango in cover on the aft side

of the launch vehicle moving toward the control panel," Riker reported, warning Spence. "He's trying to launch."

Realizing he was their only chance to stop it, Riker shifted left and took aim through one of the blown-out glass windshield panels. With steady hands, he placed his magnified red dot on the terrorist's head and squeezed the trigger. As he did, however, the man lunged for the missile launch control panel and smashed his outstretched hand against it.

Riker's first round hit the man's hip, but he shifted his aim and squeezed again, finishing the terrorist off with a headshot. Riker's heart sank, however, when the missile's rocket booster ignited. The lunging terrorist had successfully hit the launch button, and a rooster tail of flame lit up the main cargo deck. Riker scrambled clear of the flames and watched in terror as the lamppost-size missile leaped from the launcher cradle on a pillar of flames and streaked away from the ship, trailing fire and leveling just a few hundred feet off the surface of the sea.

"Oh shit," Riker said through a breath as the Chinese-made cruise missile raced east toward Israel.

"Center, Knife—one missile away," Riker reported. "Say again, the shitheads here launched a missile. The target ship is now secure, but one got away."

"Copy, Knife," came Michelle Yi's terse reply. "Secure and advise ASAP if a nuclear warhead could be in play."

"Copy, Center. Will advise," Riker said, wondering how the hell he was supposed to do that.

The KA-28 screamed across the deck again, targeted fire finishing the last of the fighters at the rails as Spence and his SEALs from Bravo advanced. Riker surveyed the bloody carnage from the bridge, his desire for murderous revenge for Saw fading now that the battle was won. Instead, his thoughts and worry redirected to the men, women, and children of Israel. Because if the missile heading east was tipped with a nuclear warhead, hundreds of thousands of innocents were going to pay the price for his failure to get the kill shot off in time.

And then Saw's sacrifice would have been for nothing.

CHAPTER 39

US EMBASSY

SENSITIVE COMPARTMENTALIZED INFORMATION FACILITY (SCIF)

RIYADH, SAUDI ARABIA

For Whitney, the déjà vu she was experiencing was impossible to ignore.

She was back in the American Embassy SCIF, sitting in the same chair, talking with the same people about Crown Prince Faisal and the cover-up. Only this time, instead of strategizing how to escape with the evidence, they were brainstorming how to sneak back into the palace to present that same proof to the King.

". . . I agree with the central premise of what you are proposing," Ramia was saying. "The King is the only man who can defy Faisal and strip him of power. But I must warn you: There are many pitfalls that you have not anticipated. Simply presenting the King with our evidence may not be enough."

"What do you mean by that?" Ambassador Harley said, verbalizing the exact question on Whitney's lips.

"I think the logic of the plan is sound, I do," Ramia said with patient eyes. "But that doesn't mean the King will believe us. And even if he does, it doesn't guarantee that he will react in the way that you are anticipating."

"Are you saying he might watch the video of his eldest son being murdered and side with Faisal?" Ambassador Harley said, his expression incredulous.

Ramia chuckled. "It is a possibility. He could decide the reputational damage to the Crown from the truth being made public is too damning. In which case, despite hating Faisal for what he's done, the King may choose to stay the course. Another possibility is that he watches but is unsure what to believe and decides to conduct his own investigation with members of his staff. He might conclude our video is a deepfake, meant to manipulate him, and have us arrested. Or maybe he becomes offended at even the suggestion that one son murdered the other, refuses to watch the video, and hands us over to Faisal. You see, there are many permutations besides the outcome that you desire."

Whitney thought of her paternal grandfather—a notoriously stubborn and difficult man who never ceased to surprise her with his ability to twist logic and deny facts to suit his worldview. Ramia was right—it was dangerous to make assumptions about how the King would react. Her stomach felt leaden on hearing this. How they framed the conversation and presented the information to King Abdul would be critical, and that meant she needed to know more.

"What kind of man is the King?" Whitney asked, probing deeper. "What's his personality like? What are his values?"

Ramia's gaze went to the middle distance momentarily as she considered the question. "Unfortunately, I don't know my uncle well. As a child, I had limited interactions with him. As a grown woman, even fewer. In general, I would say the King is a stern and serious man. His worldview was forged in a different era: It was under his rule that Wahhabism flourished, and the oppression of women was the status quo. As Ambassador, I've sat in on council meetings with him, but I have no relationship with the man. Remember: It was Crown Prince Khalid who appointed me, and Khalid who respected my opinion and sought my counsel. The King, never."

Hearing Ramia's truth only further dampened Whitney's spirits.

"What is the King's general state of physical and mental health?" Theobald asked. "Is his mind—how shall I say this—still intact?"

Ramia nodded, but noncommittally. "The King is much older than he looks on TV. He dyes his beard and always wears a thawb and ghutra, so you can't see how frail and aged he is. But from what I hear, he's not suffering from dementia or Alzheimer's disease. At his age, he's most certainly lost a step, but I do not believe he's confused or mentally compromised."

"That's an important data point. If he has faculties, the plan could still work," Theobald said. "We didn't see him during our visit, which at the time did not surprise me. But I also know that President Jarvis scheduled a call with the King, and that Prince Faisal usurped that call."

"And he's not been seen or heard from since the news of the murder leaked," Harley's Chief of Staff chimed in.

"Should we be concerned about the King's safety and well-being?" Theobald asked.

"Yes, there is certainly reason to be concerned. The silence, as they say, is deafening," Rami said. "Faisal murdered his own brother in cold blood. There's no limit to what he's capable of."

"But murdering the King would work against his goals,"

Whitney said. "Mohammed's death would trigger Faisal's ascension to King, and being Crown Prince is where the real power is, right?"

Ramia considered this. "Maybe, but not necessarily. If King Abdul *unexpectedly* died, Faisal could argue that until a suitable successor for the role of Crown Prince could be identified, he would assume the duties of *both* King and Crown Prince. He could draw this out for many months. I think the only real threat to Faisal's ascension to King in this scenario could come from other royal families in House al-Saud who could challenge him for the throne. But I assure you—they will not challenge Faisal's legitimacy while King Abdul lives, and Faisal knows this. The longer Faisal fills the role of Crown Prince under his father as King, the more it cements his legitimacy—a legitimacy he'll need when the day comes that his father does die."

"I'm going to be honest—I'm not very encouraged by what I'm hearing," Theobald said and glanced at Whitney before looking back at Ramia. "If we decide to go through with this plan—and I'm no longer convinced we should—what allies do you have inside the palace who you can leverage? I can't imagine you're the only one who has concerns about Faisal's rise to power. Do you have allies on the Royal Council, or in the King's Cabinet, or a trusted contact on the King's security detail who you could reach out to? Can we test the water, so to speak, before we jump in with both feet?"

"Yes, I have allies, but they are scared for their livelihoods and probably their lives as well. I'm not sure who I can count on." She sighed heavily. "Probably our best option is Bashar al-Hadi, the King's senior Royal Court Advisor. He's been a loyal and dedicated servant to the King for nearly two decades. If there's one person who could give us access and would be willing to watch the video and bend the King's ear, it would be Bashar."

"I've interacted with Bashar on multiple occasions," Harley said. "He's proud and arrogant, but well-informed and unquestionably loyal to the King. I agree that contacting him would be a good starting point."

"It's going to be tricky though," Ramia said, fidgeting with her hands. "I think we must assume all my communications via mobile phone are being monitored. And if the King is somehow being controlled by Faisal or locked away, then we should also assume that Faisal has threatened Bashar and is monitoring his communications as well."

"Do you have another phone? A burner, perhaps, or a private email account you could use?" Theobald asked.

"Yes. I have another private phone, but it doesn't solve the problem of Bashar being monitored. Also, there is no guarantee he will answer my call. We don't have a strong relationship."

"Normally, in these types of delicate situations, we'd use an intermediary to facilitate communications between the principals. Do you have a staffer who works in the palace, or who could go to the palace and pass a message to Bashar?" Theobald said.

"Yes, there is someone on my staff who I would trust to do this," Ramia said. "But I will need your help to craft the messages and provide instructions to minimize the chances of him getting caught. I'm not a spy, and neither is Jassim."

Theobald flashed her an *easy-day* smile. "No problem, Madam Ambassador. This sort of thing just happens to be my specialty."

CHAPTER 40

SENEGALESE-FLAGGED CARGO SHIP *DAKAR*

MEDITERRANEAN SEA

Chunk was the first operator over the rail at the fo'c'sle of the cargo ship. Access had been easy. The ship was dead in the water after the barrage of anti-ship missiles from their Tir II had torn away the better part of the entire stern just above the waterline. Chunk raised his Russian-made AK-74M assault rifle with his right hand, searching for targets aft of the starboard rail, as his left unsnapped the ascender from his kit. He swung a leg over the rail and dropped to the deck, taking a knee as he scanned through the less familiar optics of the Syrian Navy weapon he was carrying.

A squeeze on his shoulder told him that a Shayetet 13 operator was at his side. Chunk rose and surged forward along the rail, searching right on the open deck for a target.

He needn't have bothered.

The Tir II's anti-ship missiles had done their job and then some. The CONEX box was completely gone, a large hole in the deck where it had been now belching smoke, and the remaining deck was a bloodbath of corpses and body parts.

He scanned carefully anyway as he moved toward the superstructure aft of the carnage, scanning it for fire from enemy fighters. A glint of sunlight reflected at him from the railing at the O-1 level, where a metal deck wrapped around like a white balcony. He placed his red dot where the reflection had been and squeezed off a three-round burst. He never saw a body fall, but a second later, a rifle fell from the O-1 wraparound deck and clattered to the deck below.

Chunk weaved right, chopping his left hand and signaling his teammate to fan in that direction and spread out. There were four heavy cranes mounted to the deck, one of which now tilted precariously, hanging out over the port rail by more than twenty feet, explaining the slight port list he had sensed as he moved. He scanned for any movement in the carnage around the smoking hole in the deck, maneuvering behind the closer, intact crane for cover from any fire that might come from the superstructure.

"Sword One, Two," came the call from Mirashi. "Deck seems clear. Moving to the superstructure access now."

"One," Chunk said and spun a hand over his head as his three operators quickstepped toward the starboard entrance.

As he moved, automatic rifle fire erupted from the 0-4 level wraparound deck, and he scrambled for cover, raising his rifle to return fire as he did. A tongue of fire licked across the bridge level from the Tir II's deck-mounted machine guns, the barrage continuing for several seconds.

"Sword, hold," came Mirashi's voice in his ear.

Chunk took a knee, still scanning. "Neutralize the threat, Seven."

"Roger," came the reply from the Israeli gunner.

A beat later, machine-gun fire erupted from both port and starboard as the missile boat gunners poured lethal rounds into the superstructure at all four above-deck levels. When it was over, only the tinkling of glass falling to the deck remained.

"One will secure the bridge," Chunk announced and surged forward again. "Two, search below. Five, secure the deck."

Chunk and his Israeli operators ascended the ladder wells unopposed, moving up the bridge tower on the outside to avoid possible shooters still alive inside. At the O-4 level, he stopped at the top of the ladder and motioned for his two Israeli teammates to move around to the portside door. He watched as they moved low and fast, disappearing around the front of the bridge, and then he squatted low beneath the shot-out windows beside the starboard door.

Chunk popped up for a quick peek inside and dropped down again, giving his brain a moment to process what he'd seen. There had been no movement inside, but he snatched a flash-bang from his kit anyway and tossed it through the glassless window. It detonated inside with a flash of light and a loud pop.

Then he was up and moving through the door.

One crewmember was still alive, crawling through the blood and broken glass, but the pair of Israeli operators breaching the bridge via the port door ended the man's painful journey with a bullet to the head.

Everyone else inside the bridge was dead.

"Bridge secure," Chunk reported. Next, he pulled a small tablet computer from a pouch on his thigh. The screen-saver background image he'd saved was a zoomed cropped picture of Jahan Heydari's face. He committed the man's facial features to memory, then handed the tablet to one of the Shayetet 13 operators. "You two hold here and ID the dead. We're looking for this man—Jahan Heydari. He's our HVT."

"Understood," the more senior ranking of the two men replied.

Chunk turned to Tevie. "You're with me. We're going to sweep the O-2 and O-3 levels."

"Hooyah," the Israeli shooter said with a wide grin, using the Navy SEAL battle cry.

It took only minutes for them to clear the O-3 and O-2 levels. They shot and killed one tango but didn't find Heydari.

"Sword One, this is Six—the HVT is not among the dead on the bridge," reported the 13 operator to whom Chunk had given his tablet.

"Six, One—copy. Sword Two, all levels of the pilothouse are secure. No sign of Heydari," he said, updating Mirashi and the rest of the assault team.

"Crew quarters clear as well," Mirashi announced a moment later. "We found a command center on deck two below. Six enemy KIA. The space is secure. No HVT."

Chunk let out a throaty, annoyed exhale, then updated the head shed. "Center, Knife is Jackpot. No joy on our HVT. I repeat—Heydari does not appear to be on board."

"Copy Jackpot. Copy no joy on the HVT, Sword One," the Israeli intel officer Becker replied from the TOC, his voice all business.

"Two, I'm heading to you," Chunk said and gestured for Tevie to continue shadowing him.

They descended the internal ladder wells down to the level below the main deck, emerging in a short passageway where an Israeli operator was posted by a doorway, gesturing for them to enter. Chunk and Tevie entered a large room, where the coppery smell of blood was overwhelming in the stale air. He noted the air-circulation system had apparently been knocked out by their anti-ship missile barrage, but thankfully the lights were still on.

In the center of the command center, Mirashi stood, bent over a large table, scanning maps and drawings. He looked up as Chunk entered, his face grim. "Have a look, Commander Redman," he said.

Chunk joined him at the table, which was covered by maps of Israel, handwritten notes all over it in Arabic. There was a circle around Gaza City harbor.

"What does that say?" he asked Mirashi.

"It is a note about scheduling a pickup with a UNRWA 'aid truck' at this pier," he said.

"UNRWA?" Chunk asked, not familiar with this particular UN subgroup.

"Yes. UNRWA is a Palestinian aid team in Gaza. Unfortunately, we have long known that it has been infiltrated by Hamas operatives. They are meeting this scheduled aid shipment for distribution, but see here," Mirashi said, tapping a finger on another site circled in red. "This is an office building in the center of Beit Hanun, just a few blocks from the UNRWA distribution center where the aid shipment will be delivered. The office building at the corner of what appears to be Ahmad Street and Palestine Street is circled, but then do you see these lines here?"

Chunk bent over and studied the dashed lines, which had then been highlighted with a green highlighter. The lines extended north, across the Gaza-Israel border, ending a few inches later where the highlighted line formed an arrow.

"Heading north into Israel, but the route doesn't follow any roads . . ." Chunk said. Then it became clear. He looked up and met Mirashi's eyes. "Oh shit. The tunnels."

"It would appear," Mirashi agreed. "But it doesn't matter, because we stopped them. We control this ship now, and hopefully, within minutes, we'll control the *Earabat Albahr* as well."

"Yeah, I guess," Chunk said, scratching his scruffy chin.

The uncomfortable feeling he'd been wrestling with all day—that they were missing something—returned with a vengeance. His thoughts returned to the missing CONEX box that he'd tasked Yi to look into.

"Center, Sword—can you give me a SITREP on the missing CONEX box on the deck of the *Dakar* I tasked y'all to look into? Were you able to pull historical satellite data that shows the cargo deck?" Chunk asked.

"Sword, Center—we looked into this. We have no dedicated satellite coverage of the *Dakar* prior to the operation window. We have the vessel's track and AIS data, but no visual data of the cargo deck for the period you requested," Becker said.

"Okay, well, prior to coverage at 1330, when's the last imagery you have?"

"When the vessel transited the Suez Canal yesterday. I can confirm there were two shipping containers on the deck during transit."

Chunk slapped his hands together and looked at Mirashi. "Dude, something happened to that other CONEX box. There's got to be some record or something on this boat—"

"Seren Mirashi," a Shayetet 13 operator seated at a computer terminal interrupted, urgency in his voice. "I might be able to help you with this problem, sir."

Chunk followed Mirashi to the workstation, where the Israeli leaned over a laptop computer, the screen stained with a fresh smear of blood and spatter. Chunk glanced down and saw that the operator's left boot was resting on the body of a dead terrorist, half the head missing.

"Sir, I accessed the security feeds for the *Dakar* and have been scrolling through the footage from the deck. I discovered this . . ."

Chunk looked at the screen and saw recorded security camera footage looking down on the entire cargo deck from a bird's-eye position—a camera he assumed was mounted atop the bridge tower. He checked the date and time stamp in the upper-left corner and saw today's date with the time advancing in fast-forward, from midnight the night before. In the frame, clearly visible, were two CONEX boxes sitting side by side.

"Dude, there it is," Chunk said and clapped the enterprising Israeli operator on the shoulder.

The three of them kept watching as the time advanced. Shortly after 0500, ship personnel appeared on the deck, moving around the now-missing shipping container. A forklift appeared and stopped. Deckhands opened the container. A supervisor walked out to observe. The forklift operator drove into the CONEX box and backed out carrying a large crate on a pallet and moved the crate to the center of the deck. The forklift disappeared, and the deck crane swung into view. The workers secured the crate with lifting straps to the crane hook. The deckhands and the supervisor relocated to the port side of the ship, looking at something. Then another vessel, which looked like a fishing trawler to Chunk's eyes, came up alongside and maintained a parallel course with very little separation from the side of the *Dakar*. Then the supervisor waved, and the crane lifted the crate in the air, lowered it over the deck rail, and onto the deck of the trawler, where it took up almost every available bit of open surface area.

The Israeli commando working the computer paused the video and turned to look at them expectantly.

"Holy shit, they moved it," Chunk said, turning to Mirashi.

"The question is: What did they move?" the Shayetet Commander said.

Chunk turned back to look at the paused video screen. "Hit play. I want to see what happens next."

The Israeli specialist did as instructed, and the video resumed in fast-forward. Deckhands retrieved a portable ladder, hung it over the gunwale, and the supervisor climbed over the side of the cargo ship and disappeared from view. The trawler broke off and steamed away just as dawn was breaking on the horizon. Then the crane operator picked up the now-empty CONEX box and dropped it over the side of the ship into the sea.

"Wait, wait, wait," Chunk said, tapping the computer operator on the shoulder. "Can you go back and zoom in on the supervisor guy? The one who left?"

"I can try," the man said. After a few minutes, he found a moment in the video where the supervisor was looking in the direction of the camera. He screen-captured the paused image, then used a photo editor program to zoom in and sharpen the image of the man's face.

"That's Heydari," Mirashi said.

Chunk concurred. "Thanks to your guy's handiwork, looks like we've answered both questions. What happened to the crate and what happened to Heydari—they're both on that damn fishing trawler, and they got away with half a day's head start."

"Yes, but we still have one question: What in God's name is in that crate?"

Chunk blew air through pursed lips. He was just about to say that to answer that question they had to find the trawler, but another idea came to him instead. "Just a thought, guys. What if the thing in that crate is the same thing that was in the other CONEX box we blew up? I mean, you guys saw what I saw—there wasn't an inch to spare on that trawler deck.

Maybe Heydari caught wind we were coming and took steps to salvage his mission but was only able to move one payload?"

"This is very good thinking, Chunk," Mirashi said, using Chunk's nickname for the first time. "I'm going to radio my men on the main deck and tell them to conduct a post-blast analysis."

"Do it," Chunk said.

While Mirashi made the radio call, Chunk checked in with the TOC and how Gold was doing on their op.

"Center, Sword One—SITREP on Knife?" he asked.

There was a short pause, but instead of Becker, Chief Yi was the voice that responded. "One, Knife is Jackpot. Ship secured, but one missile was fired. The IDF is tracking it and will engage with the Iron Dome."

"Any evidence of nuclear warheads on those CJ-10s?" Chunk pressed.

"Negative," Yi said. "Knife has opened two containers, and those missiles appear to have conventional warheads. Assumption is the fired missile was conventional."

"Copy. Keep me posted," Chunk said. He turned to Mirashi. "This might be a good-news, bad-news situation."

"What do you mean? I think this is only good news," Mirashi said.

Chunk shook his head. "Not really. Your intelligence folks had an inkling there could be Iranian nukes in play. Heydari was on *this* ship, not the *Earabat Albahr* . . . and that crate they moved was definitely big enough to hold a nuke."

Before Mirashi could respond, their radios came to life.

"Two—Five, preliminary PBA performed on main cargo deck. We've found a radiation signature in the wreckage of the destroyed shipping container," an Israeli voice reported over comms. "Possible nuclear weapon or dirty bomb inside."

Chunk's stomach suddenly turned to lead. He rushed back to the table with the nautical chart and map of Gaza.

"Heydari's plan is to sneak it into Gaza," Chunk said, stating what was now obvious. "He's going to use the tunnels to smuggle a nuke into Israel and . . . shit, Tel Aviv is only thirty miles away from the border. They could get there in no time."

Mirashi nodded slowly, the gravity of the situation now apparent. "We can call in an airstrike to blow it up."

"Yeah, if we knew where it was," Chunk said and slammed his palm down on the table. He took a deep breath, centered his focus, and looked up at his counterpart. "Okay, we've still got time. We have to try to figure where that trawler went and when. Did it pull into Gaza City harbor or somewhere else? Did UNRWA send a truck and receive that crate? If yes, where did they truck it? We can do this, but we're gonna need help. And once we find it, we need to quickly plan and execute another joint op to intercept and disarm the nuke before it leaves Gaza."

"I agree with everything you just said," Mirashi said, his face tense and tone urgent.

Chunk quickly relayed the information and request to Center, then waited for what felt like an eternity to get a reply.

"Request routed. Your exfil air is inbound. But, Sword . . ." Yi said, and he heard a pain in her voice that caused his own throat to tighten in anticipation of the impending bad news. "Knife is one man down."

"Copy," he said, his voice cracking as he did. "CASEVAC?"

"We just got a call from the Thunder," Yi said, referring to the call sign for the KA-28 helicopters supporting the mission. "It was an urgent surgical . . ."

She couldn't finish, but the way she'd phrased her reply—it *was* an urgent surgical—made it clear. This afternoon he'd lost a brother.

"Who?" he asked, knowing he shouldn't ask but asking anyway.

"Saw," she said, and he heard her sob before unkeying her mic.

Saw? No—

"There must be some mistake. Are you sure?" he asked.

"No mistake. It's confirmed," answered Becker, taking over for Yi, his voice solemn. "I'm sorry, Sword One . . ."

Mirashi put a comforting hand on Chunk's shoulder, but it was as though that hand weighed two thousand pounds, because Chunk felt his legs give out. He collapsed to his knees. His mind filled with images of his teammate and friend, laughing beside him at Daytona, holding his daughter, and standing outside the SCIF, worried about Ellie getting little Connor to T-ball.

"This is my fault," he murmured, his lower lip trembling. "It's all my fault . . ."

Then he clenched his jaw and focused on the job at hand. The rest would have to wait.

CHAPTER 41

UNNAMED JETTY SPUR OFF AL-RASHID STREET
GAZA CITY HARBOR
STATE OF PALESTINE
1615 LOCAL TIME

Heydari stood on the jetty next to the fishing trawler as the medium-size Mercedes Axor truck pulled up, UNRWA stenciled on the side. A half dozen men climbed out of the back of the truck to assist with the cargo transfer. There were no ports in Gaza—the Zionists had made sure of that—but this semicircular jetty along the strip of beach created a pier for unloading as well as a small harbor to shelter the unrecognized Palestinian fishing fleet.

Heydari glanced at his watch.

They needed to get moving before the Americans or the Zionists figured out what was going on. He'd just been notified that the *Earabat Albahr* had been hit, presumably by the IDF.

The loss of the *Earabat Albahr* was unfortunate, considering the staggering cost of the cruise missiles they'd likely lost as a result. He'd not heard anything about a missile attack, which meant the Jews must have commandeered the vessel before the commander on board had been able to fire a salvo. No matter, the *Earabat Albahr* had fulfilled half of its strategic objective: to draw the IDF's attention away from the *Dakar* and Heydari's mission.

The Sayf Allah fighters were smuggling in a weapon that would shift the balance of power in the Middle East forever. For the fighters of Sayf Allah, the goal was killing Jews. For Heydari, the mission meant a chance for a promotion—a promotion that would take him out of the trenches and the accompanying life of sacrifice and subsistence with the jihadis. Heydari believed that a rise in power and standing of the Republic of Iran would mean a rise in power and standing for him as well.

I will become legend. Everything I have sacrificed will be repaid a hundredfold when the Supreme Leader learns that I was the man responsible for toppling the Zionists, he thought. *And soon that playboy spy Arash Reza will work for me.*

"God is great, brother," a young man called Jabril said after jogging up to greet Heydari.

"He is indeed," Heydari replied and placed a closed fist over his heart.

To the Sayf Allah fighters recruited for this mission, Heydari was Malik Abu Khatib, a lieutenant in the covert operations arm of Hamas. But to Hamas, he was a freelance fighter with deep connections in Iran who miraculously delivered them both weapons and cash. Here in Gaza, Heydari was a superstar—almost a celebrity.

"We need to hurry, Jabril. The Zionists are always watching," Heydari said, wondering how manpower alone would be able to move the crate. "Where is the forklift? I told you the weight. It is too heavy for manpower alone."

"I have a telescopic fork-loader coming," Jabril said, nodding. "It is driving down the jetty there."

Heydari followed Jabril's gaze and saw the vehicle that looked like a cross between a bulldozer and a forklift rumbling toward them a half kilometer away. "That is perfect. Good job. Soon the Zionists will feel the power of Allah's wrath, and they will know that we are to be feared. All the land promised us will soon be ours."

"Inshallah," Jabril replied with a bow, his eyes closed. Then the young man hustled back to his fellow jihadists, who were waiting with nylon straps and pry bars to help with the cargo transfer.

Heydari shook out a cigarette, lit it with the lighter from his pocket, and took a long, calming drag. For the next ten minutes, he smoked and watched as Jabril and his team used the telescopic forklift to transfer the wooden crate containing the weapon that would be the beginning of the end for the Zionists from the deck of the trawler into the truck. Once the transfer was complete, Heydari smiled as the six Sayf fighters scrambled into the rear of the truck and Jabril closed the doors behind them. Heydari flicked his cigarette into the sand and climbed up into the cab of the truck as Jabril joined him on the passenger side.

"I still can't believe it," the young fighter said.

"That we will be striking at the heart of the Zionists?" Heydari asked. He put the heavy truck in gear and began to drive the short distance back to Rashid Street, where he turned to head north.

"No," the young man said, now staring out the window. "That Allah would choose me to be part of it."

Jabril's naive optimism reminded Heydari of his own seven-year-old son, Ahmed, back home in Karaj, a suburb of

Tehran. Suddenly, his heart felt heavy. This bright young man next to him was unlikely to survive the next twelve hours. If he wasn't killed by the IDF during the infiltration, he would likely still be inside the blast zone if they were forced to detonate the weapon before it was discovered and neutralized.

"It is an honor to serve Allah beside you, Jabril," he said softly. "Your reward will be great indeed."

"Yes," Jabril said with a wistful smile on his face.

He checked his watch as they approached the circle at Bashar Street. Within twenty minutes, they would be in the parking garage of the target building. Heydari estimated it would take an hour to unload the weapon, move it into the tunnel, and lift it onto whatever track or trailer system had been set up by Sayf Allah. After that, the unknowns would pile up. What was the condition of the tunnel? He was assured the height and width would accommodate the dimensions of the crate, but was this information validated? How long would it take them to move the weapon six miles through the tunnel? Would the team with the truck show up on time when they emerged on the Israeli side? The pickup was scheduled at midnight under the cover of darkness. That timeline still gave the Israelis and Americans plenty of time to intervene.

So many things that could still go wrong, he thought.

"You look troubled. Is everything okay?" Jabril asked, shaking Heydari from his worries.

He forced a smile.

"Everything is perfect . . . just as Allah has willed it to be."

PART III

"Fear not death for the sooner we die, the longer we shall be immortal."

—Benjamin Franklin

CHAPTER 42

RANGE ROVER EN ROUTE TO AL-YAMAMAH PALACE
RIYADH, SAUDI ARABIA
2314 LOCAL TIME

Lying on her side in the fetal position, with Theobald snugged in tight behind her in the trunk of Princess Ramia's Range Rover, Whitney changed her mind. What had seemed like a brave and proper plan back at the embassy now felt rash and stupid. In an instant, all her certitude about the mission they were about to undertake dissolved into a soup of doubt and disquiet.

There's no way we'll make it in undetected.

Chief Saad will catch us, and then . . .

It's lockup, interrogation, and torture.

Like a psychic boomerang, visions of her time on the al Qadar yacht *Dauphine*—where she'd been held captive, tortured, and nearly killed—came back to her. Fresh fear blossomed in her chest at the prospect of that horror happening again.

"Are you okay?" Theobald said, his breath hot on the back of her neck.

Whitney wasn't a claustrophobic person by nature, but this was tight quarters. Getting into position in the trunk space of the Range Rover with Theobald had felt like trying to fit two puzzle pieces. They'd somehow managed, but even at their most cramped, they barely fit. She could tell Theobald was trying his damnedest to keep as much physical separation between his pelvis and her ass as possible—and she adored him for that—but right now spooning was the least of her worries.

"I'm fine . . . why?"

"You seem super tense."

She hesitated, then settled on a half-truth. "Just nervous, I guess. I hope our contact doesn't lose his nerve."

"Me too," he said.

The former Green Beret–turned–DIA field operative had been in the black ops business for two decades. She didn't know how many times he'd stared down death and walked away, but knew it had to be a number in the high double, maybe even triple, digits. His experience and confidence were a salve for her nerves. *Everything's going to be fine*, she silently told herself. *We're going to get in undetected, show the video to the King, and flip the script on Faisal.*

As if in rebuttal, her mind flashed back to the engine room of the *Dauphine*, where she'd been thrown down a flight of stairs and then zip-tied to a metal support column. She could practically smell the tang of engine oil and saltwater in the bilge, practically feel the heavy plasticuffs digging into her wrists.

Is this what PTS feels like? She wondered.

Of course it is, you moron.

She'd experienced significant traumatic stress, and now she

was living in the past. Chunk had encouraged her to talk to a counselor after getting back to London, and she'd promised him that she would, but things had gotten busy, and—

"We're arriving," Ramia said from her seat in front of them, interrupting Whitney's rumination. "Cross your fingers and toes, if you feel so inclined."

Whitney felt the Range Rover ease to a stop at the security checkpoint. They were entering the palace grounds via a gate reserved for the royal family and senior staff, the same gate Ramia used when visiting the palace without guests. The King's Chief Advisor, Bashar, was supposed to notify the guards on duty to expect Ramia, but guests were another matter. If the guards searched the vehicle, the plan would fail before it even got getting started. Whitney and Theobald were hidden from easy view by the Rover's retractable cargo cover, but if the guards opened the rear hatch, the gambit was up.

Her pulse ramped up in lockstep with her nerves.

At the same time, an intensely powerful and ill-timed itch sprouted like a weed in the middle of her back. It itched so bad she could barely stand it, but she forced herself to remain perfectly still and quiet while Ramia talked to the guards. She couldn't make out what they were saying, but the tone of the conversation sounded okay—professional, but not tense or adversarial.

The conversation stopped and Whitney felt the Range Rover begin to move forward.

"You can breathe now," Theobald said with a chuckle.

She exhaled, only then realizing that she had, in fact, been holding her breath.

"We're clear," Ramia said. "You might need to stay hidden longer, depending on the personnel situation in the underground garage."

"Understood," Theobald said.

The Range Rover drove for a little while. She felt the angle change as they took a ramp down into an underground garage. On reaching the bottom, the tires made a hollow *kerchunk, kerchunk* sound as they crossed some sort of metal grate or retracted barrier plate. The Rover then continued inside, where the sound changed again to the screech of the rubber on smooth concrete. After thirty seconds of maneuvering, she felt the transmission shift into park.

"Wait in silence," Ramia said. "I need to go in and make sure the right people are in position to facilitate your entry. If they are not, it could take a while. Do not get out until I return."

"Understood," Theobald said.

Whitney heard both front doors open, then shut almost simultaneously, leaving her and Theobald alone in the dark, cramped compartment.

Now came the worst part: waiting.

She closed her eyes and tried to visualize the outcome they wanted—making it successfully into the palace, meeting with the King, showing him the video, and Faisal's arrest. The analyst in her—the part that used data, statistics, and probabilities to make decisions—thought the idea of manifesting a positive outcome was total bunk. But another part of her, the part that had been in the suck facing death and impossible odds, only to persevere and survive by sheer force of will, felt otherwise.

Unfortunately, her attempt at manifesting was being undermined by the damn itch in the middle of her damn back.

"Bobby, can you scratch between my shoulder blades, please?"

"Seriously?"

"Yes, seriously."

She felt him squirm, then reposition a hand in the gap between his chest and her back.

"Is this the spot?" he said, scratching awkwardly.

"Up a little . . . left a little . . . now down a little . . . yeah, right there," she said, sated. "Thank you. I was dying there."

"You're welcome," he chuckled.

They sat there in silence again for a few moments. Then, out of nowhere, Whitney asked, "Do you have kids?"

"Yeah, two," he said, unfazed. "A son and a daughter."

"How old?"

"My daughter is twenty-three, just graduated from college, and my son is nineteen, a second-year at the Air Force Academy."

"Oh, that's awesome. You must be proud."

"Yeah. Except, you know, for the Air Force part," he said with pretend disappointment.

Whitney knew by now that interservice rivalry and smack talk was just how military folks bonded and connected with their fellow servicemen and -women. She'd even noticed that Chunk and the guys only tended to banter with the people they respected most, and who were confident enough to dish it right back. In this case, she could tell that Theobald was beyond proud that his son was a cadet in Colorado Springs, and he couldn't care less that he'd not directly followed his own path into Army SF.

Whitney was grateful for the conversation because it kept her mind occupied and out of *what-if* doom loops, but before she had a chance to ask him more, one of the passenger doors opened, instantly silencing Theobald.

"It's Ramia," the Ambassador's familiar voice said. "Everything is set. Ashif is going to open the trunk now."

"Roger that," Theobald said.

Whitney heard a click. Light flooded the trunk as Ramia's driver opened the Rover's rear cargo door. She waited for Theobald to get out first. When it was her turn, she rolled to her other side, sat up, and scooted aft until she was sitting on the tailgate ledge. Ramia, her driver, Theobald, and a nervous man she didn't recognize were standing in a semicircle waiting on her.

"We're going to move quickly, directly to the King's private residence. If anyone stops us, I will do all the talking," said the man in accented English, who, based on his age and appearance, Whitney decided was probably Bashar, the King's Chief Advisor. "Any questions?"

Whitney shook her head.

"Okay, we go," the man said with an anxious urgency.

They stepped from the garage into a dimly lit but decadent foyer with a marble floor, a beautiful chandelier, and walls decorated with colorful mosaic panels. She watched Theobald automatically clear corners on crossing the threshold with a quick left and right turn of the head, leaving his concealed carry pistol holstered and hidden. She mirrored his action, and only then did she see the pair of armed security guards flanking the door, standing in shadow. She momentarily locked eyes with the right-hand guard, whose gaze seemed to hold both judgment and intent, but the man held fast and made no move to stop them.

Like Theobald, she was armed, still carrying the Glock 19 that Mick had given her. Ramia knew they were armed—they'd discussed it when they'd gamed out the scenario—but Whitney wondered if their escort did.

They turned right into a darkened hallway. She and Theobald were both wearing athletic shoes, but Ramia wore high heels that clicked on the marble tile with each step, echoing loudly down the corridor. Just as Whitney turned to tell the

Princess to take them off, the thought seemed to occur to Ramia simultaneously. She stopped to remove them, before carrying on barefoot.

The group continued, quieter now. Whitney shut down her paranoia by grounding her mind and senses entirely in the present. She wasn't an operator, but right now, she needed to move and act with the single-minded focus of a SEAL on a mission. After twenty feet, she glanced back past Ramia, who was bringing up the rear, to see if they were being followed, then picked up her pace as the gap between her and Theobald widened. At the next intersection, their guide stopped short and waved for them to get behind him against the wall. Once they'd done as he instructed, the man leisurely rounded the corner, hands clasped behind his back as if out for a midnight stroll to ponder the nature of the universe.

"Is that Bashar?" Whitney asked.

Ramia nodded.

A moment later, Bashar reappeared and gestured for them to follow. As they rounded the corner, they entered a shorter hallway. Whitney stayed close to Bashar, who led them down the short hall to an elevator across from double doors into some large room, she supposed. Bashar swiped a key card and tapped the panel to select the fourth floor. The elevator chimed, the double doors opened, and once inside, Bashar entered a six-digit code into a keypad, and they began to move.

Whitney watched Bashar carefully as they ascended. Beads of sweat dappled the man's forehead, and he was tapping the outside of his right thigh rapidly with the side of his thumb, an obvious tick. The man's nerves did not inspire confidence for Whitney, nor would they go unnoticed by any of Chief Saad's security guards, if they were unfortunate enough to encounter a roving sentry en route to the King.

She glanced at Theobald.

He nodded, and his eyes seemed to say, *I know.*

The elevator glided to a stop, and the doors opened directly into a grand parlor, which was decorated similarly to the royal reception hall. Bashar stepped out and nervously scanned left and right before waving for them to follow him. They jogged quickly across the parlor, turned left, and continued down a hallway. Bashar, breathing heavy now, stopped in front of an imposing bodyguard in a black suit, standing guard in front of a pair of intricately carved doors gilded entirely in gold.

The guard reached for his weapon, but Bashar stopped him with an urgent plea in Arabic. A one-sided conversation followed, with Bashar doing all the talking and the guard doing all the listening. Whitney's knowledge of Arabic was rudimentary at best, but she didn't need to know the language to get the gist of what was happening. Bashar, who normally had the power in this hierarchy, was imploring the King's last line of defense to trust him. That the two Americans were here to help, not to harm.

The guard's eyes narrowed, and his gaze locked on Theobald. Then he spoke, asking a question in Arabic. To Whitney's surprise, Theobald answered for himself, speaking in Arabic with the same calm, soft-spoken confidence he'd addressed her with during their first interaction in Mingora. He'd earned her absolute trust in record time, and she could tell from watching the softening of the bodyguard's face that Theobald was working his magic on this man as well.

The guard asked a second question, which Theobald answered. The Arab protector chuckled, shook his head, and then bowed slightly to Bashar before turning to open the door. Whitney desperately wanted to know what had been said in their exchange, but now was not the time.

Whitney followed Bashar and Theobald into what turned out to be King Abdul's private bedroom. Her gaze went past the fluted marble columns, past the seven-tiered crystal chandelier, past the framed Picasso on the wall, taking in what was surely the most opulent bedroom she'd ever been in, until it stopped on Saudi King Abdul Mohammed lying unmoving and unconscious in his bed, hooked up to a heart monitor and IV drip.

It all made sense now.

With King Abdul in this state—whatever *this state* was—Faisal had absolute autonomy and complete control. The sham murder investigation, the false press release, the call to arms against Israel . . . all this had happened without the King's assent or knowledge.

"Oh my God," Ramia said, the first one in their party to speak—her shock and dismay as pronounced as Whitney's. She looked to the King's guard. "Bashar, what happened to His Majesty?"

The man looked both furious and on the verge of tears as he said, "They did this to him."

"*Who* did this?"

"You know who," he said, his eyes darting nervously to the gilded doors of the King's chambers and the hallway behind.

Just then a nurse, carrying an empty plastic jug, entered the bedroom from one of the connecting hallways. On seeing the group assembled at the King's bedside, she froze, fear and panic in her eyes. Bashar quickly intervened. Whitney didn't catch much of the Arabic, but the King's advisor seemed to be reassuring the woman while also demanding her compliance. After he finished speaking, she nodded, returned the jug to the rail beside the King's urinary catheter collection container under the bed, and took a seat in the chair against the wall.

"Don't worry. She's loyal to the King and can be trusted," Bashar said, turning to address them as a group.

"Is the King's mind intact, or is he a vegetable?" Ramia asked, getting straight to the only thing that mattered.

Bashar's lower lip trembled. "I don't know. I'm not a doctor."

Ramia's expression hardened. "You've put us in terrible danger, Bashar. You should have communicated the situation when we were planning this."

"If I had, would you have come?" Bashar stammered.

Ramia huffed and gestured angrily at the unconscious King. "Look at him! We can't show him the video like this. We can't even talk to him, Bashar. Oh my God, we're dead. We're all dead."

Theobald had wandered over to inspect the IV pole where two bags of fluid were hanging. After reading the labels, Theobald turned to the nurse and asked her a question in Arabic. She answered him, but without making eye contact, her gaze fixed on the floor.

"What's going on? What are you asking her?" Bashar asked.

"Tell me everything you know about what happened to the King. Everything you saw and heard."

Bashar nodded. He explained how Faisal had arranged a private meeting with the King, but Bashar had not been permitted in the room.

"The next thing I know, Faisal bursts out of the conference room screaming for a doctor. When I rushed in, the King was having a seizure. After that, the palace emergency medical staff attended to him. Then, instead of taking him to the hospital, the doctor in charge had the King put in here, under twenty-four-hour care managed by the Crown Prince. The King has been like this ever since."

Whitney watched Theobald blow air through pursed lips. He was staring at the IV bag.

"I know that look, Bobby," she said. "There's something going on with the IV, isn't there?"

He nodded. "They have the King on a propofol drip, along with fentanyl, which together are keeping him in a perpetual anesthetized state. It's similar to how a hospital would prepare you for surgery, except in the King's case, they're not letting him wake up." He shot a hard glance at the nurse.

"How do you know this?" Bashar asked, his tone challenging. "I held my tongue when you told the guard outside you were a doctor, because I assumed this was a cover story. Were you telling the truth. Are you a doctor?"

"I'm not a doctor, but I have extensive training in emergency medicine and battlefield triage. I'm well-acquainted with anesthetizing agents and their applications."

"This is good news," Bashar said, lighting up. "You can turn off the drugs and wake him up!"

"It's not that simple. The drugs they have him on are not intended for prolonged use. They're meant to be used in combination with general anesthesia to put a patient under temporarily for surgery. The fact that he is not on a ventilator suggests they're using a relatively low dose, but there are still risks. The King has been under for an extended period of time. There are cardiovascular implications with this cocktail of medications. I can reverse the fentanyl easily with flumazenil, but the propofol is more complicated. He could wake up in a half hour, or it could take several hours. I just don't know. Plus"—Theobald clenched his jaw—"I have no idea what emerging from such a long time on propofol would be like—and what the risks are."

"But we can't leave the King like this," Ramia said.

"No, we can't, and I'm not suggesting that," Theobald said.

Whitney saw Bashar nervously glance at his watch, the second time she'd seen him do it. "You keep glancing at your watch. Is there something we need to know? Are we on the clock here?" she said, pressing him.

Bashar swallowed. "I did not witness what was done to the King, but I have a good idea who is responsible. The Crown Prince has two enforcers—very dangerous killers in his employ—who could show up at any moment to check in on the King. We need the King lucid. We must wake the King and brief him on everything that his son has done. Only then can we challenge the Crown Prince."

"The guard posted at the door," Whitney said, interjecting. "Is he loyal to the King?"

"He's loyal to the King, but only because I have paid him handsomely. I would not want to gamble our lives on the strength of that loyalty if the Crown Prince were to appear with a half dozen armed men. Do you understand?"

"Perfectly," Whitney said and looked at Theobald. "We have to try to wake him. It's our only hope."

"I know," Theobald said. She could see his mind was running a silent risk-benefit calculation.

Theobald shifted his attention to the nurse and asked her a question in Arabic. They conversed for thirty seconds, then she stood and walked around the bed to unlock a medical cabinet on wheels, which had been pushed up against the wall nearby. Together they began to go through the drawers until they apparently found what Theobald was looking for. With a slightly less concerned look than he'd been wearing before, he turned and held up a preloaded syringe.

"What's that?" Ramia asked.

"Naloxone," Theobald said. "Once I stop the propofol drip, the King will wake slowly. The physostigmine will speed his recovery from the anesthesia, though it's still experimental. The naloxone will counter the narcotics in his system. Together these drugs will bring him back quickly, but it will be a shock. If King Abdul were thirty years younger, I wouldn't be concerned. But as Ramia noted, he's not a young man. There are risks."

"What risks?" Bashar asked.

"Cardiac arrest. Alternatively, he could go into shock."

"Then a real doctor should be present."

"The *real* doctor is working for the Crown Prince and is the reason we're in this mess to begin with," Theobald fired back.

Bashar nodded. "You're right. I'm just afraid—afraid for the King and afraid for us."

"You need to inform the guard outside that we're going to wake the King, and that it could be noisy. The King will be confused when he wakes. He could be in pain. He might scream. He might wail. For this to work, we need time. We need that door secure."

"I will tell him, though I would not count on our muscular friend out there to lay down his life for us."

"I understand," Theobald said.

In her partner's eyes, Whitney saw the ugly truth. If the proverbial excrement hit the rotating cooling apparatus, it would be the two of them trading bullets with Faisal's enforcers. With a nod, she pulled her weapon and checked to make sure there was a round in the chamber. She looked up. "I'm all in. Do it."

Theobald shot her a *here goes nothing* smile, walked over to the IV stand, and stopped the drip. Then he checked his watch.

"What are you waiting for?" Bashar said, crossing his arms impatiently.

Unfazed, Theobald uncapped the syringe and drove the needle into a port on the IV tubing. Then he locked his eyes on the King's heart monitor. "Not until he's ready . . ."

CHAPTER 43

ISRAELI AIR FORCE SHIMSHON (C-130J) SPECIAL OPERATIONS AIRCRAFT
EIGHTEEN THOUSAND FEET OVER THE MEDITERRANEAN SEA
2324 LOCAL TIME

Chunk checked his watch.

Six minutes until go time.

Thanks to the hard work of Chief Yi, Seren Becker, and the rest of the intel staff, they'd reconstructed events after the Iranian operative Heydari had transferred the suspected nuclear weapon from the deck of the *Dakar* to a fishing trawler. The trawler had made its way to the coast, where they'd next found coverage of the crate being unloaded onto a UNRWA truck in Gaza. The target for their HALO jump was the roof of an apartment building where the truck had last been spotted. The Israelis suspected the basement of the building was the likely origin point for a yet-to-be identified Hamas tunnel that Heydari was going to use to smuggle the weapon into Israel. Chunk hated that there was an assload of speculation upon which they'd planned this op, but if they waited to act until that speculation was confirmed, they would almost certainly be too late.

He looked across the aisle at Senior Chief Hutch and his Belgian Malinois, Thor—the SEAL and military working dog team who'd been a last-minute augment to support the mission. The pair normally operated with SEAL Team Two but had been in-theater for a training operation with the Israeli spec ops canine unit. Chunk had been wanting to add tracking capability at Gold, so he considered tonight's evolution a job interview for the handler-canine duo. Both Hutch and his four-legged partner had already earned the reputation as the best of the best, so having them at the Tier One was a no-brainer.

Chunk's gaze settled on Thor, a male Belgian with a beautiful rust-and-black-colored coat and pensive, confident eyes. The dog was wearing a custom helmet with a face shield that wrapped around over his snout to protect his eyes while providing the dog with an unobstructed view. The rig made the already badass canine look even more formidable. A specially designed funnel-shaped oxygen mask could be clipped over the muzzle to provide sufficient O2 during high-altitude jumps. Thor also wore a specialized torso harness that secured to Hutch's chest, linking them for the free-fall and parachute phases of the infil. According to Thor's bio, the dog had made over forty jumps, two-thirds of them with Hutch. Make no mistake—Thor was a special operator just like the rest of the human SEALs and Israeli operators assembled for this mission. He understood his job, was ready to work, and was ready to risk his life for the mission and his teammates.

Chunk shifted his gaze to Hutch. The senior chief nodded. *We won't let you down, Commander.*

Chunk nodded back. *The thought never crossed my mind.*

"Five minutes," the pilot's voice reported in Chunk's ear.

He pressed to his feet, rising from the bench seat where he'd been sitting between Riker and Trip. Normally, the three of them would be bullshitting and talking smack, but not tonight. Those days were over, and he doubted they'd ever return. The center of his chest felt like someone had cracked his sternum open and poured acid inside, dissolving his heart with liquid fire until only a burned-out cavity remained.

Thankfully, he didn't need a heart to run tonight's op.

All he needed was his trigger finger.

The aluminum deck beneath his booted feet tilted as the pilots made the final turn for the insertion. Chunk widened his stance, bent his knees, and leaned into the turn with the grace and balance of a downhill slalom skier. He turned to face his six Gold squad teammates and the half dozen Israeli operators who would together decide the fate of a quarter of a million innocent civilians in Tel Aviv. They'd already briefed the HALO infil and the mission. Everyone here knew exactly what the stakes were. Everyone here knew the cost of failure. They didn't need a pep talk, and he wasn't in the mood to give one.

A macabre quote, the author of which Chunk couldn't remember, was playing on repeat in his brain: *"Fear not death for the sooner we die, the longer we shall be immortal."*

Five minutes. He signaled to his teammates to don their oxygen masks, watching as they lowered their goggles and secured their breathing equipment. Once his own mask was in place, he called for buddy checks, and the operators paired off, methodically inspecting each other's gear, then their own kits. Chunk secured his weapon on his chest and powered up his NVGs.

His mind drifted to Watts, who for some damn reason had stayed behind with Theobald in Riyadh at the embassy instead of exfilling with the other members of the task force who'd arrived safe and sound at NAS Bahrain. Whatever plan the two of them had concocted, he suspected it was noble, audacious, and dangerous. Bowman had made the decision to compartmentalize both their missions so that Chunk didn't know what she was attempting and vice versa. Chunk had pushed back, but Bowman had held his ground. The CSO had also decided to withhold news about Saw from Watts until she was safely back in Bahrain. Chunk knew she'd probably be mad as hell about that, but it was the right call. He wished he hadn't known the truth until after they'd stopped Heydari.

An image of Watts grinning at him while she teased him about the velociraptor coaster popped into his mind. The memory prompted a confusing surge of emotions in him—adoration, protectiveness, warmth, and fear . . .

If you touch one hair on her head, I swear to God, he thought, threatening Death himself, *I'll hunt you down and end you myself.*

"Two minutes," the pilot said in Chunk's earpiece, snapping him back to the present.

Chunk showed two fingers and gestured for everyone up. In a moment of binational badassery, the American and Israeli operators rose in unison and followed him to the ramp at the rear of the cargo hold. Tonight Chunk would jump first.

For Saw . . .

He stopped at the yellow-and-black tape line next to the jump signal light. He rolled his helmeted head in a circle and then his shoulders. Hutch and Thor stepped up beside him on the right, Riker on the left. The SEAL breacher and self-proclaimed luckiest man alive was almost unrecognizable to Chunk. On the outside, Riker was physically unchanged. But the man inside was fighting World War III with his demons, and his rage and sadness bled through to the surface. The clenched jaw, the furrowed brow, the hard-pressed lips. And the eyes—Chunk did not envy the terrorist who got in Riker's way.

Chunk inhaled and tasted the metallic tang of canned O2.

The timbre of the hull vibration changed as the pilots—experienced Israeli aviators—slowed and made last-minute corrections based on winds and temperature to ensure that the jumpers would have a clear path to land on the target.

"Thirty seconds," came the call from the pilot on comms.

The Israeli jumpmaster on their stick stepped up to the ramp controller and pressed a button. A loud clunk reverberated, and cabin pressure immediately dropped as the rear ramp began to lower. Frigid air flooded the cargo hold, and Chunk's ears popped. He watched as the flat metal deck lowered until it stopped a smidge below level.

The jump light switched from red to yellow.

The jumpmaster gave Chunk a thumbs-up. Chunk nodded.

A beat later, the light switched to green.

Chunk walked to the edge of the ramp, spread his arms bent at the elbows, and fell into the night.

The frigid air assaulted his exposed skin, but he welcomed the onslaught. The wind raged against the fabric of his jacket sleeves and pant legs, snapping them against his flesh. But the wind, the cold, the night—they were his partners tonight. Contrary to what some people might think, the free-fall portion of a skydive was not a passive event. Maintaining the correct form and body position took work and effort. Keeping his arms out and his legs spread and bent at the knees to control the descent required strength, dexterity, and concentration.

Chunk looked right and saw Hutch and Thor falling in formation beside him.

He looked left and saw Riker.

Lit by a waning crescent moon, a silver sea of rolling cloud cover stretched for miles in every direction. Chunk's plan was to open chutes at five thousand feet, below the cloud ceiling at seventy-two hundred feet—low enough to minimize vulnerability but still high enough to navigate to the target. It didn't take long to reach the cloud deck at nearly two hundred feet per second. From here, the clouds looked like they had some kind of tangible mass, like cotton candy or cushion stuffing, but that was just the mind's imagination at work. Clouds were just vapor. On hitting the cloud deck, he felt nothing, except dampness on his neck and a warmer air against his cheeks.

A heartbeat later, the lights of Gaza materialized below. On this cue, Chunk pulled his left arm in and checked the altimeter on his wrist. The digital numbers changed in a blur as he plummeted toward the target altitude where he would pull his chute. The rest of the team would cue off him, their attention glued on him and the IR light strips on the back of his helmet and heels of his boots.

At fifty-six hundred feet, he crossed his arm over to his chest, pulled his legs in slightly for bracing, and called the countdown:

"Three . . . two . . . one . . ."

On the zero beat, he clamped his jaw shut and yanked the silver D-ring on his left chest harness. His parachute deployed and his body jerked upward, pulled by the leg and chest straps, which bore the brunt of the instant deceleration. He looked up, verifying that his chute wasn't fouled as he reached for the risers. With practiced efficiency, he grasped the handles and took control of the specially engineered wing chute, which was designed to give him precision control over his approach and landing. He tugged, slowing his descent, a confusing sensation that felt like his body was rising instead of simply falling slower.

He surveyed the LZ to manage the approach. On this jump, orienting toward the target was visually straightforward. The LZ was located inside the Gaza Strip—a narrow slip of territory slanted at a forty-five-degree angle along the southeasternmost corner of the Mediterranean Sea. The target building was located in Beit Hanoun, a township at the northern end of Gaza near the Erez Crossing—the only official access point into and out of Israel. Due to its proximity to the security perimeter, Beit Hanoun was the origin point for most of Hamas's northern tunnels. To find Beit Hanoun, Chunk looked for a particular landmark he'd identified pre-op when paging through satellite imagery: Netiv HaAsara—an Israeli moshav just north of the Gazan border. If he imagined the Gaza Strip as the body of a lowercase *i*, then Netiv HaAsara was the dot.

He quickly found the dot, then looked south a few degrees to find Beit Hanoun.

He pulled on the right riser, banking to align his heading with the vector in his mind. Then, with his right hand, he snapped open the lid of the navigation computer he wore Velcroed to his kit. The target was preloaded in the nav app with a glide-slope indicator. The more offset from the center the lines displayed, the more off he was in the approach. When these lines were perfectly centered, they formed a plus sign, which indicated he was approaching the LZ with the proper rate of descent and heading. Like an imaginary slide in the sky, the goal was to ride the glide slope all the way down and land perfectly on the roof of the target building.

Using his riser handles, Chunk made the necessary adjustments until he achieved the plus-sign configuration on the display. The rest of the team would make their own manual adjustments to match Chunk's and follow him in. He said a silent prayer that the data had been loaded correctly to account for the height of the roof above the ground so that he wasn't glide-sloping himself and everyone else into the side of the building.

"Two minutes, Vengeance," he said in his boom mic and clicked his NVGs into place, bringing the world into full daylight color.

Through the state-of-the-art X27 night-vision goggles, he could now clearly see the clusters of buildings that formed the center of Beit Hanoun. The rest of the approach he would manage himself, leveraging his experience and five senses. Just as he was about to call, "One minute," into his boom mic, the voice he'd desperately missed hearing spoke into his ear.

"Vengeance, Mother—be advised I hold a single thermal, armed with a rifle, stepping out of a rectangular structure onto the rooftop," Yi said.

Chunk growled in displeasure at this unwelcome news. During the entire observation period, the roof deck of the target building had been unoccupied. Now, with less than sixty seconds before their arrival, an armed sentry showed up.

"Check," he said, confirming with his own two eyes what she'd just reported.

Roof sentries rarely looked up, but once Chunk and his team got close enough, the element of surprise would be gone. It was hard to miss fourteen operators parachuting en masse toward where you're standing. During the final hundred yards, they would all be incredibly vulnerable, and if the fighter strafed the formation, they would take multiple casualties. Shooting the asshole while parachuting was a nonstarter—in addition to compensating for the movement and wind action while aiming, he'd have to let go of the risers. He could drift off course and miss the LZ, or worse, he could crash and ruin the mission.

Even Saw, with all his years of experience and skill, couldn't make that shot—

Hot angst flared in his chest at the thought.

Not now . . . Lock it down.

In his left peripheral vision, Riker moved up to a parallel position. Chunk glanced at the breacher, who was looking at him.

"One, I'll kamikaze that asshole. You focus on the rest," Riker said.

Chunk both understood and appreciated his NCO's valor and team-before-self ethos, but what Riker was talking about was two parts martyrdom and one part valor.

He was about to rebuke his teammate, when a crazy idea came to him. A crazy, impossible idea with practically zero chance of success without divine intervention, but a crazy idea he was going to try anyway.

"Negative, Two. I got this," he said.

Chunk visualized what he'd have to do, watching the sequence in his mind as if watching a movie, and in doing so, the seemingly impossible feat suddenly felt inevitable—like a memory that simply hadn't happened yet. With about fifty yards vertical and horizontal separation from the rooftop remaining, Chunk let go of his left riser handle and ripped off his oxygen mask. He switched hands, pulled a frag grenade from the front of his kit with his right hand, and pulled the pin with his teeth. Clutching the baseball-size bomb in his hand, he kept the safety lever depressed while he worked the left riser to keep him on slope. The Mk 67 grenade utilized a time-delayed fuse with a four-to-five-second duration. He'd burn two of those seconds in his hand. The travel time would burn the rest.

At thirty yards, he released the safety lever, arming the grenade. As he counted—*one-one-thousand*—in his mind, he cocked his arm.

On *two-one-thousand*, he threw it.

It had been many years since he'd played high school baseball in Texas, but muscle memory dies hard. Tonight his arm might as well have been a grenade launcher, because he delivered the payload on time, on target. The frag grenade exploded a few feet above the roof sentry's head just as the terrorist was turning to look up in their direction. Shrapnel ripped the fighter apart where he'd been standing.

Three seconds later, Chunk pulled the risers hard, stalling his descent over the center of the roof deck. He pedaled his feet as his momentum carried him toward the hip wall at the edge of the roof deck twenty feet away. He shifted his weight backward, kicked his right foot out as he landed, and dropped onto his left knee as he opened the quick release for his chute. He felt a momentary tug, then the chute detached and sailed away as he came to rest five feet from the edge of the building. He loosened his rifle sling and brought the weapon around and up in a quick, fluid movement. Throwing the grenade had secured the LZ, but it had also stolen their stealth. Any shitheads sheltering inside the building had most certainly heard the explosion.

He swept his red dot across the roof, then sighted on

the rectangular shed at the far-left corner, which served as the access point for stairs leading to below. Eight feet to his right, Hutch touched down, with Thor strapped to his chest. Chunk reckoned the SEAL had performed at least as many combat jumps as he had—which was a lot—because the operator-canine pair landed with expert precision. Hutch had his chute free, and his partner unclipped, with four paws on the ground in less than two seconds. The rest of the force landed in waves, staggering themselves along the surface of the roof deck. He watched out of the corner of his eye as his American and Israeli brothers landed one after another without mishap.

In less than ninety seconds, the infil was complete.

"Mother, Vengeance is Daytona," Chunk said, reporting the milestone. Tonight they were using NASCAR racetrack names for checkpoints to honor Saw.

"Copy, Vengeance," Yi came back. "Satellite imagery holds a minimum half dozen enemy thermals in stationary positions on the lower floors. Stay frosty."

Ze'ev Mirashi—the Israeli Shayetet 13 platoon commander leading the other stick—crossed the roof deck in a combat crouch and took a knee beside Chunk. "I didn't realize they were training SEALs as bomber pilots," he said with a crooked grin.

"Sometimes I just like to pretend I'm Air Force," Chunk fired back.

"Now that we lost our stealth, what's the plan?"

Chunk thought for a moment. "Instead of trying to clear the building floor by floor, breaching rooms with shooters who expect us, what if we just run-and-gun our way down the stairs and set demolition charges as we go? When we get to the bottom, we collapse the stairwell and bury access to the basement."

"I like this plan, but I think we reserve two bricks of C-4 in case it doesn't work. That way, we can still collapse the tunnel entrance after we enter to prevent us from being followed."

Chunk nodded. He chopped a hand toward the stairwell shack at the corner of the roof. With his jaw set, rifle up, and legs churning, he led the charge into the stairwell access.

CHAPTER 44

KING ABDUL'S PRIVATE RESIDENCE
AL-YAMAMAH PALACE
2329 LOCAL TIME

The naloxone Theobald injected into the King through his IV worked almost instantly. Within mere seconds, the slow, regular beep of the King's pulse on the heart monitor doubled in cadence. Next, Whitney watched as the King's facial muscles began to twitch, followed by his fingers, and soon his legs. Then the aged Saudi monarch arched his back and gasped, sucking in a lungful of air with the urgency and desperation of a man who'd been holding his breath underwater.

"It's working!" Bashar exclaimed, with joyous disbelief.

The King released a ragged exhale, then sucked in another large breath. Whitney saw that Theobald's eyes were glued to the heart monitor. As a precaution, he'd directed the attending nurse to break out and charge the portable defibrillator, but he'd not made a move for the paddles.

For the first time since she'd arrived in Riyadh, Whitney felt buoyed with hope.

Maybe, just maybe, we're going to pull this off.

The King grabbed a fistful of bedsheet with his right hand, and his face contorted with pain. He let out an awful moan—a sound the likes of which Whitney had never heard before.

"What's wrong with him?" Bashar asked.

"He's coming out of it," Theobald said, still clutching the naloxone syringe in his right hand.

The King fell still, and his grip on the bedsheet loosened. The cadence of his pulse began to slow, and his body relaxed.

Theobald watched and waited a long moment. Then he said, "I'm going to give him another dose."

Bashar nodded, but Theobald wasn't asking for permission. He took a second syringe from the nurse and administered it into the IV. The King moaned again; this time, less pained.

Finally, he opened his eyes.

Bashar clutched the King's left hand in both of his own and said something in Arabic. The King blinked twice, then tried to speak, but the effort spurred a coughing fit. Sweat dappled the monarch's forehead as he hacked away, trying to clear stubborn phlegm from his lungs. Theobald grabbed the controller for the hospital bed and inclined the King's head, while the nurse rushed in with a towel to wipe his brow, lips, and chin.

Whitney watched as the King's wits began to return to him. First came simple awareness of his own return to consciousness. Next came recognition of his surroundings and Bashar. In a voice, both raw and weak, he addressed his longtime advisor. Bashar answered the King with a slow, comforting lilt, like he was addressing a child who'd fallen off his bicycle for the first time. As Bashar spoke, the King's gaze went first to Theobald, then flicked to Whitney. He studied her for a long moment, then his focus shifted to Princess Ramia, who stood beside Whitney. She saw fear in the King's eyes.

Then anger.

Speaking in Arabic, the King asked Ramia a question. The Saudi Ambassador, probably for Whitney's benefit, answered in English.

"Yes, Your Majesty, I'm afraid it's true," Ramia said. "Your son, Crown Prince Khalid, was murdered by his brother, Faisal. And Faisal is also the one responsible for putting you into this drug-induced coma. I know this is difficult information to hear and to process, but this is the state of things. And we have proof."

The King looked visibly pained now, as if learning of Khalid's death for the first time. Whitney couldn't help but wonder if learning this news about Faisal's treachery felt like losing a second son.

"Show me this proof," the King said at last, with tear-rimmed eyes.

Whitney reached under her blouse and retrieved the USB thumb drive hidden in her bra. Pinching the memory stick between thumb and forefinger, she handed it to Ramia.

"Does the King have a laptop computer?" Ramia asked Bashar.

"Yes, yes—in his office. I'll get it," the advisor said and hustled out of the room.

The King switched back to Arabic and asked Ramia another question, which she answered in Arabic this time. While she spoke, the King's expression grew stern and dark. Once she finished, he tried to speak again, but it brought on a coughing fit. Wheezing, he spat phlegm repeatedly into a bedpan provided by the nurse. When he eventually caught his breath, the King launched into an angry diatribe.

Ramia nodded as he ranted, but she did not interrupt him.

A moment later, Bashar returned with a notebook computer—the thumb drive sticking out of a port on the side—and set it on the King's lap. He'd already cued up the video file, a time-lapse edit clip that had been cut and edited by Sam to show the "highlights" of Khalid's murder and the tremendous efforts to cover up the crime. Whitney had watched the edited clip with Ramia and Theobald back at the embassy before they'd originally set off for the airport. It was undeniably damning.

All eyes were fixed on the King while he stared at the screen. Whitney felt real sorrow for the man as he watched the unimaginable happen in his own house. When the video stopped, the King's demeanor transformed. The old man, enfeebled by age and anesthesia, roared to life like an angry lion, hoisted the laptop computer over his head, and threw it. Bashar gasped, but somehow Theobald managed to catch the laptop before it smashed into the marble tile floor.

The King didn't say anything for a long moment. Whitney wondered if his reaction was telegraphing what would be a full-on denial of the facts. Ramia's words from earlier played back in her head now: *He could decide the reputational damage to the Crown from the truth being made public is too damning . . .*

"Your Majesty," Ramia said, her tone respectful but pressing. "The lives of everyone in this room are in grave danger. Crown Prince Faisal will have us jailed or worse for waking you and showing you this truth. What would you have us do?"

The King pressed his lips together into a hard line and balled his right hand into a fist. He trembled for a moment, then said, "I hereby disavow Crown Prince Faisal's rule. He is no longer my son. Bashar, summon General Ahk—"

Gunfire in the hallway outside interrupted the King's order.

"Does the King have a safe room in his chambers?" Theobald asked, whirring to face Bashar.

"Yes, but . . ." Bashar gestured to the King. The monarch was still connected to the IV, heart monitor, and clearly too weak to walk without assistance.

"The bed's on wheels. You and the nurse take him. We'll hold them off as long as we can," Theobald said.

Theobald was already moving toward cover to defend the King's bedchamber. Whitney felt a wave of both adrenaline and fear wash over her as she moved, already several steps ahead of her partner, Glock in hand. She set up behind a marble credenza and sighted on the gilded doors separating the bedroom from the hallway outside. Apparently, Bashar had been wrong about the muscular bodyguard outside. Based on the bidirectional gunplay she was hearing, the man had chosen to fight and risk his life for the King.

"Are we really doing this?" she called to Theobald.

"We don't have much of a choice," he shouted back from the other side of the room.

Whitney thought about all the drills and missions where she'd been in the TOC while Chunk and the guys breached and cleared rooms. Numbers didn't lie: Statistically, things usually didn't go well for the defenders. Being on the receiving end of a breacher team was not the position she wanted to be in.

I don't have a rifle, body armor, or a helmet. I don't even have an optical sight on my pistol. If Faisal sends a SWAT team to take us, we're totally screwed.

No sooner had she thought those words, then the heavy gilded doors swung open. Two men with pistols entered the room. Maybe it was God's hand, or maybe it was the countless hours she'd spent on the range, or the laser-focused precision fueled by fear and adrenaline, but Whitney dropped the assaulter surging forward on her side with a double tap.

Theobald dropped the other.

Or at least, she was pretty sure he did. The second she capped her tango, she'd immediately dropped low behind the credenza. She held and waited for instruction from Theobald.

Seconds passed with no gunfire, no commotion, no pounding footsteps. She could feel her pulse throbbing in her neck, in her temples, in her ears. She realized she was holding her breath and forced herself into a four-count rhythm while she waited on Theobald.

"Clear," he shouted.

She hesitated. Was he speaking for both of them or only for himself? Was she supposed to say "clear," too, because she dropped her guy? Or did his "clear" refer only to the act of dropping his own shooter a moment ago, and now it might not be clear?

Damn it. She'd heard the guys report "clear" a thousand times on ops, and it never seemed complicated.

Why am I making it complicated?

"The entry is clear, Whit," Theobald said, apparently sensing her confusion.

She popped her head up for a scan. The doorway was empty, two unmoving bodies on the floor, and Theobald was in a crouching firing stance covering the entry. With a forced exhale, she brought her weapon up and sighted on the doorway in a kneeling firing stance, backing him up.

"What now?" she called.

"Not sure," he said as he advanced on the hallway. She covered him as he quickstepped to the threshold of the double doors, took a knee, and quick-sighted around the corner to the left, the direction they'd come from originally. Next, he swiveled, sighted the other direction, and called, "Clear."

On hearing this, she stepped out of her position and moved to join him.

"Check those guys," he said.

Good idea, she thought. She knelt beside the bodyguards Faisal had sent to murder them. The lifeless eyes, unmoving chests, and bloody black holes in both men's skulls definitively answered his question.

"Both dead," she said and quickstepped to his side.

"This dude's KIA as well," he said, taking a knee beside the fallen security guard who'd tried to protect the bedroom.

"I think the two we dropped were Faisal's fixers," she said. "I recognized their faces from the security footage. They were the ones who murdered the Mossad agents."

"Agreed."

"What now? Do we go after Faisal?"

"Hell no," Theobald said emphatically.

"I'm so glad you said that," she said. "Safe room, then?"

"Safe room."

They backed into the King's bedchamber and worked together to close and barricade the gilded doors with the marble credenza Whitney had covered behind. It was so heavy they could barely move it, but with sheer force of will, they got it into position.

"That oughta hold for a while," Theobald said.

"Ya think?" she said, catching her breath.

Footsteps behind them made them whirl, weapons up.

"Don't shoot! It's me!" Bashar said, his hands flying up over his head. His gaze ticked to Faisal's two dead enforcers on the marble floor. "You killed them?"

"It was us or them," Theobald said. "They murdered the guard in the hall."

"That means Faisal sent them to kill us," Bashar said, eyes wide in shock. "It's just unbelievable."

"He knows the gambit is up," Whitney said. "We've backed him into a corner, and there's only one option remaining for Faisal now. He has to eliminate all witnesses. That includes you and the King, as well as the two of us."

She didn't quite catch Bashar's Arabic, but she knew a curse when she heard one.

"We barricaded the door, but it won't hold forever," she said. "I'm sure Faisal will order Chief Saad to finish the job his hitmen could not. What will happen when Saad musters the palace security force against us?" Whitney asked. "Who will they obey when forced to choose between the Crown Prince and the King?"

"Saad is loyal to Faisal, but I suspect not all the staff will raise arms against the King," Bashar said.

"The two of us won't be able to hold them off indefinitely," Theobald said. "We'll run out of bullets long before Faisal runs out of men."

"You've done enough. The King owes you his life," Bashar said. "Come and join us in the safe room. It is impenetrable. In the meantime, the King has summoned General Ahkmed and special forces to secure the palace. The King has many friends and allies. Not everyone here is loyal to the Crown Prince."

CHAPTER 45

CROWN PRINCE FAISAL'S PRIVATE RESIDENCE

AL-YAMAMAH PALACE

Reza wanted to wake up.

Wake up from this nightmare and find himself in his apartment bedroom with Aliyah lying naked against him.

Unfortunately, Reza *was* awake, and the nightmare he was experiencing was real life.

On the one hand, it made perfect sense that Faisal's rise and fall from power would happen this way—meteoric on the way up, swift and catastrophic on the way down. Faisal had never been equipped mentally or emotionally to usurp the throne from his brother. On the other hand, a mere twelve hours ago, Reza had been convinced his old college mate had done everything necessary to firmly cement his future as the ruling face of Saudi Arabia for decades to come.

Strange how the fortunes and lives of men can turn so quickly.

"Are you going to answer the question?" Faisal said, his

voice ripe with impatience and frustration. "Do I pull the plug on my father and seize the monarchy, or do I continue working the charade?"

Reza blinked and wondered how long he'd been tuning Faisal out.

"What you've asked me is the one question I can't answer. It is something that you and you alone have to decide, because you and you alone will have to live with the consequences for the rest of your life."

The Crown Prince threw up his hands in exasperation. His response had angered Faisal, who despite everything that he'd accomplished still preferred the simplicity of being told what to do. The Prince had been this way for as long as Reza had known him. Making real decisions was hard—too hard for most people, in Reza's opinion—which was why the small minority of the people who ruled the world were the rare breed who were comfortable thinking for others.

A sharp knock on the door interrupted them both.

"Answer that," Faisal barked, commanding Reza to the door with a wave of his hand.

Reza did as ordered, bristling inside. He walked to the door and opened it to reveal a harried Security Chief Saad and four armed security guards.

"Your Highness, it's Chief Saad," Reza said.

"It's about fucking time! Where have you been? What took you so long to get here?" the Crown Prince shouted.

"My deepest apologies, Your Highness," Saad said, bowing his head. "I got here as fast as I could."

"Has anyone told you what's going on?"

"Yes, Your Highness. Hikmat called as soon as the guards were found dead and the Americans were discovered."

"Well, I haven't heard anything from Hikmat in over

fifteen minutes, since I ordered him to arrest the American intruders and secure my father's chambers."

Saad bowed his head again. "Neither Hikmat nor Jafar are answering their phones. I've sent a six-man team to investigate and secure the King's residence."

"And what did this six-man team report?" Faisal said with a stomp of his foot.

"I . . . I . . . just dispatched them, Your Highness. I'm awaiting word," Saad said, visibly flustered.

Faisal crossed his arms. "There's something you're not telling me. I can see it on your face."

Saad swallowed hard. "I've been informed that General Ahkmed has dispatched a military security force to secure the palace."

Reza watched Faisal receive this report like a slap across the face. The Crown Prince stood, mouth open and murder in his eyes, glaring at Saad.

"I . . . I . . . had nothing to do with it, Your Highness," Saad stammered.

"I certainly didn't call General Ahkmed. So, if you didn't call him, and I didn't call him, then who did?" Faisal barked.

"It could only have been one man—Bashar."

"I knew I should have had that traitor locked up," Faisal said with narrowed eyes. "Chief Saad, ring the general and tell him to call off his troops. Their presence is not necessary. Everything is under control here."

"Yes, Your Highness. But maybe there would be a higher probability of success if you were to contact the general directly yourself. He's more likely to heed a direct order from the Crown Prince than from me."

"Useless! You're all useless," Faisal snapped. "Fine, I'll call him, but I want you to personally go and oversee the team that is securing the King's residence. Report to me when you have the Americans either in custody or in body bags. I don't care which."

"Yes, Your Highness," Saad said. He bowed and closed the door. A heartbeat later, he reopened it. "I'm going to leave a security detail of four men outside your door—as a precaution."

"Fine," Faisal said and dismissed his guard with a wave.

Reza turned to look at Faisal. The Crown Prince, whose expression had been fiery and furious a moment ago, now looked like a terrified child waiting in his room for Father's belt. This last bit of news from Saad—that soldiers had been dispatched to the palace—changed everything for Reza. He knew that the King's advisor, Bashar, would not and could not order General Ahkmed to send a tactical team to the palace. That order could have only come from the King. And if it came from the King, then it meant the King was awake. The old man hadn't ruled Saudi Arabia for decades by accident. He was cunning, ruthless, and had made as many allies as he had enemies over the years in the Kingdom.

If the Americans had revealed the truth of Khalid's murder to the King, the King's retribution would be swift and terrible.

It's over, Reza thought, forcing his expression to remain neutral. *Faisal will be arrested, stripped of his crown, and probably executed.*

"What should I do, Arash?" Faisal asked. "Tell me: Should I call the General?"

Reza heard the question, but his mind had already shifted into self-preservation mode. He knew Faisal better than Faisal knew himself. If forced to choose between their friendship and saving his own skin, Faisal would pick the latter a hundred times out of one hundred.

And the same is true in reverse.

Faisal hadn't yet thought as many steps ahead as Reza, but the Saudi Prince would get there eventually. When confronted by the King's interrogators, Faisal would look for a scapegoat, and the most logical target was Reza. Faisal would blame Reza for filling his head with lies and unworthy aspirations. He would cast Reza as the mastermind of the coup. At the King's behest, Saudi intelligence would start digging, and with enough time and effort, they would pierce his NOC. Faisal wouldn't be exonerated, but he would take Reza down with him. And that meant that not only was his mission a failure, but Iran would be blamed for everything that had happened. His country would be destroyed in the aftermath—geopolitically and perhaps even literally.

And I can't allow that to happen.

"Yes," Reza said with certitude, meeting Faisal's eyes. "You're the Crown Prince. By title and rank, the Saudi armed forces work for you. Call the General and order him to stand down."

Faisal puffed out his chest. "You're right—the General works for me, not my father. I'm going to call him and order him to stand down immediately."

Reza nodded and flashed the prince an approving smile.

While Faisal picked up the palace phone and demanded to speak with General Ahkmed, Reza circled behind the Prince and pulled an ultracompact Glock 42 from his concealed holster. In the deepest, most Machiavellian part of his brain, the decision had already been made, and the operative in him never questioned it. With speed and precision, he grabbed Faisal from behind, jammed the muzzle into his friend's right temple, and squeezed.

The Glock kicked, and Faisal instantly became deadweight in Reza's left arm.

He let the body fall, quickly placed the pistol in the dead monarch's limp right hand, and quickstepped to open several meters of distance between himself and the body. A heartbeat later, the door to the hallway crashed open, and two guards rushed in, drawn by the sound of gunfire. They looked at Faisal, looked at Reza, then jerked their sidearms.

"I . . . I didn't know," Reza stammered.

"You didn't know what?" one of the guards said.

"I didn't know he was going to do it. If I had, I would have tried to stop him," he said.

The tears and angst came easily and naturally to Reza, because in this case, the emotions he was portraying happened to be real.

He'd just murdered his best friend.

It had been necessary, but he hadn't wanted to do it. Reza felt weak in the knees and let himself collapse into a heap on the floor. As he sobbed, the guards left him alone as they radioed Chief Saad to report what had happened.

No one would challenge Reza's story.

The Crown Prince had just committed suicide, and in doing so had solved everyone's problems—including Reza's own.

CHAPTER 46

APARTMENT BUILDING
BEIT HANOUN
THE GAZA STRIP
2331 LOCAL TIME

As he crossed the roof, Chunk experienced the strangest sensation. It almost felt as if a steel cable was dragging him forward into the stairwell, into danger. Stopping at the threshold to clear the top landing took a herculean effort on his part, like slamming the brakes to slow the momentum of a fully loaded semitrailer. But once he was stopped, the feeling didn't go away. The invisible tether was still trying to reel him in, as if a winch was connected to the nuclear weapon that intelligence had placed in a multimile-long tunnel that originated at this exact location.

In all his years as a SEAL, he couldn't ever remember feeling this way. He'd had countless missions where he'd felt a sense of urgency, the proverbial ticking clock people refer to, but never anything like this. This mindset felt dangerous, reminiscent of yesterday's warriors, who charged blindly into battle only to be cut down by enemy fire. JSOC operations were surgical. Precise. Controlled. Never wild and fueled by rage and passion.

Tonight, however, was different.

Tonight he would die for the mission, and do so gladly.

"Clear," he barked after sweeping left on the concrete landing at the very top of the stairwell.

"Clear," Riker echoed on Chunk's right.

Riker, who was now in the lead position, wasted no time descending the staircase, and Chunk couldn't help but wonder if his LCPO was tethered to the same invisible winch that he was. Rifle up and legs pumping like pistons, he followed his brother SEAL, scanning for targets down the center column of vertical empty space. In less than ten seconds, he and Riker arrived on the second-story landing. A steel fire door separated the stairwell from the apartments on level two. Riker took a knee, sighting on the closed door. In his mind's eye, Chunk imagined shooters crouching on the other side, waiting in ambush. But instead of breaching the hallway beyond, he decided that Yi would have warned them of any thermals in that location, and it was best to keep moving and minimize engagements.

Getting to the tunnel as quickly as possible was the mission.

He chopped a hand at a forty-five-degree down angle and slipped behind Riker to take the lead on the descent to the ground level. He registered Riker rising and falling behind him in his peripheral vision. Above, the rumble of a dozen pairs of combat boots descending in trail reverberated in the stairwell. Everyone on this mission was an experienced operator, and none of them were pounding the ground with their footfalls, but fourteen kitted-up shooters descending en masse made noise.

On reaching the ground-level landing, Chunk confirmed the steel fire door was shut and immediately cleared left, confirming two important details at once: First, nobody was hiding under the staircase in the back corner in ambush; two, the staircase continued down to the basement. Chunk took a knee and sighted down the flight of the switchback stairs leading to the basement, covering the approach.

"One, third-story charges set," Trip reported in Chunk's ear.

"Check," Chunk said quietly, picturing his SEAL brother unwinding det cord from the bricks of C-4 that he would have strategically placed on load-bearing points as he descended the stairs above. The SEALs had been born out of the Navy's Underwater Demolition Teams (UDT). Demo was still very much a part of their expertise and skill set.

Riker drifted past Chunk on the right, and he felt the SEAL's gloved hand momentarily on the top of his shoulder. Normally, gestures such as this were used to communicate positions nonverbally, but tonight the momentary contact sent a different message: *What we do now, we do for the fallen.*

Chunk popped up into a combat crouch and followed Riker down the stairs. Their X27 NVGs were so good that Chunk often forgot he was on night vision. The image processor automatically adjusted brightness to compensate for variations in ambient light and could even prevent "whiteouts" when encountering an unexpected light source, like the single light bulb now hanging from a wire tied to the underside of the staircase at the bottom landing. Down here, there was no steel door blocking off the stairwell from the rest of the building—just a rectangular open doorway in the concrete wall leading to the space beyond. Riker stopped short of the opening, his right shoulder against the wall. Chunk took a knee just behind him. Thanks to the light bulb, the inside of the bottom of the stairwell was lit. Which meant anyone in the basement would be able to see them.

"One, Three—charges set on level two," Trip reported.

Chunk acknowledged the report with a double click, then looked over his shoulder to get a look at the spacing of the operators behind him. Immediately behind him were Edwards and Antman. Behind them, Hutch and Thor paused on the steps, and behind them two pairs of Israeli operators. Spence and Trip, he knew, were likely heading to level 1 to set charges there. Seren Ze'ev Mirashi was leading from the rear to safeguard their six.

Chunk touched a flash-bang on his kit, then pointed at Riker.

Riker shook his head.

Chunk screwed up his face at Gold's best breacher, not understanding the dissenting opinion.

"Feels like a trap," Riker whispered, his voice barely audible.

Riker tapped one of his frag grenades, then another. Then he pointed to Chunk's grenades and gestured his intention: He wanted to throw four—one right, one left, and two center. This was a highly unconventional breach strategy, but in this case, it made perfect sense: They weren't trying to extract an HVT for questioning. Anyone guarding the tunnel needed to die, so why not breach with shock and awe and mop up after?

Chunk nodded. He and Riker would breach at the same time, he gestured, with his LCPO clearing left while he went right.

Riker nodded his agreement this time.

Chunk turned and signaled to Edwards and Antman that the two of them should clear up the middle, and got a pair of nods back. Next, he gestured to Hutch and Thor to hold, and the SEAL canine handler nodded his agreement. His gut told him that Thor had a role to play, and that role was going to involve the tunnels, and he didn't want to risk the dog getting shot in a melee before they'd even located the tunnel. If the entrance was hidden, they'd be counting on Thor to find it and find it quickly.

Riker pulled two fragmentation grenades from his kit, one in each hand, and yanked the pins with his teeth. Holding the safety levers depressed, he crabbed closer to the open doorway. When he was set, he looked back at Chunk.

Chunk pulled a frag grenade from his kit, pulled the pin, and mouthed, "Go."

Riker tossed the first grenade through the doorway into the void. A few seconds later, it detonated with a roar. He rolled the second grenade around the wall to the right and jumped clear for Chunk, who tossed his grenade to the left. They'd effectively delivered their payloads to frag a 180-degree arc of coverage on the other side of the wall, and because the wall was four-inch-thick concrete, it would easily shield them from the shrapnel blasts.

The second and third grenades detonated with successive booms, and Riker and Chunk were up and moving through the doorway. Riker went left, and Chunk cleared right, while Antman and Edwards surged up the middle.

Riker's intuition had been prescient: A pair of enemy shooters had been waiting in ambush. One was already down and squirming on the floor, while the other was frozen in shell-shocked confusion holding his rifle up but not sighting. Chunk put his targeting dot on the young jihadi's forehead and squeezed the trigger. The fighter's head snapped back, and he dropped like a sack of dirt. Chunk indexed left and low to target the wounded jihadi, aiming above his left ear, and ended the terrorist's pain permanently. Behind him, Chunk registered pops from Riker's rifle, as well as volleys from Edwards and Antman off to his left. He finished his scan all the way to the far-right corner. Finding no new threats, he swiveled left to surge forward and clear an imaginary alley next to where Edwards and Antman swept up the middle.

The basement was littered with mounds of dirt, wheelbarrows, piles of broken cinder blocks, tools, and wood scraps. Chunk quickstepped its entire length, encountering no further resistance, and joined up with his teammates on the other side.

"Three KIA," Edwards said, speaking for himself and Anthony.

"I capped one," Riker called. "Left side is clear."

"And two for me," Chunk said, taking a moment to really survey the cavernous basement. "Let's sweep for booby traps before we call clear."

"Agreed," Riker said.

"Seven—hold while we sweep for secondary threats," Chunk said.

"Copy, One," Hutch came back.

Chunk moved quickly and with purpose, looking for IEDs among the junk and rubble. In short order, the four-man team had swept the basement for bombs and found nothing of concern.

"Vengeance—the basement is clear. Fall in," Chunk said, summoning the rest of the assault force. Then, to his guys nearby, "Spread out and look for the tunnel entrance."

The Belgian Malinois, Thor, didn't waste any time getting to work. Within ten seconds of entering the basement, he made a beeline to a row of metal lockers standing along the far wall—the north wall, Chunk realized. After sniffing along the bottom and the right and left corners, Thor walked to the center of the row of lockers, sat, and looked at Hutch.

"Good boy," Hutch said and jogged up to give his partner a scratch behind the ears.

Gunfire erupted from the stairwell, and Chunk whirled to face the doorway they'd entered from. Mirashi and two Israelis who were guarding their flank were actively trading volleys, with a threat coming toward them from up the stairs.

Chunk turned to Hutch. "Can Thor smell an IED?"

"Depends, but yeah, that's in his skill set," Hutch said. "You worried they booby-trapped the lockers? That when we try to move 'em, they're gonna go boom?"

"Yep."

"Thor—Search ED," Hutch said. Thor immediately went back to work, assessing the lockers with an olfactory tenacity.

"One, Eight—we've got company behind us," Mirashi said in Chunk's ear, confirming what Chunk had already deduced.

"Copy. I assume Three and Four are clear, and the charges are set?"

"Affirmative," Mirashi came back. "If the guys shooting at us notice the det cord, they could cut it, and we'll lose the ability to detonate."

Shit, he's right.

Chunk looked over at the doorway. Trip and Spence were standing off to the side with the detonators, looking at him. He hand-signaled for them to relocate to the west wall, on the opposite side of the basement from the stairwell access. Spence gave him a thumbs-up, and they began unspooling det cord away from the stairwell. Chunk turned back to look at the group of operators assembled around him, waiting for instructions.

"Well, what do you think?" he asked Hutch. "Does Thor smell a problem?"

The canine superstar had seemingly finished conducting

his olfactory investigation, because Thor was standing beside the locker, tongue lolling in a relaxed posture.

"He didn't find anything," Hutch said, "but that's not a guarantee, boss. It's a probability game with dogs. His nose is incredible, but there are so many factors when it comes to ED interrogation."

"Good enough for me," Chunk said. "I need a volunteer to help me move the lockers. The rest of you, take cover over there with Edwards and Anthony."

A bunch of hands went up, but Riker and one of the Israelis walked over to the lockers and stood on either end.

"We got this, boss," Riker said.

Chunk crossed his arms.

"Seriously, dude. The unit needs you a helluva lot more than it needs me right now. Now git."

There wasn't time to argue. Chunk nodded and jogged with Hutch and Thor over to where everyone was huddled low in the far corner. Taking a knee, Chunk ducked his head, shut his eyes, and said a prayer that he didn't lose another brother today . . .

A loud scraping sound—metal on concrete—echoed in the basement as Riker and the Israeli operator shoved the row of lockers out of the way. The sound was like fingernails on a chalkboard, but for Chunk, it was sweet music to his ears because nothing went *boom*.

"One, Two—that dog's got one helluva nose," Riker said on the radio. "I'm in the tunnel, and it's a big one."

The corner of Chunk's lips curled up into something almost resembling a smile. "Vengeance, infil the tunnel. Three—blow the stairs when Eight is clear."

"Three," Spence said, using his call sign as an acknowledgment.

Chunk quickstepped with the rest of Vengeance platoon to the north wall, around the lockers and into the tunnel, where Riker and one of the Shayetet 13 guys were kneeling in firing stances, covering down the tunnel into the darkness.

"Eight, Eleven, and Twelve are clear," Mirashi reported over comms at the same time he and two of his guys slipped into the tunnel. "Blow it."

"Check. Blowing charges," Spence said.

A heartbeat later, the entire building shook as twelve bricks of C-4 detonated in rapid succession, bringing not only the staircase down but, by the sound of it, some or all of the eastern wall of the building. Spence and Trip ducked into the tunnel a few seconds later, their helmets, kits, and sleeves covered with a fine layer of gray dust.

"Probably shoulda blown it from in here," Spence said with a cough.

"Yeah, we didn't because we're SMRT," Trip said, wiping dust from his eyes.

"You mean SMARRT," Spence fired back, completing the Homer Simpson reference.

"Chunk," Mirashi called. "Should we set charges here as well to collapse the tunnel entrance? I don't want to have to worry about being pursued and covering our six the entire time."

"Trust me," Spence said, spitting grit from his mouth. "Ain't nobody following us now. That stairwell was the only way down, and from what I saw, it's completely caved in. It would take weeks to dig it out."

"That's good enough for me if it's good enough for you," Chunk said, meeting his Israeli counterpart's eyes.

"It is."

Chunk and Mirashi turned at the same time and looked

down the eight-foot-tall by eight-foot-wide tunnel—engineered with cinder blocks and wooden beams—that stretched off into the distance.

"Okay, boys, this is what we train for," Chunk said with a resigned exhale. "It's time to run."

CHAPTER 47

KING ABDUL'S PRIVATE RESIDENCE
AL-YAMAMAH PALACE
2341 LOCAL TIME

Whitney was sheltering in the King's safe room with Theobald, Ramia, Bashar, and the King when the report of the Crown Prince's suicide was called in by the General himself. Minimal blood had been shed stripping the Crown Prince of his power; the bloody gun battle between General Ahkmed's military response team and Chief Saad's security team for control of the palace never happened. Nevertheless, Whitney watched the King's fury instantly transform into grief at the loss of his one remaining son.

Faisal committing suicide was the one resolution to the situation that none of them had anticipated.

"It's imperative that the King release a statement walking back the false accusation that Crown Prince Khalid was assassinated by the Mossad," Princess Ramia said, pressing Bashar hard.

The King's advisor was nodding while Ramia spoke,

but Whitney could see this wasn't Bashar committing. She suspected the King still needed to be brought up to speed on everything that had happened while he'd been unconscious. Speaking of being out of the loop, Whitney had been without comms for hours with Bowman and Yi. She had no idea what was going on in the outside world. She checked her mobile phone and saw that her cellular service had still not been restored.

"I still don't have comms," she said to Theobald. "Do you?"

He shook his head.

"I need to check in with the unit," Whitney said. "Lord only knows what sort of fires they're trying to put out right now."

He nodded, again saying nothing.

"Are you okay, Bobby?" Whitney asked. Either something had his tactical antenna up, or he was upset.

"I'm fine," he said. "I'm just praying we're not too late."

"What do you mean?"

"Faisal gave the rest of the Muslim world the excuse they needed to join forces and wipe Israel off the map. It's going to be difficult, if not impossible, to put that genie back in the bottle."

Suddenly, her concern about putting out fires felt like the understatement of the year. Theobald was right: Israel's enemies had been waiting for an opportunity like this for over a decade. With a cause to rally around, they would band together and attack the Jewish homeland from all angles. And from what she knew about Prime Minister Shamone, Israel would not hesitate to defend itself. Even if King Abdul walked back Faisal's false claims, it might be too late. If history had taught her anything, it was that once a war starts, it tended to take on a life and trajectory of its own.

Before she could verbalize her concerns, Ramia walked up

to join them. The Princess looked completely spent, as if she'd just crossed the finish line of a marathon she didn't realize she'd been running.

"It was very brave what you did," Ramia said, fixing Whitney with a weary smile. "Thank you for coming back to the embassy."

"It was the right thing to do," Whitney said.

Ramia chuckled. "Then you're in an elite club. Sadly, over the years, I've learned that most people only do what's in their own best interest."

Whitney smiled. "Well, I feel the same way about you. Challenging Faisal and sneaking us into the palace tonight saved many lives. Faisal wanted to turn the clock back on Saudi Arabia and sow discord across the Middle East. You stopped that before it could happen."

Ramia pursed her lips, unconvinced. "We shall see . . ."

Whitney turned to Theobald. "Bobby, we need to get back to the embassy. I need to check in," she said, letting the urgency in her voice convey the unspoken.

"My driver will take you," Ramia said, astute as ever. "He's standing by in the parking garage."

Whitney nodded. "Are you coming with us?"

"My place is here now. Bashar and the King will need my guidance in the coming hours," Ramia said with a tight-lipped smile, then opened her arms for a hug. "After everything we've been through, I think of you as a sister, Whitney. If you ever need anything from me, don't hesitate to call."

Whitney embraced the Princess. "Likewise."

Ramia extended her hand to Theobald. "Thank you, Mr. Theobald."

"It was an honor," he said, shaking her hand and bowing his head.

"I realize you are leaving without an audience with the King, but know that His Majesty is a thoughtful man who always repays his debts. Bashar and I will make sure he knows that the two of you saved his life. You will always have an ally in the Kingdom of Saudi Arabia."

Whitney nodded to the Princess and departed the King's private chambers with Theobald at her side. As a palace staffer led them to the parking garage, Theobald must have noticed her wringing her hands.

"It's over, kid," he whispered. "Don't worry. We're safe now."

"It's not us I'm worried about," she said, wondering where Chunk and the rest of the team were, and just what kind of shitstorm they might be in.

As they reached the end of the hallway and turned right, she saw two uniformed men leading a third man, this one dressed in a suit, down the other hall. The man looked up, and their eyes locked. He was handsome, but something lit in his eyes when he saw her—something like rage.

"Who is that?" Whitney asked the staffer beside her.

"That, I believe, is the Deputy Ambassador to the Kingdom from Iran."

Whitney looked again, but the man had already turned away. She made an effort to burn his face into her memory for later.

You just never know . . .

CHAPTER 48

HAMAS TUNNEL, TWO AND A HALF MILES FROM THE TARGET BUILDING
TWO MILES FROM THE EXIT NEAR THE HIGHWAY NORTH OF EREZ, ISRAEL
2345 LOCAL TIME

Heydari gritted his teeth in frustration and stared at the high-powered radio in his hand as it gave him another burst of broken static. He knew without a doubt that whatever the unreadable message was, it was not good news. Only a mission-altering event would spur the team of jihadists back at the tunnel entrance to break his ordered radio silence.

"Say again, Abu," he tried again.

There was a burst of static, then a few words came through that tightened his chest.

". . . under attack . . . infidels . . ."

It was all he needed, and he closed his eyes, his mind reeling through the very limited options for success. Not only mission success but personal success as well. He had no intention of dying in these Gaza tunnels as a jihadist. He fully intended to play again with his little boy, Ahmed, his daughter, Yulia, and make love to his wife, Darya. Mission failure did not have to mean death, not for him.

He turned now to address the eight Sayf Allah terrorists who had been, in teams of four, pushing and dragging the 350-kilogram crate containing the nuclear device on a cart. He'd been furious on arrival in the basement to find they didn't have a motorized conveyance of any kind. It had been slow going moving the payload with manpower only. The cart was not designed to carry a load of this size and weight. Every meter of progress was a battle, trying to push the twenty-five-centimeter inflatable tires over a tunnel floor that was uneven, rutted, and full of debris.

"Enemy fighters have taken the building and have entered the tunnel. But don't worry. By the time they catch up, we will have reached the end of the tunnel and disappeared into the night," he said, doing some quick calculations in his head that made him seriously doubt his own words. "But we must go faster. We must work harder to fulfill Allah's will."

"*Alhamdulillah*," one of the younger men said, shifting his AK-47 on his shoulder and placing a hand over his heart.

Heydari mimicked the gesture and scanned the weary eyes of the men, all of whom were drenched in sweat. "I need two volunteers—two of Allah's best and most committed warriors to stay behind and ambush the Zionist fighters who are pursuing us."

All the hands shot up. Heydari pointed to the two slightly older, more experienced-looking fighters, one with a scar that started over his left eye and ended beside the tip of his nose.

"*Allah maeak*," he said, giving them a bow and then holding their eyes. "Your orders are to go back to where the tunnel splits and set an ambush. Take one of the IEDs and place it in the main tunnel before the branch. Detonate it when they approach. Then shoot any survivors and rejoin us."

The man with the scar scowled. "How can you be sure the explosion will not collapse the tunnel on our heads?"

"It may indeed collapse a section of tunnel, which is why I instructed you to set it *ahead* of the branch section. You will be safe if you wait a good distance back," he said. He was no engineer and had no idea if his words were true, but a collapse could be the perfect solution to stopping the pursuit. "If it does collapse, the debris will wall off the Zionist fighters, and we have won. If not, finish them off and rejoin us for our greatest triumph. Sayf Allah will forever be known as the warriors who ended the Zionist oppression of our people."

The man nodded, then grabbed one of the two satchels from the top of the crate. Heydari would use the other satchel to seal the exit once the weapon was safely out of the tunnel.

Or before, he thought, realizing he needed a contingency plan.

"I'm going to sprint ahead to the exit to make sure it is secure, and that our brothers have arrived with the truck," Heydari said.

"I will go with you," young Jabril said. "You need protection."

The gesture, and the young face that reminded him of his son, Ahmed, pulled at his heart. For a moment, he considered bringing the young man with him. But taking away even a single man would slow down their progress and further decrease their already withering chance of successfully delivering and detonating the bomb under Tel Aviv.

"You are very brave," he said, clapping the boy on the

shoulder. "But this is the part of the mission Allah has destined for me—to ensure you are safe when you arrive. You, my friend, are needed here." He leaned in and whispered, "Lead the others well, my young warrior."

Jabril beamed. "I will," the young man said.

With that, Heydari began his sprint down the tunnel toward the exit. He would not die for these men. He would not die for this mission. If the cart team could not beat the Zionist spec ops team to the exit with the weapon intact, Heydari would do what he always did in these situations.

I will disappear into the shadows and live to fight another day.

CHAPTER 49

HAMAS TUNNEL

2348 LOCAL TIME

Chunk ignored the growing burn in his legs as they sprinted through the terrorist tunnel. Physical readiness was a critical component of every special operator's skill set, and Chunk treated fitness the same way that elite professional athletes did: He made it a top priority and a professional obligation for himself and his team. Riker loved to tease Chunk about his stout, thick frame—the word *fireplug* had been used to describe his build on more than one occasion—and if Gold squadron was forced to field a track and field team, Captain Bowman would make Chunk the shot-putter. But Chunk was a shot-putter who happened to be able to run a 5K at a pace that would put him in the top third of a typical big-city race.

Chunk might not have been born to run, but he had grit in spades.

But this wasn't a street race. Chunk and his teammates

were kitted up, carrying sixty to seventy-five pounds of gear, and wearing boots. The tunnel, which had been impressively uniform and square at the origin, had gradually degraded the farther north they traveled. For one long stretch, the ceiling height had dropped low enough that they had to duck their heads as they ran. The floor had long since transitioned from concrete to dirt; the farther north they traveled, the more uneven, rocky, and pocked the surface had become. As hard as he was pushing himself, the group was probably averaging no faster than a nine- or ten-minute-mile pace over ground. Based on that math, Chunk estimated they'd traveled roughly a mile and half since entering the tunnel—which put them north of the 1950 Armistice Agreement Line and on Israeli sovereign soil.

As the group trudged along at a fast jog, Thor would sprint ahead in hundred-yard increments to conduct ED checks—Chunk and Mirashi had both dealt with enough terrorist masterminds to never underestimate their cunning and willingness to blow up their underlings—then wait for the pack to catch up, before Hutch would give the command to send him charging off ahead again. When Chunk had asked if the dog could handle the sprinting, Hutch had merely laughed and clapped Chunk on the shoulder. "Dude, he can run circles around us all day, every day, and five times on Tuesday. This is what he was born and bred to do."

As they caught up to Thor, who was sitting by the tunnel wall panting and waiting for them, Chunk held up a closed fist and halted the platoon.

"Problem?" Spence asked, huffing beside Chunk.

"Maybe," Chunk said, breathing hard and heavy. "Looks higher definition up there to me. What do you think?"

All night-vision systems, even the X27, worked by amplifying low ambient light to provide a high-contrast, enhanced picture. The resolution and quality of the amplified image was of lower quality than when operating in low-level visible spectrum light. Chunk had adapted to the grainier display, but now he sensed a change. He shut his eyes, flipped his goggles up, and waited. After fifteen seconds, he opened his eyes. There was a dim glow.

"I think I see light ahead," he said and flipped his NVGs back down. "They might have battery backups or generators at intervals along the tunnel."

"We'll lose our stealth unless we can find the power supply and cut power," Spence said. "For all we know, this could be power from a connection at the other end of the tunnel."

"Yes, this is a valid consideration," Mirashi said. "This tunnel probably exits somewhere in the vicinity of the Erez kibbutz, a Jewish communal settlement with a population of around six hundred people, located about a mile north of the Gaza security perimeter. Based on your estimate, we've traveled a little over half that distance. It is certainly possible that terrorists tapped a power line somewhere on the outskirts of Erez and brought the feed into the tunnel."

"Adapt and overcome. If we have to fight in the light, we fight in the light," Chunk said, in between panting exhales. "Keep your heads on swivels, gents. My gut tells me there's a surprise waiting for us ahead," Chunk said. He turned to Hutch. "Send him."

"Thor, ED search," the canine handler said, and the dog took off in a run down the tunnel.

Chunk gave everyone another sixty seconds to catch their breath, figuring this might be the last chance they had. Then he chopped a hand forward and set off. When they reached Thor, the dim aura he'd barely detected a hundred yards back was now a glowing bulb in a line of lights strung along the ceiling stretching off into the distance. Hutch sent Thor on the next survey patrol, and Chunk could see from the look on the man's face that he was less comfortable having his partner exposed and highly visible.

But it wasn't just Thor; all of them were at greater risk. That was the job and the nature of the work they'd all signed on for.

Chunk flipped up his NVGs, as did most of the team, and kept on trudging down the tunnel. The search continued, with Thor completing hundred-yard sweeps and the operators maintaining a steady pace between meetups. After a dozen or so of these, however, Thor reached a fork: The tunnel bisected into left and right passages that led off in different directions.

Hutch took a knee beside his dog, who'd dutifully waited for him. The Belgian whined, turned a circle, and looked agitated.

"Which way did they go, buddy?" Hutch asked, pointing left and then right. "Search ED."

Without hesitation, Thor took off toward the left-side tunnel.

"Left it is," Chunk said.

Before Chunk took his first step, Thor stopped, turned in a circle, and barked three times. Hutch stopped Chunk with a gloved hand on the shoulder.

"He found something. We need to—"

Chunk didn't hear the rest of the sentence. An explosion rocked the tunnel. Reflexively, he dropped prone on the ground as a plume of gray dust—moving at incredible speed—tumbled and rolled toward them down the left-hand tunnel. When he looked up, he saw Thor materialize mid-leap out of a cloud. The dog made it to Hutch's side just as visibility went to zero. Gunfire erupted a heartbeat later from somewhere ahead, enemy ambush shooters completely obscured by the cloud of dust.

Night vision could cut easily through the dark, but it couldn't see through smoke and dust. Until the dust cleared, they were blind. Chunk felt intact. He performed a quick self-assessment and felt no burning or pain anywhere on his body, but there were so many unknowns: How far away had the IED been located? How had it been oriented? What type of explosive had been used, and what type of shrapnel material encased the charge? Without being able to see his team, there was no telling what the terrorists had rigged up and what sort of damage it had delivered. Just because he hadn't been hit by shrapnel didn't mean others had been as lucky.

"Vengeance, SITREP?" Chunk shouted over the din as a gun battle erupted in zero visibility.

Everyone reported in as intact. Everyone but Thor.

"Seven, how's Thor?" Chunk called as enemy bullets zipped overhead.

"Seems intact," Hutch replied. "But I won't know for sure until the dust clears and I can give him a good once-over."

As if both sides were sharing one mind, the gunfire abruptly stopped.

Chunk's thoughts went to an unexpected place: tunnel integrity. In this section of tunnel, the workmanship looked shoddier than in the earlier stretches. Depending on how the terrorists had rigged up the IED, it was possible that the act of detonating it could destabilize the tunnel and cause a cave-in. Not only would that be potentially lethal for his team, but it would also result in a mission fail. He needed to get his guys on the other side of the blast zone.

He was just about to say this to Mirashi, when a loud bark and fierce growl turned his attention right.

The bark was from Thor, but the growl belonged to Riker.

Thor took off running north into the densest part of the dust plume and the enemy shooters, one lone operator sprinting after him as Riker followed the dog into battle. Through the clearing haze, Chunk saw the canine handler lying prone with his rifle up and a perplexed look on his face.

"Did you send him?" Chunk hollered.

"No. He did that on his own," Hutch hollered back.

A human shriek pierced the silence, followed by a growl, and a gunshot—

And another gunshot.

"Threat neutralized. Vengeance is clear to advance," Riker's voice said on the party line.

Rolling his eyes, Chunk got to his feet and led the rest of Vengeance platoon into the gray-brown haze that still filled the left-hand tunnel. When they emerged from the blast zone and the thickest lingering smoke, they saw Thor standing with his head high and muzzle bloody over one dead terrorist, while Riker was standing beside another, his booted foot on the dead man's chest.

"Damn, that animal is one fine warrior," Mirashi said with awe in his voice.

Chunk nodded, then shook his head with a grim smile. "Yeah, and so is the dog."

Friggin' Riker . . .

Hutch jogged to Thor's side, took a knee, and performed a fitness inspection. When he got to Thor's right haunch, he slowed down and pulled a flashlight for a closer look.

"Is he hit?" Chunk asked.

"Yeah, looks like he took a piece of shrapnel," Hutch said,

pulling a tube of something from his kit. "I think it punched through. Blood loss doesn't seem too bad, but I'm going to fill the hole with clotting agent."

"Is he out of the fight?" Chunk asked.

Hutch turned and shot him a funny look. "Does he look out of the fight?"

Chunk looked at the canine, panting over the dead terrorist with the ripped-out throat. "No, Senior, he does not."

"What about you?" Chunk said, catching Riker's eye. "I assume you're five by?"

"You know how I roll. Not a scratch," Riker said. He had a hard, humorless expression that Chunk had never seen from his teammate and friend.

Chunk was about to get the platoon moving, when a memory from the past popped into his brain: John Dempsey in the Iraqi desert using a masterful bit of tradecraft to fool the enemy long enough for them to turn the tables and survive the engagement.

He looked back at the two dead terrorists. "Trip, Jamie—strip off those guys tunics and caps and grab their AK-47s."

"Seriously?" Edwards said, cocking an eyebrow.

"Seriously," Chunk said.

They did as instructed. A moment later, Hutch finished up tending to Thor and gave Chunk a thumbs-up. Chunk chopped a hand, and they were on the move again. He could see Thor favoring his right leg when he ran, but the dog refused to slow down. Vengeance platoon advanced another half mile or so when Thor's ears pricked. When Hutch gave the search command, Thor lowered his head, sniffed the ground, then growled in the direction down the tunnel.

"He hears something," Hutch said, turning to Chunk. "I think we've just about caught up to them."

Chunk took a knee beside what looked like a set of small-size ATV tire tracks in the dirt. He'd assumed from the beginning the nuke was too heavy to hand-carry. The Israelis had estimated its weight at almost a half ton, so Chunk had expected a wheeled conveyance of some sort. But he didn't hear the growl of a gasoline-powered engine straining under the load, nor did he smell the unmistakable tang of exhaust.

Chunk motioned for the entire platoon to gather around him.

"Listen up. With this tunnel lit up the way it is, there's not much chance we're going to sneak up on the target convoy. We have no idea how many shooters they have. There's no cover of any kind. They could have an RPG. They could have a heavy machine gun. I know we've already briefed as much, and everyone here signed on anyway. But there's another option—"

"We already know what you're going to say," Mirashi said and flashed Chunk a wide grin. "And Shayetet 13 will provide the volunteers. Hand over the tunics, caps, and AK-47s."

"Now hold on," Riker said, shaking his head. "What if two of us want to volunteer?"

"You already got to play Superman. This is our country and our countrymen who are at risk. Besides, everyone in this unit speaks Arabic."

"He's got a point," Spence said and clapped a hand on Riker's shoulder.

Riker didn't react for a long moment, then he nodded.

Chunk had everyone take a knee to catch their breath while Mirashi and Jandy transformed themselves into the enemy. When the deed was done, they briefed the assault, with Chunk and Mirashi agreeing on a strategy in which less was more.

When in doubt, follow the KISS principle, Captain Bowman was fond of saying. *Keep It Simple, Stupid.*

"Good luck," Chunk said, extending his hand to his Israeli counterpart.

The Israeli officer nodded, then grinned. "If we're still standing when you arrive, please don't shoot us."

CHAPTER 50

HAMAS TUNNEL

ONE-FOURTH MILE TO THE EXIT OF THE TUNNEL

THIRTY-NINE MILES SOUTH OF TEL AVIV, ISRAEL

Heydari had put considerable distance between himself and the Sayf Allah martyrs, but he could not be sure of just how much. Sound traveled well in the tunnels, and for the longest time after he kicked off his sprint to safety, he could hear the muffled grunts and groans of young martyrs laboring over their impossible task.

The sound of the explosion and then gunfire was much easier to make out.

The engagement sounded brief. What he had no way of knowing was to whom the victory went. A part of him considered using the detonator immediately, grasping for at least a partial victory. Nearly a thousand Zionists would perish in the Erez settlement above, and while that was a relatively minor and inconsequential blow, it could still be used by Sayf Allah and all their other proxies as a rallying cry. Assuming that his colleague Arash Reza had been equally as successful in Saudi Arabia and an alliance had been formed, the long-term goals of the mission would still be met. There would still be a powerful alliance with Saudi Arabia, lifting Persia's might and influence in the region. Their proxies would rally behind any victory and form a caliphate of terrorists ready to bring down the Zionists and beat back the West.

But he was still in the tunnels, and unsure of how far it was to the exit. To detonate now would lead to his death, and destroying a single Jewish kibbutz was not worth martyring himself for. His beliefs about life after death in paradise were far less certain than the zealots' he now led. On the other hand, with each step, he knew the likelihood of his remote transmitter being effective decreased. The transmitter was powerful, but would it work once he exited the tunnel?

He simply didn't know.

And in any case, it was still more than possible that the ambush had worked and that the IDF special forces were now dead, buried in or blocked by a collapsed tunnel. Decision made, he left the detonator in his pocket and picked up the pace, sprinting toward the tunnel's end. According to Jabril, the exit was—ironically—inside a graveyard located a short distance from the highway leading to Tel Aviv. On reaching the exit, he would decide what to do. If the transport truck was waiting and ready to receive the weapon, he would give the Sayf Allah fighters in the tunnel as much time as possible to complete the mission.

If not, he would leave the detonator behind for Jabril and flee.

Heydari wiped sweat from his face with his sleeve, lowered his head, and pushed himself as hard as he could.

Just a few more minutes, and I will know my fate . . .

CHAPTER 51

HAMAS TUNNEL

Chunk watched Mirashi and Jandy run down the tunnel until they disappeared completely from view.

He checked his watch.

Twenty-eight seconds. I knew I was right.

To his right, Thor was whining and tugging at his lead—clearly not happy that two members of Vengeance team had gone ahead into battle without him.

Chunk looked at Riker, who seemed to be battling the same feelings as Thor. "Don't make me put a leash on you too, Senior."

This earned a chuckle from Trip, but Riker ignored the dig with a clenched jaw.

After forty seconds had passed, Chunk chopped a hand and Vengeance platoon moved out. The plan was simple: Ze'ev Mirashi and Jandy would advance with a one-minute lead, carrying unpinned grenades in their hands. Assuming the terrorists were still in the tunnel, and they let the two disguised

Shayetet 13 operators get close without engaging first, the Israeli operators would throw their grenades and engage with guns. The rest of the assault force would arrive less than a minute later and overwhelm with covering fire.

What could possibly go wrong?

"Boss, quick question," Trip said, jogging next to Chunk.

"Fire away," Chunk said.

"What are the odds the grenades accidently detonate the nuke?"

"Impossible," said the Israeli operator named Boaz. Boaz was one of two team members from Shayetet who had training in advanced EOD, defusing bombs and nuclear warheads.

"Nothing's impossible," Trip said.

"Nukes aren't like nitroglycerin. They're stable by design. To detonate, the correct geometry of the nuclear materials must be obtained in the warhead. Getting a nuke to explode at all is the challenge. It's more likely the grenades will render the bomb unable to detonate than the opposite."

"Hope you're right about that," Trip said, "because if that sucker goes off in this tunnel, we're cooked."

"We're cooked if it goes off anywhere in a mile radius," Boaz said.

"Thanks for that good news," Trip said.

A grenade detonation ended the conversation. A second grenade exploded a half second later, followed immediately by a racket of gunfire. Chunk kicked it into high gear, sprinting to close the gap and get into the fight. He and Mirashi had debated how much offset, and the Israeli had insisted on sixty seconds. Chunk had argued for thirty, and they'd split the difference at forty-five. Now he worried even that was too long, and by the time they arrived, it would be too late to back up Mirashi and Jandy.

Of course I was right, Chunk thought, gripping his rifle tight in his right hand.

When the firefight came into view, Chunk instantly determined there was bidirectional gunfire in play. At least one of his Israeli teammates was still in the fight.

No, they both are, he realized as he continued to close the gap.

They'd split, with one Israeli fighter taking a prone position along the left wall, the other on the right. Riker, despite being a decade older than the younger guys, was still the fastest man in Gold, and like a maniac with a death wish, he ran past Mirashi and Jandy, his rifle spraying fire.

Chunk anticipated what was going to happen next a split second before it did. Unlike Vengeance platoon, the enemy was in cover behind the nuke, which was on some sort of massive wheeled cart. He'd mentally noted the locations of the enemy muzzle flashes, and he knew which shooter would have the best line on Riker. Chunk stopped, raised his rifle—flipping his magnifier in place in front of his red dot—and took aim. A split second later, the terrorist shooter popped his head out to sight on Riker, and Chunk drilled him with a three-round burst to the face from seventy yards. The terrorist's head exploded in a puff of gore, and the body dropped into the dirt.

Trip dropped a shooter on the other side of the cart with a similar long shot.

Boaz dropped a third guy who tried to run away.

And Riker—well, he pulled a Riker and ran around the nuke cart to engage and kill what turned out to be the final living defender in a point-blank confrontation.

Like so many of Gold's engagements, this one was over in less than a minute. Once the site was called secure, the two bomb techs got to work trying to safe the nuke, with Trip watching over their shoulders.

"Do they have it on a timer?" he asked.

"No, it does not appear so," Boaz said, while he used a small electric screwdriver to remove screws from a housing cover.

"So, it's a remote detonator?"

"Yes, I think so," the Israeli answered.

"They probably rigged that with an anti-tamper device—"

"I know these things, Trip. This is not my first time."

"Just sayin' you gotta anticipate."

Chunk shook his head. "Trip . . ."

The SEAL looked over at him. "Yeah?"

Chunk beckoned his teammate with a curl of his index finger. "Dude, you gotta let 'em work," Chunk said.

"Yeah, but if they—"

"Trip, I'm serious."

"I'm just watching their six. I'm the EOD expert in Gold, so it's kinda my obligation to—"

Chunk put a gloved hand on his brother SEAL's shoulder. "Trip, leave 'em alone."

Trip nodded and walked away, murmuring, "Maybe you don't mind being the main course in a million-degree BBQ, but I for one—"

"Don't worry. They won't blow us up," Mirashi said, stepping up beside Chunk.

"Do I look worried?" Chunk asked, turning to meet the Israeli's eyes.

"A little . . ."

They both chuckled.

"I'm really sorry about your teammate, Saw," Mirashi said, pressing his fist against his chest.

Chunk could see the pained look in his fellow operator's eyes. He imagined there had been more than one such loss for this warrior, a man who had clearly given much for his country.

"Yeah . . . me too," was all Chunk could think to say.

"We owe you a debt of gratitude, my friend. Without you and your team, Tel Aviv would have become a nuclear wasteland."

"Well, don't jinx us. That nuke isn't defused yet."

"I know, I know. But I'm not superstitious. It's here, under our control, underground and thirty miles from Tel Aviv. Even if it does blow up, we won."

Chunk wasn't so sure he agreed, but he nodded anyway. "Happy to help."

It took another five nerve-racking minutes for Boaz and the other EOD expert to disable the remote detonator and safe the bomb, and when they announced as much, every member of Vengeance platoon let out a whoop or a holler—or, in Thor and Riker's cases, a bark.

"We should probably walk this tunnel to the end, boss," Spence said, walking up to stand on the other side of Mirashi. "A lot of people with clenched sphincters are waiting for us to radio the good news that we secured the package."

"You're absolutely right," Chunk said. He turned to Mirashi. "I say we leave a team here to guard the nuke. You and I take six guys and haul ass to the end of the tunnel."

A weary-looking Mirashi brought his rifle up, blew out a resigned exhale, and smiled. "I thought you'd never ask."

CHAPTER 52

EMERGENCY OPERATIONS CENTER (EOC)
US EMBASSY
RIYADH, SAUDI ARABIA
2359 LOCAL TIME

By the time Whitney and Theobald arrived at the embassy and cleared security, twelve minutes had slipped away. They burned another fifteen debriefing Ambassador Harley. By the time Whitney finally made it into the Emergency Operations Center (EOC) and convinced the watch officer that she was taking control, seven more minutes evaporated. When she finally established communications with the TOC in Amman, Captain Bowman and Chief Yi were already in the middle of coordinating a joint operation in Gaza with Shayetet 13 to stop a rogue nuke before a Sayf Allah terror cell could blow up Tel Aviv.

A lot had happened while she'd been out of communication in Riyadh.

And everything leading up to this moment had not come

without cost. Nick Sawyer had died on a maritime assault in the Mediterranean Sea, and the news had hit her like a sniper round to the soul . . .

Instead of focusing on how powerless, sad, and defeated she felt, she donned a headset, planted her butt in a task chair, and got to work as "Mother" in tandem with Yi. The embassy's EOC had everything that a Tactical Operations Center did, and now that all cellular, satellite, and data transmissions had been reinstated by the Saudis, her feeds and comms mirrored those in Amman. Right now, Gold squadron was underground pursuing terrorists smuggling a nuke in a tunnel that started in Gaza but popped out somewhere in Israel. The problem was twofold: One, there was no way to communicate with or geolocate her teammates while they were subterranean; and two, the Israelis didn't know where the tunnel exited on their side. With the clock ticking, and a nuclear weapon in play, there was too much uncertainty.

Which is something I intend to rectify.

"What are you searching for?" Theobald asked, looking over her shoulder as she worked the terminal.

"I'm trying to find the tunnel exit," she said, using the mouse to click and drag and zoom on satellite imagery of the Israeli countryside north and east of Beit Hanoun. Theobald was the intelligence community's version of a field marshal. He understood on-the-ground covert military operations better than anyone. She stopped clicking and dragging and turned to look at him. "Bobby, a couple of weeks ago, the Israelis reported finding a tunnel that surfaced on the east side of the Strip. I can't remember the name of the neighborhood where it came out."

"Hmm. It was Ne'ot HaNevi'im," he said and leaned to point at an unlabeled residential area, "which is here, I think. But they wouldn't dare use that one. It's compromised."

"Yeah, I know, but that was the longest tunnel discovered to date." She approximated the distance from Beit Hanoun to Ne'ot HaNevi'im. "Looks like it was roughly two and a half miles, depending on what I pick as the origin point in Beit Hanoun. So, if I use that as a reference distance . . . plus or minus a mile or even a mile and a half . . ."

"And if you make an arc . . ." he said, reaching over and tracing a rough arc with his finger, sweeping north from the end of the measuring tool, which was still showing a dot at Ne'ot HaNevi'im.

"You intersect Route 34," she said, finishing his sentence. "Which they can take to Route 4, which runs all the way to Tel Aviv."

"Bingo," he said.

"Bobby, what's the weight of a nuke?"

He scrubbed his face with his hands. "It depends on the yield and who made it. Since this one was probably built by the Iranians, it's probably a less elegant design. I don't know—eight hundred pounds? A thousand? This is not my area of expertise."

"But it's going to take a truck to transport it?"

"For sure," he said.

"Okay, so that means they're going to need to stage a truck at the tunnel exit to be ready to load it."

"They wouldn't have to stage it. It could be driving a route in a defined area with instructions to arrive at a set time. Or driving a loop waiting for a call."

She nodded. "Do you think they're that tactical?"

"Hell yes, they are," he said.

"Okay," she said, chewing the inside of her lip. "Instead of trying to find the tunnel exit, which is probably like trying to find a needle in a haystack, I'm going to look for trucks on and around Thirty-Four that could fit the bill—trucks with the right thermal signature in the arc, close to the highway in this area here," she said, tracing a short distance of road from where the highway made a sharp turn due north and back out to the east.

"I like it," he said and folded his arms to watch her work.

With machinelike tenacity, she zoomed in and out, methodically interrogating all traffic moving along Route 34. Eventually, she saw something.

"What do we have here?" she said, assigning a tracker to a U-Haul–type truck heading south on 34. She zoomed in. "Looks big enough."

"Yes, it does," he said.

"Whoa, whoa, whoa—he's getting off," she said, her voice ripe with anticipation. "I think he's going to Erez."

"Maybe. But Erez is the next exit. It looks like he's going somewhere north of Erez."

"What is that?" she said, moving her cursor to a little square patch of something off by itself, surrounded by trees.

"Looks like a cemetery," he said.

"Why's a U-Haul truck going to a cemetery in the middle of the night?" Whitney said. She switched the satellite feed from night vision to heat map thermal imagery and saw seven heat blobs—two in the cab, five in the covered trailer section. "Hello! There are five dudes in the back of that truck." She messaged Yi and dropped her pin with the coordinates. Then, keying her mic, said, "Yi, are you seeing what we're seeing?"

"Yes, the truck pulling into the cemetery," Yi said, from her terminal in Amman.

"Actually, it's backing into the cemetery," Theobald said.

"Yi, I think we found it—the tunnel exit. With Bowman's authority, we should have our air assets lock a firing solution on that truck."

"Ma'am, just playing devil's advocate here, but what if those are not terrorists in the back of that truck?" Yi came back. "What if they're gravediggers or groundkeepers?"

"I suppose it's possible, but why would they be there at this hour?" Whitney said.

"Maybe the shift starts early before it gets too hot?"

Whitney nodded. "Maybe, but I still think we ID this target with our air assets and get a firing solution read."

"Agreed, but I wouldn't be doing my job if I didn't ask the question."

"I know, Michelle. That's what makes us a good team."

"I've got a headset on, and I'm standing here with Yi," Bowman's voice said. "I heard everything, and I agree. You've got the green light, Watts, to ready firing solution, but not to fire."

"Copy and understood, sir," she said, then switched from the closed channel between the Embassy EOC and the Amman TOC to the broader tactical channel with their air and ground units. "Thunder One, this is Mother, over . . ." she said, hailing the lead pilot of a pair of Israeli F-35 fighters that were in orbit to support the operation with air support, if needed.

"Go for Thunder," the pilot came back.

"Thunder, enter and lock a firing solution using air-to-ground ordinance on a target designated Zulu 01," she said.

"Copy. Firing solution entered and locked on target Zulu 01 using Hellfire missiles," the pilot came back.

For the next seventeen minutes, they watched and waited, eyes glued to the screen. This was the worst part of the job—waiting while her teammates were in harm's way. Minutes felt like hours. She tapped her fingers on her thigh, then on the side of her chair. Yi twisted a loose strand of hair with a finger beside her and sighed away some of her own tension.

Then, unexpectedly, something insane happened. She leaned forward to confirm what she was seeing.

"Holy shit, we've got a new thermal," Whitney said, zooming in on the graveyard.

"Where did that guy come from?" Yi said.

"I think . . . he came out of that tomb," Theobald said.

"Okay, so either we're watching a zombie rise from the dead," Whitney said, heart pounding, "or we just found the tunnel exit."

CHAPTER 53

EREZ KIBBUTZ CEMETERY

EREZ, ISRAEL

ONE AND A HALF MILES NORTHEAST OF THE GAZA BORDER

Heydari walked up the ramp leading from the underground into the interior of a ceremonial crypt that concealed the exit of the six-mile-long tunnel. The structural camouflage was genius, and he took a moment to marvel at the ingenuity his partners in jihad had demonstrated. Finally out, he took a long, deep breath of fresh air, reinforcing how stale and dusty the tunnel had been. Beating a hand against his shirt and trousers, which brought a cloud of dust that made him cough, he walked out of the shed-size tomb. Brake lights appeared just a short distance away, which then became white backup lights as the small cargo truck began backing toward him. He looked back over his shoulder at the tunnel entrance, concealed beneath a large tree from above and inside a faux ceremonial crypt.

It was time to make a decision.

He pulled the brick-like high-powered radio from his pocket and raised it to his mouth.

"Abbas, Omar, Jabril, come in," he said, hailing the Sayf Allah warriors in the tunnel. "Hurry, my brothers. The truck is here."

He watched as two fighters emerged from the truck, raising a hand in greeting, ready to assist.

Heydari waved back and then clicked the transmitter again. "Jabril, come in . . ."

Still silence.

Was his team dead? Were the Israeli fighters closing in, ready to emerge from the tunnel at any moment? Or was the weapon still on its way, the Sayf Allah fighters victorious but simply not yet in range of his radio?

He thumbed the detonator in his pocket with his other hand, weighing his choices. With the weapon practically beneath his feet, his own death was guaranteed if he detonated the bomb now. He had never agreed to martyr himself on this mission—or any mission, for that matter.

But do you not put your life on the line every time you accept orders to conduct an operation in the field? A voice asked in his head. *Is dying in service of your country really any different than martyrdom?* He heard himself chuckle as epiphany cut through his self-delusion like a razor through unprotected flesh. *I'm such a fool . . . I'm no different than the men I lead. I never have been, and never will be.*

What sounded like a pair of military jets traveling fast and low streaked overhead, and his insides went queasy.

They've found us, he realized, feeling both the horror and weight of the moment. *Which means it's death by fire for me either way.*

He pulled the detonator from his pocket and said a little

prayer for forgiveness. Not for the things he'd done but for the lies he'd told his wife and children over the years—the wife and children he'd never hold or kiss again. Then, before his courage faltered, he pressed the detonator button.

Eyes closed, body tense, breath held, Jahan Heydari braced himself for what was coming next.

But to his dismay and disappointment, nothing happened.

CHAPTER 54

EMERGENCY OPERATIONS CENTER (EOC)
US EMBASSY
RIYADH, SAUDI ARABIA

"It's them," Whitney said over comms, her voice resolute. "It has to be."

"Where's the nuke? The thermal came out of the tunnel alone with nothing," Yi said, in Whitney's headset.

"It must still be in the tunnel," she said.

"So what, this guy's a squirter?" Yi said.

Dread instantly flooded every cell in Whitney's body, coupled with a moment of doubt. She didn't want to kill any innocents, but she could not let the terrorists responsible for all that had happened get away to kill another day.

"We need to take the shot," Whitney said.

Theobald stopped her with a hand on the shoulder. "Are you sure? We can track the truck."

"What if he squirted because Vengeance assaulted his convoy before he could exfil the bomb?"

"Then that means we have control of it," Yi said.

"Not necessarily. What if this guy is the one with the remote detonator?" she said.

"With all due respect, that's a lot of conjecture, ma'am," Yi said.

She felt her lower lip quiver. *I can't lose any more brothers tonight.*

"Many scenarios are possible," the Israeli intelligence officer Becker said on comms, weighing in for the first time since the truck had been spotted. "But it is more likely that Ms. Watts is correct. These are hard choices, but in Israel, we are in a fight for our very survival. There is a nuclear weapon believed to be in play. The small risk of collateral damage is more than justified here."

"We can't take the chance this guy detonates the nuke remotely," Watts said in the strongest voice she could muster. "Captain, I strongly recommend we take the shot."

"Do it," Bowman said.

Whitney switched comms channels. "Thunder One, this is Mother," she said. "Bring the lightning. Kill target Zulu 01."

"Copy. Killing target Zulu 01," the pilot said.

For a moment, nothing happened, then twin streaks of fire raced into the frame of the satellite feed from the west and turned the truck, now parked in front of the cemetery, into a massive fireball that whited out the feed.

No one cheered.

For a moment, no one said anything at all.

"Mother, Thunder One confirms Zulu 01 destroyed based on visual interrogation," the pilot reported, breaking the silence. "Standing by for additional targeting, if you need us."

"Roger that, Thunder One. Nice shooting," she said.

Theobald put a hand on her shoulder and gave it a single squeeze. He didn't say anything. He didn't have to.

Now, I just have to wait for Chunk to call in, and this nightmare can be over.

She couldn't stop herself from pacing now, or from looking at the clock. Or from thinking about Saw as she waited. She still couldn't believe he was gone. She could barely even imagine the pain that Ellie would be feeling at the loss of her husband and best friend. Did Ellie even know yet?

Then she thought of Chunk, of course. She thought of what he meant to her.

It took another seventeen minutes and forty-seven seconds, but the call finally came.

"Mother, this is Vengeance One—Jackpot, Jackpot, Jackpot," Chunk's voice said in her ear, his voice as crystal clear as if he was standing in front of her. "The weapon has been secured and is in Israeli custody. I repeat, Jackpot."

As soon as she heard the report, a wave of emotion practically knocked her over where she stood as all the feelings she'd kept bottled up since she arrived in the EOC busted the dam. Whitney collapsed into her chair and wept tears of relief, tears of joy, and tears of anguished loss all at the same time.

"Copy all, Vengeance," she somehow managed to choke out as she watched six thermals materialize in the graveyard. "Are you exiting the tunnel presently?"

"That's affirmative, and from the looks of it, you found it without me."

"Yes, I did."

"And from the smoldering remains of that truck, it also looks like you administered fiery justice from above," he said with an undertone of what sounded to her like pride.

She wiped her cheeks with the backs of her wrists, stood up straight, and, in wordplay only operators would appreciate, said, "That's right, Vengeance. Tonight Mother is God."

CHAPTER 55

IRANIAN MINISTRY OF FOREIGN AFFAIRS BOMBARDIER JET
ENTERING IRANIAN AIRSPACE, THIRTY-SEVEN THOUSAND FEET
OVER THE PERSIAN GULF
0645 LOCAL TIME

Reza stared pensively out the window of the luxury business jet, down at the coastline of his country and what he assumed to be the city of Bushehr to the south. The relief of having been allowed to leave the Kingdom of Saudi Arabia alive competed with the dread he felt at facing the Director of MOIS to debrief the mission's utter failure.

No. It was not the dread of the debrief. He had been on a very, very dangerous mission for which he had volunteered. The odds of success were known to be low, but the risk was outweighed by the enormous, world-altering benefits of success. That he had left the Kingdom with his head—but more importantly, without any provable evidence of Tehran's involvement—would be viewed as a success by Director Golzar, who was pragmatic almost to a fault.

Hopefully, the Minister of Intelligence would feel the same.

But that didn't erase the devastation of the loss. Surviving with his life was, of course, a win. That some version of his career might also survive was a bonus. But did that return the decade and a half of his life he had devoted to this project? It did not. In truth, he had been partly inside this NOC and this operation, the brainchild of the legendary Amir Modiri, for his entire adult life. He had been recruited by Modiri with this mission in mind, he knew. He had been trained extensively for this operation. He had lived and breathed it year after year, working patiently but tirelessly.

Reza sighed as the jet crawled across the coastline and the land of Persia slipped beneath them.

Now what?

Golzar would give him meaningful work, but it would not be the same. He might as well marry Aliyah. They could have a family.

Reza leaned back, pulling his eyes away from the window. Immediately, the lovely woman in a modest flight attendant uniform, replete with a little cap from which her face covering hung, rose and hurried to his side.

"Is there something I can get you, Mr. Ambassador?" she asked.

He smiled at her and felt her eyes on him in a way that suggested her face covering was a required uniform, not a symbol of the devout. In other circumstances, he felt sure he could conquer this lovely woman.

He had no such appetite today, however.

"Some tea, perhaps," he said, and she gave a slight bow, smiling at him with her eyes.

His mind went to the Americans, who had ruined everything. Faisal had viewed the tall man as the leader of the team who had destroyed everything he had built in his life. But Reza knew that wasn't true. He was modern enough, after his time in the UK, and open enough to the reality of the world beyond the borders of the Republic of Iran to shake the assumption bias and see the truth.

It was the woman. He had seen her, locked eyes with her for a moment, as he left the palace. In that moment, he knew. It was the way she looked at him—studied him almost. She had done this.

"Here you are, sir," the flight attendant said, brushing his hand with hers as she set the cup of tea on the table that separated him from the empty seat across from him. Her eyes smiled again, and this time he smiled back, making a show of looking her over slowly and closely, then holding her eyes and winking. He reached a hand out and let it rest on her hip.

She made no effort to remove it.

Reza considered a moment. Perhaps there was still work to do. Perhaps his professional life still had one more, important chapter.

"Perhaps you can sit with me and keep me company?" he said, caressing her hip gently.

"I would like that," she said, removing her cap and covering to reveal a lovely face.

He patted the seat beside him, now feeling a renewed sense of purpose as the woman slid into the seat beside him and placed a hand on his leg. If he was stuck at a desk for a time, he would spend every free moment finding just who this woman, the woman whose face was burned into his memory, really was.

EPILOGUE

TEL NOF AIRBASE (AIR FORCE BASE #8)
NINETEEN MILES SOUTH-SOUTHEAST OF TEL AVIV, ISRAEL
TWO DAYS LATER

Chunk stood beside the American flag–draped coffin in the misting drizzle.

Rain was unusual at Tel Nof this time of year. This meant the gray skies and rain had to be nature's tacit acknowledgment that a brave and noble man had given his life to safeguard the lives of so many others. Chunk had never considered himself a spiritual man, but while he waited, he swore he could feel Saw's presence.

Chunk, Trip, and Edwards stood on the left side of the casket, with Riker, Spence, and Antman ready on the right. The rest of the team stood behind, ready to board the plane for Saw's final flight home from deployment. Captain Bowman would walk at the lead, but tradition granted the honor of carrying the casket to Saw's closest brothers-in-arms.

At last, the rear cargo ramp of the C-17 began to lower—the signal to lift the coffin and begin the slow walk into the Air

Force jet's cargo bay. Chunk led his brothers, each gripping a silver handle on the side. As he stepped forward, the others matched his cadence, beginning their march just as the first real raindrop hit his cheek, blending with the tears streaming unashamedly down his face.

They had agreed Saw wouldn't want them in uniforms. They rarely wore uniforms in Gold anyway, and while digital cammies would have been the appropriate attire, these men spent most of their time—even in combat—wearing slicks or jeans and T-shirts. So they each wore unmarked cargo pants, their favorite T-shirts, and ball caps.

That's how Saw would have dressed, and it was what he would have wanted.

As Chunk carried his teammate—realizing only now that Saw had been his best friend—toward the waiting plane, he wrestled with the guilt already consuming him from the inside out. He'd been the one who'd convinced Saw to stay with the teams. He'd been the one who'd encouraged Saw to leave his family behind and deploy on this mission. It was his fault that Ellie was a widow, and Conner and Maggie no longer had a father to celebrate and participate in all life's challenges and joys. It was his fault Saw was gone.

But then Chunk remembered his conversation with Saw just before they'd deployed, the last real moment they'd shared together. "It was my decision, bro," Saw had told him. And Saw had been right. Chunk had lobbied for Saw to stay, yes, but it had been Saw—and Ellie—who had made the decision about what was right for him and their family. In the end, Saw had chosen the brotherhood, because they were a family too. Saw wouldn't have changed a thing, he'd said so himself. And Chunk guessed that Ellie would understand. She knew her husband better than anyone in the world, including Chunk.

So many brothers had given their last full measure of devotion in the two and a half decades since the towers had fallen. More than a hundred SEALs—and double that number, when you counted the SWCC operators, EOD techs, combat medics, and other support personnel who had accompanied them into battle. Far too many had taken their own lives after separating from the military, unable to escape the demons that followed them out of uniform. Each NSW death struck a blow to the brotherhood.

But until now, Chunk had never lost a brother this close to him. Saw was the first direct teammate he'd lost, and the first brother to perish under his command.

They reached the foot of the ramp, where the Air Force crew, still kitted up in helmets and connected to the jet by internal comms cables, stood at attention. As Chunk's entourage arrived with Saw's coffin, the crewmen snapped to attention. After a brief pause, Chunk took a step onto the aluminum ramp, and together, Gold Squadron carried Nick Sawyer up into the aircraft.

An enormous American flag hung from the overhead in the forward cargo hold, covering nearly the entire forward bulkhead. Two additional crewmen stood at attention on either side, snapping to attention as the flag-draped coffin approached. Upon reaching the designated area, marked by the casket-shaped space on the metal deck, Chunk quietly said, "Halt," and the detail stopped. After a moment, they took a collective knee, gently setting Saw on the deck, then rose in unison to face one another. On the other side of the coffin, directly opposite Chunk, Riker wept openly. Spence's cheeks were wet, and Antman looked like a man in shock.

The task was done—they'd delivered Saw to his final flight—but no one was ready to move. Sensing this, the aircrew stood patiently at attention, waiting. Finally, Chunk broke the spell, turning and heading aft in the C-17 cargo hold toward the rest of the SEALs and support personnel. Halfway down, he passed Bowman and Whitney standing together—the former red-eyed and unnaturally stiff, and the latter hugging herself as tears streamed down her cheeks. Not ready to engage with either of them, he gave them a wide berth, slipping out of the plane and making a beeline to where Ze'ev Mirashi stood with his team at the base of the ramp, Ami Galant behind them, all dressed in formal IDF uniforms.

Chunk reached his Israeli brothers and extended a hand to Mirashi, who grasped it in both of his own.

"I am so saddened by your loss, my brother," Mirashi said, emotion tightening his voice.

"Thank you, Ze'ev," Chunk managed. "It was an honor to fight beside you. I hope that one day our paths will cross again."

"Under better circumstances," Mirashi replied, releasing his grip on Chunk's hand and forearm.

"Given the state of the world, unlikely," Chunk said, managing a tight grin.

"Indeed," Mirashi said. "And so I look forward to fighting beside you again when the time comes."

Chunk nodded and turned to the rest of the Shayetet 13 warriors who had gathered to say their goodbyes. When he'd finished, he turned and walked solemnly back into the plane.

As Chunk stepped onto the ramp, it began to rise. Chunk scanned his team. Near the bulkhead, Riker knelt, his torso draped over Saw's coffin, his chest heaving as he sobbed. The rest of the team stood in a loose circle around him, hands in pockets, heads bowed, and eyes fixed on their dead brother's flag-draped box. These were the best warriors in the world, and pride found its way into Chunk's heart alongside his grief.

Captain Bowman walked over to meet him.

"I know the past two days have been difficult, Commander, but your strength has held this unit together," Bowman said, putting a hand on Chunk's shoulder. "I know you and Saw were close . . . I'm very sorry, Chunk."

"Thank you, sir," Chunk said.

"If you need to talk, my door is always open," Bowman said. Without waiting for a reply, he turned and walked away.

Chunk's gaze returned to the casket. He wanted to join his teammates, but he needed a minute. With leaden legs, he dropped heavily onto the orange nylon bench by himself at the rear of the plane, pushing away the memory of the most gut-wrenching phone call he'd had to make in his adult life—the call he'd made yesterday to inform Ellie of Saw's death.

He felt a tender hand on his shoulder and blinked away his tears. He looked up, not at all surprised to see Whitney, standing in front of him.

He just wanted to be alone. He was about to tell her as much, but something in her gaze stopped him—strength and compassion the likes of which he'd never felt so strongly from another human being. Had she come to him because she needed comfort? Or because she realized that he did?

"May I join you?" she said.

He nodded.

She eased herself onto the bench beside him. She didn't say anything for a long moment, and when she finally did, her words took him by surprise.

"You're wrong, you know."

"Wrong about what?" he said after a beat, pretending she wasn't reading his mind.

"It's not your fault. You didn't force him to stay. You didn't make him deploy. And even if you'd been leading that stick instead of Saw, the outcome wouldn't have been different."

"It *would* have been different, because Saw would have been overwatch in the helo, and I would have been leading from the front," he said, realizing he'd walked right into her trap.

"And then you'd be dead. Or Riker would be. Or maybe both of you. Or maybe that sniper would have targeted Saw in the helo anyway . . . You see how this game works? Do you want to guess how many times I've played it myself? How many times I've reimagined my choices on the *Dauphine* and said if I'd only done X, Y, or Z, then Lucy Kim would still be alive?" She let out a shaky breath. "Too many . . ."

He looked at her, expecting now to find her cracking, but saw only strength and compassion.

Whitney's journey since joining the unit had been a difficult one. After the trauma she'd experienced in Mingora and Bagram, she'd let Chunk support her. After the kidnapping, torture, and loss she'd experienced on the al Qadar London operation, she'd confided in him, sharing her pain, guilt, and sorrow. She'd let herself be vulnerable, and she'd trusted him to be her rock.

Now, the tables were turned. Could he be strong enough to trust her in return?

She extended her right hand and rested it on his knee, palm facing up. He stared at it for a long moment, wishing and hoping she'd just give up and take it back.

She didn't.

As a fresh tear trickled down his left cheek, he realized something about himself—something he'd not understood until this moment. Then, accepting that he did not have to survive his grief alone, he leaned his head back against the bulkhead, closed his eyes, and accepted her hand.

ACKNOWLEDGMENTS

A special thank-you to Jennifer Mullican and Sam Octavius for lending us their insights and subject-matter expertise as well as their names.

GLOSSARY

AI Artificial Intelligence

ASW Antisubmarine Warfare

BDU Battle Dress Uniform

CAC Common Access Card

CAG Combat Applications Group

CIA Central Intelligence Agency

CO Commanding Officer

CSO Chief Staff Officer

DCS Dry Combat Submersible

DDS Dry Deck Shelters

DNN Deep Neural Network

DOD Department of Defense

ELINT Electronic Intelligence

EW Electronic Warfare

Exfil Exfiltrate

GCU Ground Control Unit

GCHQ Government Communications Headquarters; British equivalent of NSA responsible for Signals Intelligence and support

HVT High-Value Target

IED Improvised explosive device

Infil Infiltrate

IR Infrared

ISR Intelligence, surveillance, and reconnaissance

JSOC Joint Special Operations Command

JTAC Joint Terrorism Analysis Center; British equivalent of the NCTC

KIA Killed in Action

MI5 British Domestic Counterintelligence and Security Agency; British equivalent of the FBI

MI6 Foreign Intelligence Service; British equivalent of the CIA

NCTC National Counterterrorism Center

NCO Noncommissioned Officer

NOC Nonofficial Cover

NSW Naval Special Warfare

NVGs Night Vision Goggles

OC Official Cover

ODNI Office of the Director of National Intelligence

OGA Other Government Agency, frequently refers to CIA or other clandestine organizations

OIC Officer in Charge

OPORD A military Operational Order

POC Point of Contact

POV Privately Owned Vehicle

QRF Quick Reaction Force

RAF Royal Air Force

ROCAF Republic of China Air Force

ROE Rules of Engagement for a military operation

SAS Special Air Service; British Special Operations forces equivalent to Green Berets

SBS Special Boat Services

SCIF Sensitive Compartmented Information Facility

SEAL Sea, Air, and Land Teams; Naval Special Warfare

SERE Training Military Survival, Evasion, Resistance, and Escape training

SF Special Forces; Refers specifically to the Army Special Operations Green Berets

SINKEX A military maritime exercise involving the sinking of a simulated enemy vessel

SIS Secret Intelligence Service; the formal name for MI6

SITREP Situation Report

SOAR Special Operations Aviation Regiment

SOF Special Operations Forces

SWCS Shallow Water Combat Submersibles

TAD Temporary Additional Duty

TAO Tactical Action Officer

TBI Traumatic Brain Injury

The Farm Slang for the CIA's training facility

TOC Tactical Operations Center

UCAV Unmanned Combat Aerial Vehicle

UAV Unmanned Aerial Vehicle

USN United States Navy

VTOL Vertical Takeoff and Landing

PARTNER PAGES

Andrews & Wilson actively promote and partner with veteran-owned small businesses that demonstrate a mission of giving. The organizations featured here donate to and support the health and well-being of US service members as well as their families. We encourage you to learn about and support our partners and to spread the word about the important and uplifting work that they do.

BONEFROG

Tim Cruickshank is the founder and CEO of Bonefrog Coffee Company. A Veteran-owned and operated premium, small-batch coffee roastery located in the Pacific Northwest.

After serving twenty-five years in the US Navy, he created Bonefrog Coffee Company as a tribute to the "Brotherhood" of US Navy SEALs, the Naval Special Warfare community and to all Americans who bravely served, or who are currently serving, in our United States Armed Forces. Each label they create tells a story to remind us of battles fought and great American heroes who answered the call.

WWW.BONEFROG-COFFEE.COM

The SEAL Legacy Foundation is a 501(c)(3), nonprofit organization dedicated to providing support to families of wounded and fallen United States Navy SEALs, educational assistance for SEALs and their families, and other charitable causes benefiting the SEAL community. The Foundation was established in 2011 by SEALs to preserve their legacy of no one left behind.

WWW.SEALLEGACY.ORG

ALL SECURE FOUNDATION

Force Tier One operator Tom Satterly and award-winning filmmaker Jen Satterly, the All Secure Foundation provides resources, education, Post-Traumatic Stress Injury Resiliency training for active-duty units, warrior couples workshop retreats, and family counseling for Special Operations warriors and their warrior families. We believe that every family member deserves tools to heal from war trauma and that no one is left behind on the battlefield on the home front.